Children
of
The Lambs

*An old myth brought to life
by rogue science!*

Pulp Fiction

by

John Aalborg

With a backdrop of human replicas, most of whom are female, willing, and dumber than dirt. A book barely ahead of its time.

—

From the original screenplay "Snuff Island"

FIRST PRINT EDITION

Copyright 2010/2013 John Aalborg
Bleep-Free Press
http://bleepfreepress.com

ISBN: 978-0-9849365-9-5

Cover illustration by Baugmo

This is a work of fiction.

Homer County, "Rasputin's Marina and Bar", the "Cremo del Mar" condo, and all the characters in this book are fictional, but the author and the publisher are not sure about the clones.

Publisher's Rating: PG-14
Home Schooler (USA) Rating: MA
Author's Rating "All Ages"

Parents are responsible for child's book choices.

AUTHOR'S NOTE

All of the unusual players in this novel are serial characters and are copyrighted.

Dr. Mannlicher's boisterous manner of speech requires that some words be spelled in bold type, to indicate his emphasizing some speech with considerable and high-pitched force.

The clones, which take less time to mature and therefore could be confused as "underage", are not considered to be human although they may appear to be so. (They can, however, pass the Turing Test). It is currently unknown, however, how many human adults — the aptly named *walpolloi* — could pass the Turing Test, but the author has a ten-year-old dog who could probably squeak by.

CHAPTER 1
Luck of The Clueless

When the unattached, blond head — beautiful, fe-male, long-haired — rolled off the cliff and skidded to a stop at his sandy feet, Jack spun around in a panic. No-body in sight. OK! It had better be okay. His 9MM Walther was out of reach, farther down the beach where he'd absent-mindedly left it with the beer cooler and the empties and the boat.

She had skidded to a stop on her mouth, and the sand on her fresh lipstick was hard to brush off. But, hey! He was a beach-comber and this head was the ulti-mate find! Young, pretty, still warm — and a hell of a better catch than a glass fishnet float. Even better than a tightly wrapped bale of Jamaican drift-bud. And whoever snuffed her thought to lift her blond mane out of the way before severing the neck at the shoulders!

Jack was ecstatic. Wait till the guys back at Raspu-tin's Marina saw this! She had bright-blue eyes, too, even if the lids were too stiff to close, plus there were her un-plucked, sexy, thick eyebrows — his favorite kind.

CHAPTER 2
A Babe Beheaded

On the urgent hike back down the beach to his boat, Miss Chernobyl, Jack considered swimming out to her and getting the can of Arid Extra Dry he kept in the cuddy cabin. The severed head, swinging by the hair in his right hand, would probably need a spray coat. It was going to need something! From the feel of the mid-day sun it could get warmer — maybe over eighty — hot for November on the northern Florida Gulf Coast. The deod-spray would at least keep the bugs off the thing but he doubted if it could stop rot from setting in.

When Jack got to the gear he'd left on the shore, he wiggled his toes in the hot sand and contemplated the cooler at his feet. Somehow he just couldn't see the chopped-off head, regardless how pretty, sharing the cooler with his remaining beer and the tasty, Ziploc'd liver-sausage sandwiches Norma had made just for him. Where was Norma G, anyway? Jack straightened up and looked ahead down the long, windward shoreline, and sucked in a deep load of the sweet, salty air. He wanted Norma to see what he had found while the prize was still in good shape, but his girlfriend was nowhere in sight.

The Marine Patrol he could deal with later. "Whaddya mean I should've called the cops? The island has pay-phones now?"

Maybe that's what Jack liked about his boat best of all, after he'd traded his marriage for it. Getting out to these barrier islands. The ones without bridges to them.

Solitude. Middle-aged Man and the Sea. Not to mention the considerable muff-factor that an offshore powerboat radiated, and what the boat said about the owner. It took a certain breed of human to give up the relative security of dry land to deal with the planet and the sea one-on-one. No Seven-Eleven on the corner. No nine-eleven. No cops to protect you or your toys. "Gee, officer," (looking down at the teenage junkie who'd just tried to rape your wife and was now spurting great gobs of blood through the bullet holes you punched through his scrawny chest), "Honest, how could I tell he was under eighteen!?"

Out here on the island you fed shitheads to the sharks.

Jack was holding the long-haired head away from the side of him so it couldn't touch his body. His arm was getting tired, though, holding it out like that, but he didn't want the grody stuff which was beginning to hang out of her neck to slap against his bare leg. A human head was so heavy!

He nudged up the lid of his cooler with a toe, and bent over for a cold one. Where to lay the head? Not in the sand again like he'd found it — that wouldn't be right.

Maybe on top of the cooler if he could lay her down on the side of her face and let the neck-gorp sort of hang over. (The cooler was a brand-new Igloo and it still looked good). Still undecided, he let the hair slip a little through his fingers as he used both hands to twist the cap off his Miller.

The beer was just the right temp! After a long swallow, Jack looked at Miss Chernobyl bobbing up-and-down out there in the four-foot sea. His bluewater, deep-vee-24 pride and joy. The wind was pointing her stern at him from the anchor line, with the outdrives on the twin three-fifties heaving in and out of the water. "Better than pussy," he said to his boat for the umpteenth time, and suddenly remembered with an adrenaline-burning crunch that he hadn't turned to check his back for at least five minutes. Jack instinctively leaned toward the kit-bag beside the cooler where his 9MM Walther P-38 was stashed, grabbed for the pistol, and turned on his heel — dropping the girl's head onto the sand after all.

"It's me!" Norma yelled. Her pretty mouth formed a perfect "O" as Jack swung the gun up and away from her. She wasn't but ten feet away, her copious red hair billowing in the humid, ocean breeze.

Jack's eyes lingered on her hands as they clutched at the skimpy bikini top. "You think your hands can stop bullets? That was close, Baby. Don't sneak up on me like that! Damn!" He eased the safety down on the P-38 and winced when the hammer dropped with a "snap" - the only thing he didn't like about the trusty, German, WW-II piece — the de-cocking mechanism — he'd never get used to it. But a killing machine it was. Clip crammed with semi-jacketed, 124 grain Federal Hydra-Shocks.

"Big warrior man, you're shaking all over. Hell, Jack, I followed you all the way up the beach and you never checked your back once. Ha! Men!"

"Yeah, well, if it wasn't for the surf I would've heard you and..."

"Yes, Jack, but there **is** a surf! Jeez!"

"And I'm shaky because I'm so horny. I'm ready to bust." Jack dropped the Walther back into his kit-bag and pulled her hands away. He buried his face in the goodies. "We need to do something about it, too, so I can enjoy the rest of the day."

"Aww, poor baby needs Mama again." Norma

planted a kiss on top of Jack's thinning hair. "Well, we're not going to do it in the boat again, unless you want to move into the bay where it's calm, and we're not going to do it right here on the sand, either."

"Why not?"

"With that girl looking right at us?"

Jack pulled his head out of her tits and looked around.

"**Her**, silly!" Norma readjusted her bikini and pointed at the head, which had landed on its back and was looking right at them with half-open eyes. "You got my top all spitty. Mmmmm, her eyes are the same color as my bikini-top you got all lickety."

"That head! Isn't she great?" Jack bent over and carefully closed his hands around the victim's hair, gathering it all up in a bunch before lifting her from the sand. "I didn't mean to drop her. I thought somebody was behind me." He brushed off the sand from the girl's chin but decided that the stuff hanging out the neck looked better frosted.

"There **was** somebody behind you, Jack, really. You did too much dope when you were a kid." Norma sauntered up and gently grabbed the head by the ears, turning the face toward her.

Jack felt proud, despite Norma's cuts about his intelligence. "When you saw me with it, you didn't think, um, you didn't wonder if I chopped some chick's head off myself and..."

"Oh, yeah, sure. You?"

"I was in Vietnam."

"Wow. Jack, I found that head before you did. How do you think it suddenly rolled off the cliff right in front of where you were walking?" Norma leaned forward and rubbed noses with the thing. "Jack, maybe you're too dumb for me." She puckered her lips but didn't go so far as to kiss it. "Lips are sandy."

"I thought somebody was up there."

"Right. I love your body, though, even if you are older and dumber than me."

"That's all?"

"And you're sweet to me. And you want me all the time." Norma turned the head up higher and inspected the neck. She grimaced. "And I love your boat."

"We were talking about making love."

"God, Jack, let's get to the important stuff first, right? Okay, if you wade out to the boat and bring back a blanket, there's some neat woods back in there." Norma turned the head loose and pointed inland, and laughed when Jack almost dropped the girl back in the sand.

"Jack, give her to me. I'll hide her in a shady place. And bring back my .41 when you get the blanket. This head had a body. Not too long ago, either. It doesn't even smell. Well, I can smell her perfume."

"I was going out to Churny, anyway. To get the deod."

"Churny?"

"Miss Chernobyl."

"Cute. Good boy, Jack."

When he was out far enough where the sea was lapping at his trunks, Jack turned around to check the shoreline just in time to catch Norma lowering the head into the Igloo. Shit. Typical chick! But he was proud of Norma G. Not only was she dream material, she was a fellow gun freak. Saw life the way he did — well, maybe not exactly — and she wasn't afraid of anything!

But minutes later when he ducked out of the cuddy-cabin with the Arid Extra Dry and Norma's .41 magnum revolver safely wrapped in the blanket, Norma was gone.

He crouched in the stern and tried to maintain his balance while he scanned the shore. Despite the splash and dip of the outdrives in the heaving sea, the silence was ominous. He shouted out to her: "Norma, I'm serious! If you're okay, holler!"

The beach was bare, pure-white sand for about twenty feet to the cliffs, which were covered with sea oats and shrubs. Jack unrolled Norma's Ruger Blackhawk from the blanket and splashed in, holding the huge revolver high and dry over his head. As he plowed toward the shore, fear pounded up in his chest when he spotted the obvious signs of a struggle. Prints of street shoes, and parallel lines dug into the sand — Norma's bare heels — the ugly trail heading straight for a low place in the cliffs. And his 9MM Walther was gone.

Jack dug in and sprinted for the cliff, tearing his way up with his feet and one free hand to the high ground just in time to see two fully-dressed men, about fifty yards away, dragging Norma Gene into a thick copse of gnarled sand-oaks. Jack skidded to a stop on his ass, steadied Norma's .41 with his elbows between his knees, and blasted a shot at the head of the man who was still pulling on Norma's arm. The creep dropped her and disappeared after his buddy.

Jack cocked the single-action and sent another round crashing into the woods behind his girlfriend. "Leave my gun!" he hollered, and the .41 bucked up into the air two more times.

"I got it!" Norma yelled back, scrambling for it off to the side on all fours, and Jack watched her twist around with his P-38 in both hands as she dumped nine rounds into the thicket. Holding his position, Jack covered her while she got to her feet and ran toward him.

As Norma flew by and disappeared down to the beach behind him he fired his last two rounds."I loved the way your tits bounced when you ran past me," he said, somewhat out of breath after rolling off the cliff. "At least I saved a couple rounds until I saw you were clear."

"T and A, the important stuff." Norma was plowing through the kit-bag for another clip, and breathing heavily. "How was I to know — that the famous P-38 — holds only nine shots."

"It would be eight if the chamber wasn't loaded."

As soon as she had the new clip shoved into his automatic and a round chambered, Norma began to shiver. "Oh, Jack." Looking over his shoulder, she kept her eyes trained on the cliffs while she gave him a quick hug. "Those people are bad, Jack. Bad! They slapped me and...and they laughed when I started crying." She shoved him away. "We need to get out of here. Quick! Trade guns!"

"Okay, but yours is empty." Jack handed her the revolver.

"One of them looked just like Saddam Hussein. Garlic breath. The whole nine yards."

"Nobody's ever been close enough to Saddam to choke on his breath."

"Jack! Can you keep your hands to yourself? We're in deep shit here! We have to split! Now!"

Jack bent over the cooler and lifted the lid. "Head's okay."

"Jack!"

"Hey! We're armed!"

"The ammo for **my** gun is still in the boat!" Norma backed away from him, her eyes on the cliff. "I'm gone! Cover me!"

Jack watched her splash into the first wave with the

.41 high in her left hand. Then he turned away and scanned the shoreline and the cliffs.

"Okay! Come on!" Norma was yelling from the stern now, shouting above the surf. "I'm loaded up. Hurry!"

Jack looked down at the cooler, the kit-bag, the empty beer bottles. It would be a shame to leave the bottles behind. To litter.

"Jack! Fuck the bottles! Get real!"

He slung the kit-bag strap over his shoulder with a sigh. The chick could read minds.

CHAPTER 3
To Kill For: Norma Gene

The cooler would take both hands and he had to lay the Walther on top of it, where it could slide off.

Norma was still yelling orders from the boat. "Jack, don't leave the cooler! Come on, I've got you covered!" She had her weapon held out in both hands, legs flexed at the knees to keep her balance. "Your gun goes in the kit-bag!"

He could barely hear her above the waves crashing near his feet, but he was glad she wanted to keep the head they'd found. In a minute, Jack was out there and handing up the cooler and admiring Norma's befreckled cleavage. It was harder climbing up the heaving out-drives, and he hoped Norma wasn't noticing what a struggle it was for him to get into the boat. She could hop in like a bunny.

A bullet screamed between their heads and the two halves of the step-through windshield. Norma hit the deck and flattened out on her stomach. Without thinking, Jack rushed for the controls and lowered the out-drives into the water. "As soon as you hear the second engine fire, go for the anchor line!"

Two more shots popped and thunked into the water on either side of them.

"Small caliber!" Jack's voice was okay, but his hands were trembling.

"I can't see them!" Norma had skidded around on her tummy and had the .41 steadied over the port engine cover. "There they are!" **POOM! POOM!** "They're gone!

13

No, wait!" Norma's arms twisted up with each shot.
POOM! POOM! POOM!

The starboard engine started but Jack's ears were ringing with the deafening thunder of Norma's huge revolver. The port unit was still cranking and he figured Norma had only one shot left. "Grab the P-38 when you run out! Keep them down!"

POOM! Norma slid around for the kit-bag and pulled out Jack's 9MM just as the other engine caught.

"Anchor!"

"Jack, damn it!" Norma handed him the pistol and dove through the split windshield for the anchor line.

"Got it?"

"Got it!"

Jack shoved both drives into gear at idle-speed and the boat shuddered.

"Pull! Pull! Pull!"

"I'm pulling!"

A head appeared through the sea-oats at the top of the cliff. And two pairs of sleeved arms holding pistols. Jack tried to aim but Miss Chernobyl was tossing too much. He could see their pistols begin to buck up-and-down just as he snapped off his first shot.

Norma flinched as two bullets whined overhead. A third smashed into the compass mount just as Jack dove behind the engine housing for cover. He tried to time his shots with the movement of the boat but he could hear and feel the incoming lead smacking into the stern and the gunwales. He squeezed off three more rounds and saw the arms and pistols disappear.

Norma yelled: "Anchor's coming up! I can see it! Go!"

Jack scrambled to his feet and made sure Norma had both hands on the line before he shoved the throttles down. The bow lifted and shuddered forward as the twin, converted Chevy 350's twisted the big, three-bladed props through the sea. Norma hung onto the anchor line until Miss Chernobyl was up on plane and slicing through the waves, out of range of the pistols on shore. Jack throttled the engines back to 3200 RPM and matched their speeds as the hull flew over the chop.

"Anchor's smacking the bow! I can't lift it out!"

"Cleat the line and trade places!" Jack dropped the speed down to 2900 - the boat could plane at 2400 - and eased forward while Norma moved around him.

"That was close!"

"You did good, Baby. You were beautiful!" Jack bellied up to the anchor and heaved it up over the bow combing. "Norma, you're a star!" he yelled. "I love you!" He lashed down the Danforth with a bungee cord and moved back into the cockpit. "I love you! You were great!" He looked at her for a reaction but her eyes were fixed on the horizon, the wind whipping tears away from the corners of her eyes. She made no motion to relinquish the helm.

"Keep on heading out, baby. Maybe they don't have binoculars handy. When we're out of sight we can head east, toward Tyndall, get back into the bay through the Lands End cut. They'll expect us to head back through St. Andrew. The jetties."

Did I have to tell her I loved her?

Jack listened proudly to the powerful and steady drone of the engines he had rebuilt himself.

Did I have to tell her twice!

But he did love her! "I love you, Norma Gene!" He was so proud. So happy. Adrenaline pumping it all higher and higher. Jack let out a long, inspired, rebel yell. "Yaaaaaaay - hooooooooo!" He saw the corner of her mouth curl down.

"Stow the anchor line, Jack, Jeez! Want that all twisted up in the props?!

"Okay! Okay! Hold'er steady. I'm going to check they didn't hit any gas lines and stuff." He had to yell because the hull was pounding and slicing and sending spray splatting into the windshield. He eased up the engine covers a little, and, satisfied with that, leaned out over the stern. The bullets which had struck the transom hadn't penetrated.

"Jack, can you take over now? I don't know where we are. Compass is smashed."

"Okay, Baby." Jack took a last look at the island, which was now a thin line of green on the horizon. He moved up to Norma and took her place at the wheel. Something was glowing, and warm on his back, running down to the waistband of his trunks. He tried to reach around to it. "Norma, is there blood on my back?"

Norma suddenly looked alive again, and twisted her body to get a look. She dipped a finger along the stuff."Looks like cooking oil." She held the finger up to her nose.

"I love your nose. Here, let me smell it." Jack grabbed her hand and sniffed. "Compass oil. Can you wipe it off?"

Norma scowled at him. "Sure, Jack, like with what?"

"Jeez, baby, are we having a problem? I mean, we were lucky! Enjoy it!"

"I'm not you're fucking **baby**!"

"Good. There's rags in that gun tube under the dash on your side."

"Rags is plural! And we weren't lucky, we were stupid."

"You never had so much fun."

"This is a gun tube?" Norma had pulled out a wad of tattered underwear shorts which Jack recycled as useful rags. She was peering down the tube. "What kind of rifle fits in here?"

"M-1 carbine with a four-round joker clip. There are — another — tube on my — side. Empty. But it won't be empty next time."

"You have an M-1?"

"Two. One for me, one for you. Thirty-round clips banded to the stocks."

Norma finally smiled. "I knew you were a neat guy when I first spotted you at the gun show."

"I picked you out, remember?"

"Is that what you think? I maneuvered myself right in front of you."

"Yeah?"

"Yep."

"Good thing I had the guts to speak up, huh!?"

"Oh, Jack, you came on to me like such a turkey! And you were so nervous. Ha!"

"Yeah, well, I always dreamed about a beautiful woman who handled guns like a warrior." Jack had to clear his throat so he could keep his voice up. "When I was a kid I used to steal book jackets from the bookstore — tape them up on my wall — like science fiction book covers — the kind where these chicks are on Mars and stuff wearing chain-mail bikinis and toting M-60 machine guns, you know, bandoliers full of ammo crossed over their tits. Dream stuff! Now I have me one! A real one! Norma Gene, you are my dream come true!"

"How much fuel we got, Asteroid?"

A pang of adrenaline stabbed Jack's gut. Both fuel gauges were on dead-E. Empty.

"Take the wheel."

From as far as he could tell by peering through the filler tubes, both forty-gallon saddle tanks were at least half full. "They must have hit some wiring."

"Well, I sure hope so." Norma shivered. "I'm getting chilly."

Jack lifted the lid off the cooler one more time to reconfirm that the prize of his beach-combing career was still there. The severed head didn't look as good as it had at first, though, but the face was still above the water, resting on the melting ice and the remaining supply of Miller beer. The tangled hair Norma could dry and brush out when they got to Rasputin's.

"Beer?"

"Beer."

Jack took the wheel again while Norma opened the beers and went down into the cuddy to get a sweatshirt to pull over. He headed the boat east, then north to the cut near the western tip of the barren and deserted Tyndall Air Force Base peninsula. The sun was at two o'clock, the engines were humming along in perfect synch, and his beautiful girlfriend's flaming hair was billowing in the breeze. What more could a mere mortal ask for?! Jack shoved in a tape of Wagner's "Die Niebelungen", Act Two. The opera boomed out of the waterproof, expensive quad-speaker system he had fortuitously installed just before the fateful weekend gun show when God sent him Norma G.

"Shit, Jack!"

"You don't like it?" Jack hung onto as much of the opera as he dared before shutting it off. "That's where Sigmund is hammering out the sword he's going to use to kill the..."

"Jack!"

Jack shrugged his shoulders. Maybe he should've

shoved in some heavy metal. He took a sideways look at her, standing so proudly, back arched, her left hand gripping the hand-hold on the port gunwale, her chest out. A dream. *Probably loves Aerosmith. What's'name? Tyler whatever. Scumbags always get the best chicks. And that old, delinquent Mick Jagger.* Jack slowed the RPM's down just enough to match the speed of the breaking wave just ahead of them. They were running with the sea and wind now, and as they crested the wave, he held the boat steady on top. Surfing. The bow leaning out way over the crest. *So perfect. So beautiful.*

"Jack, everybody else has a VHF on their boat."

"And every chick I know has a cell-phone!" *How many boats has she been on?!* "Chernobyl has stereo! And GPS navigation! And a depth sounder!"

"Mmm - hmm. So how do we radio ahead for the news team and stuff? You know — the girl. I mean, her head."

News team.... Jack let her continue.

"TV! Maybe it'll even go on **network** TV! And that BBC dude, he is so cool!"

BBC with Matt Frei? Jack thought about it. *Any-body else would be wondering how they could radio the cops. God, I'm more in love with her than ever!* "Matt Frei loves opera!" *I think.*

"Yeah? He does?"

They were nearing the Lands End inlet — one of Jack's favorite places. The cut was twisty, tricky and narrow even though it had recently been dredged, and the sea breaking over the sandbars was dangerous but always a spectacular sight. On sunny days you could also depend on the shoreline to be a carpet of basking bikinis. Some of them Tyndall Air Force Base wives.

Jack squinted his eyes. There were a few boats pulled

up on the banks, but none as slick as Miss Chernobyl.

Norma sidled up to him. "We can stop and ask somebody to borrow their radio!"

Yeah, well, the last time I tried that I got a rude what-for and I told him to kiss ass."

"That won't happen if I ask."

"No, Baby." Jack swallowed and waited for the reprimand which never came. "Norma, I don't know if I want you on TV. You'll get discovered. You are so fine! I want you all to myself."

"Oh, Jack, you really do love me." Norma stood beside him and hung onto his waist. Jack was easing the throttles back-and-forth to keep on top of their wave, which looked like it was going to roll them right up to the mouth of the inlet.

"We'll need to give the camera crew time to get to the marina, too," Norma said. "We could find a cove on the bay side here. Get the blanket out. I'll give you a quickie." She planted a kiss on his cheek. "After we find a radio."

"We'll give each other a quickie."

"Right. That boat over there — the big sportfisherman — see it? I'll bet they have a VHF **and** a cellphone."

"Hell, it's not as neat as Miss Chernobyl."

"Are you kidding? It looks like a million bucks! And it must be deep enough there to beach. We won't have to get out the anchor. You just let me do the talking."

"Yah-yah. Jeez, pretty stupid to run a boat that big up on shore." Jack saw there were some nicely-tanned ladies on a blanket parked on the sand next to the cruiser. It was a thirty-one foot Bertram, wide of beam, and deep. And expensive. Jack grinned and imagined the ladies jumping up and screaming while he held the severed head over them by the hair.

"Okay, Baby, I need both hands. The tide is running out the cut — against the wind — see it? Hang on!"

A minute later the bow of Miss Chernobyl cushed to a stop on the white sand-bank — a discreet distance from the larger craft. While the hydraulics tipped up the outdrives with a sweet whine, Norma hopped out onto the beach and headed toward the girls.

The blondes were both lying on their tummies, their little asses poking up in the air. Goose-bumps frosted Jack's forearms and rippled across his back. The books they were reading were large and flat, and both the same kind. From Miss Chernobyl they looked like picture books, like for little kids. Sesame Street stuff. Jack had a leg over the gunwale and was about to step out but stopped cold. He snapped his head toward the big Bertram to see if anyone was aboard, then turned back to Norma. She was obviously shocked, also. The girls were looking up from their books and smiling at her. Such a pretty pair. Identical twins. No, not twins. Counting the head in the cooler — triplets.

CHAPTER 4
Rasputin's Marina Bar

Jack held his breath and saw the surprise disappear from Norma's face and change to a beatific smile. She dropped to a crouch in front of the identical little foxes and humbly asked if she could use the VHF radio on their boat.

"What's that?"

Giggles. "V - H - F?"

Jack watched Norma look up at their huge Bertram and he shook his head at her. "No, baby, let's get moving! We'll find another boat!" He still had one leg in Miss Chernobyl and the other dangling over the gunwale. He wanted to holler: *We're in deep shit here!*

One of the girls said: "We have a cell."

"A cell-phone?"

Giggles. "Yeah."

"Yeah."

Jack's heart was pounding and he kept looking back and forth between the Bertram and the girls. Those dummies didn't bring that 31 footer in by themselves — beached as skillfully as it was. They sure were pretty, though. And built so nice for their age. Mid-teens? Jack swung his right leg back inboard and eased up to the controls, making sure the 9MM was within reach in the chart pocket. He called to them from where he was. "Where's your boyfriend?"

More giggles. The girls turned a little to look at him and smile. "Boyfriend?" "Boyfriend?"

"My Uncle is down there." "Down there."

A sweep of a dainty hands down the long beach. Jack could see some smaller boats down there, and a knot of men standing around. Didn't they notice Miss Chernobyl?

Norma said: "The cell-phone?"

"Oh! Sure!" One of the cute identicals got to her feet as a rush of desire and pain moved inside Jack's trunks. Too much pain. There was no reason for it. Prime young stuff couldn't be that sexy, and it wasn't like he hadn't been getting laid lately. Jack swallowed and watched the little lust-pit tap on the cabin window. Shit! There **was** someone else inside! He tore his eyes away from the triplet's chunky, young ass and reached for the Walther.

Norma was helping the other girl to her feet. They were laughing. Norma must've really needed to call that news team bad. A side window on the Bertram slid back and the third identical, no, make that the fourth counting Miss Igloo, poked her pretty head out. Beautiful, white-toothed smile. Perfect make-up. Perfect.

"Hand out the phone."

"Ohhhhhhh. We're not supposed to talk to anybody."

"Well, he said nobody would come here."

"So?"

"So?"

Norma interrupted. "Please hurry. It's an emergency."

Jack lowered the outdrives back down, cranked the engines, and calmly waited for Norma to finish yakking to News Force Eleven before handing the phone back through the window.

After the tricky backward maneuver into the swift-flowing, tidal cut, Jack shoved the throttles forward.

Miss Chernobyl slalomed between the twisting banks and shot out into the bay. As soon as they were in the clear, he looked at Norma. God, she was a beauty! So what was the big deal with his hard-on for the twins? Quadruplets. Or whatever. God.

"I love you, Norma Gene!" *I wonder where the body is that went with our chopped-off head.*

"I love you, too, Jack!"

"You do?"

"Yeah, but don't take that to mean I'm your slave now!"

"I wouldn't dream!"

"You do all the time! I got them! They're coming!"

Jack had to think.

"News Force Eleven! They believed me! I called that news hot-line of theirs. Free!"

"They coming to Rasputin's? The bar?"

"Right. And I told them we're not pulling into the marina until I see their truck."

"I'm the captain here!"

"Yeah? You better think about that!"

Jack held his tongue and corrected their course for the Inland Waterway and the Hathaway Bridge. They could discuss who was boss after he pulled into the palmettos at Redfish Point and they had the quickie Norma had promised. Thinking about jumping the bones of three identical blondes at one time had squirted a lethal dose of testosterone into his blood-stream and his lust was approaching critical mass.

"You notice if the chicks had belly buttons?"

"Hey! You're heading the wrong way!"

"I'm rounding the point! I know a neat spot in there!"

"No, Jack. Jack!"

"What did you think of the quadruplets?!"

"Jack? Stop the boat! Now! I mean it, Jack!"

The bow dropped and slowed as Jack throttled back and geared both drives into neutral. They were about a half mile from Redfish Point, with no other boats in sight. He cut the engines and Miss Chernobyl's hull bobbed and slapped gently in calm of the bay. The high sun shone down its welcome, winter heat.

"They said they were in the area and were coming right away, Jack. News Force Eleven."

"You promised me a quickie. On land. On a blanket."

"Oh, Jack. You just got your panties in a wad over that young stuff back there. Get real."

"I serve **your** needs. Like today, for national attention."

"Not if we don't get there with the goods in time!"

Jack bent over and flipped up the cooler lid. "The goods, huh? Hi there, Miss Goods!" He turned the girl's face up a little more so it could float better on top of the remaining stuff in there. Norma was going to have to lay on the make-up to cover all the discoloring if she wanted their discovery to be as photogenic as the sisters.

"Jack, don't be gross! That was a living, thinking person!"

"Thinking?"

"Well. Yeah. Close the cooler and let's get going."

"It doesn't bother you what we ran into today? And stopping to use their phone, God! Pretty callous!"

Norma narrowed her eyes at him and reached behind her back. With a snap she flipped off her bikini top, and shoved his face into The Valley of Fornicatious Freckles. "Jack?"

"Mmmmmmfh?"

"You don't take me over to Rasputin's right now, you'll never fuck me again. I mean it."

"Ohhhhh. Mmmmf."

"I need time to brush out her hair and slick her up a little — and do my own face, too — so when we get nearby we'll idle out for a couple minutes while I get us ready. I'll make it up to you later. I promise. I'll take all you've got until I taste brains."

As soon as that translated, Jack pulled his head out of the fruit and headed the boat toward the near side of the Hathaway Bridge five miles to the northwest — toward Rasputin's Marina and Bar.

At the outdoor, palm-thatched bar, Jack and a regular drinking buddy of his there handled crowd control while Norma Gene showed her ass for the News Force Eleven camera. The few patrons at Rasputin's were noisy but friendly, and it wasn't late enough for many of the regular boaters to be tying back up at the docks. Norma used the deserted pier like a fashion-show runway, and the young cameraman with his walrus mustache got right down to business. "Mind heading back and walking up to the camera again? Look right into the lens. That's it! Can you hold the head out a little farther to the side? Not **your** head — **hers!** Great! Great! I know it must be heavy!" He would stop only to bitch into the ear of his partner, a middle-aged female reporter whom everyone recognized as Vicki Jonathan from the Channel 11 "Six O'clock Report". Vicki Jonathan from the "Tri-State Church of the Week" show, the "Homemaker's Round Table" and "The Panhandle Community Saturday Morning Bulletin Board". Grim-faced and determined to get her ice-cream-cone shaped mike into the middle of everything, Miss Vicki was already dressed in full fig for her nightly News Force Eleven "Our Lady on the Street" segment. She was trying to take names and get details while the camera-dude was yelling orders to Norma G. "Can you hold her up real high now? That's it! Turn her head to face you? Yeah! Yeah! Closer! Yeah. Kiss her? On the mouth? Oh! Far out! I don't believe this! Too much! Too much! You've got it! National news!"

Norma's smile brightened along with the cheers from the onlookers.

"National?"

"I promise! We're an ABC affiliate!"

Though her arms were tiring at this point, Norma kept on standing sideways to the camera, back arched and ass out, with her lips puckered in a girlie-calendar pose — her arms high and her hands clenched around the swinging head's long, blond hair. Once more, Norma's lips went for the cold, unyielding but freshly lipsticked mouth of the victim. After the second round of clapping and cheers, everyone suddenly became aware of the distant sound of an approaching police siren. Norma swung away from the camera and judged the scene with a happy grin on her face. She heard Jack telling Miss Vicki: "No, we just found it lying there on the beach." "No, we're not married. Norma's my girl-friend." "We met at a gun show in Miami." "Yes, she is. She's so beautiful that when I first saw her I thought she was a transvestite."

"That's enough, Jack!" Norma turned to the camera dude. "We'll cut away from the sun as soon as we round the pier," she promised, "so you can get a good shot of the boat."

After yelling at Jack to get into the boat, Norma lowered her arms and finally agreed to huddle with Vicki

Jonathan. But the lady backed away and held her microphone out at arm's length.

"Norma Gene! No, gee eee enn eee!" "Yeah! Sure! Jack Rebman." "No, B, as in rebel! Rebman!" " The boat's name? Oh, for sure! Miss Chernobyl! See the transom? Spell it from that!" "Mine? Noooo. It's ours!" "The police?" Norma looked around at the swarm of beer guzzling males which had formed around her delicious body and the gruesome beach-combing drift-head. One of the men, a pink porker in low-slung camouflage trunks and no shirt to cover his pale, hangy-down tits, was arguing with the cameraman. "I'll French-kiss it but only when the camera's running and you give me a tape."

"No you won't!" Norma hollered, and as she dropped down into Miss Chernobyl, the gorp hanging out of the victim's neck slapped against a piling and tore off, the dark-red snot dangling there like a wad of exhausted night-crawlers. Jack slapped the cooler lid down over their prize and they gunned away from the dock, barreling past two "NO WAKE" signs just as a Panama City Police cruiser scrunched to a halt on the gravel beside the bar. Hanging onto a hand-rail, Norma twisted around and waved to the camera and the crowd and the cops with her free hand.

"Oh, Jack, that was perfect!" She had to shout above the roar of the engines and the outdrives. "The Evening News tonight, and tomorrow ABC! And they're going to pay me! Maybe I can pay some off on my cards! Neat, huh? Is this great or what?!"

But Jack was more worried about the gray Florida Marine Patrol boat which had suddenly appeared from behind the last slip — and which Miss Chernobyl nearly swamped — on their way out of the tiny harbor. The patrol-boat was small but had two, huge outboards — a speed-boat probably confiscated during a drug bust. A quick look back and sure enough, it was rooster-tailing after them now, its blue bubble-gum machine flashing. Jack thought he could pretend he didn't see the light, right? With a three or four hundred yard lead, he could cut Miss Chernobyl over to the abandoned cannery, idle under their low bridge and sneak through the canal there into West Bay. The man would have to dismantle his tall Bimini top to follow them that way.

"Jack! Maybe we should stop!"

"Is he gaining?"

"Can't tell!"

"Hang on!" Jack bent his knees and Miss Chernobyl took the shock as they crossed the wake of a Mercury-powered tri-hull which had just cut into the channel ahead of them and heading under the Hathaway Bridge. Jack cut the wheel hard to starboard and followed their wake down the middle. Temporarily blocked from the Marine Patrol's view by tiny Pelican Island, Jack throttled back and eased Miss Chernobyl around the pilings at the spoil bank there — and waited. Silently, Norma and Jack watched the patrol boat, the man hunched over the wheel, spank and bounce at high speed after the tri-hull's wake under the bridge.

"He'll be back in a minute once he figures it out!" Resisting the urge to pour the coal to the three-fifties, Jack idled his boat under the cannery pier, then, in neutral, they used their hands to guide the twenty-four footer around the tee to relative safety behind an abandoned barge. Sunlight streamed in dusty beams down through the creosoted slats overhead as Jack cut the engines and Norma crouched behind the transom to peer out into the bay. The cooling engines ticked as Miss

Chernobyl's own wake caught up with them and slapped soothing laps against the huge pilings. Jack moved the boat farther under the huge pier with his hands.

Norma whispered: "I can't see over the barge but I hear him coming back."

"Could be anybody."

"Oh, Jack, jeez!"

Jack pushed against the near piling with his hands to keep the boat from clunking, then slowly lifted the lid of the Igloo. Despite the bumpy ride, the girl was still facing up, her eyes looking out under the stiff, half-open lids. Jack was just as horny for Norma as ever but yet he could feel the urge building to kiss the dead girl's lips. He glanced over at Norma, still leaning over the transom, her long, straight back striped from the light shining through the planks overhead. He looked back to the girl in the cooler. But Norma could turn around any second and catch him doing it, and then forever after she would think he was kinky or something. She had kissed those lips herself, of course, but Jack was an experienced enough dude to know that Norma would judge him doing that differently. Unfair, but it was the world you got but never ordered. No refunds, no returns, and "Providence" was not the name of a shopping mall.

Jack lowered the lid. "Norma?"

"I don't think he suspects we turned in here."

"I'm horny, Norma."

"Me, too!"

Jack almost said: *You are?* He watched her hands reach behind her back to unsnap her top, and watched her turn while her long legs shucked off the bikini bottom. A true red-head and all his — for now.

"Right here in the boat," she smiled. "Out in the open. Get the blanket."

Jack didn't lower his head enough and he smacked it on the way up out of the cuddy cabin, but not too bad. He spread out the polyester, red plaid on the cockpit sole and Norma Gene spread herself out upon it.

"After all, I promised," she purred, wiggling her back and ass against the blanket, her alien, freckled opulence throbbing up at him in the slatted light.

"Well, this isn't exactly what you promised, but I'll take it." Jack dropped his face down between her raised knees and got to work. In a few minutes they were working together, gently, sweetly, face to face. Miss Chernobyl took up the rhythm with them, gently rocking and lapping against her watery berth.

He felt the inevitable and urgent release announcing itself much too soon. If it were entirely up to him he would just as soon let the Rebman armies rush up her tubes right now and the hell with it — it was going to feel so good! — but there were Norma's feelings to think about, too, and then there was the cooler. Along with the motion of the boat, the cooler was beginning to make a sloshing sound, water and melting ice, sloshing back-and-forth with the clinking beer bottles. Jack pictured the pretty head floating in the cold and clammy darkness inside the Igloo, and the emergency averted itself for a moment. Norma was picturing the head in there also, and her stomach muscles bunched, her shoulders lifted off the deck, and she came like a devil.

CHAPTER 5
The Nub Boy

Jody dug in with his heels and inched his half-naked, fourteen-year-old-boy body up higher under the twelve-foot, out-dated, fiberglass satellite dish. With darkening, sunset-pink clouds scudding overhead the unit was pointing nearly horizontal to the ground, and the top of the hill here was the only area cleared in their thickly forested area. Jody was trying to make a connection in the junction box underneath the dish framework while his mother worked the satellite catcher's controls back in his room in their double-wide.

Barefoot, clad only in his smudged-white, Fruit-of-the-Loom briefs, and girded with a pistol belt full of tools and a .32 automatic, Jody's uneven teeth chattered against the metal of the flashlight stuffing his open mouth. He keyed the mike on the two-way radio. "Mom, now!" Jody gurgled, and spit out the flashlight. "Don't forget to punch in a zero before the..." The dish began to whir and pack down against his shoulders. "Mom! Hit cancel! No, hit... Okay! Okay!"

Jody's radio crackled.

"I forgot the zero!"

"You almost killed me!"

"Didn't you tell me at supper last night you were going to kill yourself anyway?"

"Yes! Myself! Punch in F - zero - four!"

The machine whirred again, this time moving slowly the other way, coming to a stop just a few inches from its previous position. Jody pulled his good shoulder out of harm's way. (His left shoulder was deformed since birth and held an arm only half the normal length, with a hand, fingers, and a thumb where the elbow should be). Jody twirled a wire-nut onto the connection he'd just made and keyed his mike. "How's the picture? Right on?"

"Oh, my God."

"You don't have to watch the movie! Just tell me if it's coming in clear!"

"Ohhhhh. Jody! Why do you have to watch this stuff! Ohhhh. My God! It's Sylvester Stallone! Himself!"

"Shit, Mom!" Jody got out from underneath, wobbled a little in the chilly, evening breeze, and looked up at the sky. "Sylvester Stallone? Mom, I don't get it! The dish is pointing in the right place!"

"No, no, no, oh, my God!"

"Mom!" Jody clasped an arm and a half around his shivering ribs and stared down the slope at their double-wide sitting on concrete blocks off in the distance, part-way down the hill through the woods. All the windows were glowing with the bluish, flickering haze of television, computer, and security monitors.

Jody picked up the big flashlight and switched it to his left paw. He keyed the mike again. "Mom!"

"Oh! Yes, son! Perfect picture!"

"Sylvester Stallone? What channel? Did you mess with the channels?"

"No, no! Oh. Neat. Now he's — ohhhhh. Jody, no, it's Sly Stallone about twenty, thirty years ago! In a porn flick. Oh, would you believe? Where' your blank tapes? Jody?"

"You wouldn't let me buy anymore last time, remember?" Jody tapped the battery compartment on the two-way. "Mom?"

But Jasmine, his mother, had abandoned her radio and was already tearing her way to the living room for a cassette tape. Jody calmly screwed the waterproof cover back onto the junction box and began to whistle through his broken teeth. Jasmine was a news and video freak, and she would have that fresh tape slapped into his VCR in seconds. No, now she was going to catch SatCom-4 with her own dish — the largest one on their hill — record Rocky Hard Stallone on DVD — and Jody stopped whistling to listen to the giant, sixteen-footer whine into position. His mother had it painted a dumb-looking brown to match the plastic shutters on her trailer, and the bushes around it which Jody was supposed to keep trimmed were snapping and breaking as the giant, steel-mesh parabola reached deeply into the ether for the fuck-movie channels. Well, he could watch Rambo come in a dead starlet later — from his mother's disc. It certainly wasn't anything he wanted to view with Jasmine right there and gushing all those *oh-my-gods* and stuff. Like she knew who her god was.

On his way back down the grassy, tire-track road to their trailer (with the flashlight on so he wouldn't step on any of his step-father's broken beer bottles)(broken because neither Jack nor Jody could resist target-shooting every one that turned up) Jody stopped once to stare farther, past his mother's double-wide, down into the valley at his adopted father's camper — the little RV where Jack went to live after the divorce. Jack's tiny clearing was barely visible in the twilight, hidden in the cypress forest the way it was, but when the man was home you could see the lights twinkling and reflecting off the swamp, and hear Jasmine's pump go on and off every time Jack used water. Despite the quickly cooling air, Jody stopped once more to look down there and listen. The swamp was noisy with bugs and bullfrogs, but he thought he'd heard something more. And he heard the pump click on briefly.

Sometimes, when the pump would run for a long time, Jody would sneak out of bed and ease down the path to his father's place to watch the girlfriends take showers. The camper was too small for indoor plumbing and the shower was out on a deck Jack had made, which also sported a gleaming, pink commode and an electric hot-water heater with the faces of pretty ladies from all around the world glued all over it. Beauties of all races and colors, smiling and looking out at you from under the clear epoxy coat which Jack had applied after clipping them from magazines. And a bright lamp on a post, of course, so Jack's current poke wouldn't get paranoid about the snakes and centipedes which shared their modest chunk of hilly, Northwest Florida territory.

As deformed as he was, Jody had a genius IQ but seemed to be short on common sense. And it always surprised him that his dad could reel in all these foxes when there seemed to be so little to offer them down there. The ladies sure were fun to watch, though. *Oh, god!* as Jasmine would say. And Jody would fall in love with every one of them. Later, in his room, he would look at his deformed body in the mirror and cry. But not for long. Fuck it. None of them would go with a fourteen-year-old anyway, deformed or not, unless he were rich. And rich is what Jody had decided one day he would be.

On the back porch of the double-wide, Jody checked the matching-brown drier to see if his only decent pair of jeans was dry, and listened for the sound of a distant, approaching vehicle. Jack had promised to take Jody out in the boat the next time, which would be today, and then forgotten. Jody reminded himself that he was glad Jack was not his real father. There would be no chance of ever succeeding big-time if he had inherited a four-cylinder brain. And without money, no chance ever to score pretty girls who fucked for money.

Jasmine was standing tall in the light of the glowing monitors in their large living room. She was shaking a DVD disc at him, her aging, six-foot, muscular, iron-pumped body busting out of the quaint, flower-print, sun dress she was wearing. "Got him!" she yelled. "The last part of it, anyway. Tomorrow during my work-out with this on the monitor? Ha!"

"Mom, don't be gross." Jody adjusted the laden pistol-belt which was digging into the waistband of his Fruits while Jasmine patted and poked at her short, menopause-red pixie-cut.

"And I've got your father and his new air-head on disc, too."

"Mom, you already showed it to me."

"How much do you think they'll pay me for it? You think that head's real?"

"Maybe, yeah, but when I came in a car was banging up the hill. Sounded like Dad's pickup with the trailer empty."

Jasmine quickly handed Jody the disc. "Put this in the rec-room for me. I have to fix my face."

"Mom, there's nothing you can do. You got old. You got like my arm. Nothing you can do."

"He might bring her up here. I don't want the new bitch to see me without my make-up."

Jody shook his head. "Especially this one."

"Oh? Describe."

"Mom. You saw her on the news."

"Yeah, but what else can you tell me. It can't hurt me, you know that, what Jack does."

"Oh, sure. Okay. Her name's Norma. She looks even better in real life than on TV. Gorgeous. And smart, too. And young — much too young for Dad — and built like a brick shit house. And she's..."

"That's enough. I get the picture. A real opportunist, in other words. Doing her best to get as much as she can out of Jack."

"Mom, Dad doesn't **have** anything!"

Jasmine was eyeing the security monitors. "Good. They're not stopping. Yup. Trailer's empty. Jack sank the boat. I knew it was only a matter of time. They had the boat this afternoon when the news shots were taken, though."

Jody was turning the DVD around in his hands, no case, staring at it. "Sylvester Stallone's really in this fuck movie?"

"Jody! Watch your language around me, please! Yes! Oh, look at this. A police car! Sneaking in behind them with the lights out!"

Jody rushed to the perimeter-road monitor and saw the tail end of a cruiser just passing their last yard light. It was following down the road to his step-father's camper, the brake-lights blipping on-and-off and blanking-out the black & white security monitor.

"I'm getting dressed."

"Please do. And take the videocam when you go down there. The new Sony. There might not be much light. Oh, and if she takes a shower."

"If she does, the movie is mine."

"After I dupe it."

"Deal, but I keep the original!"

The secret path Jody had cut through the woods, parallel to but out of sight of Jack's twisting, downhill driveway, was close enough, however, that Jody had to stop running and walk in a crouch when he neared the police cruiser. He was glad to see that it was old Sheriff Eastland, parked half-way down and apparently alone with the window open. Jody wondered why the man had snuck in with the lights out since he was family. Jack's father no less.

The head! They must still have it!

Jody decided to take a chance and force his way through the huckleberry thicket to the side of Eastland's car. When he neared the window, he was surprised to see the sheriff twisted in the seat and looking out the back.

Jody whispered. "Uncle Cletus? It's me."

The sheriff jumped, and nearly knocked off his big cowboy hat when he turned. "Hey, Nub-man! Hey. Don't worry, I'm not after Jack. I'm just making sure nobody followed. I can see your mother's place from here, too. But I didn't see you! Come on, get in. It's getting cold."

Jody waved the Sony in his face and shook his head.

"Oh. Going for more outdoor shower movies, huh? Well. You ever tell Jack you do that?"

"Noooo. The head. They still got it?"

"I hope so. I need to take it back with me. Everybody knows about it, now. You see the news?"

"Yeah. Neat, huh."

"Not for me. Go on then. You can tell them I'll be down directly."

"They don't know you followed them?"

"No."

"I think I just heard the pump turn on."

"Well, I guess I can wait that long. Hurry up!" Eastland slipped the boy a manly wink. "Don't forget, I'll need a copy. Just between you and me and the Siamese computer in that camera."

"Uh-huh." Jody headed down the drive to a place he knew where he could access his path without getting all scratched up from the undergrowth. As for the video, if he could get some good shots of Norma in the shower it would be a cold day in hell before anybody else got to see them besides Jody, adopted-name Jody Rebman, alias Nub-man. Uncle Cletus was pretty smart, though. *Siamese computer. Made in Thailand? ha ha!*

Sheriff Cletus Eastland, the oldest sheriff still in office in the world. Homer County, Florida: terminally rural with a population under twenty-thousand souls, so-to-speak. Souls who were quite happy and proud to keep this cooperative, good-old-boy in office (with a few, short-term exceptions) decade after decade. Cletus was eighty-five, still sharp, and relished the fact that just about every other law enforcement officer and agency in the State of Florida and the federal government was praying for his death, natural or otherwise.

Often, when Cletus was alone on a stake-out as he was now, he would review his life with such total satisfaction and joy that it made his head hurt.

CHAPTER 6
The Sacred Shower Deck

At first Jody did not recognize the metallic noises coming from behind the camper — and the clinking of chains — until he realized they were unhitching the trailer. But from his vantage point at the edge of the shower-deck clearing, their voices were plain enough.

"You could've let me bring some clothes!"

"Norma, the cops have got to have your place staked out."

"And not my boat slip? Duh."

"Give me a break. They probably don't even know your ex had a boat, okay? Anyway, I have some stuff that'll fit you. For now."

"Oh. Yeah. Some ex-girlfriend's crawly-crab infested jeans, right?"

"I washed them before I put them up."

"Jack, forget it! No way!"

Jody heard the creaking of the boat trailer and pictured his step-father lifting it off the bumper hitch. The moon came out from behind the clouds and cast the eerie scene in luminescent blue and gray. Norma, in sight at the side of the camper with her arms crossed over her chest. Bare legs? Wearing a sweatshirt? The glare from the light at the shower deck, which was on the near side of the cabin, hindered Jody's vision.

Oh, please, Norma. Please feel all funky. Please want a shower real bad.

Think of how good the hot water will feel!

Oh, please, God! Please make her want to take a shower!

The crippled boy's prayers were answered immediately. It was a miracle. Sitting in the darkness at the edge of the clearing, Jody held the Sony with his good arm steady against the inside of his knees so he could look over the viewfinder for long, hormone-crunching intervals. Despite the night chill, he wished he hadn't dressed before coming down here, though. There simply wasn't room enough in his jeans for what was happening to him.

Jody stumbled back to his mother's trailer through the dark woods. He was in love, only this time it was the real thing. *Norma. Norma. I love you, Norma!* He tripped several times because he was off of his trail, but the new video, safe in the Sony under his good arm, was precious now. Sacred. Just before he reached the clearing of their big double-wide, Jody tripped on a scuppernong vine and slapped headlong to the ground, partially breaking the fall with his nub hand while protecting the camera with his good arm. The Sony survived the crash but not Jody's nose. He entered the trailer, bleeding, via the back door after hiding the camera behind the giant Tide box on the back porch shelf above the matching, earth-tone brown, Kenmore, washer-drier ensemble.

"Jody! Oh my god!"

"Which god, Mom?! Shit! I tripped."

"Oh my god!" Jasmine steered the boy to the bathroom and shoved his head under a stream of cold water from the shower head. "God, Jody, you're bleeding to death!"

"I don't think so, Mom. I have a reason to live now."

"Twenty minutes. The pump ran twenty minutes. She must not have plumbing where she lives."

"Mom, she lives in a fancy Condo. On the beach. The Cremo del Mar."

"Cremo del Mar. How dumb! Where's my Sony?"

"Safe. I didn't drop it."

"Nose stopped bleeding. Go get it."

"After I dupe the video."

"I want it now!" Jasmine slung a towel at him and glared, hands on her hips, her steroid-fertilized deltoids rippling under the straps of her tight sun-dress.

"No."

"I'll slap the fire out of you!"

"Go ahead."

The two stared at each other. Then Jody looked down at the blood and dirt on his shirt and pulled the sticky material away from his chest with his nub-hand. "Mama, that video is the closest a man like me will ever get to a lady like her."

"Lady, huh?"

"Yes, Mom. Maybe if you weren't blowing so much snow and munching gorilla biscuits when you conceived me I'd have a chance. I'd have a real body."

"Jody, if I'd had my shit together back in those days you wouldn't even be here. You'd be a dried-up stain on some whorehouse wallpaper!"

"Yes, dear, sweet mother."

"So what took you so long down there? After the shower of paradise."

"I wanted to see what they were going to do."

"And?"

"Norma's sitting in Uncle Cletus's car right now. He's going to take her back to her condo after he straightens everything out with the Bay County sheriff. Bay County is still hunting them. She needs to be near her phone in case movie producers call and stuff like that."

"She's dreaming."

Uncle Clit's taking the cooler with the head, too. It's in the trunk. He let me look at it. It doesn't look as neat as it did on TV. I guess it's going bad. The ice is all melted. They slid empty beer bottles all around it so it doesn't roll around."

"He shouldn't let a fourteen-year-old boy see stuff like that. I'm going to tell him, too, if he stops here. What else?"

"That's all."

"You take your shower. I'll dupe the video for you, don't worry. I'm sorry I got mad, Jody."

It wasn't coke or Quaaludes I did back then.

Just a little angel-dust rolled into every joint. PCP.

Poor Jody! But it wasn't my fault. I didn't know.

"The camera behind the Tide?"

"Mom, if anything happens to it, I'll know it wasn't an accident."

"Jody, I love you. Really! So what else happened down there?"

"Nothing."

But there was more, and after Jasmine closed the bathroom door Jody inspected his throbbing nose, felt to see if it was broken, and gently probed the swelling. Then he shucked off his shoes and clothing and got in the tub under a good stream of hot water and jerked off. He pictured the headless, female bodies in the Bay County morgue that he had overheard Uncle Cletus tell his step-father about after putting Norma in the car to wait. "There's more than one." Uncle Clit had described them in detail, after which Jack said, so typical for him: "Young and built. What a waste."

After Norma's shower, Jody had taken up a position

at the window on the far side of his step-father's camper, where the little bed was and the dumb, little, thirteen-inch TV with the coat-hanger antenna. Where Jody could see and hear everything.

Eastland had let himself in and was leaning back in the big rocking chair — which barely fit in the cramped camper — his pointy-toed lizard-skin boots propped up on the tiny, stainless steel sink, which Jack used to store his socks and the colorful bandannas he used for hankies. The sheriff felt good, and proud. "Yep, Jack, when I go out, it'll be with a bang! Not the kind of bang you and your horny little Nub-man like, although I'm not too old for that kind of stuff yet, no, not yet. Not ever. Nope. Not ever."

"Dad, it's not right to call him Nub-man. It's not his fault."

"Hell, Jack, that's **his** idea. Force people to look him in the eye when he's around instead of pretending the little crip's not there! He's smart, Jack. Real smart. And way, way ahead of his age group if you ask me. It's wrong for you and Jasmine to make him go to school, too. He hates it and he doesn't need it. This dumb-little country school here. All those insensitive little rednecks."

Jack thought about it. "And the clones are dumb, huh?"

"You wouldn't believe. We've got this Jap who has that part figured out. But production got out of hand and we need another safe place to feed them and put them all up. So, if you want in, your first job is to throw off the feds. Keep them off the island. Tell them you picked up the head on Tyndall. I noticed on the news you didn't say more than the word beach. Am I right?

Think, now. This is important. They'll be up in the air at first light. And the FLIR chopper is already looking."

Jack had to think. "No, unless Norma told."

"She says no. And she didn't say what island on the news."

"I'm supposed to make out we found it on Tyndall, huh?"

"Call it Tyndall Island, which is what the peninsula looks like from a boat if you don't know any better. Pretend to be dumb. Forget your ego on this one. Near the base yacht club. Only you think its a private club, not part of an air base."

"Yeah."

"Meanwhile, I'm flying over the island tomorrow. Herd up the runaways with the dope chopper." Eastland leaned back and laughed, the bookshelf behind him edging the brim of his hat down over his eyes. "Just like they herd cows out west. With choppers. I want to see for myself what Manny's doing out there. I can't believe he was planning to ship that reject pod. Now he's claiming a couple of his buddies kidnapped them and took them out there, but I'm not so sure."

"Pod?"

"Litter. The bunch you ran up on. They're rejects. Too smart. Starting to think on their own. The ragheads don't want them. They're not virgins."

"Rejects. Virgins." Jack scratched his head and tried to get a feel of the reality of all this. If he hadn't actually seen a few of them himself, or found the severed head, it would all sound like so much senile bullshit. Deadpecker bench fantasies. His father so much older than him. No ass and no brain left to mind the store.

"I want to go along."

"No, no, you go out to the feed-lot with Jackson

tomorrow. Meet Doctor Mannlicher. Meet Monday, his wife. Oh, Jack, Monday. You won't believe Manny's wife!"

"Dad, then your pilot will know!"

"He's in on it."

"Shit Dad, that sucks. All this time your own son doesn't know shit what's going on and some smart-ass chopper pilot you hired off the street knows everything! I'm your son!"

"He's your step-brother, Jack. One of many". Eastland sighed. "Too many already know about it. Look back, son. All the times I told you to straighten up, make some sense of your life, get your shit together. See? What did I get? You can't blame me. When were you ever serious about anything? Huh?"

"I can't believe somebody finally figured out how to make fuck clones and nobody knows about it. Nobody gets caught. All those cute little slaves. I can't believe you never told me."

"Okay. I was wrong. Right now you're just the right man for this. We need a hand and I should've thought of you sooner. Because you're blood. Family. Okay? But I ain't stayed in office for half a century by being careless. You understand? I hope so, because I love you, Jack. I love you."

In his mother's bathroom, Jody turned up the cold water and shivered. He could still hear Eastland's voice when he'd said, "I love you." And then Jack's voice, cracking, with a meek tone Jody had never heard before. Jack, leaning back on the pillows on his camper bed, looking up at the low ceiling, almost turning toward the window before Jody could jump away in time.

"Clones. Barbie doll clones." Sounding like he had

just discovered a real pot full of gold under a rainbow. Finding out that his father loved him and that he knew where there was an endless supply of young pussy. Finding out about all that in the same, precious moment.

"Oh, Daddy, I can see them! I can see myself just a rollin' in 'em! Just a rollin' in an acre of 'em."

It was times like this that Jody felt happy and proud that Jack had adopted him. Even with the exaggerated rebel embellishments the man felt obliged to use when he was excited.

"And no AIDS, Jack. Think of what that means, boy!"

"I'm thinking! I'm thinking!"

"The world price of rubber'll go straight to the bottom!"

"Just like the price of pussy."

CHAPTER 7
The Cremo del Mar

As soon as Sheriff Cletus Eastland dropped her at the Cremo del Mar, and after he had checked out her apartment for thugs, Norma shucked off the ladies jeans Jack had lent her.

So tight!

Must've been some undernourished, air-head, high-school slut.

She reflected on the lonely elevator ride up to her fifth floor with the antique lawman looking every bit the part, and as silent as a wax statue of a mustachioed Jack Palance. Yet he seemed to be perfectly at home when they had entered the fancy high-rise. Well, he ought to be used to everything at eighty-five years old! Norma looked at herself in the full-length foyer mirror, tugged down the sweatshirt just a little to cover her neatly-clipped bush, and wiggled her manicured and painted toes in the thick carpet.

"Home sweet home!" she said with a happy voice. "Indoor plumbing! Thick, warm, snuggly carpets! A thermostat on the wall!"

Jack's outdoor shower was kinda neat, though.

She padded to the living-room and drew the long draperies over the twinkling scene below: the yachts at berth in the small, man-made harbor which was the pride of the Cremo. Miss Chernobyl looked so forlorn and, well, low-bucks down there. But the boat sure did the job! Norma sighed and tugged at the open slit between the draperies so that no sickos on the piers could

48

watch her with binoculars, then reached for the note-book on the end-table next to the blinking, retro answer-machine. Flinging herself full length and bare-ass on the long couch facing her huge TV, Norma arched her left index finger over the play-messages button. Blood-red, vampire nail, poised over an electronic servant. The finger dropped. Norma grinned and wiggled her bottom deeper into the couch, shoving her back against the armrest so she could jot down notes. A little zippy sound, and a beep:

A sweet, virginal, female voice: "Hello, this is Melanie Pedway. You don't know me. I'm from the First Holiness Deliverance Church on Back Beach Road? I saw you on the news and I know the Lord will forgive you if you..."

Norma fast-forwarded the ancient, micro-cassette machine to the next message.

...tweedle-de-deedle-de-deep...

Another unfamiliar, female voice: "Indecent whore! Necrophile! My family's been putting in at the boat-ramp right next to Rasputin's since before the Devil inseminated your mama! My husband and I have children! You may not know this but forcing a kiss on the mouth of a dead hooker is against the law and my husband is going to file a complaint with the Panama City Beach police, and..."

...tweedle-de-deedle-de-deedle-de-deep...

"Hello, this is Vicki Jonathan, News Force Eleven? I'm sorry I missed you but if you could call me back at..."

Norma happened to glance up at her dark television set and her mouth opened in disbelief. Missing the "Stop" button on the answer machine, she froze. From a reflection on the blank screen, her foyer door was open a crack and a wire-like object was trying to fish the chain off the hook. And she was sure she had carefully locked the knob and the dead-bolt after Eastland left! Her heart pounded up so furiously that Norma became oblivious to everything Vicki Jonathan was saying: "...waiver forms to be signed on the release of their interview for ABC...a follow-up report tomorrow on the local news with a plug for the national coverage...a follow-up on the investigation... Are you aware that the head you found has been tentatively matched with two bodies at the morgue thought to be twins?"

My gun's in the boat! Is it? Shit! I left my .41 in the boat!

Norma let Vicki Jonathan run on as she eased off to her bedroom for the little .22 mag derringer she kept in a slit in the upholstered headboard of her king-size bed. Should she rush out with it before they got in? Cock the gun and wait behind the bedroom door?

The answer machine switched to an impressively confident, male voice which was extolling the owner's love for her, his destiny, referring to Norma as "...the chick with the red hair and nice ass." He truly loved her body, and he loved her spirit. A date as soon as possible would be of great benefit to both of them. "Stand you on your head and eat you till the cows come home."

Behind the half-open bedroom door now, with the double barreled pistol cocked, Norma heard someone switch off the machine. Her mind was scrambling for answers. The first thing they'd do is slap the bedroom door wide open, smacking it into her and eliminating her element of surprise. She needed to move, and fast! Sucking in a deep breath, she bolted from her hiding place and burst into the living room. The first man was already so close to the bedroom that she nearly smashed into him and the top barrel of the gun went off into the middle of his pudgy gut. The sound was muffled so effectively by the gent's fat stomach that Norma thought it was a hang-fire and forgot to cock the pistol for a second shot. Both of the men were swarthy and middle-aged — in Hawaiian shirts and shorts — different clothes but the same men who had tried to kidnap her on the island. The first one who took the bullet in the gut screamed as he slumped to the floor, hanging onto her bare, smoothly-shaved legs as a lock of his greasy, slicked-back hair caught on her wiry-red bush. Norma eyes fixed on the other dude who was still in the foyer and apparently just as shocked as she was. The pistol took Norma two hands to cock because the hammer was so small and hard to grip, and just as she was raising it to fire, the loser at her feet let out another yell and wrapped his arms tighter around her legs. Without thinking, Norma lowered the muzzle and dumped her second and last shot into the top of his balding head. He shuddered and slumped, still on his knees, and pitched forward onto the white shag rug as dark, venous blood quietly leaked from the tiny, black hole in the top of his scalp. A brighter, more vivid gush of blood suddenly burst from his mouth but Norma didn't have time to appreciate it.

Jumping to the side, she crouched and cocked the empty derringer again, hoping against hope that the other guy would be terminally stupid.

He wasn't. "You fock up," he grinned. His eyes darted up and down the length of her before he stepped over his dead partner and drew a bloody, old 9MM Astra out of the dead man's waistband. "Abu is my first wife brother. You fock up bad, even if he is a asshole."

"Was — an — asshole." Norma dropped the derringer and backed away from the man until she ran into wall.

Her head bumped and tilted the framed picture she had hanging there of the ex-dictator of Panama, Manuel Noriega, in full military dress complete with his fifty-mission-crush flier's hat.

"He like pink nipples, too?"

"I'm sorry I shot him! Please. I didn't mean it. I panicked." Norma pressed her back against the plaster as the Astra's muzzle touched her Adam's apple.

"Noriega. How much he pay?"

"Ten grand," Norma lied. She heard the hammer cock back with a smooth click. "Please don't shoot me. I didn't mean it, I swear!"

"Ten grand." His eyes briefly left hers and scanned the naked territory below her sweatshirt. She was looking past him, chin up, holding her breath and shaking as he lifted up the hem of the sweatshirt Jack had lent her.

"Okay! Pink! Nooooo, maybe better say, strawberry." He backed away. "Remove shirt and sit. I play with your tits later."

Norma could smell his heavy breath and a hint of BO. Alcohol breath, like Jack's was whenever he drank too much Old No. 7. "I have to go to the bathroom."

She watched him drag one of the chairs from the kitchen over to the TV and face it toward the couch.

"I have to go bad."

"No, no, not so fast. Shirt off!"

Tears were rolling down Norma's eyes now as she pulled the sweatshirt over her head. What she hated more was the fact that she'd left her revolver in the boat. So stupid. So helpless!

"I'll piss myself."

"No, no, not now please. Wait for my friend come. He like that stuff. Gold shower stuff. You wait for him."

"Oh, Christ."

"Please, no Jesus. No pork, either, okay? They make me convert to Islam. Sit!" His voice was high and effeminate, Norma thought. Like a foreign Michael Jackson. With a Cuban accent.

The kitchen chair had a tubular, bright chromium frame with a small, vinyl-covered seat and a curved, vinyl back support. The plastic was a light green and covered with white-petaled daisies with yellow centers. The thick man grunted as he kneeled before the chair and pulled at the coil of rope in his left hand with his teeth. The gun, still in his right, never wavered from pointing at Norma's face — right between her eyes. Once, when he had turned the muzzle just the right way, she caught a glimpse of the bullet down in the barrel, the copper jacket reflecting the overhead light — the missile chambered and waiting for launch.

"Please."

"Sit!" I want to see your ass on this cold plastic.

Norma complied. Shaking again. "Could you turn the thermostat up a little?"

A kink. Watching my ass spread out on the chair. I'm as good as dead, anyway, after killing his friend. His brother-in-law. I should go for his gun. Now!

But Norma's courage failed her. He looked so — like he would do anything. "Please, I'm shivering. And I still have to pee bad. Is your friend coming soon?"

"Hands behind chair."

The palm of his hand felt cool and alien and sticky as he pulled on her wrists. He was wrapping the cord around her elbows, pulling them painfully close together and forcing her shoulders back.

"Make your tits stick out better," he explained. "I have to make video."

"You're sick."

53

"I'm a man."

"Allah is maybe not so great? Oh, I'm sorry. Please. I'm so scared."

"You mean." He moved around her, still on his knees — still plenty of rope left. He was smiling for the first time. Yellow, narrow teeth. "I know what you mean." He wrapped the cord around her legs just below the knees, then strung it around the chair legs. Norma tried to concentrate on him, rather than her fate. The oily, black, tight waves of hair at the sides of his head. The chewed-down fingernails. The gun which was lying now on the thick, white pile of her carpet so he could tie a knot. The gun looked like a brown-metal water pistol. Norma had seen that particular model at gun shows many times. Single action auto, she thought. Spanish army surplus? Sometime in the last few minutes he must have lowered the hammer back down.

Losing her concentration, she pictured the man's stubby fingertips probing up into her. She shuddered.

"Where's the camera?"

"My comrade. He come soon."

"What will you do with the video?" She wanted to ask what she had to do on the video but was too afraid. "What's your name?"

Still on his knees, he grunted his way over to poor, silent Abu, and leaned over to look at the darkening pool of blood seeping into the white shag. Then he began to feel under Abu's Ocean Pacific tennis shorts. "My name is Hector."

"Hector." Norma had once been raped by a Cuban named Hector. In Miami. Well, she called it a rape, since he ran off without paying. Before she met her husband, of course — god rest his soul. One time she told her husband the story when they were both drunk, and he became furious. Even more so when she remarked: "Well, you never pay me, either!"

Hector grunted to his feet with Abu's wallet, stood behind her chair, and slowly cupped his brown hands just underneath Norma's breasts. But he didn't touch. Just a long, painful sigh and then he was headed for the kitchen and the fridge. When he came back with a cold Miller his erection was obvious under the long, flowery Hawaiian shirt. He flopped himself back into the middle of the couch and faced her, and tilted his head for a long pull.

"You thought I was Arab? A sand nigger? Shee-it!" Another long pull. "I am a Cuban Jew."

"Oh." Norma tried to picture one. *Hell, I'm looking at one!*

"No goat humper. What you call them? Camel drivers? Rag heads?"

He looked so relaxed that Norma began to feel her own tension ease, but not by much. The guy with the videocam was coming. Soon. "But you said Abu was your wife's brother."

"One of them."

"One of her brothers, or one of your wives?"

That desert kingdom smile again. Not enough water to waste on brushing teeth. "Yesssss, I have many wives."

"The law says four, right?"

"Depends which country. The law? Ha! You interest in the law, Miss Norma?"

"Please let me go to the bathroom. Please? Before he comes?"

The knock on the door came before Hector could answer.

Ten minutes later, still alive, Norma winced when

the new guy, a hunk, whipped out a knife and cut the section of carpet they'd decided to wrap her in. With all her credit cards maxed out and no husband to pay them, there'd be no way to replace the white shag. If she lived.

Norma had been fearful of what was going to happen when they first cut her loose from the chair. Maybe she was better off when she was tied up. Were they planning to kill her?

She had been even more terrified when the hunky guy grabbed her and held her up-side-down by the ankles to take a good look.

"Lay down!"

Norma's mind jolted back to the present.

"No! On the square. No, on the carpet square! We roll you up in it now. Arms at your sides!"

Rough pushing, and tucking of the white shag as they rolled her into it. At least nobody was pulling on her with pliers, or putting out their burning cigarettes on her.

The German-sounding guy probably doesn't smoke.

Did they have to roll her up in such a big piece?

But the darkness inside the rug, and the lush thickness of it around her nakedness, was a comfort. Temporary, but nice nonetheless. She tilted her head back to breathe better but hated the little bit of light that the movement let in from the rolled end above her head. She tried to remember what they had said about where they were taking her when the younger dude was performing his crude little medical exam. "Spread wider!" German accent. ("Vell, zat'z nice. No herpes. No varts. No tuna. You douche today?")

"None of your fucking business, asshole!" Not an easy thing to spit out when some huge, muscular dude is holding you up-side-down in the air by your ankles and scoping out your twat. He looked like Arnold Schwarze-negger but much younger. Just the opposite of Hector, who had chug-a-lugged the last beer while Klaus bitched about his drinking. Klaus.

When Hector let him in, Klaus had walked right up to where she was lashed to the kitchen chair, bent down, and with his face inches from hers, said: "Hello, my name is Klaus. Pleased to meet you." Arrogant fucker! Pepsodent breath. White Levi's. Gold-trimmed sandals. White T-shirt filled to bursting with clean, iron muscle. Big, jade crucifix on a heavy, gold chain. Who the hell did this big jock think he was? At least he didn't twist and pull on her tits or anything crude like that. Just the up-side-down, eyeball-only, amateur gynecologic — quick and to the point. Remembering what Hector had told her about him, she neglected to inform him she needed to pee.

What were they waiting for? In the snug and safe confines of her carpet roll, Norma tried to hear what they were saying.

The little Cuban guy: "I told you, they grow them from the focking tail now. We don't focking need her parents!"

"Who said parents? I said the man wants her baby snapshots!" The younger man sounded so much like Ar-nold! ("...vahnts har baybee znapp-schatz!") Norma could hear muffled sounds of dresser drawers being yanked open and slammed shut.

"No sisters?"

"One. One focking sistor. Live in Tampa or some-place."

"And no more Corona or I pinch your fucking head off! Okay, let's get her out of here."

"All she had was Miller. What about Abu?"

"Fuck Abu! If there's time, we get a hacksaw and bag him up for the garbage chute."

Norma braced herself. Footsteps on both sides of her head and feet. She could feel the bulging muscles of Klaus reaching around under her shoulders. Wherever she was going, she'd have no clothes.

A more feeble attempt at her feet. "Fock! The carpet make her too heavy, men!"

"Shit. Wait. Roll her on the side. We carry her out the elevator on her side. You just keep her feet up. Under one arm, like this."

Norma sensed the struggle and tried to help by shifting her arms. Klaus's arms were as long as they were powerful and she felt cramped and squeezed as she and her jerking cocoon left the floor.

"One arm, Heck! One arm! Make it look light as a feather." To Norma: "Straighten up in there!"

Her ass bumped into the doorway on the way out.

"Straighten up in there!"

"Shhhhh!" Hector said.

Some faint, unfamiliar voices. Then Klaus said: "No, no, thank you. You go ahead. We wait for the next car. This carpet is polyester. Very light. The one they want us to install, though, well, that will take four of us!"

Norma heard the elevator door open and close while the two men waited. They readjusted her under their arms. Should she have tried yelling for help? She could feel her tail sagging — lower than the rest of her now — and she wasn't going to be able to hold her urine any longer. It had become beyond enduring and she was going to have to piss on herself. But that would add weight and make the carpet even heavier for them. No, that's stupid. Dumb. ahhhhhhh. So warm and good. Let it all go. She was a dead bitch, anyway.

Klaus's voice: "Press B"

"Basement?"

"No, basura, garbage-for-brains."

Norma cringed. In all the time she'd owned her apartment at the Cremo, she never pressed "B". Never thought much about the basement. It was where the plumbing was, she assumed, and the end-of-the-line for the garbage chute in her kitchen, and storage areas for the machinery and chemicals the maids and janitors needed — all that yucky and best-not-thought-about stuff.

They had tossed her keys into the opening of the carpet roll near her head and the ring with the Playboy Bunny medallion was working itself down and digging into her shoulder blades. She tried to squirm the keys away.

Klaus: "Be still."

"The keys hurt."

"The least of your problem."

"Kidnapping is a federal offense. The FBI will get you for this!"

"If it make you feel better, I was kidnap, too. ("vass kit-nap") When I was twelve year old. Not even one little clue of your FBI."

When the elevator stopped at the bottom, Norma could definitely smell the dank, cool atmosphere of the basement. She supposedly had a storage bin down here with her apartment number on it, which she had never seen or used, and she was guessing they might want to dump her in there temporarily since her keys were along for the ride. But they kept going on and on, with a brief struggle down some kind of dark, narrow place which was even more musty smelling, with no light at all sneaking in above her head now. Then up about two steps to another basement level. They kept on shifting her weight around and sometimes it was hard to breathe. Another building? The next door building — The Viking. An older resident from The Viking whom Norma had met at the supermarket once had bitched about water in her storage area, among other complaints. Bitched about all the new, foreign residents The Viking was getting, the new people rudely speaking in neither English or Spanish in the elevator. Their expensive, extra vehicles always stuffing the parking lot to capacity including the long, antique, Chevrolet Impala blocking her BMW's numbered parking place whenever she was out — complaints to the owner's organization notwithstanding. Norma had not replied to any of this because the Impala, a mint, fully-restored '64, was hers — parked at the Viking to avoid repossession.

Norma could hear their feet splashing through a wet section.

"Fockin' bitch is heavy!"

"Bullshit. Trade ends?"

Norma had to squirm again to relieve the pain of the keys digging into her flesh. Apparently they hadn't noticed yet that the middle of the carpet was soaked with her piss.

"Where are you taking me?"

"To the shipping department."

"Ohhhh.... To where?"

Hector's voice, muffled through the carpet: "To a harem someplace nice."

"A harem where?"

Klaus: "You can get there from Baghdad."

"Nice, waterfront harem. With a focking view."

"With a nice balcony." ("Viss a nyze balconie.") Perfect match of Arnold's voice! "You can watch the ships

60

go by. Ships full of oil."

"Please."

"Please what?"

"Please let me go. I'll do anything you want."

Hector laughed.

Klaus said, "You are doing anything we want anyway, baby."

She could feel them making a real effort now, Hector grunting and cursing as they worked the carpet roll up over something. Level ground again, their feet still on concrete, though, but no more sounds of water. A whiff of a breeze at the foot end of her cocoon and Norma felt warmer air. But just for a moment.

Hector could not stop bitching. "You think you're so focking smart. We can dump her out here. Make her walk. Make her carry her carpet, like they make Jesus carry his own cross. You think of that?!"

"Shut up. This is as far as she goes. They don't want her up there now. They have a guest today. Some big shot."

They were lowering her to the floor. A spear of light appeared briefly above her head. From a flashlight?

"Where am I?"

"On your back. Roll over!"

"How can I, god damn it!" Norma screamed as Klaus's sandal thumped into her side.

"Yell all you want, Baby. Nobody to hear you here."

They both were shoving her from the right side and she rolled onto her tummy, carpet and all, arms still pinned to her sides. The keys which had been digging into her shoulders fell up against her chin.

"You sure nobody to hear?" Hector said. "What if junkies use this place? Sleep down here? You don't think of everything!"

61

"Yeah? You sweat too much."

Norma felt hands poking around the wet part of the carpet, the urine now cold. *What were they doing?*

"Don't move!" Klaus said. "I'm cutting the rug here. With a knife. Shit, you piss like a horse!"

Norma froze. They were cutting into the carpet right above her ass.

They're going to fuck me through the carpet!

"Nooooo!"

"Shut up! It will only hurt for a second."

She felt a quick prick in her left ass-cheek, then a growing burn inside the muscle. They were injecting her with something!

"No! No, please!"

"Too late, baby!"

"Bye bye," Hector said.

A wonderful rush suddenly began to course through Norma's veins. Her empty stomach glowed with it, then her shoulders. It pulsed through her neck. Her legs lost their weight and she began to float. "Ohhhhh."

"She no say goodbye back," Hector said.

Norma heard him but it didn't matter. It was all so peaceful now.

CHAPTER 8
Jasmine in Boots

Jody watched his step-father trudge up the path toward him through the early-morning mist. That's when Jody realized that he'd left the long-distance, directional mike for his army surplus surveillance outfit leaning on the porch railing, right where Jack would see it. Well, good. Let him bitch. Then the conversation could swing toward this clone stuff. Jody wanted to know more. Much more. No matter what.

"Hi, Pop!"

"Hey, Jody! How's m' man?"

"Nub-man."

"If you insist." Jack was about to climb past Jody up the porch steps of the big, tan double-wide when he spotted the microphone. As a coincidence, Jack was wearing one of his favorite T-shirts, the shirt younger people didn't understand but used to be common. The one with a scoped, long-barreled rifle silk-screened on the front. Above the scope were the letters:

LONG DISTANCE

Underneath the rifle:

"The next best thing to being there!"

The smile left Jack's face. "So you and your mother heard it all, huh?"

"Not her. Just me."

"The phone calls, too?"

"Just me. She has a new fuck movie to play with now."

"That's nice. Where is she?"

"Making breakfast, remember?" (From Jack's last phone call).

"So you got them all, huh? Recorded?"

"Yeah, but we need to erase it." Jody pulled out the audio cassette from his shirt pocket and was about to plug it into his portable when Jack stopped him.

"Right, but let me have it, okay? I always wanted to know how good that thing of yours works."

"Okay. But I get the phone stuff from a direct tap. Good thing Mom was busy, huh? I only used the mike for when you and Uncle Cletus were talking — in your trailer — and all that randy stuff you were yelling to Norma when she was trying to take a shower." As soon as he mentioned the shower, Jody knew he'd screwed up. The shower wasn't on there. It was on the video tape.

"Shower! You were sneaking around when Norma was..."

"Just kidding, Dad! Check it out. There's nothing from her shower on the tape."

"I will. Check it out."

Jody smiled. "It's the clones we need to talk about, Dad."

"Oh? Yeah, well. You're sure your mother didn't hear any of it?"

"Positive. I'm not stupid. Besides, we need to be buddies now. Trust each other. One day you'll be glad you've got a high-tech kid."

"Maybe, but you let her have the tape she used in court to prove infidelity, which wiped out my property settlement."

"You were going to rip us off."

"Not you. Her."

"I like it this way."

"Both sides against the middle."

"I use what I got. Like you. Like she does. Like everybody does. Sit down, Dad."

"Breakfast."

"She'll come get us when it's ready. Need to warn you, though, she's wearing her Phantom outfit."

"The black-leather bikini with the leather bra? The gun-belt with the holster with the flap? Ha ha."

"Right."

"She's goofy. Big time. I could get custody of you now, you know?"

"Please don't."

"You'd like living with me."

"You need your privacy, Dad. And you don't have room for me, remember? I got half a double-wide here with plenty of space for all my stuff. Three squares a day. An allowance. Indoor plumbing. And Mom and I are both into electronics. Can you top that? Mom keeps her promises, too. Up here there's no lovers to compete with. You were supposed to go boating with **me** yesterday."

"Last time we had this discussion you called them whores."

"Norma's wonderful, Dad."

"It's only pussy, son."

"Yeah? Well, this time you got really lucky."

"It's not just luck, boy. Anyway, I'm sorry about yesterday. I couldn't help it. Norma begged to go."

"It's only pussy, Dad. But this one's luck. Pure luck. She looks great, you look old. She has money, you're always broke. She lives at the Cremo, you live in a camper next to the swamp."

"She loves my place down near the pond."

"Pond."

"And she loves my outdoor shower deck. You've

65

seen her condo?"

"No, but I heard."

"Oh. Yeah. Well, anyway, she's broke. Her plastic's near maxed out. As for me, some changes are being made."

"Sure. How?"

"I can't tell you right now, but..."

"Dad, I heard everything! So tell me how you're going to make money on it. I could even help! Remember when you asked Uncle Cletus about the DEA spotter planes and how the clones can't be outside much to sun and stuff like that?"

"Jeez, Jody, I should confiscate your equipment. All of it."

"I could rig up a sound detection system, or radar, or tap into the Fort Rucker flight-line computer, you know, where they keep the choppers. Early warning. Shit, that alone would help. You guys need me."

"Too young."

"Jeez. You know you need me."

"I'm not sure I believe any of it, yet."

"What? Oh, the clones? Even after finding that head? Uncle Clit showed it to me. It was real! I don't see how Norma could kiss it, though. On the mouth." Jody closed his eyes, leaned his head back against the upper step, and pictured Norma's lush, vampire-red mouth opening to receive his own lips and his tongue. He shivered.

"You need to wear a sweatshirt over when you're chilly. You're so thin, Jody. She feed you enough?"

"I said before, three squares a day. You're the one I'd be fighting with over scraps. So where does the money come in."

"Getting ambitious, Jody?"

"You better believe it! Okay. Reality time, Dad. When I'm older. Right now, if I could..." Jody stifled a nervous laugh. "As long as I live, for me, a cripple, an ugly cripple, the only way I'll ever get nice girls is by having a lot of money. The sooner I start, the better. Comprehend?"

"No, Jody, that's not true."

"Fuck it, Pop. We had a deal."

"Okay. Partly true. Maybe."

"So. What's our cut in all this clone shit?"

"Jody, could you please watch your language? At least until you're of age?"

"Tell me about the money. Tell me about the rabbits, George."

"Okay, Lenny. Nub-man."

"Bunnies would be a better word."

Jack laughed and finally sat down, on the same step. "You sure are a smart kid, Jody. All right. With the boat, I figure we can get in on some of the problems with getting the clones out. The whole coast of Florida is being watched for dope. They've boarded my boat so many times in the past, when I was just out there with some chick or other, they don't bother Miss Chernobyl anymore. Now. And apparently they haven't even noticed the clone stuff yet, and..."

"Clones which we haven't even seen. Which may or may not exist. It might be just one of Uncle Cletus's little jokes."

"You just said you saw the head yourself."

"I'm being the devil's advocate here, Dad. Listen. Technology's not up to making human clones like you're talking about. The clones would have to have time to grow up and stuff."

"That's here. In Homer County. The feedlot, he

called it. The lab and stuff is in Bay County. Panama City. Or used to be, I think he said. Shit. Moved to Fort Walton Beach? But the feedlot...."

"Feed lot? Gross! So when do we see them?"

"I see them. This morning."

"Oh, yeah, Jackson's coming to pick you up. You ever meet her?"

"No, Son. You wanted to know how we can make money on the clones."

"Actually, I'd be satisfied just to get a fuck off some of them."

"Jody!"

"Sorry. Bet I took the words right out of your mouth, though!"

Jack turned a little and took a long, fond look at the cripple he had adopted. So smart. When Jack himself was going on fourteen years of age, he hadn't a clue. Of course he hadn't been born crippled like Jody, either, spending all of his free time reading instead of playing with other kids. For a moment, Jack wondered just how smart Jody's real father must've been. A genius? Maybe, since Jasmine was no push-over back then and yet she didn't know who Jody's father was. So she said. Some guy I met at a party.

"Earth to Jack."

"You're all right, kid."

"Nub-man."

"Nub-man."

"Earth Woman to Jack and Nub-man."

Jack and Jody both flinched. Jasmine had eased open the screen door without their hearing it.

"Breakfast is ready."

Jack grunted and looked up at her. His ex looked so virile, so fit and alive, and so happy. He wondered how long she had been listening, and decided to squelch the desire to poke fun at the black leather bikini and the studded, tall, Captain Hook pirate boots. As her long legs stepped over them on their way to the front yard, Jack looked up. She'd shaved. Not a pin-feather. *Don't say anything. Not now. Jody's used to her shit, anyway.*

Jasmine turned to face them, high-lighting herself in a spot where a shaft of early light pierced the trees. She was a scene out of a Heavy Metal comic book. A Crepax Valentina with short, red hair. Jack even felt a twinge of horniness for her and promptly tried to forget it. He would be rejected instantly. For punishment.

"Let's eat out at the picnic table," she said. "It's so nice."

Jack forced his middle-aging body up off the steps and ignored the pain with a smile. He headed for the door to help with the breakfast logistics.

"No, no. You two go sit at the table. Brush the leaves off the benches. I'll take care of everything."

The males did as they were told. Jody picked the bench on his mother's favorite side where she liked to face the hill with the antenna farm. The antenna-towers and the dishes were Jody's pride and joy, too, including the tallest mast with no electronics on it. Their lightening rod. The tallest items were visible above the treetops.

Jack sat opposite and leaned forward to whisper. "She's sure acting cheerful."

"She worked out with that ancient Stallone tape this morning. I guess. That doesn't bother you?"

"Hell no. I was thinking about the clones again."

"Like what?"

Jack sighed.

"Yeah. Dad? You can tell me."

"I don't know anything yet." But Jack wanted to

keep the conversation going, too. He could feel that this was a special moment between them and that Jody felt the same way. A permanent bonding. Jack was sure.

"Tell me about the bunnies, Dad."

"Jody, the way I see it, well, 'course I haven't been out to the feedlot yet, is they need to get the mature clones out. Out of the country. And they're afraid they'll get caught by the DEA or the Coast Guard dope patrols. So I see myself doing a lot of off-shore runs, empty, just beach-combing stuff, you know, but I go way out there into the shipping lanes. Frequently. To get stopped frequently, until they get used to me. Which they already are, actually. Label me as some harmless eccentric."

"And."

"I'm getting to that." Jack paused, and a vacant look crept across his eyes.

Jody leaned closer across the planks of the picnic table. "I'll bet you dreamed about them all night."

"Laid awake staring at the ceiling was more like it. Like you probably did."

Jody smiled. Man-to-man stuff. "Dad, they were dancing across my ceiling. Up-side-down, right-side-up. Doing splits. Flitting over me like a bunch of Tinker-belles, flying so close I could feel the air from their wings. Sometimes their tits brushed across me." Jody paused. "That do it?"

Jack slapped the heel of a palm against his forehead. "Jeez, ..." He was going to say: kid, but he caught it just in time. "You are beyond your years, Nub-man."

"So what did **you** see?"

"Huh?"

"Last night. On your ceiling?"

"Oh. Yeah, well."

Jody had to jump-start Jack again. "Like how are

you going to pack a pod into the boat. Did you think about it? You know. Fantasize? The boat only has that little cuddy-cabin under the bow deck, remember?"

"Pod. Ha! But that's what Cletus calls them, doesn't he? Well, I figure I'll have to get a larger boat eventually."

"If they want you to run them at all, Dad."

"Yeah."

The two of them shut up as Jasmine approached with a large tray while a collection of brindle-colored house-cats followed in her boot-steps. The bright studs embedded in her boots flashed in the rising sunlight.

"Don't let the cats jump on the table," Jasmine said.

A platter full of bacon and eggs and grits and buttered toast. Jody stuck a finger from his longer arm into the puddle of apricot jam on a side dish.

"I have to go back and get the plates and napkins and stuff," Jasmine announced, and loped back to the double-wide in the long strides which belied her age. Jack was picturing her receding body from the front, tits bouncing. *Old tits, though. Sort of wrinkly.*

Still.

"Dad? The rabbits?"

"Uhhh."

"Dad, listen. I pictured them being packed. Last night. For shipment? A whole pod? I pictured these guys sliding them naked into big oil drums. Spraying them with Pam and packing them down into the barrels like naked sardines."

"Naked sardines."

"Yeah. A slave ship full of these big oil drums on deck. Hosing them down when the sun is up, you know, when it gets hot."

"Jeez, kid. Nub-man."

71

"That could be my job. Hosing them down. After I let them out, of course."

But Jody could see that the spark which had ignited the conversation had died. He should have kept the fantasy real. "Dad? Seriously, I was thinking, though. Don't the clones have to be destroyed if something goes wrong and they can't make it to market? The defective ones, too? I was wondering about that."

"Me, too. Yeah."

"You should ask them about that this morning."

"Yeah. I will!"

"That would be murder. Wouldn't it? I mean, even if they are clones and stuff. Maybe they should contract out for somebody like us to build a place where they don't have to be killed. And you could charge so much per head for running down the ones that get away. Like you do with bounty hunting. Only instead of hauling them to jail you bring them here. If they hollered or screamed, nobody would hear it. Where we live."

Over Jody's shoulder (the stunted, nub-arm one) Jack could see Jasmine flashing her way back to them. "Yeah. Somebody has to do the dirty work in the world, huh Nub-man? Shhhhh. Just kidding."

"Just kidding, what," Jasmine said.

Jack raised his voice. "Hey, before I forget. I left the boat tarp up here when I moved. In the barn. Do you mind if I bring my pick-up here soon and get it? It snaps all around the boat. It doesn't fit anything else, so."

Jody wished Jack wouldn't act so humble when he was asking his mother for something. When she needed anything from Jack she came right out with it. Demanded it. Jody ignored them as an argument developed between them regarding the tarp.

"Just let him have it, Mom!"

Clones under a tarpaulin!

The argument ended and Jack was awarded the tarp. Jody pictured the boat with that heavy, impregnated, burgundy cloth snapped tightly over the open cockpit. Underneath were all these cute girls, their heads bumping up little bulges in the material. Their eyes peeking out from little gaps at the gunwales.

Jasmine snapped a hardened, crimson nail on the top of Jody's head. "Eat!"

The breakfast was good and Jody was hungry. But he never got the opportunity to ask Jack if the clones had belly buttons. He hoped they all did. That's how he always pictured naked girls. With navels. Nice, deep, dark ones. Or the other kind would be neat, too. Knots that stuck out, like foxy colored girls had sometimes in X-rated videos.

CHAPTER 9
Miss Desirey Jackson

Jack barely had time to buckle up before Deputy Desirey Jackson stomped the throttle and gunned the white and green '79 Lincoln backwards without hitting anything. With a flick of her black wrist (and a jangling of gold bracelets), the huge, four-door, converted-to-police-cruiser Continental barreled forward down the long driveway. Jack looked out the side window for a second to watch chunks of rock and gravel hop and bound down the side of the hill toward his little camper. Well, nothing to worry about, right? He was remembering an early, childhood, backwoods maxim:

You put a little colored gal behind the wheel for the first time and in fifteen minutes she can drive! Stick shift, clutch, all of it!

Especially the tall, skinny ones.

No food-stamp or Twinkie poisoning.

But Jack couldn't really relax until they were on good, solid blacktop. He snuck a glance at the speedometer (80) and Jackson (a babe).

"This car!"

"Yeah, it got a de-smogged po-lice interceptor V-8, too. A four-sixty-two! I love it! This used to be Cletus's last wife car until he give it to me."

"His wife drove a police car?"

"He put the light-bar and the siren in for me, and the cage an' all. It use' to b'long to a dope dealer, you know. It was my present when I gra'jated from the police 'cademy. An' my Beretta nine. I didn' want none of them

74

plastic Glocks like the other deputies got. I need a gun what look like a gun. I wanted me a 9-mill with some steel in it."

Jack looked down at the large handgun at her side, a Beretta 92-F. He noticed how nicely Jackson's uniform fit. The dark, tight, black-striped trousers, the tailored, tan shirt with the top three buttons unbuttoned, the tiny waist. Jack had to wonder if her git-go belt had been custom made. None of that cutting the leather shorter and punching-in extra holes for her, he bet. Then there were the spotless, black, original Reeboks.

Little feet, too.

A doll.

Daddy's no fool.

A shiny-black, fucking babe!

"You thinkin' good, clean thoughts over there, white man?"

"Hell, no! I was thinking how smart old Cletus is."

"Mmmm - hmmmm."

"You confiscated, too? Like the car?"

"Well." Jackson laughed. They were driving more slowly now — sixty-five — and were whooshing by the empty school-bus shelter in front of a white, clapboard church. The hand-painted, amateur sign said:

TRIUMPH FAMILY CHURCH

"Family church," Jack grumbled. "What other kind is there? Huh?" He looked at her, his heart pounding up a bit. He had never actually sat this close to a good-looking, healthy, breeding-age, black woman before and he could feel the fire. He was nervous, anyway, with the knowledge that his arrival at the clone farm was only minutes away. And then there was the fact that Norma wasn't answering her phone at the condo.

The trees on either side of the road thinned out a

little, then opened up on two, large ponds, one on either side of the road. Lily pads. A large cypress here and there.

"My daddy used to take me fishing here when I was little," Jackson said. They were down to 40 MPH now. "It still weren' integrate' way-back here and we knew the deeper pond, the big one on the norf side, was the white pond so we kep' to our little bream bog. They bofe on private land."

Jack shivered.

"You look nervous, Whitebread".

"I'm cold."

Jackson quickly reached for the AC control and shut it off. Her fingers were loaded with heavy, gold rings and they flashed when she shoved in the cigarette lighter, and when she poked a butt into her crimson mouth. The window on her side whirred down. They turned onto a remote stretch of old Highway C-10-A, the "Old Spanish Trail". "You nervous **and** cold."

"Well, yeah. Were **you** the first time?"

"When he show me the farm? Well, I didn' know 'head of time so, no, but I sure got hateful about it at first. Then I got scared 'cause I thought if he figured I was agin' the whole thing he'd pro'bly want to snuff me before I talked. You know what I'm sayin'? Cletus **would**, too. In a heartbeat. Remember that."

"Naw. He tell you to tell me that?"

"Well, not in so many words. Listen, he didn' get to be no eighty-five on the sof'ball field."

They passed by a few, ramshackle homesteads set back from the road and Jack noticed she was careful not to speed past any of them. He mentioned it.

"They got pets cross the road. And Cletus like to get re'lected."

"Doesn't sound like hard-ball to me. He is the oldest sheriff in the country, though."

"In the world!"

Jack was getting giddy on her exotic perfume, which seemed to be all the more invasive with the window open. He tried to concentrate on the important stuff, like why was her radio squelched down. Then he pictured her without the uniform. Pictured her as firm as neoprene rubber. But the burning lump in his chest was a growing fear, not lust. They would be out of the county soon, over into Walton, and he knew the feed lot was in Homer.

Any minute now.

"So — you didn't answer. Were you confiscated?"

"He didn' tell you, huh? Well, I was a present. From a pimp he busted. Firs' I was kidnap' by him, the pimp, then I was confiscated by the sheriff. Fresh off the school playground. No AIDS or any of that there stuff. Cletus love me, so you keep this in the family, hear? He say I'm werf money."

Jack noticed how easily she could revert to ghetto-speak when she wanted to, then switch back. "I believe he's right."

"You wouldn' know."

"Well, just the same, I'm going to ask him to put you in his will for me."

"For you? Ha! Don' hol' your breath!"

They were down to thirty now, and had collected an old pickup truck behind them.

"I'm waitin' for that old honky to pass."

"So what did you hate about the farm at first?" Jack tried to sound nonchalant.

"Me? Think about it! Oh, well, you can't 'cause you ain' seen it yet. Okay. Picture this. Me still a teen and as pretty as they come. So I thought, anyhow. Hell, I thought, my papa and mama didn' name me Desirey for nothin'!"

"I thought your name was Desiree."

"Mama wanted me to be Desire-ee. But when I'm in a social situation, you know, with a bunch of shirts, I introduce myself Des-er-aay. Fuck 'em."

Jack was trying to listen as his brain tried to picture what lay ahead. The clones. All around him. He was wallowing in them. He was rolling around in a pile of female, little-girl bodies, all squealing and squirming with the delight of his presence. Jackson cut the wheel to avoid a pothole and Jack bounced back to Earth. "So what turned you off at first?"

"What I didn' like? Picture me then, thinking I'm such a hot little number myself — property of the high sheriff no less — an' comin' up on all these little girlie clones made specifically — specifically, mind you — for sex objects for men. Okay? Okay. Nothin' wrong with a new system to drain off all this male egotism and horniness so the world can get down to seekin' after the importan' things in life, right? Well, but, at the farm, all they was raisin' was these little **white** devils. Like black or yellow or in-between ain' worth nothin'! Get my drif'? But SiblTek's come a little ways since then. Since they got Klaus."

"Klaus?"

"Oh, honey! Yes. Klaus! Now there's a whitey I can do something with. In my dreams! God! Looks and talks just like Arnold, too!"

"Arnold."

"Arnold Schwarzenegger!"

"Oh! Of course. The Terminator, et cetera."

"He can terminate me anytime!"

"Wonderful for you."

"Like I said, in my dreams. Shit! You can keep that to yourself, too. I don' want Cletus getting all upset. Hear?"

"I understand."

"Good."

The pickup finally pulled out and began to pass the Lincoln, which was down to 25 per. An old, robin-egg, blue, sixties Chevy. No tail-gate (two old tires and some hay and a few, loose, oil cans in the back), with a maroon passenger-side door, no right-front fender or headlight. The old duffer took a long look at the Lincoln as he passed and raised a hand to wave. On the back of his head was a black, one-size-fits-all baseball cap with CAT POWER embroidered on the crown in yellow letters. Jackson waved a dainty, bejeweled hand back. "Honky mother-fucker," she smiled.

"Cletus loves you, huh?"

"Lord, yes. He should. He's sixty-five years older than me! An' I get it up for 'im, too!"

"I'll bet you do."

"You'll never know."

"Oh, Yeah. Right. I forgot."

Jackson checked the mirrors and turned the '79 Lincoln, the last of the big hogs, south onto an unmarked dirt road. Unmarked except for the DEAD END sign.

"Show time, Whitebread."

"Whitebread?"

"Oh. I was s'pose' tell you. That your new code name when you're on the radio."

"Wonder who thought of that one?" Jack watched her long fingers punch in a few strokes on the communications keyboard and the radio crackled. "You keyed in a macro?"

"Yes. The frequency's a secret."

Smart as hell, too.

"Your hand-held is in the glove box. Keep it on you at all times. When I take you back, remind me to get you a charger out of the trunk. And when you get a chance, bring in your boat radio so we can set the frequency on it."

"Oh. Yeah." Jack's heart speeded up as he examined the unit. VHF.

They're planning to use Miss Chernobyl!

His eyes re-glued themselves to the windshield.

A clone farm.

A real clone farm!

Woods to the left of the long, dirt road, and a fallow cornfield to the right. Then pasture grass for as far as he could see. Rolling hills in the distance and a three-story, white house coming up on the right, with clean-looking barns in the back. Way in the back. Everything Cyclone-fenced with ivy covering the barbed wire on top as best it could. And on one of the hills, a radio repeater tower.

A couple of wooly-black sheep dogs were suddenly bounding happily along with them on the other side of the ditch, inside the fence.

Warning signs appeared on Jack's side of the car.

NO ENTRY WITHOUT A PASS

SiblTek Corporation

BAD DOG

"They use sheepdogs for watchdogs?"

"No, no. They're for heading any runaways back to the barns."

"Oh. Yeah."

"Besides, they raise sheep here. There's four-hundred acres of pasture."

"Sheep? In Florida?"

"You don't want to know why."

They pulled up to an electric gate and Jackson punched in another code on the keyboard. "Let the cartoon begin," she said. She was smiling and her teeth were the whitest teeth Jack had ever seen. He thought she was a dead ringer for Desiree Washington, the black beauty-pageant contestant that the boxer Mike Tyson felt compelled to drop a load into. The two established eye-contact for the first time, and Jack fell in love.

The electric gate was lurching along its tracks to open.

Jackson said: "Now you won't have this computer when you come and go, so, just identify yourself with your hand-held."

"Whitebread."

"Right. The kind that's not good for you."

"Right."

Jackson dropped him near the back yard of the big house on a path that led to the back porch. Jack saw that she was not going to get out with him.

"Radio."

Jack leaned back in to snatch the unit and say goodbye. His eyes copped a hint of a lacy, black bra and his throat developed a major lump. "What channel?"

"You only got one. Don't look so worried. I'll be back in a little bit."

Jack watched the Lincoln execute a neat U-turn and rooster-tail a plume of dust down the road they had just traveled.

Oh, fuck you in a heartbeat.

He looked at the radio and keyed it.

"Whitebread, here. I'm at the path to the back door. Should I proceed?"

No answer. He looked around for a moment, his feet rooted to the path. The barns were huge, tan, metal Butler buildings, and he could see that each had its own, fenced-in enclosure. And the ivy covering over the fence webbing and barbed wire made the whole thing look perfectly normal, even picturesque. He sucked in a breath of what smelled like newly-mown hay, and listened to the late-summer hum of bees.

Jack looked down and saw a swarm of green bottle flies paying homage to a steaming heap of sheepdog shit near his feet. His radio crackled.

A foreign, female voice. "Proceed, Whitebread."

With a tight grip on the radio, Jack began to move toward the back porch while his thumb flicked at the little, rubbery antenna. From the barns he thought he heard a burst of laughter, like the kind you hear sometimes when you walk past a school.

The radio crackled again. "Just wait in the kitchen, Whitebread." The accent was unfamiliar, but definitely female. "Pour yourself a cup of coffee or check the fridge. I'll be with you in a minute."

Portuguese, maybe? No.

Whoopi Goldberg?

CHAPTER 10
Kidnapped

Norma regained consciousness in a sitting position, in the dark. Still in a basement area — she could feel that instinctively — but the circumstances were not clear at first. She had been dreaming. She and her sister Sandy had been kidnapped and were locked up in an old log cabin somewhere. Sandy kept on hunting around the place for tools, for weapons, while Norma remained tied up in the corner. Sandy was dressed, Norma wasn't, but in the dream the two situations seemed perfectly normal. Sandy was going to get them out of this.

For a second or two Norma was so relieved that their kidnapping had been just a dream! Then she realized where she was. The reality of it was crushing.

"Oh, Sandy."

The carpet roll they had brought her in was open but leaning up against her, and the weight of it was pressing against her shoulders. Norma was sitting on part of it, the large area which she had apparently wetted again in her sleep. Or coma or whatever, induced by the injection. Well, at least she wasn't tied up. She reached for the injection site, lifting her ass up slightly so she could feel of it. Not too sore. Her eyes darted about, hunting for the least little glimmer of light. But the darkness was total. A suffocating blanket of hollow black.

What time is it?

Norma felt a headache clamping up in her forehead as she tried to think, to trace back.

Relax. Breathe.

It was almost as if her older sister Sandy were still there from the dream. "Relax. Be cool!"

So thirsty!

And stiff! Her back and knees made popping sounds as Norma leaned forward and freed her shoulders as the carpet wrap slumped to one side. On her knees now, she felt the floor with her hands. Cold, gritty concrete. The smell of chemicals, or...industrial soap? She crept forward and bumped her head against a thin stick of wood. She touched a bucket, with wheels. A mop and pail! Shoving that out of the way, she felt through the air with her hands and contacted a grimy mop sink.

Water! Using the edge of the sink for leverage, Norma slowly worked her way onto her feet but as soon as she could stand she felt faint. She waited for that to pass before feeling for the faucets. *The cold will be on the right.* She twisted the knob and heard the gush splash into the bottom of the deep sink. Not very cold, but... Norma bent her head into the sink, puckering her lips for the flow, and jumped back with a scream. The water had turned scalding hot.

"Motherfuckers! Dumb fucks don't know what side to put the cold on!?" Her hand burned on the valve when she felt for it but she found the handle and cranked it off. The cold water on the other side became icy almost immediately and after a long drink, Norma felt of her lips for blisters. As far as she could tell she was okay, but when she found the door to the tiny cubicle locked tight, she began to cry.

During the next, few, hopeless hours Norma resolved to cooperate fully, even cheerfully, until she had a fighting chance.

If they don't leave me here to starve to death.

84

Pulling on the overhead-light chain produced nothing and her probing-about of the tiny, filthy room only turned up the dry, crackled remains of dead roaches and spiders. A blind search for tools to work open the door proved futile, also, as were her occasional screams for help. When she finally did hear footsteps, and Hector and Klaus still bitching at each other, she slumped back down onto her carpet and flung a corner of it over herself just in time. Klaus's flashlight was excruciatingly bright and Norma scrunched her eyes shut while they jerked on what used to be part of her white, shag rug. Dutifully, she pressed her arms to her sides when they rolled her back up.

They could kill me and nobody would know.

If they were going to kill me, I'd already be dead!

A dim light appeared above her head. They were leaving the basement? There was the groaning and creaking of an elevator.

"Quiet, bitch," Klaus said. "Or I shoot in the rug. Nobody will hear it." She felt the steel of a gun barrel slide down the right side of her head, snagging in her ear. It slid down to the hollow between her neck and collar bone and rested there. "The bullet will go down you the long way. Blow your cunt out."

They met no one on the elevator and Norma was not able to tell how many floors up they were traveling. The light around the top of her head became brighter as they humped her down some kind of hall and into what seemed to be a large room. A room with a very pleasant scent. Almost like the distant smell of roses. Norma tried to readjust her weight.

For the first time, Klaus sounded really angry, even through the muffled darkness inside the carpet-roll co-coon. Angry with Hector rather than her, however, despite the problem that her urine had never dried and they couldn't set the carpet down.

"Don't let it touch the floor! You're so fucking out-of-shape! Grab the side! Grab the side! Just dump her out!" ("Yhas dahmp her auss!")

Norma cringed and tightened her stomach muscles for the fall, and show-time came immediately with a burst of intense light. As the back of her head thunked against the floor her eyes opened to the brilliant dazzle of a huge, cut-glass chandelier hanging from the high ceiling directly above.

She was once again reminded of her brutal naked-ness. Naked and exposed under thousands of dollars worth of cut glass and electric incandescence. Not that Klaus and Hector seemed to be interested, busy as they were with trying to keep the piss-soaked carpet square from touching the precious rug she'd been dumped onto.

"We can leave it in the focking elevator," Hector said. "They got janitors for shit like this."

"And then the fucking cops know what building to look for the bitch in? On the kitchen floor. Kitchen floor! Back up, you dumb-fuck Cuban. Soon as we tie up the broad, we take the carpet back. For Abu."

"Oh, man. You're a focking robot, you know that?"

"And then you can mop the kitchen floor."

Norma heard some chairs scrape back in another room — sounded distant — and the carpet thud to the floor. She quickly turned on her side and drew her knees up to the fetal position. Klaus's gold-trimmed zori pad-ded up to her face, his pedicured toes poking through the thongs, inches from her eyes. Norma scrunched her lids shut.

"Open eyes, little American strawberry tart."

His voice sounded suddenly so friendly. Kindly. She opened her eyes and shivered. "Asshole."

"Oh. You're cold. I'll turn down the AC."

"And get me something to put on. Please?"

"No." His voice sounded distant after he walked away, like the AC thermostat was in that other room. The suite of rooms must take up the whole floor, Norma thought. And the thick rug she was on, laid on top of the wall to wall carpeting. A real Persian? Like she would know.

He returned. "Get up, little princess."

"I'm not little."

"Come here." Klaus was standing between a pair of white, fluted columns which reached to the tall ceiling, near enough to the center of the room to almost touch the chandelier. His teeth flashed a white grin as he beckoned to her. The way his huge arms burst out of the T-shirt, the muscles like ropes, reminded Norma of the picture in her family Bible, when she was little and still believed in the church-god. Samson chained between two columns in this huge feast-hall or whatever, before he brought the columns down and the whole ceiling with it, crushing to death all the people God was pissed-off with at the time.

"Come here now or I let Hector de-clit you with his rotten teeth. He doesn't brush or floss."

"Fock you! I brush every day!"

"Shut up garlic breath."

Hector was somewhere behind Norma but she didn't feel inclined to turn and look as she got to her feet.

Hector's voice got closer, like he was sneaking up. "You smell like a big cheese. Not you, Miss. Klaus. You smell good, killer lady. Piss and perfume."

"After we take care of Abu you can have a shower, baby. Come here!"

Norma's arms were crossed over her chest in an attempt to cover her breasts. She took a quick look around before approaching Klaus, who was dangling a heavy-looking gold chain from his fist.

"Between the posts." He backed away so she could stand between them.

"Posts," Hector snorted. "Columns! A post is a focking stick."

Golden rings protruded from the two columns at various heights and there were chains attached to some of them. Norma noticed that the silk-covered divans and couches which circled the room all seemed to be facing the spot where she was standing. The couches were floral patterned and looked expensive. A large painting, a Gauguin, hung above one of them: a tropical feast, alone in a vast expanse of egg-shell white wall.

"Turn around."

Norma turned to see Hector sprawled out on one of the couches, facing her and grinning. He quickly pulled a hand away from his crotch.

"Arms out."

"No."

Norma's brain bounced inside her skull in a flash of light as Klaus punched the back of her head with the heel of his hand.

"Arms out."

Norma reminded herself that she had decided to cooperate. She saw Hector's grin broaden as she complied.

"Farther out. Higher." She felt her breasts lifting and a cold cuff ratchet over her right wrist. She turned her hateful stare away from Hector and looked. A gold hand-cuff. Smooth and heavy. Solid gold? A slap on the bottom and Klaus was pulling on her left wrist, chaining it to the other column with another golden cuff, her arms stretched out just above shoulder height. A slave on the block. And all because she absentmindedly left her revolver in Jack's boat. Stupid. Stupid. Stupid.

"No gag for my mouth?" Norma immediately regretted what she had just said. More stupidity. She made an attempt to get them to forget about the gag. "No ball and chain?" *Not enough.* "No ..."

"Shut up. Spread your legs."

A golden cuff ratcheted around her left ankle. "Spread father." He was pulling on her right leg so he could chain it to the other column. "There, baby. No. No gag. Don't even think about screaming for help. Just because I say so. Nobody could hear you, anyway. Nobody who would help, that is." He laughed. His laugh was just like Arnold's. "You know where you are now?"

"No." She figured the suite was somewhere in The Viking, the next-door condo, but she was going to have to play dumb. Even dumber than she really was, apparently.

"Guess."

Norma sucked in a deep breath as Klaus moved around to the front of her, his face so close now her nipples touched his chest for a second. He did smell like a new cheese.

"This is (*Dis iss*) a high-class torture chamber."

Hector laughed.

"Not like one of those Cuban dungeons they dig into a hill so nobody can hear. This place is insulated with high-tech stuff. Very energy efficient, too. Swanky. Not one of those Miami Little Havana basement deals where the yard is so small and full of chickens they have to bury the bodies under the basement floor when they're done. Right, Heck?"

"No focking basements in Miami." Hector was vigorously pointing a finger upward. Norma spotted the camera lens recessed in the woodwork of the valance above Hector's head, and the glowing, red dot.

"Show-time, baby." Klaus backed out of the way, baring Norma to the distant video camera. Naked and spread-eagled vertically before a cold, electronic eye.

Hector got up and made a wide circle around her to avoid the camera. "Snuff flick," he whispered with a grin.

"Don't worry, baby. No tape. No disc. Not yet, anyway. Relax. I'll be back."

For the first time, Norma raised her voice. "Who's watching?!"

"Shhhhh. Behave. A million dollar piece of ass does not make so much vulgar noise."

Far behind her, kitchen chairs scraped out of the way as Hector and Klaus worked the urine-soaked carpet through the doorway.

Norma tried to calm her voice but it came out as a half-scream anyway. "Who's watching me?"

"Hasta la vista, baby."

In the silence of the bright and huge empty room, Norma could not bring herself to speak out, to cuss out whoever was monitoring her with the videocam in the wall. The red dot underneath remained on except for a momentary flicker she thought she saw once.

What the hell is taking Klaus so long?
They have to get rid of Abu's body.
That's it. Abu's body.

Norma was grateful that neither of the two seemed to be overly upset about her shooting Abu or whatever his name was. At least they didn't seem mad enough to kill her over it.

Hector is a creep.

But smarter than he looks.

Norma spent some time inspecting the cuffs on her wrists and ankles. The chains. Had to be solid gold. She calculated what they might be worth in dollars. If only she had thought to take her gun out of the boat before saying goodbye to Jack and going to her apartment. She pictured the big Ruger .41-mag bucking up with each shot. Pictured Klaus's brains splattering all over her doorway. All over the hallway walls. She saw his body hurtling back from the force of each two-hundred-and-ten grain jacketed-lead, soft-point bullet ripping into him. His body slamming back out of her doorway, slamming back against the far wall of the hallway, his body slumping down and painting a wide smear of blood down the peach-colored wall-paper.

She stared at the camera lens, the red dot under it, and spoke to it. "You see that? Huh? Motherfuckers?"

Norma pictured herself post rescue (so she hoped). On TV again. That would be so cool. She would be wearing something more elegant than her bikini this time. God, she'd kill to have that bikini now, though. Or a summer dress. A white hat to accent her billowing, red hair, well, her wonderful hair would hardly be billowing in an airless studio now, would it? She would field questions with her usual, quick, smart-ass style, her wit, and then lecture the audience about guns. There was so much anti-gun talk on TV. So dumb! How else do you defend yourself? Have a cop for every person? No, three. Three eight-hour shifts. Plus more to work weekends. So dumb. Those riots last year. That shop where the husband and wife were shooting back. Nobody fucked with

their store! Norma remembered cheering when she saw that film clip on TV and that couple shooting back, keeping the looters and firebugs out. She had cheered and clapped although she was alone at the time.

Solid gold.

She was inspecting the chains and cuffs again. Real gold was supposed to be softer than iron. Softer than steel. And heavier. Maybe she could...

Norma struggled with the cuffs by straining against them first, and trying to pull her arms together. The cuffs bit into her wrists and hurt terribly and the pain was even worse when she tried to jerk her ankles away from the two columns. It was no use. Still, the cuffs didn't feel or cut like steel. And the chain didn't clang or ring like steel.

Solid gold.

Bird in a gilded cage.

Norma stared at the camera lens again. So still and hard and uncaring. The red dot so sure of itself. She tried to readjust her body to ease a growing pain in her back but the columns were so far apart and the chains so short she didn't have much choice but to shift just slightly in the spread-eagled position she'd been left in.

"My back hurts!" she yelled at the camera.

Rich mother fuckers.

Oil sheikhs?

She hoped her captors looked and smelled and acted better than Abu.

She wondered how far away the monitors were. Probably on the same floor. Maybe even in the next room, or suite. Yeah. probably right next door. Norma sucked in a deep breath and jiggled her breasts for the camera, but just for a moment. Motionless now, she thought she'd seen the red dot flicker a little when she'd done that. Did it? No. She must have hallucinated that. Try it again? No. Fuck 'em. Don't give 'em a thrill.

She wondered how many might be watching, and pictured a small, dark room with a security guard type, all alone, sitting behind a bunch of monitors, hers in the middle, in color. She pictured herself from the front. So bare. So clearly bare. Her nipples began to grow and harden.

Shit!

She could see the guard's body wiggling behind the desk while he jerked off.

"I'm hungry!" she said calmly. The lens did not answer. "May I have something to eat, please?"

They called me a million-dollar piece of ass.

A million dollars!

Norma suddenly realized how she was going to escape. Struggling against the chains was stupid, especially with the camera on. She was young, smart, and beautiful, and men were so dumb.

"Please?"

The red dot looked back at her, unblinking.

"Please, my back is starting to hurt. Can somebody come in here and let me sit down or something?"

The lens, with just a hint of purple in its glossy reflection, seemed to soften a little. It was a large lens for a video camera, Norma thought. About the same size as the big lens in her Dad's Nikon F1.

"Please?"

She waited, not expecting any reply.

"I'm warm enough and everything, since Mister Klaus adjusted the AC. But I need a shower, too. I'd be proud if somebody would come and let me have a shower. I promise to be good."

The more she stared at the lens, the more Norma

93

realized the videocam was a high-dollar unit. It could probably pick out individual hairs at this range. Good thing she had shaved and clipped her bush before going out with Jack. Million dollar ladies could be reduced and put on sale if they looked like a plucked turkey.

She looked into the lens and puckered her lips.

"Please?"

CHAPTER 11
The SiblTek Farm

The woman let Jack finish his banana and the best cup of coffee he had ever tasted, then led him out the back of the big kitchen toward the first, fenced-in enclosure. Jack followed at a respectful distance and noticed that she had to key her radio before opening the small gate. He figured she must be a Seminole or Miccosukee Indian, except for the puffy, Filipino sleeves of her blouse and the large, gold ring through her nasal septum. The nose ring was unusual in that it had two, squared-off corners before coming together at the bottom. Jack winced at the thought of her having to spread the gap to insert it (and then turning the ring through the hole in her flesh). Himself, he couldn't stand to have anything touch the inside of his nose. Just the hairs there were a pain in the ass. You clip them and then the sharp, stubby ends grow longer and poke you on the inside and make you sneeze. It was a cruel world and there was little justice to be found in creation, something he'd always known but would never get used to.

It was her dress that looked Indian: row upon row of horizontal patterns of intricate patches and bric-a-brac of many, different colors.

"Are you a Miccosukee?"

"Cuna. Panama. Manny met me there when he was studying the rain forest. Bought me. Not from my family but from a Brazilian slaver. Brought me here about twenty years ago. Married me."

"Manny?"

"Dr. Mannlicher."

"Oh. Yeah." *Must be an asshole. He could've bought her and then returned her to her tribe.* Jack pictured her as a little girl, with nipples like lug-nuts. Would he have been able to return her? Well. *Get real Jack!* Okay, well, no.

They passed near two empty boat trailers grown over with weeds and Jack's heart fell, but just for a moment. The tags were out of date and the trailers were rusting. "No airplanes?"

"No."

"And your name is Monday."

"Monday." She turned to face him and Jack bumped into her. Skin dry and brown. Thin, almost nonexistent eyebrows. They were eye-to-eye now, above the gold nose ring gleaming in the sun. Her eyes were powerful and steady. Irises muddy and flecked with gold. Surprisingly wide pupils considering the bright sun. Her eyes were looking into him.

Jack sucked in a deep breath but held his gaze. "The day he met you?"

"Manny thinks so, but it was a Sunday. He was out in the jungle too long and his calendar was off."

"Your English is perfect."

"I had to fuck a lot of Anglos when I was a kid."

"Ohhh!" Jack lost it and looked away. Monday turned and moved ahead. Jack was glad that chigger season, aka red-bug season, was over because the two of them were walking through tall grass, off the beaten path now which led to another barn on the right.

"We could take one of the electric golf carts but I love to walk," Monday explained.

"Barefoot."

"Why not?"

"Pin worms, for one thing."

"Uh-unh. We spray — for everything. Very high tech."

"The chemicals could absorb into your body through the soles of your feet."

"You an expert, Jack?"

She knows my name. "What is your code name, Mrs. Mannlicher?"

"Monday, Whitebread. My birth name is too long."

"Try me."

"Twenty Two Horse Yonson."

"Far out."

"Far outboard."

They both laughed, and Jack could see the friendly fire in her eyes. "I forgot to ask what Desirey's code name is, too."

"Andrew."

"So feminine."

"For Jackson."

Jack followed Monday through another electrically protected gate; a gate too small for a golf cart to squeeze through, he noted. But he could see other, larger gates farther down the fence where the hedges broke for them, and winding, one-lane, blacktop roads.

"Why are the roads so twisty?"

"So the DEA or the FBI or whatever doesn't get the idea we can land planes here."

"Can you?"

"Choppers. But they can be picked up on radar immediately. Fort Rucker isn't far from here. They're just north of the line in Alabama. Big helicopter train-ing base." Monday stopped in front of a lower fence, a wooden rail fence that any child could easily manage. The remnants of what appeared to be vines hung all over the white-washed wood. "We let the girls grow pole beans

97

along the fence here in the summer. The building just ahead of us is where we have the Model T's housed at the present time — what's left of them. Model T's are the earliest successful clones. Very successful. In fact, they've financed everything else to come."

"Model T's, huh?" Jack turned and looked back toward the house when Monday lifted her voluminous skirt to climb over the fence rail. He was surprised to see that they had walked a good distance. "My, how the miles fly when yer havin' fun," he said as he hopped over to her.

"Smart-ass, aren't you. So is Manny. You two should get along just fine. Anyway, the Model T's took a lot of thought other than the science which was required, and I'm glad Manny didn't involve me in the business then. He's settled down quite a bit since the early days, although when you meet him you'll probably wonder how I can say that." Monday pointed to the other side of the enclosure, a roped-off compound which Jack figured to be about two acres. She was indicating several picnic tables with huge, yellow umbrellas over them. Jack's heart speeded up when the two young ladies, the sole occupants there, looked up and dashed back to the building and around the corner. The same, long, blond hair streaming behind them.

Two clones!

Jack swallowed hard, and tried to sound relaxed. At least they were properly clothed this time. "Building looks like an airplane hangar."

"Manny got all these hangars government surplus — the materials, the plans — when he first started. His parents were rich and he told them he was investing in an aqua-culture farm. Experimental. Fish farming was hot stuff back in those days. You probably recognized the girls. Not many of that bunch left. Third pod. The last of the Model T's. A lot of stuff went wrong with Pod Three but the problems only showed up recently. Plus, we're having difficulties with some of our foreign personnel. To say the least. I think that's why you got the job. Bounty hunter, huh? Really!" Monday spread her skirt out across one of the benches at a table and Jack plunked down opposite her. Monday sighed. "You ran into them on the island."

"Yeah. My girlfriend. They tried to kidnap her. They tried to kill us when we left the island and we tried to kill them."

"And that doesn't bother you? No, I guess not. Eastland briefed us about you. But. Well." Monday's dark, fierce eyes locked into his again and she leaned forward across the table. "Mister Jack — Whitebread — I don't figure. I need to know, like, why aren't you mad about it? And why did you two look so — juvenile — on TV — the news — like it was some kind of joke. Or game? You guys even looked happy about it."

Jack's nervousness suddenly evaporated. Juvenile? If he were juvenile he wouldn't be sitting here at this picnic table in the middle of nowhere with rolling hills and sheep grazing off in the distance, and with all the cards on the table.

"I thought I got hired because Norma and I found that head."

"Sheriff Eastland had already talked Manny into hiring you before your incident on the island, he just hadn't approached you, yet. With your man-hunting experience. You really make a living doing that? Bounty hunting? People who skip bail and stuff? Anyway, your chick finding the head was a coincidence. In a way."

Jack had to smile, and he risked eye contact with

Monday again. "Chick, huh?"

"Chick."

"Are **you** a chick?"

"I'm a mink."

Jack nodded his head appreciatively. "The bail bondsman I work for leaves me the tough ones, so I don't score much money with it most of the time. Beats working at the 7-11 on the night shift. And it helps to have Cletus in the family."

"That man-hunter gig turns on chicks like Norma? They love that macho, predator-hunting stuff?"

Jack was maintaining a lock on those dark, golden eyes. Hawk eyes. "You are a smart one," he said. He wondered whether she knew Cletus was his father. She must.

"Yes, and don't ever try to bullshit me."

"God forbid!" He shook a limp wrist and waited for her to reply to that, but she didn't. "You guys are getting to the end of your rope, huh?"

Monday finally looked away, over his shoulder. "You took the words right out of my mouth. Are you telepathic? Psychic?"

"I've read everything Castaneda wrote about Don Juan, the Yaqui sorcerer." Jack felt proud about the way that had simply rolled off his tongue.

"And you're thinking: well, as an Indian, I would be telepathic. Be able to read minds, signs. Know all about Castaneda."

"Yeah."

"Wrong. Besides, he made up that Indian. He and his wife." Monday pulled her radio out of a pocket in her voluminous skirt and set it upright on the table. "Listen up, Whitebread. Out there between the cattle fence and the woods Manny used to have some land

100

mines planted. Don't know if he got them all, so stick to the paths if you ever decide to go wandering. One of the Pod Two's got blown to bits a couple years ago. We have it on video, too. Manny just happened to be making a tape of the pod for a prospect, a Saudi, when the little virgin decided it was a good time to go over the hill and try freedom in the Redneck Triangle out there. Boompft! Zoom lens right on target. Manny's a steady hand in a crisis and he caught parts of her flying up and parts of her landing. One of her legs dropped back down out of the sky up-side-down and the exposed femur stuck right into the ground, foot sticking up in the air out of the grass, toes all curled up like her brain had a moment of ecstasy there. I wanted to shrink the head to wear on my belt but Manny wanted it to keep it under his pillow so we ended up burying it with the rest of her stuff. I mean, parts."

Jack was gazing at the distant pasture, and the hillside with the specks of sheep. But he wasn't looking at sheep. He didn't smell sheep. He smelled the sea. The swells and the chop. The spray breaking over the bow of Miss Chernobyl and slapping over the windshield. Miss Chernobyl. Her twin three-fifties droning in unison. Jack and Miss Chernobyl plowing valiantly offshore with a load of cute, frightened, naked girls destined for a secret rendezvous with a ship at sea, the girls' clothes safely stashed under the bow-deck where they'd stay dry. The girls all giggly and squirmy and slick with salt-spray.

He felt Monday's eyes and abandoned the fantasy.

A video of one of the clones blown up with a land mine?

She wanted to shrink the head? Dr. Mannlicher wanted to keep her head under his pillow?

These people are sick!

She's just trying to scare me.

Am I getting in over my head?

The fear had returned. Jack tried to act normal — to be cool.

Wonder if they'll let me watch the video.

"So why were you glad you didn't know Doctor Mannlicher back then. When he invented the Model T's."

"Tell you what. We'll probably run into Manny in a few minutes. You ask him. You watch the gleam in his eyes as he goes over it all."

"Okay."

"He even licks his lips. Disgusting! You'll see."

"But you guys love each other, right?"

Monday tilted her head and studied him. "You're weird, Jack. Not as flaky as you looked on the news show, but, yes, we love each other. All these years. But not like at first. When he first bought me, rescued me, really — I was headed for a brothel — I thought he was a god."

I looked flaky on TV? Flaky? Jack wished he could see the tape of that show Jasmine had made. Right now.

"He should be out here now. He can't stand to stay inside during nice weather."

"Did he ever try to take you back to where you were stolen? Back to your family? Your village?"

"Yes. We are the American natives still unconquered and still living on the territory we had originally before Columbus. Territory which the women of the tribe own, by the way. In marriage, the man goes to live on the wife's property."

"Female chief?"

"Chief? We are democratic. Always have been."

"And you left all this to stay with him?"

"Of course." Monday shook her head, and her elaborate earrings rang like tiny bells. A ring pierced each ear lobe, and from each earring a trapezoid hung, and from the trapezoid: three, golden cages with monkey's in them. Tiny, golden monkeys. Jack squinted his eyes. They were each different, the monkeys, but two out of three (on each side of Monday's face) were crouched and grasping the bars of their little prisons. They looked mean.

The faint sound of girls giggling and laughing came from inside the barracks behind her. Monday looked down and Jack realized she was wearing necklaces hung with gold coins, some of them apparently quite heavy.

Jack said: "So gold is the coin of the realm for Cuna females?"

"For human females."

"But not shoes."

"Oh, a new V-12 Jaguar convertible now and then. Indoor plumbing. Electricity. Disposable douche bags. Now then, are you ready for some **real** orientation?" Monday's mouth curled up a little and her lips parted. Strangely shaped but brilliant, white teeth, the tips capped with gold. It was her first smile.

If a crocodile could look beautiful and smile pretty, that would be her.

CHAPTER 12
The 4-Filipina Bath

The pain in Norma's back disappeared when she heard a door close. In the next room in front of her? She held her breath and thought she could hear the door open and close again — with a whiff of a breeze across her bare chest — but she could not be sure whether it came from the room behind or ahead. She twisted her head as far as she could. The large, open entrance to the room behind her streamed with light from the windows there, but because of the archway's position she could see no furniture. A bedroom? The sudden sound of voices caused her to face front with a jerk. There, too, the archway to this other room revealed nothing except light shining upon a patch of thick, peach-colored carpet.

Something higher up caught her attention and Norma narrowed her eyes. There, above the archway's brocade valance, was a second camera, with a longer lens. The red dot glowing on the camera face was new. She was sure. The unit had just been turned on. Without another thought, Norma stuck out her tongue at it.

The instant burst of male laughter from behind the wall curdled Norma's blood, and as her heart pounded up she became aware that she was pulling in against the golden chains stretching her arms. Her wrists screamed with pain.

Don't be a fool! Don't put marks on yourself!
Relax! Save your strength!
She took a few, controlled, deep breaths.

104

Pretend you don't give a shit.
What are they doing in there?!

The silence after their burst of laughter was chilling. And some bastard had turned up the AC again! Well, fuck them. Let them count goose-bumps.

"I'm cold!"

A conversation followed — muffled and incomprehensible — but the voices (in Arabic?) sounded like a bunch of junkyard dogs barking. Barking into a pile of pillows, to be more precise.

Then Hector's voice. Norma's spirits lifted when she heard his familiar sound, his Michael Jackson falsetto. In English, such as that was. Norma held her breath and strained to catch every word.

"Ahhhh, when if poor Abu be here now."

Klaus's voice: "You dumb fuck, you're looking up at the ceiling and expect to see him? We should put a monitor on the ceiling for you?"

Then: Three or four dogs barking into pillows.

Hector's voice: "We were up on the roof day before yesterday. Big sheet of aluminum blew into East satellite dish, so I climb up there and pull it off the horn and Abu, he look up in the sky and I say, Abu, you can look up there and get stuff from the satellites with your brain? What you see? And Abu say: 'Somewhere way out there is these planet with these alien women, all so-horny redheads with cherry lips. These planet is very far away and it is all jungle. No men. Gorgeous, horny redheads hanging from the trees like monkeys, with long hair, green eyes, strawberry nipples. In the sunset their nipples glow like bubble-gum.'"

silence....

Norma realized they were thinking about her hanging by one arm from a palm tree in a clearing in the

105

sunset with her nipples lit like two fireflies trying to attract a mate. Like two wads of glowing, pink bubblegum. She tucked her chin and looked down, and saw them growing again.

Damn it! Asshole motherfuckers!

Klaus's voice suddenly: "I didn't know Abu was such a poet." With Klaus on the other side of the wall, he sounded even more like Arnold. Norma could **see** Arnold Schwarzenegger there, looking at her on the monitor. "...vass soch ah poe edt!"

Hector: "Focking **dead** poet!"

Klaus: "His dream killed him."

Hector: "Oh, the strawberry bitch, yah, well, the Mutawin back home were going kill him anyway. Islamic morality police. Very powerful. They make sure your girlfrien' all cover up from head to toe, so no air get in. You can spray her with deod, though, but not in public. The Mutawin look for satellite dishes on your roof. They don't want you see foreign stuff. Christian stuff. Or pictures of girls and tits and pussies. Or videos of Pat Robertson. None of that stuff."

The chill in the suite, at least where Norma was strung up in chains, was becoming unbearable. She sucked in a breath.

"I'm cold, dammit!"

"You're not dressed properly."

Norma shuddered. Under the archway appeared a vision from Hell. A tall, hooded woman dressed in a black, full-length abaaya, her face covered with a Bedouin veil. All Norma could see of her were her blue eyes ringed with black mascara, and a hint of flesh above her black, high-heeled shoes. And her hands. Her right fist was clenched around a two-foot length of galvanized pipe.

The lady approached, keeping the hunk of pipe raised and pointing up, at chest height. Norma hawked up a gob of spit as she got closer.

"You spit on me and you're dead." Brooklyn accent.

Norma swallowed. "Please. Don't hit me with that thing. Please."

"Shut up." The woman circled her, inside the two columns, ducking under the chains stretching Norma's arms. "Too bad you shaved your pits recently. It'll just make it that much harder to remove all your body hair." She faced Norma, lowering the end of the pipe and briefly touching it's icy iron to the tip of her pubic mound. Norma flinched.

Klaus burst into the room and the lady in black stepped back.

"I told you — no herpes, no warts, no nothing!"

"Had your nose right up in there Kraut Man? She killed my husband!"

"Forget it. I know you don't give a shit. You get your freedom after the funeral. I think. Maybe."

"You don't know them. The family will never let me go. I'm as doomed as you are." The pipe snicked out and tapped up hard between Norma's legs.

After Norma's scream, the barking behind the wall intensified. "Jump up and down," the woman demanded.

"Bitch! I can't! The chains! I can't move! Klaus, come back! Don't leave me in here alone with her!" Norma watched him disappear behind the archway. There were three red dots now, one high in each corner of the room and the original camera facing her. Norma tensed as the woman moved behind her.

"Jump. Up and down."

"No."

Norma cut her eyes down and to the right and

watched the tip of the pipe circle her rib cage and stop just under her right breast. Without warning it tipped up and lifted the flesh, then withdrew and let it bounce. Twice more, then the pipe reappeared on her other side and bounced the left breast.

"They're real!"

"No silicone?"

"No." It was only a partial lie. On her eighteenth birthday, Norma had had her nipples done at the same, Miami clinic her sister Sandy had visited the year before. Numerous, tiny, silicone injections with a needle, to raise the nipples in two stages. Just the nipples. They had called the job a "Balanchine".

Klaus reappeared.

"Get this lesbian bitch away from me!"

"Make a blow-job mouth for the camera. If he doesn't like you I have to waste you. You know too much."

"No! Okay, but get her away from me first!"

"Hey! They don't care how much tongue she gives you. Just don't let her fuck you."

"Klaus!"

More barking from the other room and the woman hissed, turned on her heels, and left.

Norma looked around the bathroom for cameras but if there were any, she could not spot them. Were they going to do something to her in here so gross that the assholes couldn't watch? At least the water was nice and warm, and as Klaus fastened the last chain, her left ankle, to the far corner of the step down tub, Norma quit her bitching and let her body settle down, keeping only her shoulders above the water to protect her hair.

As he left the room, which was a big as a living-room, Klaus said: "Well, I leave you to the ladies now, and their girlie business."

"What girlie business? No, wait!"

He was gone. No doors, though. Just these gaudy, wide, entrance ways from room-to-room. Archways draped with brocade valances. Huge folds of material, enough to make a tent. That's what they looked like! Entrances to huge tents in the desert. The material at the opening rolled back and tied. Dumb camel-drivers!

The tub was shiny black, and square, and the fixtures were gold, or gold plated. A narrow border of aquamarine tiles, then more, thick carpeting, the color of sand, and leather covered benches against the walls. A stack of thick towels and stainless steel, lidded canisters, which looked like surgical instrument containers — what could be in those? Norma shivered. But the hot water sure felt good and it would feel even better if they had turned the jets on, the openings of which were visible on all sides. Norma wondered how long she was going to soak here, before her arms would begin to ache with her wrists shackled to rings behind her head. At least the little pool had a built-in head rest. How thoughtful. Above her, the glass baubles of a chandelier twisted ever so slightly, and glittered. From the movement of air! Norma tried to twist her head back but couldn't turn far enough to see if people were sneaking in, padding quietly on the carpeting behind her to steal looks at her. Fuck them! Nothing she could do now, anyway, but wait. Right?

No soap in the water but it had a strange scent. A pleasant scent. Some kind of perfume?

She thought of her father, back in Tampa. The neighborhood where she grew up. So normal. High school. The junior college. Years of growing up, waiting

109

to get the hell out of there! See the world! Often, sitting on the front porch as a teenage girl, she would envision her future life, where she would go, where she would travel. Her sister Sandy, a year older, who looked just like her but was smarter, and sweeter, too, in a way, would sit with her and they'd talk. Once they talked about Egypt. And Sandy had said: "Oh, but if they caught me with a joint, they'd lock me up and throw the key away. Or is it Turkey they do that? You don't go to a jail there, you go to a dungeon! Gosh, a real dungeon! Gruel to eat. Rats. Water sloshes around your straw mat during high tide. The guards come in on you in the middle of the night and string you up-side-down from the ceiling and fuck you in the ass."

Sandy never went anywhere without her gun and never left it out of reach at home. These people would never have been able to kidnap **her**!

But in all their dreams, the sisters never came up with a bathroom like this. Tears began to roll down Norma's cheeks, and she heard herself whisper, out loud: "Sandy." Her sister had killed one man (that Norma knew of — Sandy's step-son no less) whom she had witnessed raping another girl. Blew his ass away — blew his head apart with one shot.

Once, at a party, Norma was listening to Sandy telling everybody about their father, how he trained them in self defense, and how to shoot, and this drunk guy grabbed her by the wrist and he said: "Yeah, but what about right now. What're you gonna do right now?" And Sandy twisted around and had her derringer shoved up his right nostril so far he bled all over the nickel plating. Other people in the room were clapping, and Sandy was grinning and saying stuff like: "Well? What else is a poor girl to do?" That was Sandy. Smart and beautiful — with a sister just as pretty, but dumb.

Four, identically dressed women appeared in the doorway. Norma immediately guessed they were servants. Hooded, and gowned in black to the feet, at least their faces were visible. No veils. Young but plain faces with no make-up, like nuns. Dark eyes and black eyebrows. Speaking in Spanish! Norma cursed herself for sleeping her way through Spanish I.

They commenced to open the stainless steel canisters to get out soap, razors, what looked like bandages, and some squeeze tubes of depilatory.

"No, please, por favor, no depilatory! That stuff makes me break out! Klaus! Klaus!"

But to her surprise, the girls complied and shoved the hair remover aside. They began to soap her down, all four of them on their knees, both sides, rubbing the soap into her pits, and around her private parts. Her legs. They scrubbed with little brushes under her fingernails, and one of them said, in English, "So no germs if you bad girl and you scratch!"

Then, slowly and surely, they shaved Norma from the neck down as slick as a baby dolphin.

"This is so humiliating." Norma raised her voice. "Humiliating!"

One of the girls said: "Shhhhhh." She drew a finger across her Adam's apple. "Be good girl."

"Where are you from?"

"Philippines."

Another of them said: "Mmm-hmm. Philippines."

"Slaves?"

"Oh, no, Miss. Servant."

"Mmm-hmm. Servant."

One of them began to thread a length of nylon rope through the cuffs on Norma's wrists, and unlatched the two chains from the rings in the tub.

"Sit."

"Sit up, no, stand please."

"Rinse." Their voices sounded so sweet. Innocent.

Norma got to her feet, a struggle since her ankles were still chained to the far end. But as soon as she realized the chains on her arms were loose, however, one the of girls cinched the nylon rope tight and Norma found her hands bound behind her. Obviously, this was not the first time for **them!**

The women stood back and one of them turned a valve. Warm water came gushing down in a torrent and Norma fought the stream to look up. The shower head was concealed in the center of the chandelier. One of the Filipinas giggled.

"First class, ay?"

CHAPTER 13
The Crittercam

"Mama, you sewed the rings on the wrong dog. I told you when you did it. If you would've used Jack's dog you'd have movies of every fuck he's had since you divorced him. He lets Candy watch." Jody looked up from petting his huge St. Bernard and studied his mother's hiking outfit. Jodhpurs. Riding britches that flared out like a manta ray at the sides, tapering down into tall, English riding boots. Cotton, camouflage turtleneck shirt. Expensive, mail-order shit. A camo bandanna covered Jasmine's dyed, menopause-red hair.

"Jody." Jasmine didn't want to hurt his feelings, but sometimes it needed to be done. "Jody, I don't care how smart you are, in some ways you're as dumb — and I mean **dumb** dumb — as every other fourteen-year-old. Bernie here'll run when they see the camera on him. Candy would walk up to them and wag her tail while they unstrap it. The best piece of equipment we have, gone. **And,** Candy's too small. The camera would be noticeable a mile away. **And,** we'd have videos of Candy digging up cat-shit mounds and videos of Candy digging up the gladiolus bulbs in my garden and movies of Candy sniffing the mailman's crotch. Up-side-down movies of Jack's girlfriends while Candy rolls over for them to scratch her tummy. Bernie will circle all around that clone place. When he smells Jack he might run up to him but just so far, remember? The only way they'll be able to get the camera off Bernie will be to shoot him first."

113

"Yeah, well, what about that? I love him!" Jody dug the fingers of his longer arm into the dog's thick neck.

"Yeah. They better not!"

"Or?"

Jasmine sighed.

Jody said, "Call the law? 'Gee, officer, I was busy video-taping my neighbor with this camera I sewed to my dog and the man shot him!'"

"Wrong, Jody. It goes: 'Gee, Uncle Cletus, that asshole so-and-so shot my dog! For no reason!' See, Jody? See?"

"Yeah. I see Bernie dead."

"Hey! Are we going through with this or not. You want to see what they look like, don't you? Worse than I do, I expect."

"Mmm - hm."

"So shut up and help with this stuff."

"Mommy dearest."

"You don't know how lucky you are. Picture it. You. Only with a normal mother who goes to church. Checks out the TV GUIDE for the movie ratings before she lets you watch. Makes you go to school. Hangs a picture of Jesus on your wall right where your Miss Borneo centerfold is. Was."

"Miss Tanzania." Jody continued to ruffle his fingertips through the long, tan hair at Bernie's neck, raking it aside and checking the hardened-silver rings. It had been several years now and the rings no longer bothered the dog, no longer caused the flesh in which they were embedded to bleed and fester. "That was cruel, Bernie," Jody said. He kissed the huge animal on top of his massive head.

Bernie's tail wagged and knocked over the bowl of glue they had mixed for the receiver/repeater. Jody dropped to the floor to tip the bowl back up and Jasmine ran for paper towels. They had been sticking dried weeds and grass to the sides of the repeater, and to the antenna. It could pick up signals from the miniature videocam if it was within a mile or so of the dog. Inside the box it amplified the signal, running from batteries, and transmitted the boosted signal to their antenna farm where another receiver, with a monitor, made the tape. Compared to the camera, the receiver/repeater box was heavy and bulky. Old technology. Attached to the back of it were two bungee cords which they were going to use to attach the unit to a tree. The whole assembly was Jasmine's favorite toy, and also the most expensive.

Once, with Jody's help, they had dropped Bernie off near a little-known nude beach near San Destin on the Gulf of Mexico. After editing out about fifty-percent of the tape (the blurry parts where Bernie is either bounding up to people or running away)(picture tall grass and sea oats whipping past a lens which is attached to a running St. Bernard's neck, behind a mouth whipping froth into the wind)(plus Bernie liked to pause for refreshment at cat-shit mounds, too) the mother-son team had nearly an hour of edited film left. Naked humans, all trying to sneak up on Bernie while their mouths spoke cute stuff, like: "Want a treat?" "Oh, you're such a handsome boy!" "Here, doggie!" Or: "Is that thing working? Are you taking movies of me? Yeah? Watch this!"

Jasmine loved the "watch this" stuff best. Jody loved the young, bouncing tits. The blow jobs. *How do those guys get them to do it?* Jody was convinced, of course, that the males, being blessed with normal bodies, had an edge.

"I'm sorry, Jody."

Jody jerked and looked away from his dog, which

115

they had originally bought for him to ride, and wondered about how good this new movie would be. He hoped the clones would not be afraid of such a big dog. He hoped they would call out to him, reach out to him with maybe a dog biscuit in each hand. Bernie would get close, then. It was too much to hope for, though, for the girls to do the "Hey, watch this!" kind of stuff.

But, hey, you never know.

Because he had to do it on the run without being seen, the homing device Jody had slapped inside the bumper of Desirey Jackson's big police cruiser was a crude type with a magnetic base. Not the GPS tap Jody had been working on to track individual vehicles, Miss Chernobyl in particular — a device which could give them an exact position on a map or chart without having to physically follow the unit with a homing device. But with the transmitter on Jackson's cruiser, Jody and Jasmine had to follow the signal by chasing the vehicle in Jasmine's El Camino, Jody yelling at her to stop from minute to minute at every fork in the road so he could jump out with his hand-held directional receiver and get a bearing. And each time they stopped, Bernie the St. Bernard would go sliding stiff-legged and sideways across the bed of the El Camino and **whomp** into the rear window. The camera, which they planned to attach when they found the clone farm, lay at the bottom of a pillow case on the carpet at Jody's feet. The make-shift cloth bag also had a live snake in it. They were hunters and sellers of exotic snakes. That was their cover, and it had worked before. "What you got in that bag, lady?"

"Oh, just a rattlesnake we just caught. Want to see him?"

At their last stop for a fix, closer to the SiblTek

farm than they knew, Jody suddenly jumped back into the car. "Signals getting stronger fast! She must be driving straight at us!"

Just as soon as Jasmine got the El Camino moving, Jackson's Lincoln topped the hill ahead, red light-bar flashing. She whooshed by them without a look.

"Alone. She must've dropped Jack off."

"Or he's dead, Mom."

"Oh, Jody, they wouldn't kill him!"

"He knows too much now."

"Jody, you watch too much TV." When they crested the hill, Jasmine spotted the **No Trespassing** warnings and the SiblTek Corporation sign. The **DEAD END** sign. Jasmine slowed down to turn around.

"Mom, go past! Like we don't know any better!"

"Yeah." Jasmine stomped the pedal and **whomp!** Bernie went sliding into the tailgate. The dog was so huge and stood so tall, Jody looked back to make sure he hadn't flipped over and onto the highway. It had happened before.

At the bottom of the hill was a small creek and bridge, and Jody hollered again, this time to stop. "Here, Mom!" God, if his mother would just stop taking so many pills! "We pretend we're hunting for snakes here!"

Whomp! Bernie again. Jasmine had crunched to a stop at the far side of the bridge where there was enough shoulder to get the El Camino off the road, Bernie smacking into the rear window again. Jody hopped out with the snake/camera bag, and leaned into the open window. "Mom, maybe this isn't so good. We should find a tree on a hill. Transmit better."

"No, no, this is fine! I'm heading to the woods right now and I'll hike back up the hill with the transmitter on my back."

A pickup behind them slowed down and made a U-turn. Two hicks in overalls and an up-side-down john-boat sticking out the back. As soon as they were gone, Jasmine disappeared into the woods with the video re-peater and the bungee cords. As she headed deeper in and up the hill toward the SiblTek farm, Jody took Ber-nie down into the ravine and began to strap on the tiny videocam. "Time to pay your dues, Bernie. I'm sorry. I'll take it off you as soon as we're done."

Bernie wagged his massive tail and stood still while Jody adjusted the straps on the camera, and set the ti-mer. He figured thirty minutes was about enough for his mother to find a tree at the top of the hill and bungee the transmitter to it, and another fifteen minutes or so for Bernie to start hunting for Jack at the farm. The tape at home was good for two hours and forty minutes be-fore somebody had to be there to switch cassettes. Good enough! Jody wanted the camera to start recording be-fore Bernie actually got there. See what the surrounding territory looked like. He might want to go crawling in there himself soon. Sneak into the dormitories at night maybe.

"How long is this going to go on I wonder!" Jas-mine made no attempt to disguise her anger with her son. The two of them were sitting in Jasmine's living-room in the double-wide, the floor a jumble of cables and connectors. There was too much daylight coming in through the windows and Jody was leaning into the black & white monitor, trying to make sense of the blurred scenery flying by Bernie's flapping ears.

"Mom!"

"Jody!"

"Mom, I'm worried about the homer I stuck on

Miss Jackson's bumper. How am I going to get it back before Uncle Clit sees it?"

"Shit. That thing is so low-tech. Why did you set Bernie's camera to start so soon is what I'm wondering!"

"Low tech? Your videocam setup still uses analog tape technology! Anyway, my homer found us where Miss Jackson was going. Where the farm is."

"Farm? **Miss** Jackson?! Get real, boy!"

"Nub-man."

"Sit back so I can see! Oh, here we go! We're out of the woods! Don't stop now, Bernie!"

Bernie jumped up from the rug he was snoozing on and looked at the two of them, the brow on his massive head furrowed.

"All those buildings up ahead. Place must be a thousand acres. You'd think the choppers at Fort Rucker would've figured it out by now."

"They're looking for reefer, Mom."

"Oh, Bernie, no! Don't stop now!"

Jody chimed in: "We don't mean **now,** Bernie!"

Bernie cocked his head at them and let out a little whine.

"Sorry, Bernie." Jody leaned to the side and scratched the top of the dog's head with his longer hand. "We mean when you were making the video. Mom, we have two more hours of tape. It doesn't matter if the first few minutes are wasted."

"Bernie, no!" Jasmine yelled.

Jody turned back to the monitor. The picture was more-or-less still now, just wiggling from side to side like it usually did when Bernie was wagging his tail. Staring at them was a large, black, sheep dog. Large, but not as large as Bernie, of course. The dog Bernie was trying to stare down suddenly turned and ran, with Bernie taking

119

off in pursuit. The movie became a blur of grass, Bernie's spit, and fleeing, sheep-dog ass.

CHAPTER 14
Empty Bunks

Long before Bernie snuck in on the farm with the videocam, Jack had jumped when the outdoor PA system sounded two, short but piercing beeps. He looked at Monday who was getting up from the picnic table, swinging her legs over the bench along with that colorful, voluminous skirt. It looked like she had just punched in something on the keypad on her radio to activate the signal. Jack looked around for the speakers and spotted them on top of the windmill way back near the big house. "What was that for?"

"Two beeps mean: get ready for inspection. Listen."

Jack keened his ears. Feet trampling on wooden floorboards. The **clunk** of — a foot-locker? Then silence and no more sounds of laughter. Old memories of boot camp flooded his mind.

"Come on, bounty hunter. Let's pull an inspection!"

Jack's heart pounded and flopped in his chest as he followed Monday around the corner of the freshly painted, white building. The windows were small but there were plenty of them, swung out on hinges and open to the fresh air. No screens but too high up to look in.

"What do they do in there all day?"

Monday hesitated at the double front-door, one-half of which was wide open. "Watch videos, play games, iron clothes. Erotic videos. X-rated. They're only required to stay inside during certain hours or when the visitor light is on. In this case, you." She motioned for Jack to proceed.

Not as cheerful as outside but the overhead incandescents were bright enough. The girls were standing at attention, facing each other across the single aisle. In crisp tennis shorts and ironed, white blouses, shoulders pulled back, each girl stood rigidly to the left of her foot-locker, the locker open at the end of the bed. Boot camp — almost. Toilet articles neatly arranged in the top tray, socks neatly rolled and lined up, a stack of bikini panties in pastel, Neapolitan ice-cream hues. Plenty of empty cots, though: foot-lockers closed and bare mattresses.

Jack sucked down a deep breath, and tried to banish the memory of the head he and Norma had found, picturing it sloshing around in the ice and the beer bottles of their cooler. *Be cool! Handle this like a drill sergeant!* After a quick count of them — eight, and as many empty beds — Jack moved up to the first girl on his right, pivoted on his heel, and stared into her face. It was the face of a perfectly made-up store mannequin, the blue eyes cold and still. But alive! A beautiful face, too, almost too perfect. Jack's eyes dropped but quickly returned to her face, and he felt his right ear begin to glow and turn red.

They were so young, so firm, so identical to...

...the head on the beach.

"What's your name?" A smile, the eyes coming to life, a slight slumping of the shoulders. A giggle.

"C-14"

"Nobody said at ease!" Monday barked.

"At ease, C-14," Jack said. The girl brought back her smile and moved her feet apart, clasping her hands behind her. There was a dark smudge on her white, left Nike sneaker. "Your shoes could use some work."

"Yes sir."

Jack moved down the line. "What's **your** name?"

"C-1."

"C Number One! Well. Who belongs to the empty bunk beside you, C-1?"

"C-3, sir."

"Where is she?"

"She's dead."

"Dead? What happened?" Jack knew Monday was moving along right behind him and expected her to stop him at any moment.

"My sister ran away."

"Is it easy to run away from here?"

"Oh, no, you can get killed!"

"The runaways had help," Monday said.

"Who helped them?" Jack's face, inches from the frightened eyes of C-1. Her breath was sweet and Pepsodenty.

"I don't know."

"Abu," Monday said. "I told you!"

"Abu."

"So how do you know your sister is dead?"

"Because that's the punishment."

"For running away."

"Mm-hm."

"Do you ever think about running away?"

"Oh, no sir!"

"Good. At ease, C-1." Jack knew he sounded and looked foolish, doing this drill sergeant bit, but what other act could he have pulled out of the hat? How could he have prepared for a scene like this? He turned back to Monday, who was smiling.

"Come on, Jack. Next barracks."

Jack followed her to the door, turned, and shouted

back to the pod: "As you were!" Giggles and a blur of movement. Laughter like little girls make. Only these little girls looked like fifteen or so. Or whatever. Jack felt Monday's hand on his wrist as she pulled him outside. The sun was blinding for a moment, but not bright enough to wash out the image in Jack's brain of the severed head on ice in his Igloo, the severed head hanging from the hair in Norma's clenched fist as she held it out to the News Force Eleven camera. His brushing the sand away from the cold lips and Norma's planting a kiss on them.

He would have tested a kiss on that mouth himself if Norma hadn't always been looking.

"This next building has Klaus's favorites. But if he ever touches any of these in here, he's dead. He's a walking corpse, anyway. You, too. Hands off. You so much as get a hard-on in here you're history. Dead meat, so-to-speak." Jack was following closely behind Monday's swirls of color. Despite her ominous tone, he noted happily that no such warning had accompanied the visit to Pod T-3.

The Pod Threes are probably already spoiled. Fucked by everybody who works here...

"I'll be watching."

"Yes, Ma'am!" Jack was happy now, the nervousness gone. Special stuff coming up! "Klaus. He work for you? He must be the dude Desirey was telling me about."

"Oh?"

"The Arnold Schwarzenegger look-alike? Jackson's got the hots for him."

"Over my dead body!"

"Oh. Sorry. Guess I should keep my mouth shut, huh!"

"No. I thank you for the information. If Eastland

124

didn't have his head so far up that darkie's ass. I was against him bringing her here to start with. We have to trust everybody who knows. Pure trust. And I didn't trust her from the start." Monday spit. No trajectory, just a straight, sizzling shot into a dandelion, blowing its feathery seeds to kingdom come. "On second thought, maybe Manny should be the one to show you the Model-F's." Monday stopped and Jack was following so closely he almost smacked into her again. Their eyes clashed.

"Oh, don't say that!"

silence....

"I'll behave. How much more tempting could they be?"

"The Model F's are an improvement. The "F" stands for final and also for female. Not very scientific, but. You see a tall, black gardener on a tractor when you first drove in?"

"No."

"He was out there somewhere, mowing. My egg, his sperm."

Jack's mouth opened.

"One Cuna egg and one, brave little African wiggler for each pod. Only one just happened to turn out boys. M-pod. Those are going to be marketed as rich-girl toys. One of the F-pods is already sold."

More movies popped up in Jack's head. He remembered the Eurasian in Bangkok he had fallen in love with once. The night-clerk at his hotel. What a wonderful mix of races! So fine! The one time he was drunk enough to hit on her, though, she spit. Spit on his face right there in the lobby.

"He doesn't know it. What we did with his sperm."

"Huh?"

"Tyrone."

"Oh. Original name!"

Her spit had tasted like a Cert and he could still taste it. Jack fished in a pocket and shook a Cert out of the plastic box he always carried and began to savor on it.

"Okay, we'll look in on the F's. Or the F-5's I should call them. We have five F-pods." They had rounded the corner of the next building which had a door similar to the Model-T unit, but this door was shut tight. Monday dug in a pocket for a key. "We'll just look in. From the doorway, here. You'll know why directly. Each of the five F-pods came out great but Manny and Klaus like these the best. Separate barracks for each. Slightly different ages, et cetera."

Jack's heart was pounding again. It was all going to be too much. A shot of Jack Daniel's would help. Just one shot, though, since he was on the job. If he had come in his own vehicle....

Monday cracked the door, which had not been locked after all, and peered in. "Damn!" The lights were out but there was enough illumination from the high windows to see that not a soul was there. Jack quickly counted twenty cots, a row of ten on each side. All made-up, but not with the precision of the Model-T barracks.

"Manny took them to the creek again! Come on!"

Jack took a last look and scraped the sole of his shoe against the concrete walk. "Gum."

"They're not as neat as the T's."

"Yeah, but gum on the sidewalk?"

Monday laughed. She had taken a path which angled off from the row of hangars, down toward a wooded area. "Come on! You'll see. They love to chew gum! When they're not busy sucking on the dildos we

126

provide. Some of them Klaus whittles out of bay-wood and then dips them in that rubbery stuff they coat tool handles with."

Jack followed, trying to catch up without breaking into a run. Dildos. Barracks after barracks filled with living copies of cute girls. A live Barbie Doll factory. On this very Earth! Watching fuck movies so they know what to do! A man would kill for a couple of...

"Remember, when you see them, don't even **think** about sex. Not with these, anyway. Simply not in your future."

"Okay!"

"Uh - huh." They rounded a curve in the path, the air humid and heavy in the dense shade. Laughter coming from far up ahead. As they got closer, water splashing. Little-girl shrieks of delight. A deep yet reedy-sounding male voice: "Careful now! Don't dive on top of each other! One at a time on the board! Hey! Okay, bust your head open! Piss off Miss Monday!"

Monday grumbled. "Miss Monday!" The path opened up into the sunshine on a narrow but sparkling-clear creek. The diving board was across the wooden footbridge over the creek, and a dark, blur of a girl had just sprung from it, arcing into the water with a squeal. Jack took two more steps and stopped, his mouth open. On the banks of the creek, on both sides, were basking, or running, or jumping, a passel of luscious, identical, naked, and glistening-wet girls the likes of which Jack had never seen. Not even in all his horny dreams. Golden-brown, happy bodies with full heads of wavy black hair. Near blue-black, poky nipples, and chunky-little meat-ball asses. Long legs, and narrow-little straight-hair bushes, like little paint brushes. Deep, deep navels.

"Easy, boy."

Jack could not breathe. He hardly noticed Dr. Mannlicher on the other side — his shock of red hair — the man in tattered Levi's cut-offs — so tall and lanky, and scruffy-looking. Suddenly, Jack slipped on the stony ground at the bank's edge, and grabbed for Monday's arm with his left hand. He caught it and hung on. He tried to blurt out the word *Sorry!* but only a squeak emerged from his dry throat. He was in the Garden of Eden. It had been found. Not between the Tigris and Euphrates Rivers like the Bible said, but right here in the fucking Florida panhandle, just fifty miles north of Florida's "Emerald Coast", a.k.a. "The Redneck Riviera". And only he and a privileged few knew where it was.

The girls noticed the two of them and were waving and smiling, jumping up-and-down, their little, rubbery tits bouncing. Still hanging onto Monday, Jack pulled his right hand out of his pants pocket and waved back.

CHAPTER 15
Blood Test

Her hands still bound behind her with the nylon cord, Norma waited for the chains cuffed to her ankles to be released. The Filipina servant girls giggled and moved around her with huge, fluffy-pink towels, once pushing just a little too hard on one side and nearly causing Norma to slip in the wet tub.

"I'll break my legs with my feet chained like this!"

More giggles. The one fluffing her hair was so brisk but gentle it could be easy to forget that in the past few hours Norma had not only killed someone, she had also been kidnapped and hauled away to another building in a piss-soaked carpet. So clean and dry now, Norma was barely paying attention to how good all these new attentions were feeling. There was an escape window coming up — or so she hoped — not much of one but maybe the only one. Would Klaus be coming back to shackle her to the pillory posts in the other room again? Or were the girls going to do it?

Could she overpower all four of them?

Which room to run to if she could? If she fucked up, she'd end up cornered in a place with no exit to the hall and the elevators.

For a moment, Norma also thought about how she'd feel out there in the real world, stark-naked as she ran for her life.

I'll worry about that when I'm free!

"I want a robe!"

"Shhhhh!"

129

The Filipinas seemed so nice!

"I'm tired of standing here stripped in front of everybody! And those cameras!"

"Shhhhh! No cameras in here, Señora."

"Ohhh?" Norma looked up and around. Suddenly, she felt the nylon rope behind her, binding her wrists, loosen.

"Please, Missy, no fight. Okay? This way. Out of tub?"

The girl speaking was dangling the original, gold chains for her wrists, a smile on her face as Norma held out her arms. She could feel the tugs at her feet as the other girls worked open the padlocks on the other two chains fastened to the tub. If she could hold off on the arms for a second until her ankles were free.

Norma pulled back her hands. "Wait." She faked a shiver.

No such luck. The activity around her feet stopped while the Filipinas waited for the cuffs on her wrists to be fastened.

No dummies. Norma gave up and held her arms back out.

"Good. Thank you, Señora."

"Yeah. Good doggie. Do I get a bone? How about a robe!"

Norma felt sure that there had been a moment there when she was close to an opportunity to break away, but it was gone.

There's a way. There has to be a way.

The Filipinas were leading her to the opposite entrance, not the way she had been brought in.

That little opening on the side must be the kitchen.
What next?!
The chains are so quiet and heavy. Real gold. Gold is soft.

Didn't pirates bite gold pieces to see if they were real? Could I break them?

What if they're just gold-plated? With steel underneath?

Another large room. The only furnishing was the huge bed, ominous and black, in the center of the vast, sandy-peach colored carpet. You could ride a camel around it. Black, satin sheets. Black, satin pillow-cases — lots of them — with tacky, peach-colored roses embroidered in.

One for shoving under my ass.

On the far side of this room was another archway similar to the others, draped with the same material which reminded Norma of pictures of tents in the desert. Enough material to cover a parking lot. And sand-colored drapes and valances over the sliding-door closets.

"Up! Up!" The face of the Filipina giving the orders looked the youngest, and the most worried.

Norma balked at the side of the four-poster. She peered up under the canopy and saw the full-length mirror. In a minute she would no longer be restricted to just her imagination; she would be able to see just how a peaches-and-cream, freckled white-girl looked spread-eagled on black satin. "No."

"Yes, Missy, please, or Señor Klaus come."

"Any cameras in here?"

"Oh, no, Señora. Master's room."

"The master."

"Yes."

"Si. Yes."

In a moment, Norma was lying on her back, a real shiver shaking her for a second as she slid on the cool silkiness of the bed-cover. Overhead, she shone in the mirror, her hair spreading out behind her head. Her hair that way looked kind of neat, though. But her shaved pussy, god!

Stainless-steel clips snapped as the Filipinas fastened her chains to the four posts. They were fastening the clips through the links rather than the ends, keeping the chains short, with Norma's legs and arms stretched out on the king-sized stage. When they were satisfied, the girls headed for the near archway, three of them anyway, turning back with little, embarrassed waves of their little, tan hands.

The youngest was pretending to arrange the pillow under Norma's head. "Gun under mattress," she whispered. "This side."

Norma's heart speeded up. She tried to hold her voice down. "But I can't reach it."

"Shhhh. Master take chain off when he come. You know how to use pistol? Shhhh."

"Uh-huh."

"Please — no kill?"

"Yeah, sure, okay!"

"Just scare for escape?"

"Sure! Wait! Which way is out?"

But the Filipina had already turned to go and seemed not to hear her.

Then another of the girls was back, with a gift box in her hands. And a big smile. "Present for you. From my master."

The box was the size of a thick, paper-back book, covered in pretty, gold foil with red, diagonal strips. Expensive looking. Norma tried to sit up but her wrists, pulled back behind her head by the chains, kept her pinned down and all she could do was raise her head.

"I could rip it open with my teeth if you hold it."

"I open it for you."

"Thrilling."

"Please, Missy, I'm sure it is very nice."

Norma could see the other three girls watching from the archway but her eyes focused back on the package. With a snick of a long nail, the Filipina released the lid from the paper. Out of the tissue inside, she pulled out a heavy, thick, gold choker.

"Ohhh," they both said. Norma sucked in a breath.

"I put it on for you? So pretty."

"God, solid gold? Looks like about two pounds of it! A thousand dollars an ounce? What's the plan? He fucks me while I wear his dog collar and then he gives it to the next twat they drag in here?"

"Oh, no Señora. It is yours. To keep!" This Filipina's English was near perfect.

"Oh, yeah. Sure. Like when they close the lid on my coffin, like I should get a coffin. I get it. Mine to keep until they dump me in a ditch somewhere."

"Oh, no! No ditch!"

"Coffin was closer?"

"Oh, no, the master is very kind to his ladies."

"Find 'em, fuck 'em, forget 'em"

The Filipina's breath was sweet and her cheek soft and smooth as she looked behind Norma's neck to fiddle with the clasp.

"He fuck you? The other girls?"

"Oh, no Señora, no fuck us. The master sleep only with special ladies. Like you. He let the man servants have us. If they are good he gives us to them sometime. Or when his friends come, or his — pariente? They have servants and he gives us to them. When they visit."

"That sucks."

"No, they don't do that. But we have to for them. It's not too bad."

133

"It sucks. You ever get pregnant?"

"Oh, no, we go to hospital to get fix. No fix, no job. It's okay. The scar is small. No babies. No period. Ready to fuck all time."

"Wonderful." With the girl's face out of the way now, Norma could inspect the impressive, heavy chunk of gold around her neck in the canopy mirror. She had always wanted a solid-gold choker, but she'd be damned if she would admit that now. "A fucking dog collar."

The girls in the archway giggled, their hands over their mouths.

"Are you fixed, Señora?"

"Yeah, but for a different reason."

"Different reason?"

"Yeah, so I'm hot to trot when I want to. Big, big difference."

"Not different now."

"We'll see."

"Soon," the Filipina said over her shoulder as she left with the gift wrapping. On her way out with the other three, an older man in a gray business suit walked in, a little, black bag in his hand.

Not different now. "Who are you?!"

"Doctor Zamahdi." His eyes averted Norma's nakedness as he sat down at her side and opened the bag. "I need a little blood." He held up two syringes, one empty and the other filled with a yellow liquid. "If you fight..." He drew a finger across his throat and pantomimed a thrust with the loaded syringe at her neck. Leaning over now, he unsnapped her near wrist from the bedpost.

He wound the rubber tourniquet around her upper arm, his eyes avoiding her breasts. "Make a fist."

"Why should I?"

"We are looking to see if you have any parasites. Fist please."

Norma felt the prick and, after he unsnapped the tourniquet, she watched her dark blood push up into the barrel of the syringe. Surprisingly painless and quick. She breathed a sigh of relief when he got up. Her relief was short-lived, however, as he moved farther down the side of the bed and brought out the magnifying glass and the largest, chrome-plated, speculum she had ever seen.

"No!"

"Relax, Miss." His voice was high-pitched and foreign. "Relax. They all look the same to me. Let me warm this up a little." He blew on the two cold, flat blades of the speculum and whipped a handkerchief out of his breast pocket to wipe off the mist which had formed.

"They're not sterile!"

"Sterile?" His dark-brown eyes glowed behind puffy, shiny-brown cheeks. "I saw you on TV. With your lips on the dead girl's mouth. Yes? I don't think you know about sterile." He laid the instrument down for a moment to snap a rubber glove over his left hand. His finger thrust up into her without warning, and Norma could feel the nail through the latex.

"Asshole motherfucker! You're no fucking doctor!"

"No worry about sterile today, Miss. Not today."

When he was finished with her, the doctor left without any further ceremony. In fact, he exited the room leaving Norma's left wrist free, not even turning to see her quickly flip her arm up to make it appear shackled.

Dumb-ass goat humper!

After being alone for a minute, not a sound to be heard anywhere, Norma stretched herself as far as she could to the side of the bed to see if she could get that free hand under the mattress. Not even close. So she would have to wait for the "master" to unchain her after all.

Master.

Some rich asshole oil sheikh.

Norma's mind flipped back-and-forth between her stupidity at leaving her revolver in Jack's boat, the pistol here supposedly hidden under the mattress on the side of her free arm, and the injustices of the world in general. Injustices in particular regarding half the world's oil sitting under some smelly tents in the desert.

She began to mumble to herself. "God. Speaking of, why did You give all those sand monkeys all that oil? How come everything underground doesn't belong to everybody? The oceans belong to everybody! They should change the law!" Whispering now: "The pistol. How far under the mattress? An automatic? Jack said you have to cock the old ones for the first shot. Single action. Okay."

The safety on the old military pieces usually points down the barrel when it's OFF. Okay. Toward the victim, Jack said. Usually. There'll be a little lever, usually on the inside, flipped down if the safety is ON. Or up. You have to flip it toward the victim. Down the barrel.

"Okay. I hope so, Jack. I hope I can find the safety lever."

Think! Shut up! There might be microphones in here!

'Course it'll be a thumb lever on the left side and me being left handed — I'll have to use two hands the first second, anyway, to flip it.

If it's a revolver.

Revolvers don't have safety levers. If it's single-action, pull the hammer back for each shot. I'm used to that! My .41's sin-

gle action. Double-action, just pull the trigger for each shot.

I'll have to figure the gun out quick once I get my hands on it.

I'll have just a split second.

If it's an auto, do I feel for the safety lever? Look for it? Will I have time?

Maybe it'll be a P-38 like Jack's — I know where the safety is on that one!

I should be so lucky.

Will there be a round already chambered?

The silence in the blur of Norma's desperate thoughts was broken by the whine and thunder of a low-flying aircraft. From another room, the sound of a window rattling. *Where is everybody? Assholes are probably on their knees somewhere on some old mats praying to Allah. "Oh, dear God, forgive me for fucking all these unwilling white girls!"*

No, it's Christians who get out of their sins that way.

Her body shivered in the air-conditioned, sterile air.

Get a grip, Norma!

Not one fucking window in here!

What time is it?

Wonder what he looks like. The fucking master.

Norma pictured the Emir of Kuwait. Black robe trimmed in gold. Old and dried up. No ass. Skinny. Hawk nose.

Probably has an uncircumcised, smelly cock.

Norma shivered again and gave her right arm, the one still chained, a hefty jerk. ***Crack!*** The wood of the post made a startling noise and Norma cringed, her body scrunching up in fright. Did anybody hear that? She sucked in a deep breath and held it, waiting, and then noticed that her right arm had more reach. Could it be? She could twist around on her right side now and she studied the post and the chain clipped to it. How dumb could she be!? The chain wasn't padlocked but clipped — she knew that — clipped with a steel snap and she should've remembered she could reach it with her free hand! In seconds both of Norma's arms were free, although dangling lengths of very expensive chain, and she quickly bent over to unfasten the chains on her feet. The cuffs on her ankles and wrists were locked, but the other ends of the chains were all loose now and she was free. Free!

Norma gathered up in her arms the four chains she would have to carry with her. They were so long that she had to coil them all together around her forearms in a heavy bunch. Heavy, soft, quiet gold.

Enough to pay off all her credit cards. Enough left over to buy a new car?

Or the fucking things were just gold plated brass. That would be just her luck!

Norma adjusted the coils of chain so she could use her hands. Now, to find something to put on and get out of here!

No, first find the pistol!

CHAPTER 16
Bernie's Video Tape

Mother and son. Jasmine and Jody leaned forward, their eyes fixed on the monitor as Bernie's video-tape of the SiblTek farm got to the good stuff. Jasmine slapped a palm to her forehead, trying to dispel the dizziness she often felt from watching the St. Bernard's jerky camera technique.

"There's two!" Jody shouted. "Just ran around the corner of that building!" He tried to snatch the remote out of his mother's hands and got sliced by her vampire-red fingernails.

"Dammit, Jody, we can always play it again later!" Jasmine was intent on the distant couple in the upper right of the screen, walking away down a path into the woods.

"It's Dad."

"No, son, Jack doesn't walk that way. Who's that woman?"

"Yes he does, Mom, when he's with his girlfriends. He walks totally different."

"She looks like a gypsy from the back. Some refugee from the Sixties."

"Like a sailor on a deck. I've seen it. That's Jack."

"Well. Go, Bernie! Run over there and show her from the front!"

Bernie looked up from the carpet, his brow wrinkled.

"It's okay, Bernie. Mom, we don't need to see that lady from the front. We need to see clones!"

"Black arms and legs. That dress looks like Everglades hippie. Dumb. What happened to the sound, Jody?"

"I don't know. Tan, not black, Mom."

"Sure."

"There's some!" Jody was half out of his chair, his short, nub-arm pointing while his long arm flicked back for balance. Jody's eyes had a short focus-field but at the proper distance from the monitor he could see everything perfectly. The girls had belly buttons, they were cute, and they were naked. The picture began to jolt and flip as Bernie trotted up toward them, the girls getting prettier by the second as he got close. Four, no, five of them, all looking at the huge dog approaching. They did not seem the least bit scared, considering the dog's size. Bikini-clipped little bushes. Pokey nipples. "Mom, when they get scared, do their nipples grow?"

"How should I know! Shhhhh!"

"There's no sound, remember?"

"That was your department. You fucked up. I want to see the clone **boys!**"

Jody swallowed and hoped his mother would not notice the erection in his jeans. Oh, god, they were beautiful. Leaning forward now, their long, blond hair hanging down, their tits hovering and quivering.

"Maybe they didn't make any boys, Mom."

The picture would have been even better if some of Bernie's saliva hadn't sprayed onto the lens on his earlier run after the sheepdog. But the clones were so wonderful! Bernie stopped, about ten feet away from them. The girls' lips were moving, and Jody tried to imagine their sweet voices coaxing the dog to come closer.

"They're too dumb to see he's got a live camera on his shoulders."

"They don't look so dumb to me."

"They're dumb little twits. Nub-man, listen to Mama. These people who did this, they're kinky. No way they didn't make a bunch of little boys."

"Kinky. Oh. Like you're not?"

"Right. Compared to this, I'm Doris Day. These people are dangerous kinky, Jody."

"Look! Look! She's kneeling! Her legs are apart a little!"

"God, Jody."

Bernie could not be coaxed to come closer. Which was perfect, because he was at the best distance and the clones just filled the screen.

"The picture sways so much because the camera had to be mounted so high."

"I think we should try a new way, like under his neck, but not like last time, letting it swing like that, I mean, some new kind of harness..."

"Mom, the battery-pack is under his neck. Do you think Dad will let me have one of the clones?"

"Oh, Jo... Nub-man."

"I'll never get a real girl, Mom. Not unless I'm rich. You know. But one of these. One of these would be just right! They're not human, are they? I mean, have rights and stuff?"

"Oh, Nub-man." Jasmine suddenly shrieked. The movie blurred as Bernie swung his head, then focused on a horde of little boys, like a swarm of gnats, running toward the camera from a distant building. A whole pack of little, perfect boys. Sun-tanned boys. Well, maybe not so little. Hairless pubes but hung they were, their bodies rippling with pubescent muscle. The movie blurred again but remained pointed at the approaching herd.

Jody turned to his mother who was trying to swallow. "The picture!" she bitched. "If he'd only hold still!"

"It's jerking because he's barking, Mom. He's barking at them."

"Shut up, Bernie, oh, please, shut up!"

The camera steadied but just for a second and the boys, much closer now, came into perfect focus. There was a swarm of them, it seemed. Jasmine gasped audibly but the camera swung away, the picture bouncing wildly as Bernie began to run from them all.

"Bernie!"

The dog jumped to his feet and looked from Jody to Jasmine.

"He had to run, Mom. It was either that or bite the shit out of them!"

"I'd be biting the shit out of them," Jasmine said. Her voice lowered. "Ohhhh. I'd bite and nip and bite and nip..."

"Disgusting, Mom."

"You wouldn't know, son!"

CHAPTER 17
Dr. Mannlicher

Mannlicher strode across the footbridge, square jaw set in a narrow, jaggedly handsome, clean-shaven face. There were a lot of miles on that face but the brightness of his pale-blue eyes belied the end of middle-age. Jack tried not to be intimidated by Mannlicher's stare when the man stopped dead, three feet in front of him. Jack had to look up a little.

"Dr. Livingstone, I presume."

"Uhhh, okay."

"Oh, **yeah?** I don't **think** so!" Mannlicher's voice was commanding, with a wide range which arose from deep down but emphasized the words "yeah" and "think" with a high-pitched near-scream.

"Right. You're right. Livingstone was shorter." Jack quietly sucked in a deep breath and stood his ground. He had never seen such light-blue eyes. So bright. And that uncombed shock of red hair!

"A **lot** shorter!" Mannlicher broke into a large-toothed smile. "Plus **Livingstone** was a **gentleman!**" Again, the deep voice raised to near-scream to emphasize certain, individual words.

Jack grinned, and had to bend his head back a little more to keep from breaking eye contact. Besides, to look down would mean confronting Mannlicher's bare, reddish, befreckled chest, pink nipples poking through swirls of strawberry body hair. The man's lanky frame seemed to be leaning forward on the balls of his feet, his face bending closer to Jack's.

"So you're Jack?"

"Right. And you're Doctor Mannlicher?"

"Name's Manny! You been fucking my **wife**?"

"No, I, uh..."

"Well? What's your **last** name?"

"Jack Rebman."

"What do you **think** of her, **Jack**? Huh? **Huh**?"

"Monday? She's beautiful!"

"You're **right**! It's too bad she got so **old**!"

Jack lost it and looked away to Monday. Monday was smiling, tiny wrinkles around the corners of her mouth, her nose ring skewed to one side.

Dr. Mannlicher lifted his long, freckled arms and turned his palms up, flopping them around and shooing Jack and Monday back toward the path. "Come **on**! Let's get the little **cunts** back in their **barracks**!"

Jack started out behind Monday but turned momentarily to look at Mannlicher again. Tall and thin, with ropey muscles. Arms long and dangling, the fingertips well past the ends of his cut-offs. River-rat sandals, fancy and brand-new. A short, hooked, well-worn machete dangling from a loop from his waist.

"You think I'm **weird** or something? Come **on**!"

"No, I... Yeah. Weird!"

"Glad to **hear** it! Bet you never saw so much prime **pussy** in all your **life**! Huh?!"

"Not even in my dreams!"

"Dreams? **Dreams?!**

Monday was moving down the path quickly and Jack tried to follow close behind her. She kept moving even when her multi-colored skirt would snag momentarily on bushes along the path. Jack had to turn back once more, just for a second. Mannlicher was right on his ass, and behind him were the girls, trotting along single file, some with their arms crossed over their chests as branches and leaves flicked at them. No laughing or talking now. Their young, tan faces looking so serious. Jack was stunned by their appeal.

"You want to turn into a pillar of **salt?** Come **on!**"

Jack swallowed hard and vowed not to look back again. He had to smile to himself. So far he was doing OK. He could handle Dr. Mannlicher, he thought. In fact, Jack kind of liked him. The smart-ass stuff he said. The kind of things Jack would say himself if he had major balls.

Suddenly: "How'd you **get** here, Jack?" Mannlicher's voice still loud but with less of an edge.

"Miss Jackson drove me. The deputy."

"Oh, **Jackson!** Fuck her in a **heart** beat! But I guess she isn't worth catching one of those two-hundred-and-fifty grain lead **slugs** from your daddy's forty-**five,** is she? Huh? **Huh?!**"

"Took the words right out of my mouth."

"No, I pulled them out of your **ass!**"

The path opened back into the bright, open fields. The barracks were all gleaming and shimmering in the distance in their neat rows. Jack squinted his eyes. The sheep, barely visible, were grazing along the fence on the far side and there was the faint smell of steaming manure. The sun beat hot on the top of Jack's head and shoulders and he imagined the cool water of the creek — with the girls. Despite his vow he turned again as he walked. The girls were still strung out behind Mannlicher, single file. Still not talking. Several of them waved and Mannlicher, who had also turned, saw it.

"**Friendly** little critters, **aren't they?**"

"Yeah."

"Eat your **heart** out! You're **looking** at a cool twenty **million! You** got that kind of **money? Huh?**"

"No."

"You even **think** about fucking one of them, I'm gonna **charge** you! **Ten-thousand** just for **thinking** about it!"

"I get the picture!"

"They're **cherry!** All **twenty** of them!"

Monday turned and stopped in the middle of the path and Jack caught up to her. "After this morning, Manny, I'm going to check!"

"Check **now!**"

They had all stopped, not a one of them an inch off the narrow, beaten-down path through the pasture. Monday, looking grim, brushed around Jack and Dr. Mannlicher.

"Any of you fuck Manny?"

The girls, all looking down at their feet, shook their heads.

Monday singled one out. "You. Come here."

Jack winced at the tone of her voice. The clones all seemed so young. The little clone Monday was pointing at stepped onto the grass and walked slowly toward her, suddenly flipping onto her hands. Her dark, smooth legs spread and wavered in the air, the soles of her little feet much lighter, almost pink. Monday grabbed the girl's ankles, steadying her. Then she freed one hand and looked in.

Manny laughed at Jack's discomfort. "Take a **look** Jack?"

"No. That's okay, I..." Jack was glancing around. Here they were, out in the middle of this open field.

Like I would know what a virgin looks like!

"Can't **handle** it?!"

"I wouldn't know what a virgin looks like."

"Good. **Okay!** Come **on,** wife, let's get these little **bitches** put **up!** I've got some shit I need to show **Jack** here! Hup hup, hup, let's **go!**"

Back toward the F-5 barracks, single file. Jack saw himself in a documentary on PBS. The movie filmed like they do on a National Geographic series of the Sahara Desert. Or the opening shot of "Nature". He and Monday and Mannlicher and the girls all walking single-file in slow-motion. Walking the ridge of a sand dune or the crest of a mountain, silhouetted against the setting sun. If Jasmine could only tape this with her video camera! Twenty million bucks, just for this one pod! Who'd have that kind of money? Then, thinking about it, Jack realized what kind of deal he was getting into. The kind that if you back out, they kill you.

Snuff you without a thought.

As they approached the open front door of F-5 they could hear laughter coming from the last barracks in the row. A huge dog appeared from behind the building as it bounded away toward the perimeter fence. Bernie! Jack recognized Jody's huge dog, with Jasmine's old, Russian, ex-KGB mini-cam strapped to him, the battery pack bouncing under his neck. Chasing after Bernie was a herd of naked little boys.

CRACK!

The gunshot, right behind Jack's ears, buckled his knees. Jack saw Bernie gave an extra burst of speed as the little boys, all screaming, veered off like a flight of birds and swooped back toward their dormitory. Jack turned, his heart racing.

Mannlicher looked at the revolver in his hand, cocked for another shot, and lowered the hammer gently back down with his thumb. Big, toothy grin. "Never **could** shoot a damn **dog!**" Mannlicher paused. **"Dogs** are better than **people!** Right? Huh? **Huh?!"**

Jack nodded, his ears still ringing. *He didn't see the camera?*

The single-file line of girls behind Mannlicher had stopped, the girls waiting patiently. They acted as if a gunshot was part of life-as-usual. Hands on their hips or arms crossed under their pokey tits. Jack had to force himself to look away again. He caught Monday's sly smile. What did that mean? Everything seemed so quiet now, except for the distant sound of an approaching helicopter. Suddenly an alarm-bell went off, loud and high up. Jack spotted the alarm atop one of the electric poles just as the whole mob of cloned girls broke ranks and raced past him for their barracks. They ran around Monday in a frenzy and in seconds had poured through their open doorway and were gone. Monday and Mannlicher stood still.

Monday explained. "It's okay if the chopper sees us. Not the girls."

The alarm-bell stopped and Jack looked off toward the chopper noise and saw two. A Huey flying directly under a Cobra gun-ship.

"Practice," Monday said. "From Fort Rucker in Alabama. This isn't their regular training area but once in a while. Our radar is supposed to pick them up before you can hear them. The gunshot must've thrown it off. It can pick up the reefer spotter-planes, too. We have the girls trained to disappear before they can be seen from the air."

Mannlicher's voice bellowed. "You **see** them **run?** Do we have them **trained** or **what?!** Huh? **Huh?!"**

Jack had seen them run, all right. All he had to do now was figure out a way to erase the sight. Their dark hair flying as they ran, and their beautiful, long legs and

148

their firm-little asses.

A squawk sounded from underneath Monday's voluminous, rainbow skirt. She pulled out her radio and keyed. The radio beep-beep-beeped with an urgent tone. Mannlicher and Monday looked at each other.

"Urgent, confidential call from your **father!** Our Jurassic **Sheriff!** Mister **Eastland!**" Manny winked at Jack and took off toward the house, the dangling machete slapping his thigh. Now Jack knew where he had concealed such a large pistol, the barrel jammed down under the waist-band of the cut-offs, pointing into his groin.

Jack watched him with awe, the long strides and the absolute confidence of the man. "He serious? The call is urgent?"

Monday nodded, but with a gold-toothed smile. "That's why he wouldn't use the radio with us here to listen, he's been getting paranoid. It took Manny so many years to get to this point and now I think he worries it could all fall apart. Come on, I'll show you the male barn. The boys get excited over me, so bad lately it's kind of scary." She turned away from Jack. "I love it, though. Anyway, they seem to respect Manny's authority. Maybe they'll behave with you here."

Jack followed Monday to the second, long row of hangars, toward the one at the end which Bernie had run from. Still trying to erase the re-plays in his head of the clones from the creek-bank, Jack mentioned how beautiful the creek was and the stillness of the forest there, and missed several of Monday's small-talk questions. Finally her voice broke through his rambling.

"...loggers come in from time-to-time. They nose around and beg us to let them cut, give us a percentage. Manny calls the trees 'toilet paper on the hoof'. Don't worry, their boss never gets past the front gate." Monday stopped and faced him again. "You could be valuable to us. I hope we can we trust you."

"Maybe I'm getting in over my head."

"As long as you remain loyal, you'll be well rewarded. Don't worry. You can follow simple instructions, I'm sure. That's all you have to do. Nothing complicated. As for the rules, what's left of Pod-3 can help you keep from breaking any of them."

Jack felt his throat dry up as he kept his eyes locked into Monday's golden irises, the dilated, black depths of her pupils. He had read that the eyes were an extension of the brain and the only part of the brain that is visible on the outside. Monday's brain was too much. He felt himself needing to break away. "So Doctor Mannlicher's talking to the sheriff now, huh?"

"Manny. He'll crawl you every time you say doctor, even though he probably loves it. Yes, he's either at the house right now or he's using the scrambled cellular phone. Keep your eyes open with him, Jack. I mean, the sheriff."

"He's my father!"

"You heard me."

Jack broke the fierce eye contact. He concentrated on Monday's nose ring. Did it ever snag on stuff? If she's running around a corner or something and has to stop fast, does the ring swing forward like a door on hinges?

Monday turned her face away, stuck two fingers into her mouth, and let out a piercing whistle. Instantly, little Klauses came spilling out of the next barn, totally naked, little hairless dicks and balls, laughing and gamboling, some of them reverting to trotting on all fours. Monday allowed some of them to pull on her skirt and climb up into her arms and slobber all over her in various states of erection, hungry fingers hunting for her zipper and fighting over her tits. Her nipples protruded like black walnuts and once again Jack wished there more room in his jeans.

Monday, smiling, struggled with them as she tried to speak. "They're in the video stage now, like the girls in the adjacent barn only they're farther along. Oh, that's right, you haven't seen them yet. They're equal to age ten now. These little dudes maybe six or seven."

"How old in real time?"

"A little over four years. The boys. At a certain point, they stop growing in age and intelligence. They aren't human, they're, like, manufactured. The word age does not really apply."

"Video stage?" Jack was doing his best to remain cool.

Monday was pressed to keep on shoving her spitty breasts back into her dress and fighting off the boys, but she didn't seem to be trying very hard. "They learn to long for sex by watching porn flicks. We also deny them any physical contact with the opposite sex during this stage."

"Except for you."

"There has to be **something** in all of this for me!"

CHAPTER 18
Abu's Widow

With her leg and wrist chains gathered together in her arms, Norma nearly panicked during the first few seconds of freedom. The padlock on each wrist and ankle shackle was small but Norma didn't see a way to break any of them. And with those lengths of chain attached to her, even if she could find a robe or something in the closets on the far wall, how would she quickly thread all those heavy links through the armholes and sleeves?

The gun! Look for the gun!

Norma dropped to her knees on the right-hand side of the bed to feel for the pistol. The mattress was heavy and difficult to pry up with thick coils of chain around each forearm. Shit! She stopped long enough to slide the mess of leg chain from her left arm and thrust her hand back under. Her heart pounded in her chest as she probed. Did that little slave know what she was talking about? Any one of them could be back any second!

Just when she was about to give up and run for it, Norma felt the nail on her middle finger snag and break on the under-side of the mattress. "Fuck!" And her heart beat even faster as the tip of that finger brushed against cold steel.

Her arm was as far under the mattress as she could reach with her wrist trailing the chain shackled there, and Norma had to pull out momentarily to free-up more of it so she could reach in farther. This time she was just able to catch the lanyard ring on the butt of the pistol with her fingertips and get a better grip on the piece. Some kind of automatic, smaller than Jack's P-38. As she slid out the weapon, her mind flashed through all the instructions she could remember about the workings of automatics. Then, whipping her head around, she saw a huge man coming through the entrance behind her. Klaus!

He stopped about ten feet away. He was grinning.

"Don't bother to get up for me, girlie."

Still on her knees, Norma lowered her head and her long hair fell over her hands. She could almost see herself even though her heart was near to bursting. She could see herself bent over, kneeling, as if in shame, as if to cover her breasts, as if she were a frightened virgin.

"I'm sorry," she whimpered. Trying not to move her arms as her fingers worked at the pistol she hoped Klaus had not seen. She was trying to turn it around so she could get a grip on it and at the same time locate any lever or button that could possibly be the safety.

"The doctor told me he forgot to chain your arm back up."

"Fuck you!" Norma spit out the words, keeping her body and head bent over her knees, then cringing as if she expected a blow. Her fingers worked fast. The lever was on the left side of the piece, as she had hoped, and she was able to snap it forward with her right thumb without a sound. Now she had to hope there was a round chambered.

"Fuck me? Okay."

"You know what I mean!" Norma faked another cringe, drawing herself up even tighter and pressing her forehead into her knees. The trigger-pull was non-existent. A single-action. She faked a few, frightened sobs as she positioned the pistol in her left hand and cocked the hammer with her thumb. Two clicks — almost inaudible but she had heard them — did he?

"Asshole!"

"Get up!" That heavy, German accent. "Gett hahpp!"

"No!" Klaus was behind her but she dared not move her head to find out how far.

She could hear his sandals slide closer on the carpet. Toes slid under her left elbow and up to her chin, toes poking out of a fancy, gold-trimmed zori. Above the foot, the white-jeans pant-leg.

"Up!"

Norma whimpered. "Please. Please let me go."

"Yeah, sure." His foot slowly withdrew and before Norma could think, the heel kicked out and boxed her ear, knocking her sideways. Flipping onto her back, Norma spread her knees and with both hands on the gun, pulled the trigger — *click* — nothing! Without a thought her right hand gripped the slide and chambered a round, and she snapped off a shot at Klaus's head just as his arm was reaching down to grab the pistol.

CRACK!

He crumpled to the floor in a heap. Out cold. The bullet had ripped along the palm of his hand, nicked his right ear, and plowed an upward, diagonal channel through the scalp.

Norma's ears rang with fuzzy stillness. The gun had discharged with such a thunderclap, with the four walls to echo the blast a hundred people must have heard it! Glancing at Klaus, whose ear-wound looked like a point of entry, Norma dropped the automatically cocked pistol on top of the bed so she could re-gather her chains. She considered trying to shoot the padlocks off the shackles.

No time!

Move!

MOVE!

When Klaus had entered the room, he came through the doorway that she and the maids had used. Norma headed for the unfamiliar exit on the other side, both arms loaded with chain and the pistol. The next room had windows and Norma was barely conscious of the golden, late-afternoon glitter of the city outside as she dashed through looking for a way to the hallway, or the elevator or stairs. It was a room full of silent, ornate furniture, and just as she reached the far side and another one of those draped archways, the end of her right leg-chain caught on the arm of a chair and she went down. Half-way through the fall, as if she were in slow motion, she thought she was going to make it. Still gripping the pistol in her left hand and with the palm of her right extended to break the fall, her body slammed into the carpeting. But her hand was not strong enough and Norma's forehead smacked hard into the pink-marble threshold plate. The gun, which had skittered toward the wall when her body hit, discharged just as her brain lit up with a blinding flash of pain.

For a minute, Norma thought she was dead. Or hit in the head and dying. Dragging a length of chain with it, her left hand timidly felt of her forehead. No blood.

No hole.

Could it be? Norma lifted her chin from the scratchy pile of the carpet. Feet. Pairs of them. Bare, small — the Filipinas — all standing over her, their voices audible now. Hushed. Norma cocked her head gingerly and pulled her right arm out from under her. Under the closest chair, turned sideways so she could see the hammer cocked for another shot, was the pistol. Out of reach.

"Señora, are you okay?"

Norma turned on her side and looked up. The youngest, the one who had told her there was a pistol under the mattress, was kneeling beside her face. Two others were at her feet, each holding the end of a chain. The oldest-looking of them, the one who had fastened the gold choker around her neck, was straddling Norma with a raised baseball bat.

"Please." Norma felt herself on the verge of being overwhelmed by her naked helplessness.

She wouldn't smash my face with that bat, would she?

"The gun, Señora"

"Please don't hurt me. I hid it in the bathroom."

The youngest got to her feet and started to take off but the Filipina with the bat yelled something in Spanish and another followed the first, leaving only one holding the ankle chains.

They don't see it under the chair.

"Please put the bat away. I'll behave. I'll get back on the bed."

Norma could hear the toilet tank lid slide open in the bathroom.

Could I shoot them?

Abu's widow came in, her brows furrowed in an angry scowl from the hooded, black abaaya. She snatched at the ball bat and the girls stepped back. There would be no pleading with this one! Norma said: "Okay, okay, I'm getting up. I'll go back to the bed."

Very slowly, Norma rolled over and began to raise herself on her hands and knees.

This time there's a round chambered, the safety's off, and it's cocked.

Easing her right foot over to and against the doorjam, Norma faked a wince of pain. Then, without warning, she propelled herself forward and with the reach of her life, nailed the gun with her right hand — no time to switch — and twisted around. The first shot went wild, missing the woman. The bat came down and grazed the gun, sending the next shot into the floor. Norma screamed, and as Abu's widow raised the club for a second strike Norma snatched the pistol with her good, left hand and swung it toward the woman's face.

CRACK!

Abu's wife's head snapped back. The bat fell to the carpet and the shrouded woman crumpled on top of it. She twitched once and held a rigid posture for a few seconds. Then her knees began to draw up slowly in a tense shiver as the pupils of her eyes dilated. Norma swung the pistol around the room, her wrists flicking out the golden chains.

The Filipinas had run for it. Gone.

Sitting up now, Norma saw the tiny, black hole above the hooded woman's nose. Not much blood, but.... Norma caught a deep breath and slowly lowered the hammer of the pistol down to half-cock. She left the safety off. Four shots? That meant three or four left – with luck, five. The butt was too narrow for a staggered clip.

No time to drop the clip and look! Get MOVING!

The dying woman shuddered once more and went limp. As the body slumped to the side, Norma heard the distinctive sound of a ring of keys.

Keys! On her hands and knees, Norma clawed at the black robe. Pockets! Where are the pockets in these stupid things? She located the bunch of keys through the material but found no opening. "Christ!" She went down to the woman's feet and snatched at the hem of the Moslem uniform to pull it up. The hem snagged in one of

157

the high-heeled, black shoes. *She wears stockings under this thing, Christ! Dumb-fuck rag heads!*

It was a struggle to haul the volume of material up the dead-weight body. Desperately, she felt up the legs with her hands.

Christ, she's pissing! Norma yanked her hand out of there and tugged at the robe again. She stopped, but just for a second, at the sight of the red garters and red, bikini panties. Real stockings. *God.*

I killed them both. Husband and wife.

The keys were hanging from Abu's wife's garter belt on a brass ring. Norma unclipped them, ignoring the wetness of the involuntary urination.

Gold ring.

Gold, gold, gold.

Only one padlock key was there, the smallest on the ring. First the right wrist, then the left. *Hurry! Hurry!* The key had to be turned around two complete twists before each hasp would snap free. *Dumb fuckers!*

She bent forward to reach the ankle shackles and heard a distant door slam shut.

Laughter, and the guttural sound of that foreign language. Norma gritted her teeth and twisted the key, which was difficult to do with the key so small and the ring so large.

The laughter and talking did not come closer. She heard them calling for the Filipinas. "Marie?" "Marcie?"

They don't know yet.

"Rita!"

The voices sounded like three rooms away. *One more leg to go!* Norma glanced back-and-forth from the job at hand to the pistol lying beside her to the archway on the far side of the room.

"Klaus!"

They'll find him in a second.
Free!

Norma grabbed the pistol and got to her feet. For a split second she considered the heap of chains — a shame to leave all that gold behind — and then she took off.

I still have the choker.
All these rooms!

She almost lost hope in the last room because it was different from the others. The lights there were off but even in the dim light from the single window she could see that it was a storeroom of some kind, no, there was a small door at the other side, behind some big crates! She tried the knob. It turned but nothing happened. Muffled shouts coming from the way she came.

There was a deadbolt with a knob. Two of them, one high, one low. They clicked loudly when she turned them. She was out!

The hallway looked dingy and it dead-ended at a steel door with a panic-bar across it. An exit door! Above it, the red EXIT light was out, but the bar pushed in with a raspy groan. Stairs! Another light-bulb out but she could see well enough from another bulb which was burning farther down. At the next landing was a door at the side with another panic bar. This one was chained so it couldn't be used. Regular, steel chain. Norma tugged at the Master padlock but no luck.

She headed down another flight. The floor and steps were gritty and damp on her bare feet. A service entrance? At the next level, another door at the side but the panic bar here was chained also. The sign above the door read: FIRE ESCAPE.

Dumb rag-heads!

The next landing was the same only this time there

was a small hunk of carpet in front of the chained door. Ground floor? Norma headed down again, once scraping the back of her heel when she nearly missed a step. Now the steps were really dirty and gritty, and the air suddenly felt damp and cool and stale. The smell was familiar — the same she had noticed when they had carried her to this building in the rolled-up shag rug — and she knew she was heading into the basement.

Oh, for a flashlight!

At the bottom of the stairwell the door was to the side and the chain there was off, hanging limp on the panic bar. Stopping to listen for a moment, she held her breath just long enough so she could hear. Nothing! The door eased open. The basement was lighted, not brightly but there was an overhead bulb on here and there. A row of washers and driers. Padlocked, wire enclosures housing plumbing supplies and tools. Hot water heaters with numbers on them. Stopping under one of the bulbs still burning, Norma scouted the cement floor for traces of the way they had brought her. There had been cussing about the water then, and she had heard their shoes slapping through it. Surely that would've left a trail on higher ground.

Wait! They brought her up in an elevator!

Moving along quickly now, she scanned to the right and left as she traversed the damp bowels of the building. She stopped once more to hold her breath and listen. Couldn't they figure out which way she escaped?

Moving fast again, across a large, open area, Norma crossed the trail. And to the right of her was the elevator with its banged-up, dirty doors closed. At the instant she discovered it, there was a clunking from behind the doors and she heard it begin to move. It was coming down. A whirring noise and soft clunking, closer and

160

closer! She turned to run and with a squeak of her feet, turned back. She had seen the electric box beside the doors but that hadn't computed instantly. Rushing up to it, she pulled the lever down with a rusty-sounding snap.

The elevator stopped. The voices up in the shaft were close. A bunch of them and they sounded like they were just a half a floor away! That foreign language again, but she could tell it was cussing. And a curse in English. "God damn!"

Not only could she see the dirty trail, some of the tracks were still wet. She followed along it quickly, and stayed to the side hoping she would not be leaving footprints of her own. It led between rows of brand new crates, some of them six-feet high. What was all this stuff?

Suddenly, Norma heard a door scrunch open, and close. A metal door she hadn't seen. A second of silence and then a buzzing sound as the overhead florescent lights struggled to come on.

Norma was running now, naked and exposed, not knowing who had just entered but she could hear the slap-slap-slap of a pair of sandals. Close. She skidded around a rough, wooden crate as the trail turned, and caught a wood-sliver in the palm of her hand which she hardly felt.

slap-slap-slap

Getting closer!

The trail, wetter and more visible than ever, turned again. If it had been a straight shot she would have already been sighted.

slap-slap-slap

God, how big is this place?

If I could only get outside.

161

They couldn't chase a naked woman right out there on the street!

She hoped. During her brief glimpse from the window above, the parking lot had been nearly empty. Too early for the evening rush hour?

Still glancing from side to side looking for a door, she saw that the trail ahead looked straight now. If she didn't make another turn soon. A door! Norma slid around some smaller, plastic crates. Japanese beer stacked head high. The door opened quietly and she slipped inside. It was just another room, small, with no way out. A single bulb glowed overhead and the doorknob on the inside had no button, no way to lock it. She pushed the button on the outside, knowing that wouldn't work, and heard the lock click back open as she eased the door shut. Some old beds, spaced apart as if people had lived in here at one time. Several chests of drawers, one pulled away from the gray concrete wall — could she hide behind that? She tried it but no matter which way she positioned herself, some part of her was sticking out. *Oh, please God.* Well, she could fire over it and maybe the drawers were full of stuff to absorb bullets coming her way.

No! She could get behind the chest nearer the door. Maybe have a closer shot and a chance to get back out if she could nail whoever it was.

She jumped out and changed her mind and turned back to her original position and waited.

Her chest was heaving for air and she had to hold her breath from time to time to listen. Nothing. It had sounded like just one person, on foot. Had he gone past? Following the trail? Would she be that lucky?

It didn't matter. He'd come back.

Her nakedness began to bother her more and more,

and the thought of it intruded upon all her other thoughts. As the minutes went by, she would forget and then remember the choker, holding the pistol in her left hand and feeling the tight necklace with her right. Once, she even switched hands so that she could assess it with her left-handed fingertips. So heavy. She tried to remember what it looked like as it came out of the box, what it looked like around her neck in the mirror above that bed. The gold so heavy.

Get real! I'm not getting out of this!
Not alive!

Maybe it was time to start thinking about leaving the room. The trail would take her to her own condo. How long did they carry her? Surely it was just a few minutes. Through some kind of wet tunnel.

Norma looked around. Four beds, just bare mattresses. Stains all over them. Pecker tracks, as Jack would say. Her knees were beginning to ache and Norma stood up from her crouch behind the chest. She could always drop back down quickly enough. She shuddered. There were handcuffs fastened to the steel frames of the cots.

That's why the door locks from the outside.
Need to get out of here before they lock me in.
All somebody has to do is push the button in!
They could let me starve to death in here!

Norma was thirsty now, and she felt the unlikely urge to brush her teeth. Rinse her mouth with cool water.

Would they let me starve till I'm dead?
They chopped that poor girl's head off and we didn't even care.

Norma's breathing settled down to normal now, and she no longer needed to hold it to tell that there were no other sounds. It was time to take a chance.

Sneak out.

There might be clothes in the drawers!

Norma eased out from behind the chest with her gun aimed toward the door. Looking away for just a second, she slid open the second drawer from the bottom, where jeans would be placed back in her own bedroom.

Tube tops! T-shirts! Norma sucked in a deep breath, checked the door again, and cocked the pistol, laying it on top of the dusty chest. The shirts were folded neatly and looked too small, but the tube tops might stretch. She slid out a purple one and pulled at it. Thin but stretchy! Memorizing the exact position of the pistol, Norma riveted her eyes on the door as she pulled the top down over her eyes and face, freed her hair, and slid and stretched it over her chest. Tight, but OK. Now the bottom drawer. With luck some pants or jeans and she was outta there. If they spotted her she would drop down, take careful aim even if they started shooting first, and kill them. Head shots. Aim, squeeze, and kill!

But it wasn't to be.

Just as she was sliding out the bottom drawer, Norma looked back and saw him. Klaus. Just inside the doorway. He was grinning, and in his huge, bloody hand was the largest revolver she had ever seen. As she straightened up she was looking right up the barrel, the black hole ready to launch an incredibly lethal hunk of lead. Norma had seen what her own .41 magnum would do. This was a obviously a forty-four.

She watched, frozen, as he pulled back the hammer.

"No!"

"Blow your fucking cunt out!"

"No, please, please!" Norma clamped her hands over her shaved mound as Klaus's gun barrel lowered at it.

One shot would blow out an area the size of a football. Even if somehow she didn't bleed to death, there would be nothing left for emergency surgery to fix.

"Please."

CHAPTER 19
Norma's Video

Jody was disappointed with Bernie's video of the SiblTek farm. The cute blond girls were on camera for only a minute and then those clone-boys had to chase the dog away. At least his mother understood enough to rewind the tape all the way back to the girls each time she re-ran the naked boys.

Hearing the clanging sounds of his mother on Valium or equivalents in the kitchen, Jody looked out the window of the TV room and was surprised to see how long the shadows from the surrounding trees were, how fast the time had been flying. In the bathroom, however, he debated with himself whether to take the other new video, of Norma's shower, to his own room or re-run it where his mother might see him. The big color monitor would be better but then he could get caught masturbating. Fuck it. He opted for the big screen. Norma's video was so great! On Jack's outdoor shower deck: fifteen minutes of soaping, rinsing, soaping, rinsing, prancing around with the towel. How did Dad do it? The chicks had to be dumber than him, that's all Jody could figure.

He turned the sound down, such as it was — bullfrogs in the pond, cicadas chirping, the squirting of the shower head — and settled back into his overstuffed chair, the remote clutched at the end of his shorter arm. Bouncy tits. Nothing would ever replace firm, bouncy tits. He could kill for a set of his very own to play with but all his father had to do was invite the chicks over. Promise them a ride in his boat.

duhhhh..

That day the boat trip had been promised to him, but his adopted father had forgotten. There was pussy to entertain.

Thanks, Dad!

He could almost hear his father answer his thoughts. *Bullshit. You understand!*

Well, yeah.

God, what a gorgeous red-head! The video color was nearly black-and-white from taping in the artificial light over the deck, but the picture was sharp. Jack had told him she had a sister, too. Sandy, or something like that. A year older. "Even more beautiful, Son. She killed a guy not too far from here recently. Remember that on the news? That was Norma's sister! She terminated some big, retarded misfit, I think. Both babes are gun freaks like us. Their father taught them how to shoot, just like I did with you."

But it wasn't their expertise with guns — or the notoriety of the shooting which had been in all the papers and the local TV channels — it was the words "retarded misfit" that had stung. Jody knew he was not retarded and that, if anything, he thought about everything much too much. He could never really relax because of it, not at any time during his fourteen years. But the "misfit" fit. He was so deformed that the only way to live with it was to let it all hang out. And force everyone to call him "Nub-man". Trouble was, no girl would ever give in to a man with a hand sticking out of his elbow. He would have to be either rich enough to buy a woman occasionally, or bad enough to hunt one down and kidnap her. Lock her up somewhere on the property. But how could he do that without his mother finding out? Would she do anything about it? And if his dad found out, he'd have to share. The only way Jody was going to score a girl was to buy one. He was sure. Maybe import one from some third-world country.

"Jody!"

He jumped at the sound of his mother's voice as she entered the room, but Norma kept right on smiling, and soaping with the juicy sponge.

CHAPTER 20
The Projection Room

Dr. Mannlicher, wild-eyed and grinning his toothy smile, stormed into the huge kitchen where Jack and Monday were sipping coffee. He grabbed Jack by the sleeve.

"You still trying to fuck my **wife**? Come **on!** I got stuff to **show** you!"

Jack got up quickly and looked at Monday for a hint, a clue.

"Is everything okay?" she said.

"Nothing we don't already **know!**"

"Where are you taking him?"

"To the **projection** room!"

"First? Shouldn't he see the..."

"The **projection** room!"

Jack shrugged his shoulders and followed Mannlicher to a door off the kitchen which led down the basement stairs. "A basement," Jack said. "I haven't seen a basement anywhere in Florida for years."

"**You** hain't seen **shit** yet!"

The wooden steps creaked and clunked as they hopped down them. Lights clicked on automatically as Jack tried to keep up. They raced around the boiler and hot-water heater, past an obviously unused laundry room, and stopped before an ancient row of shelves stuffed with musty newspapers and old magazines.

"Check it **out!**" Dr. Mannlicher yelled, his reddish face glowing in the incandescent light. He mashed a button on the keyboard of his portable radio, a unit which

169

looked identical to Jackson's and Monday's, and the wooden shelves shuddered and began to slide down the wall. The movement revealed a steel door the color of gray cement.

"Like in the **movies!** Right? Huh? **Huh?!**"

"Neat," Jack said.

"Come **on!** It's **marvelous!**"

The doorway led down a brightly lit hallway. Long. Nearly white, clinical-looking floor tiles. Clean. The steel door clicked shut behind them and the damp, basement smell gave way to the scent of filtered, mechanically driven air.

"Come **on!**"

Mannlicher's sandals slapped against the waxed tiles as Jack followed past several more closed, steel doors painted the same, bright-cream color as the walls.

"Keep a tight asshole now!" Mannlicher led him through the third door on the right. Jack counted and committed the location to memory. Not just to be competent, but because he was sure there would be questions later. A test. *"Do you remember which **door?** Huh? **Huh?!**" Mannlicher screaming the emphasized words.*

Overhead lights clicked on, then dimmed down. It was a tiny lecture hall. Several movie projectors in the aisle and a slide machine, flanked by about ten seats on each side — no, twelve — anchored to the floor in three rows of four each. Expensive-looking seats, upholstered with maroon velour. Beyond the podium a large movie screen. Jack was amazed, as he always was when confronted with anything which had obviously cost a fortune, amazed at what people with money could do. Their toys.

...and all this shit underground.

"See? Huh? Isn't it **marvelous?!**"

170

"Shit yes! I'm impressed!"

"You **better!** Oh, oh, you have to see **this!** Monday snapped it last **week.**" Mannlicher rotated the carousel on the slide machine and switched on the projector. A large, color picture of two Arabs flicked onto the screen. The colors somewhat faded by the overhead lights which were still dimming out.

"Look at **that!** Don't **puke** though!"

Jack could see that one of them looked like the Emir of Kuwait, with the same gold-trimmed black robe he had seen on TV during the Gulf War. It looked like he was urinating into a fancy urn being held by the other man in the picture. In the background Jack recognized the terminal buildings of the Panama City airport.

"The Emir of Kuwait?"

"No, but it **could** be! Assholes! Motherfucker has all these servants, makes them hold a fucking jug while he **pees!** Kill him in a **heart**beat!"

"But you deal with them, right?"

"Hey! They have so much **money!** You can't **imagine** how **much!** They have more money than **God!**"

The screen went dark and Mannlicher plunked down into one of the aisle seats, the remote in his hand, without bothering to bring the lights back up. "Sit! Sit **down!** No, where I can **see** you!"

Mannlicher moved over, thankfully two seats over, and Jack took the aisle seat. He was glad of the semi-darkness, too. The man looked freakish in his shorts and bare upper body in that plush movie-theater chair. It was cold in the room, too, and Jack thought he could see goose-bumps under the man's freckles and hair.

"You a **good** bounty hunter? **Huh?**" Before Jack could answer: "You ever have three girls in **bed?** At the same **time? Huh?** Monday's had three **guys** in bed!

171

Down in Panama where I **met** her! Panama, the **country!** I **killed** them! Well, no, **one** of them jumped out of the whorehouse **window!** Then I went down-stairs and I killed her **pimp!** Big **Brazilian!** Ever hear a man begging for mercy in **Portuguese? Huh?** Sounds just like when you stick a hot **knitting** needle up a **parrot's** ass! Well? **Well?!"**

Jack began to feel panic, and tried to keep focusing on the money, the opportunities. "Well, what?"

"The three **women?** You didn't answer my **question!** Wait! Wait! You don't have to **answer** shit like **that! Do** you? Huh? Huh? **No!"**

"No."

"Did you ever **want** to? Huh?"

"Yeah. After I read Hemingway's 'Islands in the Stream'. He has three Chinese women in bed with him in there."

"**Three** Chinese **women! Hemingway?** Anyway, you **think** about it. In **reality** this time!" Mannlicher held out the remote past Jack and aimed it at the slide machine. Two or three slides flicked past on the big screen before he stopped at one showing the same, rich Arab again, same airport, only this time he was flanked by three others in western suits. Two of them short and swarthy, with Saddam Hussein mustaches.

"See the big **tall** dude? The Arnold **Schwarzenegger?"**

"Yeah."

"I want you to kill him **first!"**

Jack's heart speeded up. "I said I was a bounty hunter. Bail bonds. Not a hit man."

"So go back to school and **graduate!"**

There was a long silence. Jack stared at the big screen with the faded airport scene, the Arnold S. look-alike smiling down at him.

Hasta la vista, Baby.

"Then, those **other** two! Don't **worry!** I'm not asking you to harm **innocent** people! I'm not asking you to compromise what you **believe** in! I just want you to snuff some **assholes!** They **betrayed** us! They're **kid**nappers. They sodomize underage **girls!** Even **God** wants them dead!"

Jack studied their faces, a million thoughts rushing through his mind. All of the men were smiling down at him except the rich-looking Arab, who looked stern, almost pissed.

Jack had thought they needed him because of his boat. Because of Miss Chernobyl.

"What about the Arab?"

"See? See?! I **knew** you'd do it?!"

"I..."

"Maybe after I get my **money! Then** you can snuff that **towel**-head. **If** I get my money! Fucking **goat** humpers! Huh? **Huh?!**"

"I..."

"Three women in **bed** at the same **time!** Young! Blondes! Willing to **please! Trained** to please! **Huh?!**"

"I'm getting older," Jack said, trying to calm his voice. "I'm more mellow now. I don't let stuff like sex rule me anymore."

"Oh? Three girls at the same **time?** They'll even fuck that **red**-head I saw you with in the **news!** If you **tell** them to! You keep that strawberry stashed some-where **good**, I hope! And there's more money in it for you than you've ever **seen!**"

"Yeah? Not enough to pull a David and Bathsheba."

"David and Bath-**sheee**-ba?! Enough money to hit **ten** fucking whatsisnames!"

"Uriah."

"**Uriah! I love** it! **Ten** Uriahs! You'll need your **boat** for this! Too many **bodies** strowed all over dry land **already!** You **dig?** I could buy **ten** boats like yours, or a **Cigarette** or a or a **Donzi!** You know **what? Huh?** The Coast Guard would **spot** it!"

"They won't alert on mine? Miss Chernobyl."

"Miss **Chernobyl?** Too insignificant! Miss Chernobyl! I **love** that name! And I want my **Bertram** back!"

"We saw it. A Bertram 31."

"I want it **back!** It's an original **Moppie!** We just put new **engines** in it! Twin Crusaders!"

"It was stolen?"

"**Stolen?** My Moppie was **kid**napped! I want you to get it **back!**"

"Three girls like the chopped-off head we found? Like the ones in the Bertram? For me?"

"See? **See?! I knew** it! I **knew** you'd go for it! Yeah! Model-**Tees!** Pod **Threes!** Tell me about the **bounty** hunting! How you **do** it! Not how you **find** them? How you **get** them!"

"I wait for them." Jack had to concentrate, and he reminded himself to stop working his hands together in his lap. "I wait for them to come out of their house and get in their car." Jack's mind was rolling around with three blondes, their hungry lips sucking onto him like sea lampreys. "I stick my nine millimeter Walther in their face and I get in behind them and they drive themselves right up to Daddy's office." Jack was proud of it. "Or the jail or the bondsman's office. Whatever."

"What if they say **no!** You **shoot** them?"

"I slam the side of my pistol against the side of their head and it goes off. Bang! They think they've been shot right in the head for a minute. They think they're dead."

"Then they do what you **tell** them?"

"They think they've been shot in the head every time." Jack had to smile because it was pretty much the truth, and a very slick trick.

"You slam your gun right up against their **heads?** And it goes **off?!** I **love** it! Your daddy. Eastland! You know how **rich** we made **him?**"

"Nooo."

"He gets a **percentage!** Did you know **that?**"

"No."

"Good! We don't need loose canons and we don't need loose **tongues!** Your daddy's **rich!** You didn't **know?** You ever see his **girl**friends? Huh?!"

"Jackson."

"Fuck **Jackson!** You ever see the **others?** Huh? **Huh?!**"

"Well, he was shacked up with this model last year and..."

"Model? **Model?!** You know how much that whore **cost?** You think a bitch like that is going to fuck an eighty-five-year-old man for **free?**"

"I, uh, no, uhhh."

"You slam your gun right up against their **heads** and it goes **off?** I **love** it!

As soon as Manny left, Jack had to wonder if he had been locked in but decided not to try the doors. At least not at first. While they had been talking, a young man, looked Japanese, had poked his head in and Mannlicher assured the startled fellow, who looked like an exchange student, lab coat and all, that Jack was cool. "...a new **coolie!**" Then, to Jack: "Are you **insulted?** I said that to insult **him! He's** been fucking up, **too!**"

Alone in the projection room now, Jack studied the

two, antique movie projectors in the dim light. When he was a kid, even though his high-school had acquired modern video equipment, Jack had been the assigned projectionist for the school's archival movies, a trove of mid-century newsreels. Working these machines here would be easy. Manny had told him to view the rolls of 8MM first. "That projector is an **Ampro!** An Ampro Model A-8 **Precision!**" Nobody **makes** stuff like that anymore!" There was a stack of 8-millimeter movie reels and some 16's. "Don't leave the **room!** Start at the **beginning**, you know, the order we **took** them in! In case I don't get **back** soon! We took these for our**selves** but you can use them like an orien**tation. Dig?** Check out how foxy **Monday** used to look!"

Old but expensive for it's time, the projector had little side-lights that you could switch on when you threaded the film through all the sprockets. Jack made sure he had plenty of loop above and under the lens shutter before flipping on the "LAMP" and "RUN" switches. Quickly, he dumped himself into the nearest seat and settled back. While the white leader flickered through, Jack wished he also had a control for the AC. So cold!

In a moment he forgot all about the temperature. And yes, Monday had been a looker! So beautiful in a crocheted bikini top and short shorts. Manny, handsome and conservatively dressed in a Hawaiian shirt and white ducks and canvass deck shoes, constantly turning back toward the camera lens to ham it up. The scene changed but the woman's image lingered in Jacks head.

Jack was startled when Monday quietly slid into the seat beside his. She had worked her way down the room to him from the other side, and Jack glanced at her with a smile.

"It's been several years since I've seen these," Monday whispered. The movies were silent but in color, and the only sound in the projection room was the whirring of the machine.

"Why film?"

"Oh, Manny's father left him all this professional equipment and Manny had to be a pro. He's since switched to video, though."

"God, you were a babe!"

"Still am." Monday said it with another whisper, and Jack shut up and concentrated on the new scene.

Monday and Mannlicher were chasing through a field of cropped grass now. In the jerking picture — apparently the person taking the movies was running after them — they were chasing sheep, one in particular. An ewe, about to give birth. Except for Mannlicher's constant looking back toward the camera and smiling and waving — *What a jerk!* — the camera maintained its focus on the ewe's hindquarters. The picture steadied just as the amniotic sac burst and a baby lamb squirted to the ground trailing its umbilical cord and placenta. The ewe turned and pulled at the remains of the sac, freeing her newborn offspring. Monday, running up, partially blocked the view for a moment as Mannlicher, facing the camera, bent over and picked up the baby. A human baby. Glistening with slippery fluid, the baby squirted out of his arms and was caught by Monday just in time. Now the two of them were facing the camera, Monday holding out the baby and pulling open the legs to show that it was a girl, and Mannlicher grinning and waving. Mannlicher suddenly took off and Monday was gently placing the baby on the ground underneath the ewe. Now they were both running, the camera jerking along behind them. Up ahead was another ewe throwing, and

177

another. For the next few minutes Jack watched, with his mouth hanging open, the gift of clone life bursting all over the pasture and Monday's bell-bottom jeans streaking after each and every one.

The screen flashed bright white.

flap-flap-flap-flap...

Jack jumped up and shut off the projector.

"Don't rewind it now. I want to see another one. And by the way, they are **not** in order!"

"Jeez. So that's what the sheep are for."

"Now you know. Ever read James Dickey's poem 'Sheep Child'?"

"Noooo. Were the ones we saw the Model T's?"

"No. Actually, the first ones didn't live long. Where is Manny, anyway?"

Jack tried to concentrate on threading the new reel through the sprockets. "Some Japanese-looking kid came for him."

"Oh. Hiro. Not his real name, but. He's not as young as he looks, but so brilliant! If you think this clone stuff is unique, get Manny to show you what we're doing now."

"No more clones?"

"Well, not exactly. You'll see. Anyway, we're getting hot. As soon as the ones we've got are marketed, we're outta here for a while."

"And the new stuff?"

"We'll take that project along with us. Easier to transport. Like I said, you'll see."

Jack eagerly switched the projector back on and dumped into his seat beside Monday. When Monday's warm, dark hand reached toward his, Jack surprised himself by hanging onto it.

A row of little blond girls, not more than three

years old, in cute, white dresses. Smiling and waving at the camera.

"They look happy enough. Where are these now?"

Monday was shaking her head. "We almost got a divorce over this bunch. South American style. A bullet in the head type divorce. Manny sold them before they were five years old in Manaus. A city on the Amazon. He didn't like them. Same for the Pod-2's. The 3's he kept for the staff. Just weren't part of his fantasy, I guess. I still get pissed about it. Would you believe I cried? But he could afford to make mistakes back then. Now we need the money."

The movie switched to the blond girls swimming in the creek. The water looked lower than when Jack had seen it, but the activity was the same although on a younger level. Mannlicher looked so civilized! The movie switched back to dry land, the girls dressed in blue jumpers and sitting at picnic tables. Tilting their heads back, drinking something out of the ends of large, rubbery-looking dildos. Jack shuddered.

"You better get used to it."

The screen flashed bright white again and the end of the film struck the table.

flap-flap-flap-flap...

"They're not really human, you know."

"Well, they must be part human."

Not in a legal sense, we don't think. Manny says they can't pass the Turing Test. And if they are not legal, I don't want to find out the hard way."

"Yeah, but..."

"But what? Were the Iraqis we killed human? The Japanese in Hiroshima and Nagasaki? A hundred-thousand at a clip?"

Jack did not know what to answer but he had the

next reel ready. This one looked like it had more film on it. "Here we go!"

"Okay, these four guys you're looking at are the germ behind why Manny changed the genetic material for the Model B's and up. The Model T's were the first success, though, named after the old Ford Model T. Back before we knew how serious the whole project was going to get."

Jack was looking up at four men facing the camera, all grinning. The one on the left looked like a short, ro-ly-poly Mexican. Next to him a tall, black African. Then a blond Swede or German, and next to him, Jack was sure, was a male, teen-age, Australian aborigine.

"These guys and Manny got a federal grant and used FSU's mainframe to compile statistics to prove or dis-prove the existence of a model in the human brain which would satisfy the sex-drive of all races of human males. Can you believe it? They worked on this shit for almost three years! Stuff any madam could've told them but, of course, that wouldn't be as much fun. That truck there, see? That used to be the customs holding area at Miami International. They're transferring a ton of por-nography from all over the world. All legal for the re-search."

Jack glanced at Monday, who seemed to be quite proud of it all. She gave his hand a squeeze.

"Your tax dollars at work! I can't wait to tell you the punch line!"

"Which is?"

"Wait. Wait for the end of my story!"

The scene switched to a computer lab with the men eagerly opening crates of books and reels of film. Manny turning to face the camera again and again with his happy, toothy smile. White shirt and tie.

"For three years they looked through stuff, including some help from male students of as many races as they could get represented in the study, and they poured over all this infantile, manly, billy-goat drivel while they recorded each guy's reactions. Like people do with that scale of one-to-ten shit. The Mexican dude, if I remember correctly, had a tendency toward the plump women — but not always! So did the Germans sometimes. Manny is German, too, even with that red hair, but they were finding out things, like he and the German were scoring a lot of the African porn very high — and European porn featuring African models — and a couple times they had to rearrange the program, rearrange how they were compiling their data. Finally Manny decided that they would have to focus on body parts of women and then make one up from the results. That took the whole third year! The punch line? The computer came up with me! Or a woman like me. But with narrower, Nubian hips. Younger than I am now, of course. A woman who looked like me would score high by the males of all the races represented. I was near to the universal, desirable female."

flap-flap-flap-flap-flap-flap...

"Want to see me naked?"

Jack had just jumped up to switch off the projector. He caught his breath. "What if Manny comes back?"

"Jeez, Jack. I mean on the next reel. When I was young!"

Jack's ears flushed red, but not for long. After they finished the last of the 8MM movies, they started on the 16's. Longer. More professional photography. Lab pictures. Rows of dark embryos pulsing in clear sacks hanging from plastic umbilicals. The movie switched to the funeral for Mannlicher's partner, an old oriental which

181

Monday refused to elaborate on or name. Cremated behind the house on top of a pile of wood decorated with wreaths and flowers, Mannlicher appearing in a suit and tie for the last time. Monday in a black dress and hat.

They must have loved him.

Jack turned to see tears in Monday's eyes. She pulled her hand away and dabbed at her eyes with a corner of her rainbow skirt.

A moving van unloading beds and furniture at one of the buildings, the interior already converted from airplane hangar to dormitory. Movies of birthday parties. Rows of identical blond girls giving way to rows of smaller, identical darker girls. Some with wavy, black hair like the clones Jack had seen at the creek (only younger in the movie). Some with corn rows or plaits with ribbons. All pretty and all bringing out the lust in Jack. Was he a pedophile and didn't know it? No, because every time the movie switched to things like new lab equipment arriving or the corralling of the sheep so they could be dipped or get their shots, all Jack could see dancing in front of his eyes was the last of the 8MM reels: Monday posing. Naked. Glamour shots. Dancing. Stripping. Showering. So beautiful and desirable it hurt. Hurt bad. Movies in his head which Jack knew he would carry to the grave.

Once, while Jack was changing reels and Monday was listening to Jack extol her virtues, Mannlicher poked his head into the projection room

"Well, are you impressed? Huh? **Huh?!**"

"I'm impressed," Jack said. It sounded inadequate but it was all he could think of. "I'm very impressed."

"Wasted my whole, scientific **career** on this shit! **Wasted!** All those years and years of **work!**"

"Wasted?"

"**Wasted!** Can I share all this shit with the scientific community? Huh? **Huh?!** I've blown my **life!**"

"Yeah, but you spent your life doing what you wanted to do, right? Right?!"

"Jack. Okay. If it doesn't end with jail. Okay." He was gone as quickly as he appeared.

And all Jack wanted to do right now was come in Monday. It didn't matter how long ago those movies of her had been taken. He wanted to come in her. Now. Chew on those long, blue-black nipples while he did it. Come in her forever.

"Ready?"

He flicked on the projector and slid down in his seat beside her. With a mind of its own, his hand slid into her blouse and felt the toughness of her warm, heavy meat. The few times he had taken girls to the movies when he was young he'd never had the guts.

Monday did not resist, except to say: "Watch the movie. Manny wants you to see them all." Then she moved back in her seat a little, bent over, unzipped his fly, flipped her big nose-ring up out of the way, and went down on him.

Now, Jack knew, there was no turning back.

CHAPTER 21
Klaus & Norma

Klaus moved a step closer, the lowered gun-barrel of his .44 never wavering from its target. Norma's hands clutched tighter over her shaved, pubic mound.

"Please, no."

"You think your fingers can stop a bullet?"

"No. No, please."

He took two more steps, standing now so close that Norma was tempted to snatch at the barrel with her hands. But she had shot a raccoon once — with her .41 mag — back when she was living outside Tampa. An animal whose only crime was stealing dog-food from her pet's bowl. The bullet had torn the raccoon's right-front leg almost completely off, leaving a ragged, bloody pit where the shoulder had been. The raccoon was blown back by the blast, rolling over in the grass, and when it regained consciousness it screamed with the most anguished, horrifying sound Norma had ever heard. It tried to lick the wound, the arm hanging by a thread of flesh. After it bled to death, Norma never aimed that pistol at another starving raccoon again.

Klaus' gun was even bigger — a .44 magnum. One shot would turn her clenched hands and everything underneath them to hamburger. She remembered the small, cocked automatic behind her. The Filipinas had missed seeing it earlier. Had he?

Klaus was angry. "Please? Did you give me a chance to say please when you tried to kill me?" Klaus turned his head just enough for her to see the long, bloody furrow her bullet had carved through his scalp above the right ear. The hand wrapped around the huge revolver was also covered with blood where the bullet had hit the palm first. Underneath that hand, a gob of fresh blood was forming and ready to drip from the pistol butt.

"I didn't want to kill you! I was just trying to get away!"

"Lay down on the bed."

"No. No, please don't."

"What, I should be — sympathetic? Did you feel anything for that girl got her head chopped off?" His thick accent sounded so angry, so moral. "...gott her het chopt off?"

"Well yes, but."

"Bull shit! I saw you! Smiling. Laughing. Holding it up for the camera. You and your boyfriend. Laughing like it was a big joke. Did you care about that girl? Bull **shit!**"

"That's not true! I cared about her!" Norma pressed her back against the chest of drawers, hoping that she was exactly in front of the pistol lying on the top. She pictured the position it was in, lying on its right side and pointing away so she could grab it quickly with her favored, left hand.

"Take off that top. Who told you to get dressed. The party is over!"

"Please."

"Move!"

"Yes sir." Norma pulled her hands away from between her legs and stood tall. She slowly reached for the hem of the tube top and began to pull it up over her head. As she did so she could smell the fear in her armpits, the body odor strong and funky. She decided to go for broke. Just as the top freed her hair and head she would come down on his revolver with both hands and knock it away, then turn and grab the automatic on top of the chest. Not much of a chance, but...

Her arms over her head now, Norma slid the top past her eyes. The barrel of Klaus' gun suddenly raised and he thrust the muzzle hard into her naked, left breast. Norma squealed with pain and the purple tube-top snagged in her hair.

"Don't even think about reaching for that gun there! Get on the bed!"

Blinded with pain, Norma did not see him lower the hammer of his revolver. He tossed it on the nearest cot, on the bare, spotted mattress. "Go for that one. It's bigger."

"I — don't want — your gun."

"See this?" Klaus held up the ripped open palm of his hand. "Look at it!"

Norma tried to straighten up and look through the tears in her eyes. The pain in her breast was so intense and unremitting she thought she was going to pass out. His wound was right in her face now and he punched her in the mouth with the heel of that hand. Her head flicked back, a bloody smear on her nose and chin. His blood. He snapped a punch into her stomach with his left and when she doubled over he reached for her automatic and tossed it onto the bed beside his own piece.

"Now you have two guns to think about. Want to go for it?"

Norma began to retch but there was nothing there to come up.

"Stand up straight!"

"They want me. They'll kill you if you hurt me. Put marks on me! I'll get cancer in that breast now, you son of a bitch!" Norma turned to swing at him but he caught her arm and flung her to the floor. Before she could react, his gold-trimmed, dirty zori was standing on her neck. She tried to suck in a breath, and made a croaking sound as he shut off her wind with his foot. This was a new kind of pain. A desperate, frightful thing clamping her windpipe and bulging her eyes. And if she moved, he could crush her throat.

"Tell me why you weren't scared when you had the head. Why you were laughing. What about the police? You weren't afraid of the police? Tell me. You have some kind of protection? What do you know that I don't know. Tell me!"

But Norma couldn't talk, and just as she was about to risk bringing her knees up and attempting to grab his leg with her hands — get out from under his foot — he backed off. For a moment he stood away from her, his good hand on his hip, watching her suck for air. Then he kicked off a zori and began to toy with her injured tit with his toes. Norma screamed and grabbed at his foot.

"Tell me. Why weren't you afraid?"

"Jack, my boyfriend, his father's the sheriff."

"Guy Tunnell?"

"No, sheriff of Homer County. Cletus Eastland."

"Eastland?" Klaus withdrew his foot. "You telling me the truth?"

"Jack's his son."

"One of his sons."

"Well, whatever. Asshole!"

Klaus stood over her and watched her palpate her injured breast with her fingertips. "Well, it's too late now," he mumbled.

"What?"

"Get on the bed!" He pointed to the bed on the far wall, away from the door and the guns. "That one."

"No."

A grin spread across Klaus' chiseled face. "You like to be a tiger cat? You know about cats do you?"

"Please."

"Before they mate they have to fight first. You ever notice that? They have to fight before they do it. If they don't fight, an egg won't come down the female's tube."

"I'm no female cat."

"Maybe not, but I see to it an egg comes down first. Okay? Now, on the bed!"

"Ohhhhh.." Norma scrunched her eyes shut and crossed her arms over her chest. She waited in the pink darkness inside her eyelids.

Nothing.

Then: "If you and your fucking boyfriend wouldn't drink so much you'd have some fucking brains. Get up and put some clothes on."

Still on her back on the gritty, concrete floor, Norma slowly opened her eyes part way and looked up at him through the slits. He was still standing there. Grinning.

"If you weren't drunk you would've felt sorry for the girl."

"The girls. There's more at the morgue. What were you doing with them out there?"

"We fucked up. You ever fuck up?"

"Well."

"You fucked up today, didn't you?"

"You don't drink?"

"I haven't had a drop of that shit for years. I ask the questions."

"Really? You don't drink ever?" Norma turned slowly and felt a stab of pain where the gun barrel had poked into her breast. Her mind was racing for another chance.

"Do you feel sorry for me?"

"Not much. Pick out some clothes."

Norma whimpered: "Okay. Thanks."

"Thanks," he repeated, laughing. "Don't even think about any shit this time or I stick my gun up your cunt and pull the trigger. Hear me?"

"Yes."

"Louder!"

"Yes sir!"

"That's much better."

"Yes sir." Norma got to her knees and pulled at the bottom drawer. In her mind's eye, she saw her guts exploding upward into her mouth, and she gagged.

"We'll get some fresh air. Good, salt, sea air. You'll feel much better."

"Okay. Thank you."

"You're wearing **my** collar now, hear?"

"Yes sir."

"No need to thank me."

CHAPTER 22
Nub-man & Sandy

All through their early supper in the spacious kitchen of the double-wide, Jasmine would interrupt a mouthful of fried shrimp with another grump about Jody's video of Norma's shower. The shrimp, bought frozen and pre-breaded during their last trip to SAM'S CLUB in Panama City, was their favorite, and Jasmine had fried up a bunch. In some ways Jody was proud of his mother. For her outrageousness and courage, for instance. At SAM'S CLUB he was the only thalidomide kid look-alike, and she was the only booted, S & M leather-and-chain babe pushing a cart. But her criticism of Jack's latest girlfriend was unfair.

"Mom, she's beautiful and she has a pleasant personality."

"Like you would know."

"You don't know that she's not nice!"

"Well, don't get a hard-on with no place to go."

"You do, with your Stallone tape."

silence....

"Mom, if I knocked a girl in the head and hid her out here, what would you do? Especially if I got you a cute boy to go along with the deal."

Without a thought, Jasmine had an answer. "We'd get caught. You think I want to spend the rest of my life in jail?"

"No concern for the girl or the boy? For what's right?"

"For what's right? Does anybody give a shit when

African women have to fuck soldiers for food? When Vietnamese women used to have to fuck our troops for money? Get real!"

There was a frozen Sarah Lee chocolate cake for dessert. Even through that, Jody persisted with his fantasy and Jasmine persisted with her griping about Norma in Jack's shower. But only after they had finished eating and Jody refused to wash dishes did the argument boil over.

"That does it, Boy! You're leaving! Take a shower and get dressed. You're leaving!"

"Yeah? Where?!"

"I'm driving you to the bitch's condo!"

"Yeah? Like you know where she lives!"

"You think I don't know things? Too dumb to know what's going on? Go! Shower! And pack one little bag!"

"Mom."

"It won't kill her to put you up for one day. I need some space and you need to get real! When you come back, you can tell me how nice she was!"

It took only a minute for Jody to realize that his mother was serious, and that maybe there was a god who loved him.

The Cremo del Mar sign buzzed pink neon as Jody reached into the back of Jasmine's El Camino and grabbed his backpack.

"Hurry up, Jody, it's dark already and you know I don't see well at night!"

Before he could even say goodbye or collect his goodbye kiss, Jasmine burned out of the circular drive.

He yelled at her receding taillights through the spray of the ornamental fountain: "What if she's not home?"

But as young as he was Jody knew that his mother was frustrated, too. Well, he hoped this was the right building.

Knowing the apartment number would be nice. Just a floor number!

Maybe Jack would be here with Norma, no, his pickup hadn't been moved all day and was still down there next to his camper. And his dad had left in the morning with Jackson to check out the clone farm. Jackson. Jody tried to picture his father with the black, female deputy but all he could see was Sheriff Eastland's .45 Colt shoved into Jack's stomach.

The Cremo was a swanky-looking place and Jody knew now why his mother had insisted on the shower and the clean clothes. He also knew that no matter how white his sneakers were or how crisply ironed his short-sleeved shirt was, he still looked like a freak. At least his mother and father never let him know if it bothered them. Jack, especially. Even adopted him, a thing which Jody would never forget.

Mostly last names on the mailboxes. Some code names, Jeez.

"Who are you looking for?" A friendly-looking couple, the girl speaking. She looked drunk and the young man with her looked pained, giving her a jerk on the arm.

Jody thought the girl looked nice. Tennis shorts, tanned legs. Kind of flat chested though. But she had looked away quickly when she spotted his nub-arm.

"I'm looking for my aunt. Aunt Norma."

"Hmmmm. What floor?"

"Come on, baby."

Jody sensed that the man found his five-fingered elbow-extension grotesque. "Don't know. Long, red hair. Real pretty."

"I think I know! Norma, huh? Real pretty?"

"Yeah."

"Fifth floor — she gets on the elevator there sometimes." The woman motioned drunkenly with the swing of an arm, her purse dangling from it. "That side."

"Thanks."

Jody was glad there was no one near the elevator when the doors opened. The fifth floor hallway seemed even more deserted than the lobby, and the only sound came from one of the doorways he passed — soft music turned down low — as he hunted for name tags. Some doors had them, some didn't. He hoped Norma's would have her first name. Just as he rounded a corner he heard the elevator doors behind him clunk open again and Jody speeded up. Out of sight.

Longer spaces between the doors here, and the hallway had different colors. Pink walls and light-blue doors and carpeting — Miami Vice colors — and brass holders for the name cards, most of them empty. Jody stopped at one which held a pastel-blue card neatly typed in red letters:

BUTTAFUOCO

No, it couldn't be Joey and Amy.

"It's not Joey and Amy!" a cheerful, female voice said behind Jody's shoulder.

He jumped, and turned around. It was Norma. Walking right past him in a white dress with big, dark-green polka-dots. Long, brisk strides in cork and leather, platform shoes. Norma, God, what a beauty! Jody's heart pounded up as she turned her head back to him and winked. Built like a brick shit-house. Freckled face

193

framed in that wild, long red hair. Big, heavy hand-bag slung over one shoulder. She stopped at a door near the end, where the walls had been recently repainted a light peach color. Jody sniffed the fresh paint and watched the lady fish in her purse for keys.

Jody, paralyzed for a second, rushed up to her. She was even more beautiful than ever! "Norma?" He had to look up at her a little, she was so tall in those cork plat-forms. "Guess what! My mother, I mean, Jack's ex-wife..."

"Norma? Oh, heavens no, I'm her sister, Sandy! Do we look that much alike? I'm just kidding. Who are you?"

"I'm..." Jody had to stop to swallow. "You're more beautiful. I'm Norma's boyfriend's son. Jody."

"Oh, well then, Jody, thank you! I can't find my keys!" Sandy resumed her digging in the huge purse, glancing back at Jody frequently with a bright smile. "Well, actually, I don't have any keys to the condo but this is her door and it's locked and I rang the bell, but I guess she's not home!" Sandy laughed and took a long, hard look at the hand protruding from Jody's left elbow. "So! I guess it's just you and me! In this empty hallway here alone!" She laughed again, and didn't sound the least bit nervous. "Do you have a key?"

Jody was mesmerized by Sandy's face: her full, red lips, her green eyes, her brilliant, white teeth. So beauti-ful! "I, uh, no. But I can pick locks!"

"Oh! Great! Pick away, then!" Sandy looked to the right and left down the hallway, but it seemed to Jody she was just pretending to be concerned about others who might see.

"I didn't bring my pick set with me, but if you have a paper clip..." Jody bent down to examine the locks. "...or a hair-pin. And a small screwdriver, but I know you wouldn't have that, so..."

"Oh, silly, how would you know what I have in here! Which hand do you use?" Norma slipped the purse off her shoulder and plunked it to the floor, squatting down beside it.

Jody had to swallow again — the sight of so much firm, freckled cleavage! "The long arm." His mouth turned dry. "That was neat, mentioning my nub. My real name is Nub-man."

"Oh, well, okay, Nub-man! But I saw the fingers move — it's not really a nub then, is it? I mean, if it's a working hand, your name should be Short-Hand! Huh? Here it is!" Sandy looked up, still smiling that happy, wonderful smile, and handed Jody a tiny screwdriver. "It's for fixing my sunglasses. Now for that paper-clip. Here's one! Gosh, this is just like Christmas!"

"Shorthand." Jody liked it and was surprised that the name had never occurred to him. Especially with all the thinking he had done about it. "Short-Hand. Yeah!"

"How old are you, Nub-man? You'd better think about that short hand stuff before you adopt that."

"Oh, yeah, you mean like: short arm? I'm fourteen."

"Yes! You know what a short arm is, I'm sure! Do you have one of those, I mean, is that stuff normal?"

"Oh, yeah, and I'm horny all the time." Jody cringed at the sound of his own words. If he had only thought about that for a minute first...

"Well, not too horny to pick a lock, I hope!" Sandy was back up with the purse on the floor clamped between her feet. She reached out and took Jody's empty, short hand in hers. "Oh! It's a real hand and it has everything! Neat! It's smaller, though, isn't it?" She bent over and smacked a lipsticky kiss right into the palm of it. "Well, go on! Pick-pick-pick!"

Jody had to hunch his shoulders a little so that both hands could meet and work together, and he hoped that wouldn't turn Sandy off. He stretched out the first bend in the paper-clip and knelt before the door. With the tip of the screwdriver just inside the lower portion of the keyway in the lock, Jody inserted the end of the paper-clip farther in above it. If the dead-bolt was locked also, he could get that one next. He began to fiddle. This lock would be easy, he hoped, and Sandy would be impressed. He needed her to be. He was in love.

CHAPTER 23
Jack & Mannlicher

The next time Dr. Mannlicher poked his head back into the projection room, Jack could barely speak. At least Mannlicher stayed back there at the door! Monday had just finished with Jack and he didn't know whether her husband's question was just his usual banter or a test of Jack's honesty.

"Jack, you fuck my wife yet? Huh? **Huh?!**"

Could he know?

Is a blowjob fucking?

"What?"

"No, Manny!" Monday said. "He wouldn't dare!"

So much for the truth. Suddenly there was room in his jeans again and Jack felt Monday's fingers deftly zipping him back up with one hand. Just in time, too, as the movie ended and the screen lit up with blinding light. Jack jumped to his feet.

"You guys go on a-**head!** As soon as you're done, **holler** and we'll get something to **eat!** How many **more?**" Mannlicher was gone without waiting for an answer.

"Well, what do you think so far," Monday said, as if nothing unusual had happened.

"You're wonderful." Jack looked down at her sitting there — at his new, exotic lover. "I love you. You're — wonderful."

No expression. "I meant the movies. Our place here. The operation."

"I'm, uh, impressed." Jack tried to maintain some

197

kind of composure. "I'm sure there's nothing like it in the world! It's more than, well."

"You bargained for?"

"Something like that. And then, you. Why did you do that? That was so great!"

"Welcome to the family, Jack. The movie?"

Jack was unnerved by her business-like demeanor and he forced himself back to what he was doing. "Two more left," he said. "The leader is ripped on this one — the sprocket holes — I have to thread a little of it through." His hands were trembling and he hoped she would not notice.

"There are more but these are what Manny picked out for you."

"Yeah, well. Ready!"

"Wait. Let's see the video first."

"Video?"

"Look at the lectern on the podium. See it?"

Jack looked. Under the top of the lectern was a video projector, a big one. "Is it loaded?"

"Yup. The remote for it should be right next to you somewhere. Between the movie projectors."

"Yeah!" Jack grabbed it and tried to make out the keypad in the darkness.

"The PLAY button is the big one in the middle. You have to aim it at the lectern."

Jack swung the remote around and mashed PLAY, then plunked down beside Monday and let his left hand rest in the lap of her skirt. He hoped she would take his hand and she did. Her hand did not feel like any other, though, something he'd noticed earlier. Although Monday was not fat, or even plump, her hand was warm and meaty, with no feel of any bone in it. As if she were a different species of animal — something unfamiliar.

Maybe she's using my hand as a kind of detector...
...to see how shocked I get at different stuff.

Jack promised himself to remain calm, to show no emotion at what was coming up. This was the video where the girl gets blown up by the land mine. He was sure. Taken after the girls grew up, with a videocam.

The picture came on, but smaller. Model-T's. Teenage size. Their faces had matured enough to become the same face as the severed head. Jack was amazed to see how many of them there were — there had been only a few left in the barracks. Here it looked like there were thirty or so. Outdoors. Another birthday party!

"Their twelfth."

"They look so happy! All wearing dresses." Jack clucked his tongue. "Whose idea was the cute dresses?"

"Both. We were ready to take their marketing video. You'll see in a minute."

Jack was relieved. So it wasn't the land-mine video after all. Maybe that had been just a story to shock him, to test him.

But what about the chopped-off head, the bodies in the morgue? Can't get more real than that!

The scene switched quickly from the outdoor birthday party to what looked like studio shots: plain, dark backgrounds with just a few of the girls at a time. A group of them wearing tough-looking leather mini-skirts with open, bolero tops — a glimpse of a tit here and there — blond hair so showy against the black leather. A group of them walking a runway, single file, all identical except for their costumes. Another runway shot showing the girls emerging single file from a slit in a curtain, nude, identical, one right after the other, stepping briskly with their young breasts bouncing ever so slightly. Eyes riveted on the camera as they walked up to the lens and blurred past with wicked, little-girl smiles. One after the other after the other after the other. Jack became dizzy, faint, and realized that he had forgotten to breathe. And after he sucked in a deep breath he realized he was squeezing the piss out of Monday's hand.

"Sorry!"

"Well, at least we know you like chicks."

"Chicks."

Mannlicher promised me three of them.

Three of these!

Jack eased himself back against his seat. What a life this was going to be!

The scene switched again. Back outdoors. Sunbeams filtering down between clumps of dark, low rain-clouds. The pasture grass blotched with patches of light and dark. A knife-like pain stabbed into Jack's stomach. At first he had not seen her because of the mottled sunlight: the girl crouched near a low, white-washed fence. She was up now and over it, running. You could only see the back of her but Jack knew the face well. She was running for all she was worth, wind whipping her hair and the hem of her dress. She was headed for the perimeter fence, and the only sound was the weird woofing of wind in the videocam microphone. In the foreground a tree branch, whipped by the wind, thrashed in-and-out of the picture, out-of-focus. The lens zoomed closer to catch up with the clone.

Suddenly the ground boiled up underneath the girl and her body blurred straight up into the air inside a mushrooming plume of dirt. Debris flew toward the camera, blocking the picture for a second. More detritus came raining down from the sky after the main portion of the clone's body bounced to the earth splashing blood. The loud, rumbling sound of the blast diminished as the lens zoomed farther into the deluge of falling stuff.

"I told you, Jack. Manny has a steady camera hand. If I were to take a pistol and shoot him while he had the camera in his hand he'd take a movie of the bullet."

A pale, slender object had just arrowed back into the earth and the camera focused on it. Part of a barefoot leg, up-side-down, had impaled itself into the soft dirt, the femur exposed near the knee where it poked into the ground – the intact, bare foot in the air. Jack leaned forward in his seat. The toes were curling. Curling like his own did when he was coming in Norma.

"Jack! My hand!"

"Oh!" Jack released his grip. "Shit, I'm sorry!" He drew her hand up to his lips and kissed it, without turning away from the projection screen.

A bolt of lightening and a sudden, heavy downpour. The rain obliterating the view of the girl's remains.

"Manny told the Pod-2's. They had all been watching from the windows in their barracks — they stand on their beds which is against the rules but we let them when we want them to see something — only we don't let them know we know they do it... Where was I?"

"What Manny told them." Jack squirmed in his seat and did his best to sound relaxed.

"He told them God was angry with her for trying to run away and he sent a bolt of lightening after her dead body, and dumped rain on it, and stuff like that. They believed him. By retarding their brains when they're developing, they're just like little primitives."

"Uh-huh." The video was on the next day now, a ritual burial, home-made pine box and everything. The Pod-2's and 3's attending in solemn, well-disciplined rows. Flowers.

"She **means** they're **dumb!**"

Jack had not seen Dr. Mannlicher come back. The man dropped down into the seat in front of Jack and twisted around. "**Dumb** as **ducks!**"

Jack moved his head a little to see the screen. He remembered he had been holding Monday's hand and was surprised to find it back where it belonged, in his own lap. Had Mannlicher seen anything?

"Nothing to **see!** Just a **funeral!** Clue, Jack. Klaus, you know, the Arnold **Schwarzenegger** guy, and Deputy **Jackson** have the **hots** for each other! Nail them both **together** and we won't piss off **Eastland** if he finds **out!** Huh? **Huh?!**"

"Eastland's my father!"

"Hey! We'll fly him a **new** whore in from **Uganda** or someplace! He won't even **remember** Jackson, what's'ername, **Dee** Jay or something!"

"Desirey." Monday said.

"See what I **mean** Jack? Huh? **Shark** food!"

"Uh-huh. Where do I find him?"

"Huh? You're a **bounty** hunter! That's **you're** job! Find them **together!**"

"Does he ever come back here?"

"If he **does** I'll snuff him my**self!** He stole my **Moppie!**"

"The boat? The Bertram?"

"It's a **classic** now! I just got **through** putting new **engines** in it and he **steals** it! He and that fucking **Hec-tor** and **Abu!** What can I **do?** Call the **law?** Jack! **We** need to get **rid** of all the loose **ends! You** and **me!** Pare things **down** to the **essentials!** Keep this operation down to **family** members **only! Jack! You** look like you're going to **puke!** Hey! You're **family!** You're Eastland's **son!**"

"Yeah, but you want me to snuff the woman he loves."

"Woman? **Loves?** Jack, we're **talking** about **pussy!**"

Mannlicher turned to Monday with an obviously affectionate smile. "**Jack!** Look what **pussy** is getting **you** into **here!** Huh? **Huh?!** Am I **right!**"

Mannlicher continued to keep his smile fixed on Monday and Jack turned to look at her. Even in the semi-darkness, she was beautiful to him now. She had created, in a few, rutty minutes, a bond he would never be able to break.

Monday caught his gaze and smiled. "Like I said, Jack. Welcome to the family!"

They sat outdoors at one of those concrete, South Florida tables, round, with the broken, colored tiles set in circles and patterns, the curved, concrete benches with Corinthian borders molded in.

The tiles gleamed in the dull but sparky, purple light from the numerous, electric bug-zappers hanging all around. Jack looked away over to the full moon rising large and heavy at the eastern horizon over the pasture. The air hissed and buzzed with the death of electrocuted moths and flying beetles, and he had to wonder where the time had gone. How many hours of lurid movies he had watched without losing interest for a single minute.

"Foreign fuckers **forget!**" Dr. Mannlicher said. "That **moon!**" He paused to raise up and scratch his ass. **We** landed **men** on the moon! **Years** ago! Americans! They said it couldn't be **done!** So we did it **again!** Then we did it **again!** And **again!** Americans!"

"Manny, you just got lucky being born in the USA. You had nothing to do with it." Monday looked at Jack and winked.

A coffee-colored old lady in a French-maid uniform had just laid out a spread of hot Danish and tea. The table was on the side of the house which faced the pastures near the distant front gate, and the closeness to the house blocked the view of the barracks. Jack had not seen what was in all of them, of course, the other barracks, and he kept his ears keened for any sound coming from them. But all he could hear was the thunder and excitement of Mannlicher's voice. There was little doubt that the man was excited about everything he was doing. And Monday seemed to be as happy about it all as he was.

...but they're murderers....

"The fucking **people**, they said we shouldn't spend the **money** to go to the moon! They said there's too many **poor** people! We should spend the **money** on the **poor**! You know what the **poor** would **do** with it? Huh? **Huh?!** The **poor** would piss the money away on **booze** and Little **Debbie** snacks and **drugs** and **Twinkies!** Am I **right? Huh?! Now** they don't want us to waste public **money** on the **space** station! **Huh?** Fuck **them!** I say we'll **always** have losers! That's Nature's **plan! Right?** I say, let's keep the Hubble telescope running forever **and** go to **Mars! Now!** Whose money **is** it? Huh? **Huh?!** Let's give the Russian **space** program everything it **needs!** They look like us, they dress like us, they have better music, they write better books, they have better rockets, and they fucking **love** space! If God wants the poor **fed** let the **Pope** feed them! Let the **manna** rain from **Heaven!** It wouldn't cost **God** a **dime!**"

Jack attempted from time to time to keep up his end of the conversation, alternating between smiling and grabbing mouthfuls of pastry. He was hungry despite what he had seen in the projection room. He liked the raspberry Danish the best. "You don't ever feel sad when they get killed or go missing? The clones?"

"Huh? Missing, **yes!** That means we have to **find** them! Kidnapped by our own person **el! Yes!** Asshole mother **fuckers!**"

"I missed the first pod when Manny sold them," Monday said, sending her husband a dirty look. "So young they were then. But by the time the others got to be smart-ass pre-teens? Sheeeit."

"We start with so **many** of them! But before seventy-**two** we **stop!** Only **Allah** is allowed to make seventy-**two!**" Mannlicher's sudden laugh sounded like a braying mule.

"The smart ones and the real dumb ones have to be culled," Monday explained. "So we start out with a bunch. The goal is to end up with ten or twenty eventually old enough to market."

"Culled." Jack said, his mouth full. The blue-berry wasn't nearly as good.

"**Murdered!**" Mannlicher laughed. "Just **kidding!** They're not **human!**" He leaned forward across the table, his mouth spraying strawberry and dough. "You a philosopher, Jack? Huh? Listen! Monday! **Tell** him!"

Monday winked at Jack again and folded her hands in front of her on the table. "If a clone starts out..."

"I **saw** that **wink!**" Mannlicher screamed with a smile.

"If a clone starts out as a single person, especially since we grow them in a culture from a single egg, does the original egg have a soul? If it does, does that soul divide up among the clones? Are the divided-up souls all the same soul or just a fraction? Is the soul ethereal, in another dimension? Is it only connected to that one, original body? If not, when does ensoulment take place? Does the soul know where to go if the body is inside a sheep? Do Alzheimer's victims lose their souls while they are alive? Is there a soul at all? The Jehovah's Witnesses say the brain is the soul."

"Does the **soul** close it's eyes when we **fuck?**" Mannlicher yelled.

Jack wiped off the spray which had hit his forehead. "How do you get rid of the brains?"

"Did you **know** that when the Supreme Court was working on Roe versus Wade the justices were **arguing** with each **other?** Whether a **fetus** was a **person?** Huh? **Huh?!** The **majority** didn't **think** so! How do we make them dumb? We **fry** their **brains!** No, no, just **kidding!**"

"We subject the ectoblast to sudden temperature changes at precise times," Monday explained. "Remember that Jap you saw down there? Hiro? That's his job. He had us fooled at first. We thought we had a high-priced gene-splicer when we hired him. Doesn't know shit about it! But he turned out to have other talents equally valuable."

"Monday **dotes** on the tiny dude a little too **much!**"

Jack suddenly felt a pang of jealousy. As soon as it welled up he recognized the jealousy for what it was but he couldn't stop it. It was there. Monday was probably fucking Hiro.

She's evil. Get out of here now! While you can!

But she had gone down on him when he needed it. Just like that! And he had gotten a glimpse and a good feel of those tits and those incredibly long, tough nipples, and he had seen them chewed on by all those bratty little boy clones.

Jack said: "Does he keep his mouth shut? Hiro?"

Mannlicher leaned back. "Monday keeps him loyal.

And he gets to play with the Pod-3's. He's cool. I trust Hiro."

"You can, too, Jack," Monday said. "He's very interesting, too, once you get to know him. He lives in the house with us, but up on the third floor with his mother."

"His mother? Third floor?" Jack looked up at the tall, ginger-bread building. A window glowed in a roof gable.

"See the gables? All four sides. It's pretty up there. He'll be glad to show you. His mother is an invalid. Doesn't speak a word of English, either."

"She watches Tee **Vee!**" Mannlicher said. "Never misses 'The Bold and the **Beautiful'!** Twelve-thirty on **CBS** every **day!**"

One raspberry Danish left in the pile. Jack poured himself another cup of tea and looked at it.

"Go ahead," Monday said. "Take it."

"Yeah, Jack. Take it. I like the cherry, anyway, and she likes the strawberry."

A normal sentence!

Jack reached for it. A cool breeze licked up and the skittering leaves on the lawn blew with the fresh smell of fall, so late this year. Off in the distance came the faint but happy sounds of children laughing. Jack wondered what their bedtime was and leaned back and took a bite.

Just like family.

CHAPTER 24
Nub-man & Klaus

The lock in Norma's door gave in to the deft manipulations of the deformed boy's paper-clip pick. Jody turned briefly to look up at Sandy, so gorgeous!

"Why, Nub-man, you did it! That's so neat!"

Jody's heart beat with the passion of first love. "Yeah, but I still have to do the dead-bolt." Jody tore his eyes away from the beautiful red-head and shifted his position a little on his knees. The dead-bolt would be a cinch, too, he was sure.

"Gosh, I hope we don't get caught!" Sandy sounded cheerful, as if she were voicing the possibility just to make small talk.

"My grandpa is the high sheriff. Well, not of this county but the next one. The sheriffs are all buddies and..."

But Sandy had already started talking about something else, and Jody shut up and listened. Her voice was Heaven. And her perfume! Jody sucked up a deep breath of it as he worked. The pins inside the lock dropped into place one-by-one.

"Norma and I both married rich guys, well, not super rich, but, you know. Only hers died. I still have to live with mine. And her husband's insurance! It's taking her forever to collect! Sheriff Eastland is your grandfather?"

"Yeah!" It was a chance for Jody to glance back up at her and drink in another look.

"I know him! He's so old, too! Isn't it wonderful?

Being so old and knowing so much about everybody that nobody can fuck with you? I love him!"

I still have to live with mine.

She's not happy about her husband.

Jody still had not succeeded with the dead-bolt. "He's so old he told me once that when he was a kid he had to take his bath in a canvass bathtub."

Rapunzel locked in a tower.

"He said when they got their first radio it was as big as a refrigerator, no, their ice-box, and it took five minutes for it to warm up and he used to look behind it and watch the tubes warm up and start to glow before the sound would come on."

"Oh, really?" Sandy sounded genuinely interested. "That's a long time ago! Gosh!"

She's so nice!

"Ooops! Almost had it!" The screwdriver had slipped and Jody started over, tripping the lock pins one-by-one again with the paper-clip. "He's my adopted father's father, actually. But..."

"Oh, Nub-man! Eastland's sired so many kids around here he could still be your real grandfather! Did you know he's the oldest fucking sheriff in the world? Oh shit. Sorry about my language!"

"You're not sorry. Anyway, my computer at home can handle the word fuck so why shouldn't I?"

"Fourteen? Gosh, you are a smart one!"

Sandy's sweet, genuine laugh rang in Jody's heart and the dead-bolt cylinder gave with a pleasant click. "We're in!"

"Hope there's no alarm!" Sandy picked up her purse and dropped in the screwdriver which Jody had delibe-rately offered with his short arm to get her to bend over.

Tits with real freckles!

Jody swallowed. "I don't see an alarm key-pad."

"Yes, but what if hers is one of those radio remote things?"

Jody got to his feet. "You're smart, too!"

"Oh, for sure!" Sandy crowded behind him and Jody felt the crush of a generous, warm breast against his good shoulder.

"Well, Nub-man? Guess this is where we find out about that alarm!"

Sandy stepped in first and without looking, reached for the foyer light switch. In that instant she forgot the worry about an alarm.

"Ohhhh!"

Jody was right behind her. He had never been in such a fancy apartment. "What's wrong?"

Sandy was apparently familiar with her sister's place. "Look! The carpet!"

Jody stood with her in the middle of the living room and studied the two, roughly eight-foot square holes in the white, shag rug.

"Blood?" Sandy said. "Is that blood?" She charged into the bedroom. "Ohhhhh!"

Jody rushed in behind her. He knew he was in the middle of some real shit now but the new love beating in his scrawny chest colored everything with a sweet, mental fog. "Gun," he said, pointing to it with a freshly whitened Reebok. "A derringer."

Sandy wheeled around and bent over. "It's Norma's," she said, kneeling now and sniffing, without touching it. "It's Norma's. Don't touch anything!" She jumped back to her feet, no easy task with those high, cork soles. She began to thrust her arms under the mattress of Norma's unmade bed. Jody pictured Sandy in it. Then he pictured Norma and Sandy in it. Then Norma and Sandy and himself.

"Jody!"

"Nub-man!"

"Nub-man, shit, get real!"

Jody's ears burned with shame. He swallowed and tried to speak.

"I'm sorry, Jody, I mean, Nub-man. Really, I'm sorry." Sandy touched Jody's hot ears with both hands and her hands were cool and heavenly.

"Nub-man is as real as me."

"Oh, I know. We have a problem and I got upset. My sister! I mean, you've been here before, you know how neat Norma usually is."

"No, I was trying to explain in the hall. I..."

"Well what were you doing here?"

"My mother dumped me. Said my father's girlfriend could put me up. We didn't know she would be gone."

"She told me the other day she'd be home tonight, waiting for me. 'Course that was before she got on the news and everything. And this carpet. What do you think... And is this blood here?" Sandy was on her knees again, this time examining a dark smear at the edge of the cut-out closest to the bedroom door. She sniffed it. "So why is it cut out? We need to call the police! Right away!"

Jody could still feel her cool, wonderful hands cradling his head, his hot ears. "I think, well, maybe I shouldn't say. Just a guess."

"What?!"

"That somebody rolled her up in it. Got her out that way."

"Ohhhhh.. And her big ol' .41 is gone! Oh, Norma! I told you to hide it in a different place! You mean, rolled her up in the carpet dead? Dead?"

"Or kidnapped her alive. Take her down the elevator."

"Yeah, except there's two chunks of carpet missing." Sandy stormed around the living room, then barged into the bathroom. "No blood in here."

"Maybe they carried two people out. Alive."

"Oh, Jody, what are we going to do? Let's call the police right now!" She stopped talking when she saw the cord partially wrapped around the legs of one of the kitchen chairs. Jody tore his eyes away from her and went back to the bedroom.

"There's a whole smear of blood on the bedroom door," he said. "On the inside. No, it would be the outside if it's closed."

Sandy had the phone in her hand. "Dead," she said. And I don't have my cell. Ohhhh."

Eastland arrived before either one of them could leave to score another telephone. After a quick check of what Jody and Sandy had already found, he said: "Just an accident. Just an accident."

"Oh, get real, Sheriff!" Sandy said.

Eastland pulled on the tips of his dishwater-white handlebar mustache. "I meant my coming back. She wasn't answering her phone."

"Oh! I'm sorry!"

He keyed his radio, made a face, and opened a window. "No screen." He held the radio out and called out a code and asked for the Panama City Beach police chief.

"Roberts."

"This is Sheriff Eastland, Homer County."

"The chief's in Tallahassee, back tomorrow afternoon. Can I help you?"

"No, forget it."

"Can you give me your twenty?"

"No. Thanks. Forget it."

Eastland pulled his arm back into the room and dropped the radio back into its holster.

Sandy faced him with her hands on her hips. So gorgeous, Jody thought, in that white dress with the big polka dots. So tall and wonderful.

"Sheriff Eastland!" She stomped her foot like a little girl and Jody had to grin. Sandy was perfect!

"I don't want just any cop in here right now, Sandy. I can explain later."

"We're talking about my sister! She might even still be in the building!"

Eastland's head snapped back perceptibly.

Jody was untangling the phone cord and he found the wall-jack. "Wire's not cut at all! He pushed in the plugs and Eastland quickly grabbed the handset. "Working!" He punched in some numbers. "Tracker? Well, where is he!? Well get him. This is Cletus Eastland."

A new voice on the telephone, so loud and rednecky sounding that Jody and Sandy could hear what he was saying. Something like: "Well, I could bring Cooter!"

"How soon can you get to the Cremo?"

"The Cremo del Mar on the beach?"

"Right. The condo, the number is."

Sandy hollered: "Five-twelve!"

"Five twelve."

"Take Cooter right up the elevator?"

"Right up with the cream!"

"Gotchya! Fifteen minutes!"

"Cut the lights and the siren before you get here."

"Gotchya!"

Eastland was running a fingertip about an inch above the buttons on Norma's answer machine. He looked over to Jody. "You know how to work this?"

"Sure."

"I do," Sandy said.

"Jody. And use that pencil with the eraser. No extra prints."

They listened to the messages in silence, including the one from the unknown admirer who had concluded with: "Stand you on your head and eat you till the cows come home."

Jody reluctantly took the elevator alone down to the ground floor. It wasn't fair. Everybody said that his grandfather had gotten into more women than anybody in the county. What did he need Sandy for? Why did they both have to tell him to get lost?

Well, they didn't actually say get lost. But it was what they wanted, and Miss Chernobyl would be easy to hot-wire. He'd done it before, his father always losing the keys.

Jody had seen the boat from Norma's living room window, the only dark hull out there in the dance of lights at the pier.

I should've told them it was here.

Fuck them!

Mom thinks Jack sank it or something — coming home with the trailer empty. The night Norma took her shower.

That's what Sandy looks like. Only better.

The elevator jolted to a stop and the doors clattered open. The real world: a deserted lobby. A cab driver sitting on a couch reading a newspaper.

That tracker'll be here any minute with his dog.

Wonder if Cooter is a bloodhound.

Wonder if he spells it C-o-u-t-e-r!

Jody looked around and headed out the back way,

toward the breakwater and the boat slips. Double glass doors, smaller than the ones in front but... The air had a whole different character back here, the smell, the lapping of waves, no sound of traffic. Jody walked past the "OWNERS AND GUESTS ONLY" sign and padded out onto the large, T-shaped pier.

Miss Chernobyl bobbed gently in her own darkness, berthed between two larger sport-fishermen. Lights from the other boats twinkled happily as Jody looked down into his father's pride and joy. He knelt, and looked over the pier-plank to locate the ladder down. The twin three-fifties under their engine covers were still ticking with heat.

Dad must be around!

Jody was puzzled. When his mother was in such a hurry to dump him here with Norma, Jack's pickup was still parked beside the camper down in the gully. Deputy Jackson hadn't brought his father back yet.

Something under the bow-deck clunked. Inside the cuddy cabin! Jody sat at the edge of the pier and unlaced his Reeboks. Jack was particular about the boat, and shoes that might make marks. "If they squeak, they mark!"

He dropped down onto the cockpit sole without a sound. The boat rocked to that side and Jody waited for a second to catch his balance, the rhythm. The keys were in the ignition. Both sets. Two engines, two ignition switches — that's the way Jack wanted it. Jody, still hurt by Eastland and Sandy wishing to be alone, considered cranking them up. He wished he had paid more attention to navigation whenever Jack had taken him out in the past. He could be out of here in a heartbeat. Fuck everybody!

Jody froze. Another sound had just come from behind the hatchway to the cuddy. A whimper. He dropped to his knees and slowly cracked the louvered door, peering in. Balancing with his nub-hand spread flat on the deck, his heart pounding, it took a few seconds for Jody's eyes to adjust.

"Nr-r-m-mmmm-ah!"

"Norma?" She was huddled up in a ball against the peak of the V-berth, her knees lashed to her elbows. A knotted sock in her mouth. Jody flicked on the cabin light and crawled up to her. He pulled at the sock but the knot was so large it was catching on her teeth. "Open wider!"

Norma's lips were bleeding but she kept on nodding for him to pull harder. The sock and knot snapped out with a wet slap of saliva. Jody wiped his face with the back of his good hand and dug into a pocket for his knife. His Gerber "Gator".

"My gun!" Norma could hardly speak at first. "It's under the bunk! My .41! Quick!"

Jody reached across to flip up the opposite bunk where they stored the anchors. There was a huge, canvass sack on top of it and it was so heavy he had to brace a foot against the hatchway to roll it off. It was a body!

"Abu," Norma said. "Hurry!"

Jody swiveled around and felt the boat move under him. Side to side with a little forward surge. Before he could turn back toward the hatchway, a long, thick, white, Levi's encased leg lashed out toward him, catching him in his good shoulder. SMACK! The gritty sole of Klaus's sandal slipped off and slid up against Jody's ear. Jody flipped backward over Abu and slammed into Norma's bound and sweaty body.

"Fucking asshole! Take your shoes off!" Before he could say more, Jody caught another kick, in the jaw.

Through the haze of semi-consciousness, Jody could hear a dog barking. Or thought he did. Like a hunting dog baying through the woods: a low, guttural howl rising and ending in a high-pitched riff. And he heard one of the three-fifties crank up, idling, the exhaust gurgling through the water at the stern. Then the other. Both of them idling now with that throaty sound of confident, V-8 power. Together. In unison. A familiar sound.

Up until now, that sound had been one of Jody's favorite things.

CHAPTER 25
Body Bag

Norma was surprised when Klaus backed out of the hatchway after kicking Jody in the head. Hadn't he noticed her gag was missing?

And where was he taking them? She heard a familiar voice, a Spanish accent. Hector! The memory of those first moments of her kidnapping flooded back. Her apartment. The answer machine and Vicki Jonathan from Channel 11 wanting more.

Rolled up in the carpet. Having to piss in it...

The boat shifted into forward and Norma pitched into Jody, who was slumped at her feet. He stirred. She wished she could put a hand over his mouth but her elbows were still bound to her knees. At least she had clothes on this time. Tan shorts and that dumb, purple tube-top, the stretchy material mashing painfully against the breast Klaus had jabbed with his gun barrel.

Jody stirred again and Norma wondered just how hard that second kick to the boy's head had been. Suddenly she felt a hand or wrist slide up her shin. And something hard. A knife!

"Jody," she whispered.

"Shhhhh."

He rocked the blade back-and-forth between her left elbow and her knees and Norma felt the strands of rope give way one by one. God, that felt good! Now what was he doing?

His body slid up over hers and he whispered in her ear. "Are you left handed like Sandy?"

218

"Sandy?"

"Shhhh... She's up in your condo with Uncle Clit."

"Uncle Clit?"

"Eastland. The sheriff. They know you're missing."

"Jody, the gun. Under that berth. No, forget the ropes, get my pistol first." Norma wiggled her left arm free while Jody went back to the berth with Abu's body. Just then the boat lurched forward as the engines throttled up. Norma flew back against Jody and the both of them fell across Abu. Norma's head clunked against the V-locker.

Klaus looked in. "What's going on!"

"You killed him! He's unconscious!" Fortunately, Norma had landed on her left side across Jody and the cut rope was not visible. She hoped.

Jody did not move.

"I can't stay put if you're going to mash the throttles like that!"

Klaus shut the hatch without a word. Hector shouted something to him in Spanish.

"So don't power up so fast!" Klaus yelled back.

"You're so focking smart we have make more trip for the other body?"

Norma rolled back off Jody and held her breath while he cut the remainder of her bonds.

God, Klaus forgot he gagged me? Not possible!

She stretched for the forward end of the V-berth and lifted the cushion. Nothing! Extra life-jackets. The flare-gun kit. No .41. The flare gun! Norma slid the plastic kit out and clawed at the snaps. Christ, did she know how to use it? At least they left the cabin light on. She breeched the barrel and grabbed the clip of flares – three red ones and a white (what was that for?) and she popped in one of the reds. Just as she closed the breech,

Jody handed her the .41 mag. It had slid back down the berth locker when the boat throttled up.

"You know how to use a flare-gun?"

Jody nodded and they switched weapons. Without a word, they crawled back to their original positions. Jody stuffed the loose ends of line under the near berth cushion and grabbed the extra flares.

Miss Chernobyl was spanking right along now, and since Jody and Norma were crammed up against the bow, their bodies slammed with each bounce through the choppy sea. Norma tried to lean over Jody to whisper in his ear, but he moved up instead. In fact, he moved up far enough so he could rest his head against her chest. She took her hands and moved his ears a little, to get the weight off her injured tit. "Asshole poked his gun barrel into that one."

"Oh, I'm sorry."

"Shhhhh."

Was the kid trying to cop a feel at a time like this? Yes! God.

"Jody, let's wait until they slow down before we open fire, or wait until one of them sticks his head in."

Jody nodded, his head nestled in her warmth and softness.

Shit, he must be scared! He's only a kid and I'm talking combat!

"Save the flare for if I fuck up," Norma whispered. She smoothed back Jody's hair and let her eyes rest for a moment on his peculiar, right elbow. The nub hand. So small. But he sure seemed to do okay with it!

"I'll shoot first, Jody."

He nodded again and sank his ears deeper between her breasts. Norma winced in pain but it lasted only for the time he moved, and she let him be. If it weren't for him they wouldn't even have a chance. She bent her head down farther.

"Sandy?"

Jody nodded. Nodding and copping a feel.

"Jody. I killed that guy down there." She kicked a bare toe at Abu's body in the sack. "And I killed his wife. I've already tried to kill Klaus. They don't have any reason not to kill us. Understand?"

"Yeah," Jody whispered. "Is my Dad okay? Jack?"

"I don't know where he is."

Klaus looked in. The night sky was black behind him. No lights. Either they were heading back toward shore or they were out of sight of land. Norma yelled at him, glad that she had time to bring her knees up. "You blinded him with that last kick! He can't see!"

"Good."

"Asshole! At least he's still alive!"

"Not for long. They don't want **you** anymore, either."

Klaus was gone, only this time he left the hatch open. The little, louvered door began to bang back-and-forth on its hinges. Norma felt Miss Chernobyl slow down a little and heard Hector say something in Spanish.

"Jody, you're hurting my chest. I have to keep my knees up to look tied up." She felt the boy move away slowly. "That's enough, Jody. Thanks," she whispered. "That's fine. Jody. I chickened out when he poked his head in. I thought: wait until we can get both of them."

Jody nodded. The boat was slowing down more. Maybe they were in a NO WAKE area. That meant other boats were anchored nearby. Civilization. The sea air wafting in through the hatch took on a warmer, funkier odor.

How far had they gone? Thirty, forty miles?

Jody whispered: "Lights!"

"Shhhh."

Now Norma could see lights winking over the stern each time the hatch would bump open. The way the helm was designed, Hector would be standing at the wheel, on the starboard side of the hatchway, and Klaus would be standing on the port side. She was reminded of Jack telling her, just a week ago, that he didn't believe in helm seats in an offshore boat. As with the day she and Jack had found that young girl's head, it all seemed like such a long time ago.

She could crawl past Jody, poke out of the hatch, swing to her right, and blow Klaus away with one, close shot. By the time Hector could think and get his hands off the wheel she could turn and nail him.

But Norma hesitated. She didn't know where the boat was. If this was a marina they were entering, it was a small one. A private one. Klaus and Hector might have buddies looking for them on the dock. Better to wait.

She felt of the heavy, gold choker around her neck. *You're wearing my collar now, hear?*

Norma remembered that once the boat stopped, Klaus would see that Jody had cut her bonds, and there would have to be a shoot-out on the dock anyway. She had forgotten that, but just for a moment.

222

CHAPTER 26
Sandy at The Cremo

Sandy stood alone in the empty lobby. The cabdriver, who had been buried in his newspaper at the couch near the front doors, was leering at her now. Poor fella! Sandy sent him a sweet and phony smile, and turned her back.

Eastland had insisted he go with Tracker and the dog, Cooter, alone. But they had all come down the elevator together, Eastland guessing the trail led to the basement. But when the doors opened automatically at the lobby, the oldest sheriff in the world told Sandy that this was as far as she could go. He was sorry but this was law enforcement, there was more to this than met the eye, he didn't really know her all that well, and goodbye, nice meeting you. Stay at a motel, don't go back up to Norma's apartment. That wouldn't be safe. The Panama City Beach Police would be sealing it off as soon as they got here, anyway.

While Eastland was telling Sandy this, the dog had lurched forward with a little whine, pulling that awful redneck Tracker (the dog's father?) right out of the elevator. But then the bitch stopped. Looking confused. Sniffing and circling but toward the sliding glass doors in the back, not the front. Then sniffing her way back inside the elevator where Eastland was patiently waiting, convinced the trail would lead to the basement. How could he be so sure?

And how could he expect the Beach P.D. to get here if he hadn't notified them yet?

Cooter was kind of neat, though. Sweet in the face. White, with black spots sort of like a Dalmatian but with one of those Budweiser, English-bulldog black eye patches. Just the opposite of her master, Tracker, whose potbelly protruded over his jeans with the navel sticking out from under the front of his short, black T-shirt. Wobbly, fish-belly white in contrast to the shirt, which had bright yellow writing on the front. ZERO TOLER-ANCE. And bright-yellow handcuffs on the back. Also in the rear, a good three inches of Tracker's ass-crack showed above the curled-down waistband of his Wal-Mart designer jeans.

Back when Cooter jerked him out of the elevator into the lobby, Tracker farted a generous, wet one, upon which he excused himself to Sandy with a wink and a smile.

Christ!

The cabdriver's vacant stare was reflected perfectly in the night-darkened glass of the rear, patio doors and Sandy stuck her tongue out at his image as she exited the lobby. Cooter had momentarily headed this way for a reason. Following Jody's scent? Poor Jody! Now Sandy was sorry about the way she and Eastland had sent him away.

And where was she supposed to stay? Take care of that first? Call the police herself? Nooooo. Better give the sheriff a little more time.

A light breeze came up for a moment, clanging the halyards against the aluminum masts of the few sailboats tied up at the slips. Powerboats here, mostly. Macho stuff. Sandy loved the funky, sea air and the glitter of expensive boats — her husband had recently promised her one soon — and she found herself wandering out to the pier. But not without rearranging the .22 Beretta automatic in the big purse she had slung over one shoulder, keeping one hand on it. Not without clicking the safety off-and-on one more time with her thumb. The safety had a nice, light but positive feel. The feel of a well-made little machine. A tiny gun, but in the right hands....

The breeze died but not before lifting the hem of Sandy's polka-dot dress as she stepped out onto the pier. She heard a low whistle from the darkened cabin of the sport-fisherman on the right, then foreign-sounding voices from farther down near the end of the row. She stopped and turned to her left to look at the ketch tied up opposite the sport-fisherman.

From behind her, a low, manly voice. "You don't want a sail boat, lady. Too slow."

"Oh?" Sandy whipped around. A tall guy, thirty something, standing in the cockpit of the fisherman, his body and face dimly lit by the pier lights. An athletic look about him if it weren't for the uneven stubble on his unshaven face. The cabin lights were on now. The large hatchway open. Way down below, neatly-made berths.

Sandy studied the surprised look on his face. "I'm not Norma, I'm her sister, Sandy. Have you seen her?"

"Uhhhh, I've been napping, but. You know those dudes down there at her boat? Uh, Norma's boyfriend's boat?"

"Chernobyl?"

"Miss Chernobyl."

"Em Es Chernobyl."

"Yeah. Not your type. I've seen both them at the slips next door at The Victor but never over here. Until a few minutes ago. Cocky bastards."

"Ohhh, I'll bet you're a cock-of-the-walk yourself.

Let's go look!"

"Uhhhh.."

"Then **I'll** go look! Jeez!"

"Okay, beautiful. Wait! Let me get my gun!"

Sandy did not wait for him to hop onto the pier. She heard engines running now and was guessing it was Miss Chernobyl. She'd never seen the boat but Norma had described it over the phone, and she got to within three steps of it just as Hector was casting off the last line.

"Hey, wait! That's my boat!"

The big one looked just like Arnold Schwarzenegger. He paused just long enough for Sandy to realize that he was momentarily shocked by her resemblance to Norma.

She stomped a foot. "Stop!"

Klaus shot her a bird and Sandy reciprocated. She wanted to draw her little Beretta but how could she know that they didn't have permission to use that boat. It wasn't Norma's, and Norma was no where around to let her know.

"There they go!" The sport fisherman guy had a small, shiny revolver in his hand, his hands hanging at his sides.

Sandy did not know what to say. She stammered. "My — sister's disappeared — and..."

"Disappeared?"

"Probably kidnapped, and..."

"Kidnapped? How do I know you're not her? I did see them haul a big sack and shove it down in there."

"Did it look like a rolled up carpet? White?"

"No, and I saw this little deformed kid run down there before you came up."

"Christ! Your boat run?"

"Yeah."

"You got fuel?"

"Yeah. Why?"

"Let's go!"

"Uhhh, no, I think I'll pass."

"I'll pay! Whatever you want!"

"Yeah, sure. You still owe me a hundred bucks. Remember?"

"I told you, I'm not her!" Sandy dug down past the Beretta and pulled out a roll of bills. She snicked out a hundred. "See? I'm not Norma! Here!"

His hand flicked out and snatched the bill with the joints of his second and third fingers. "You want to follow them?"

"Yeah. Now! Come on!" Sandy had to bull her way past him toward his big fisherman. She wheeled around. "I'll pay you when we get back! Are you in a coma or something? Move!"

The guy came to life. "Bill. My name's Bill. I'm a Bill fisherman. Three hundred dollars plus fuel plus a hundred an hour." He dropped bare-footed down into the cockpit and reached for her shoes, then her hands as she hopped in.

"Go, go, go!" Sandy hollered. "And lights out! They won't see us but we'll see them. Go!" Sandy felt one of the diesels crank up to idle under her feet. Then the other. The cockpit sole throbbed with power.

"Go!"

"Well get the lines!"

"Lines?"

"Ropes! Yup, you're not her, that's for sure." Bill moved past her and had the stern and bow lines secured in seconds. He dropped both engines into forward and idled the boat out of the slip.

"Faster!" Sandy yelled.

"This is a no-wake area."

"Fuck the no-wake area!"

But Bill did not relent, and he kept the big diesels idled down until they had passed the tee. Then, with power to spare, the thirty-eight footer gently climbed up on plane and headed out toward the disappearing stern light of Miss Chernobyl.

"They're heading south," Bill said.

"What's there?"

"San Destin. Fort Walton Beach. They could be headed anywhere."

"We're losing them!"

"Be cool, lady. There's a sea tonight. They'll have to run slower. Wet Dream can take rough water but their boat can't. Not as well, anyway."

"Wet Dream?"

"My boat. This boat."

"Wonderful," Sandy hollered. "Go!"

CHAPTER 27
Evening at The Farm

Dr. Mannlicher, still in his raggedy cut-offs, stormed into the guest room which Monday was showing Jack.

"First I can't get Eastland at **all!** Now he can't find that ape-girl **Jackson! I** know where she is! She's with that turncoat **Klaus!** I should **tell** him!"

"No, don't," Monday said. "And it wouldn't kill you to drive Jack back home yourself."

"Leave the **fort?** At a time like **this?**"

"I'll be okay here," Jack said. "Really."

"Yeah? Hoping my **wife** will come slithering down the hall in the middle of the **night?** Huh? **Huh?!**"

"He didn't bring any clothes so I got him some of your stuff to wear after his shower."

"O-**kay!** Jack! I got some neat **shit** to show you if you're staying **over!**"

Jack grinned, and pictured the three clones he had been promised.

"Not the P-**threes!** You nail Klaus **first! Business** before **pleasure!**"

Jack nodded and involuntarily lowered his head and shuffled his feet, realizing instantly what that must look like and hating himself for it. He raised his chin, tried to meet Mannlicher's deadly, fiery-blue stare, and spoke up. "I'm horny **now!**"

"Didn't your **mother** ever **tell** you? The **longer** you **wait** the better it **is!**"

"Manny, quit. Is your mother still living, Jack?"

229

"Yeah." It was a relief to look away to Monday. And over her shoulder to the windows of this second-floor room, which overlooked the outdoor patio below. The circle of electric-blue bug zappers out there flickering in the glass.

"She's got **Alzheimer's** Monday! Eastland **told** you! You ever **visit** her, Jack? At the **home? Huh?**"

"Yeah, I..."

"Can she still **talk?** Does she just sit there and **drool?** Don't be **offended! My** mother has it! She won't ever see **me** again! All she does is fall half-way out of her **wheel**chair and **drool!** She goes: 'Guh-guh-guh-guh' and **drools!** I bitch to the **nurses** and they say: 'But she's your **mother!' So?** She **could**'ve done the right thing! When she was dia**gnosed! Daddy** when he found out he had cancer, he put a pistol in his mouth and **blew** off the back of his **head!** He even went out**side** so he wouldn't make a **mess!** He even underlined in his old **life**-insurance policy where it says they pay **off** if the suicide isn't in the first two **years!**"

Jack kept on nodding his head, noting the pleasant sparkle in Monday's eyes. He said to her: "Is your mother still living?"

"I don't know."

"We should go **back** there! The bitch won't answer **letters!** I want her mother to **send** me some of those curare-tipped **arrows!**"

Dr. Mannlicher bolted from of the room. Monday opened the closet and showed Jack the extra blanket on the top shelf, and said she would be back in a minute with a robe and pajamas and stuff.

Jack grabbed an elbow and stopped her. He got close to her ear, her earrings, and the monkeys in their golden cages stared at him. Jack whispered: "Will you come slithering down the hall tonight?"

"No, but I'll give you your bath."

She was gone. Jack paced the room, his heart pounding. He stopped at the window and saw that the tray with the Danish crumbs was still at the table down there. The faint sound of voices from the ceiling. Hiro and his mother?

The bathroom she led him to was roomy but the step-down tub took nearly three-fourths of the space.

"The water's just right," Monday said. She eyed him as he clumsily pulled off his shirt. "Boots, pants, come on, Jack you're not going to be shy, are you? Bounty hunter?"

Fuck it. Jack's clothes were off and heaped on the floor. The water was steaming but she said it was okay, so... *God it's hot!* He grimaced when his balls submerged. Sitting up to his neck now, he watched Monday step out of her colorful, rainbow dress. No underwear. Thick waisted with a bush of soft-looking, straight hair parted in the middle. Jack had never seen anything like it and he felt his loins throb with heat. But it was the nipples, the nipples.... So puffy and long and dark.

They sat opposite each other for a moment, water up to their necks, one of Jack's feet up against Monday's so-soft bush. Jack was in Paradise. Not in his wildest dreams did he ever think he would be sitting one day in a hot tub of water with a female so exotic. With an Indian from South America. He watched her mouth curl into a smile under the big, gold nose-ring. Her lips parted and bared those weird teeth.

"If a crocodile could be beautiful, that would be you," Jack said, without a stutter, proud of himself now even though he had come up with that one earlier in his thoughts.

"We can soap each other up after," Monday said.

After?

After we have sex here in the tub?

The door popped open and Jack's heart slammed in his chest. It was Mannlicher. Tall, pink, hairy, and naked. He looked even taller from down where Jack was languishing in the depths of the tub.

"Whose **side?**" he yelled. "Huh? **Huh?**"

Monday quickly scooted over to Jack, sloshing water over the rim and across the varnished, wooden floor. Jack was grateful for that, at least, as he watched Mannlicher plunge in on the other side.

"Just like the hippie days, huh Jack? Huh?"

"Yeah." *Except I was in 'Nam while you guys were sewing G-strings and jock straps out of American flags.*

Mannlicher was polite about where he put his feet, but Jack's spirit was crushed. It wasn't just losing the private moment in the tub with Monday, but what he had just learned about his new employer. Mannlicher was hung like a red-headed mule.

The bath had been a bust as far as Jack was concerned, but getting to know Hiro became the highlight of the evening. Yet as pleasant as Hiro's constant chatter was becoming, half of Jack's brain could not tear itself loose from the memory of Mannlicher's intrusion in the bathroom. Monday scrubbing her husband down first and then Jack after Mannlicher stepped out, without any way to rinse. Monday giving Jack's shrinking penis a snap with her middle finger when she got to that part. "Well, Jack, the Pod-3's won't know any difference. Or they won't mind."

He had never felt so humiliated. Brilliant or not, the both of them were cruel and heartless. He should get out of this business now, while he still had something of a chance. Was there a chance?

He knew too much.

Real estate was still a bargain in some parts of Idaho, Montana, Wyoming. If he could just come up with a down-payment, who could find him there?

A friend of his had told him once that Jamaica was nice.

Hiro turned out to have been born in Milwaukee of a Japanese father who was not interned during World War II because he was working on a private project near Tomahawk, Wisconsin, where they were training apes to set off car bombs. Jack had always thought car bombs were a Muslim invention.

"Mother would shave them and dress them! Live with them, sleep with them. Sew their clothes! Get on them when they wouldn't walk straight or when they'd revert and drop to all fours. This was before they knew much about dolphins. The military." Hiro lowered his voice. His mother, on the other side of the room, was sitting quietly in her rocker with a shawl over her knees.

"The female apes, when they're shaved they look like ugly girls with droopy tits."

Jack had to laugh. He liked this guy! His age? A real slope in the face but so funny! Coke-bottle glasses. A thin, wisp of a mustache that a teenager might have.

Sometimes Hiro would mimic Mannlicher. "Huh? **Huh?!**" The two men were sitting next to each other on the couch, going through a photo album, Jack in his borrowed pajamas with the pant-cuffs rolled up. His feet slopping around inside a pair of Mannlicher's roomy slippers. Well, maybe Hiro was born in the USA but he acted and looked foreign. Jack had to wonder, though,

233

why he felt so comfortable, so at home up here in the huge top floor with the four gables. North, south, east, west. In one, the window would brighten momentarily whenever an unusually juicy bug would stray into one of the electric zappers down below.

Hiro's mother kept on looking at Jack across the room, her tiny head nodding and her wrinkled face smiling. Her face was a mass of scars (Jack hoped it wasn't from an American bomb), and her black hair was thin and you could see patches of bald scalp. Occasionally she would let out these measured little farts. **...put-put-put...** Their sound muffled by the pillow on her rocking chair. Her bed was beside the chair, and not a mat on the floor, either. Hiro's was near the couch on the east side of the room, the window there glowing bright with the moon still rising.

The only thing Jack didn't like was the temperature. Just a little too warm. Kept warm because of the old woman's age, he thought.

Hiro was saying: "...and this one is the Emir. Fucker has so much money! Almost as much as the Saud family or the Sultan of Brunei. When he and his sons go hunting in Pakistan, they use the game preserves. The Saudis, too. They have all the officials bribed. They have huge, walled estates in the Punjab and they fly their camels over in C-130's. Camels, servants, even tanks! They hunt endangered species in the national parks. Got their own airstrips.. They use choppers with machine guns. Fly in hundreds of their own troops to guard their hunting camps. Huge, tent cities. They buy women for the troops. They fly in air-conditioners from France for their tents, electric generators from Germany, frozen cakes from Austria, pre-cooked goats from New Zealand. You know who trained their troops? You know who gave these assholes all that money? Every time you pump a gallon of gas."

"Fuck it. I don't feel guilty," Jack said. "It's God gave 'em the oil."

"No, well, ha ha, maybe **your** god did. It's a mistake of geography. The rag-heads are the losers in the evolutionary race. They can't compete in a mechanized world without people like us — their clothes would get caught in the machinery. They were living in the desert before oil was discovered because the other races of man would kill them everywhere else. So they moved to where nobody else wanted to live. They'll lose again one day. Survival of the fittest will come back. The real 'New World Order'."

"As soon as the rest of us quit helping the losers." Jack hoped his meager contributions to the conversation were sufficiently apropos for his new, brainy friend. "Like keeping premature, retarded babies alive in neonatal trauma centers."

"Well, yes, but evolution comes up with so many surprises. What if being a loser and getting help gives you an edge? Huh? **Huh?!**"

They both laughed. Hiro closed the book of pictures half-way through and got out another, larger scrapbook. With a pink cover, a black string tied in a bow at the binding. "This," said Hiro, "ought to be burned. Evidence. But, it's how I make money, so."

"Are you rich?"

"No, but comparatively speaking Manny made us all well-off. He couldn't have done it without my help, though. He's says he's getting twenty-million a pod from the Emir, but it might be more. Or his sons. Princes. Loose change for them. It's good for the country, too! We're bringing back American dollars by the freighter load! Better than selling dope, these clones. Except for the dark ones you saw at the creek — they're already sold — some rich European Manny found. Yup, if it weren't for me...."

Jack was happy with Hiro and didn't mind (but noted) the lack of modesty.

Hiro looked past him and Jack also noted he had yet to catch the man's eye. "What about the boy clones Monday likes so much?"

Hiro shrugged his shoulders and shook his head. "Not my idea. Ask her."

"So what's in it for me? Is that hint Dr. Mannlicher made to me about three women in bed for real?"

"For sure. Money, too, which we can't even deposit anywhere close by. Even gold bullion. Bars of it! You wouldn't believe just how much these fools pay for this shit. Yeah, count on it. We need you to help us get some personnel problems straightened out so we can hang on here just a little longer before we move out. So we don't get busted big time. So I can retire in Hawaii. That's my dream. Retire in Hawaii with all the toys." Hiro opened the book. Looking at them from an 8 X 10 color print was a face grinning out from an array of monitors and keyboards.

"Dr. Mannlicher?"

"No, no relation, either, they just favor each other. This is Turbo. Turbowski. He's the electronics freak. At the Walton lab. He lives in there. Never leaves. See the refrigerators in the background? There's one or two in every lab. Klaus has to bring him groceries and stuff every week, well, I don't know who's going to be doing that now, but... Turbo's the one got Manny convinced years ago that there is a model in the human brain as to what is the most desirable fuck."

"Fort Walton?"

"Fort Walton Beach. It's a neat place but we're moving everything out of there. Turbo's going to have to come here. He can work in the basement labs. Manny and he went to school together — they go way back. But he's crazy now. Klaus wanted to snuff him but Manny wouldn't hear of it."

"Yeah? Why?" *I'll be next.*

"Because he went crazy. I don't know, too many drugs? Like the place is on a canal, right? Sometimes neighbors or boaters come to the door. Can Turbo be trusted to say the right thing? Shit, he can hardly talk straight anymore. He's developed these 3-D goggles, similar to virtual reality but like you've never seen! He has his computers constantly refining the perfect-woman images he made from all the body parts they photographed and collected over the years. He's so close to what must have been man's original, wired-in model that it's scary."

"You believe in it?"

"No, and now Manny isn't sure, either. Turns out the computer models which turn on the most lust aren't the average woman but more near the extremes, but only if the extreme is at the other end of whatever male is observing. Look at me, I've got Jap genes obviously, right? So you'd think that I'd respond most aggressively to the image of a most beautiful oriental woman, right?"

"Uh, no, um, I'd guess you'd respond the most to a female different from the one you've got at home."

"Correct! **If** you haven't been brain-washed by the culture you were brought up in, sure, but it goes deeper than that. Okay, I like exotic, too. I love those blondes. I would've quit this place a couple years ago when Manny started hiring these jerks like Hector and Klaus, but he keeps me happy with the threes. Anyway, the Pod-3's are crude compared to what we can raise now. We're just keeping what's left of them for toys now."

...**put-put-put-put...** Hiro's mother looked at them and grinned. She was struggling to get up, it looked like, and Jack noticed for the first time that the comforter over her legs was tied to the back of the chair.

"She would get into things, hurt herself, if I let her loose on her own."

"Yeah."

...**put-put...**

We have a pair of Turbo's goggles over here if you want to see how far he's gotten. That helmet over there. It's amazing! Want to see?"

Jack could tell that Hiro was anxious to show him, and besides, it was something he wanted to see. Bad.

"I wouldn't miss it for the world."

"Great! Wait till I get Mama to the bathroom, then see if we can network Turbo's lab." Hiro got to his feet and Jack politely rose with him. Hiro was nearly as tall as Jack was, despite Mannlicher's description of him as "tiny", and Jack turned toward the window to watch the bugs fry down below while Hiro bent over to loosen the tie behind his mother's seat-back. The moon was higher now and Jack had to stoop and look up to see it. Such a clear night! In a reflection in the clean window-glass he could see the gable on the other side. And Hiro's mother's empty chair, still rocking gently from her getting out of it, and Hiro's mother heading for the bathroom with an easy, bounding lope on all fours, knuckles to the floor.

CHAPTER 28
Nailed to The Wall

With the hatch open, Norma could see that the boat was swinging her stern toward the dark opening of a wooden boathouse. Miss Chernobyl's stern-light glared white in her line of vision and she could barely make out the Bertram already berthed in there. They were backing up alongside a pier on the outside, the engines at idle speed. *Klaus will jump for the pier in a second.*

Nail them both now!

NOW!

Norma poked a finger into Jody's side and whispered it.

"Now!"

Jody nodded and moved to the side, and Norma plowed past him on all fours, the .41 mag in her left hand. There was no headroom in the small cuddy cabin, and since her elbows and knees were still stiff from being tied up, Norma faltered for a second and her head bumped the cabin light, busting out the dome lens. She clawed for the hatchway with her right hand but breaking the cabin light gave her away and before she could swing the huge revolver Klaus was already kicking out a leg. Her first shot blasted past him, splitting the air with a deafening roar. Her forearm pinned now, she managed to cock the piece again but Hector nailed it with a barefoot kick and the Ruger Blackhawk skittered to the side onto the cockpit sole.

"Ow! Focking bitch!" Hector was dancing in pain, bending over and grabbing his bunged toes.

239

Klaus picked up the revolver and was about to toss it into the bay.

"No! That's a good gun!" Norma yelled. "Saltwater!"

Klaus hesitated, and suddenly ducked. Jody's flare hissed over Norma's shoulders, which were nearly plugging the hatchway, and arced into the boathouse where it sizzled into the dark water beside the Bertram. The Ruger still cocked, Klaus shoved the barrel into the hatchway over Norma's body.

"Freeze! Don't even twitch, you little freak!"

"Shoot me. Just shoot me then." Jody rolled to the side to reload as Norma grabbed Klaus's legs. The pistol came down sideways on top of her head and Norma's brain flashed in a blaze of white, the white bleeding to red, then pink. It seemed like only a split second — the numbness, how long she was unconscious — but when she came to she was crumpled against the starboard engine cover and Jody was in a heap under the wheel. Klaus must have jerked them out. The engines were still idling but the boat was in neutral with the port side gently bumping the fenders on the pier. Blood was trickling down the corner of Jody's mouth.

Norma looked up. Hector was standing on the pier directly above her, the cocked .41 aimed between her and Jody.

"You killed him!"

"You're a focking broken record, you know that? They want him."

"For what?"

"For the computer. Don't worry about it, fifty-cent strawberry."

"Asshole!"

"Get up."

Norma looked back to Jody. She felt faint and

wasn't at all sure she could get up, anyway. Why couldn't she have waited for a better moment? Why couldn't she ever think?

Jody was breathing.

Klaus walked up with a long line which he attached to a stern cleat. "Cut the engines, bitch."

Norma sucked in a breath and crawled forward, mashing against Jody's doubled-over body. She reached up and turned the key switches. The resulting silence was strange, almost peaceful.

As Klaus pulled Miss Chernobyl toward the boathouse, Hector backed away from the boat but kept the revolver trained on the two of them. "Get out! On the focking pier!"

"He's unconscious! Where was he hit?"

"No place! Lift him out then."

"Me?"

"He don't weigh shit!"

"Hurry up!" Klaus added. ("Hory opp!")

Norma bent over Jody, on her knees. The silent engines ticked as they cooled down, and the sea lapped at the hull as Miss Chernobyl clunked against the pilings. "My stomach's on fire," Jody said quietly, his throat sounding hoarse. "He kicked me. A bunch of times. In the stomach, in the neck..."

"Shut up and get up!"

"Okay!" Jody got to his hands and knees and pulled himself to his feet using his longer hand on the wheel. His mind was racing for an option but if there was one he couldn't find it. Norma got to her feet also and helped him crawl onto the pier. She readjusted the tube top and the stupid khaki shorts she was wearing, and using the step at the split windshield, got out onto the bow-deck and took a quick look around. It was a private dock, and all down both sides of the little bay she could see the winking lights of anchored sailboats and bay-front homes. But they all looked so distant and unaware.

Klaus was tying the stern and bow lines to the pilings. "Not enough room in there," he said to Hector. Norma nearly lost her balance as he jerked the bowline. "Get on the pier, bitch! No, you don't have more options."

"You focked up!" Hector chimed in. "Again!"

A single outdoor lamp lighted the narrow boardwalk around the boathouse to a two-story, gray clapboard building. Klaus led Jody and Norma through the screened-in back porch (leaning against a washing machine was a bicycle with a luggage-rack and handle-bar basket, a broom and a mop leaning against the wall), through a dark kitchen (with a single, dull light glowing from the canopy over the electric stove), and through a small but neatly kept living-room with the standard stuff, the TV, a big couch. On the table beside the couch (with the only lit lamp in the room) was a dusty array of computer magazines.

Klaus stopped at the foot of the carpeted stairway. Hector was following behind them with Norma's pistol, cocked. "Klaus. I no go up to the lab. That focker make me nervous."

"You'll miss watching him die."

"You're focking crazy."

"We agreed. No? Okay, Castro. Suit yourself. But you stay right here. This is the only way out from up there." Klaus pulled the pistol from his back pocket, the one Norma had used on him at The Victor, and waved his two prisoners past him to the stairs. "Up! Up! Slow!"

Norma winced at the sight of the automatic and as

242

she stepped past him her eyes were drawn to the jagged, still-weeping gash so evident along his ear and the side of his scalp.

"This is the gun I kill you with later."

"I'm sorry. I didn't mean it."

"Up! Slow! No, the freak first!"

"Yessir."

"Wait. Take that necklace off your girlie friend, you're tall enough now, that gold dog collar, no, wait, you can take it off for me when she's dead."

"Please," Norma said. "I'll be good."

"Yeah, sure. Up!"

It was bright up above, and the stairs led to a long hallway, white walls and doors on either side, the doors all closed. The homey atmosphere of the first floor was completely missing here, and there was the faint smell of bleach and formaldehyde. The big fear pounded back into Norma's heart. It was all too clean, too neat. She was going to die here.

I could whip around and throw myself down on him.
If he drops the gun Jody might be able to...
"Move!"

Norma made it to the top and stood beside Jody, shivering. It was so cold! You could hear the sound of the air-conditioning — the only sound — no, she thought she heard a voice down the hall, like a radio, no, like a telephone voice.

"Go!"

Jody and Norma shuffled along. Even the thick carpeting was cold on their bare feet. A dull, cold beige.

"Stop!" Klaus worked around them, the end of the gun barrel never wavering from Norma's head as he si-destepped. He knocked at the last door on the left and, without waiting, turned his fist around and pounded three good ones. Then three more good knocks before he turned the knob and walked in. He motioned for Norma and Jody with the pistol.

"Ohhhhh! Real ones!" A red-headed Abraham Lincoln got up and turned away from the monitor at his desk near the door. Bare, hairy legs poked out from underneath his lab coat. Feet in cheap, worn, orange flip-flops. Big grin on his face. A knot of reddish beard at the end of his chin.

Norma sensed the man was not wearing anything underneath the starchy coat. "Another red-head," she said, smiling, doing her best.

"Oh, well, no coincidence. Manny and I met because I saw the only other red hair in our physics class and I properly introduced myself. I'm Turbo." He looked away to Jody. "And you must be some wayward result of genetic engineering, huh? How interesting. Let me look, please." Turbo reached out for Jody's nub hand.

Jody raised it. "My mother was a druggie when I was conceived."

"Oh, yes, well. Curl your fingers around my thumb as hard as you can, will you? Don't be afraid to hurt me."

Jody reached for Turbo's thumb but Klaus slapped the little hand away. "Cut the crap, Turbo. I want these shitheads cuffed to the wall. Then we have work to do."

"Well. In the work room?" He looked at Norma's face, then scanned her body. "Both of them?"

Norma thought his voice sounded friendly, although the man had not cracked a smile or shown any emotion yet. Well, there was a hint of a smile when he said: "Ohhhh! Real ones!"

"In here where we can watch them."

"Oh, well, I moved a whole table full of stuff in front of the specimen wall but I guess we can shove it farther down." He turned his back and walked bowl-legged down the aisle between two, long lab tables. A chemistry lab but with electronic equipment and cables everywhere, even a humming CPU sitting in an empty sink, soft pilot-lights glowing. "Yes, yes, we can shove it farther down." Norma watched him give a pull on the corner of a long table laden with printers and tractor-feed paper and to her surprise he moved it easily.

Built like an ant.

Klaus grumped from behind her: "Don't you ever go to bed, Turbo?"

"Noooo. I can't sleep anymore. Sometimes I find myself asleep, usually just before dawn. Maybe for an hour. There! Plenty enough for two! See?"

Klaus thunked Norma forward with a fierce blow between the shoulder blades. She lurched into Jody and the two of them bolted forward. Both of them hanging their heads in a submissive pose. Smart kid, Norma thought. She had already seen he was a fighter. She looked up. A bare wall with electric outlets at about waist height every three feet or so, and sets of leather wrist-cuffs embedded in rings, some of them above eye level. Christ!

"Turn around!"

Friendly voice or not, Turbo quickly reached out and grabbed Jody's longer arm and fastened his wrist to the wall above his head.

"Hang him from the short one. He tried to kill me."

"Okay!" Turbo sounded happy about it. As Norma watched, with tears forming in her eyes, Jody was easily hung from his nub, the cuff clamped where the elbow grew the hand, toes of his right foot just barely touching the tiled floor.

Jody said, "It's okay, Miss Norma."

"Next!"

Last chance...

But the heel of Klaus's hand caught Norma in the jaw and snapped her head into the wall. Momentarily dazed, she felt herself shackled with her wrists just behind her head. She noticed another set of cuffs set in the wall on either side of her ankles. Cracks surrounded the eye-bolts there. Had somebody else struggled to get away here?

No gold this time.

"Can you use those down there? So I can sit? Please?"

"Shut up. I need the market file, Turbo. The one with the addresses and phone numbers."

"Oh, well. What would Manny say, I don't know."

Norma would have thought the man was gay with that voice so soft and gentle, but he kept on staring at her, looking her up and down. She noticed his eyes were a light brown. Strange. The same color as his freckles.

"Well, I know. Mannlicher's going nuts. He's on that shit again, that..."

"That old stash of Ibogaine? Yes, well, I would have to access the computer over there so why don't you just go over to the feedlot and do it that way, or call, no, Manny took away all my telephone handsets, remember? So I can't talk on the telephone to anybody, you know, he said I fried my brain, but, well."

"You can type! Don't try to bullshit me. Come on!" Klaus de-cocked the automatic and shoved it into his back pocket with a wink to Norma. "Later, baby." He began to head back toward Turbo's desk but stopped when the man didn't follow.

"It's just pussy, Turbo. You can have her later."

"Promise?"

"Promise. After you cough up the market file. Two, three pages? How long would that take? A split second from there to here?"

"But it's not her I want. I just need to get into a babe again with the goggles on. I'm closer now to the model than ever. It's a split model, now, and I have the computer refining it down, all the images, they change their value when they're melded with both extremes but now I have a program that's programming itself. Very slow, though, but if Manny would get me that new unit I ordered I could crunch some numbers, yes, and then one day. But then she would be in the machine, listen, Klaus, she would be inside the machine, well, she's already in the machine but, and, oh! Hiro is online! He wants to see how far she's coming along, too! I haven't seen how she's maturing myself for the last couple of hours, but it looks like she's becoming an alien. You know, the model woman? Our original model? From somewhere else. Machine can't get her hair color right. Keeps on coming up with this bizarre stuff, the colors, the styles. Silver, last time I looked. So beautiful! But it might be an error. Maybe we didn't input enough data on stuff like hair, or maybe, just maybe, our Eve is from another planet! The **real** Eve? Yes. I could send the feed to his set and to my goggles here at the same time. I don't mind stopping the process for that long. I..."

"Shit, Turbo, shut up! Snap out of it! Do something!"

"Do something?"

"About Hiro! You just said he's online!"

Klaus was down at the end of the aisle, staring at Turbo's monitor. On it was a simple message from Hiro.

247

Klaus glanced at his watch. He sent this ten minutes ago! Do something!"

"Hell, there's no hurry, Klaus. He's very laid back. Does he know you're here?"

"No! And you're not going to tell him, either! Shit, man, he needs to know **you're** here!"

"I'm always here. I don't leave anymore, you know that. Did you bring my supplies? My groceries?" Turbo took a step closer to Norma. His breath had the odor of garlic on it.

Jody hollered: "My wrist hurts! Can you turn my hand around?"

"I know!" Turbo exclaimed. "And these two are for me?"

"If you print me the market file. Not before."

"First an experiment."

"And feed Hiro what he wants. He likes to scare himself with the goggles. Do that first."

"Yes, well, Klaus, you don't understand. If I have to stop the process so I can tap into it, I might as well kill two birds with one stone." Turbo pulled his eyes away from Norma and began to rummage around for something. He came up with a home-made helmet with a set of goggles attached to the brow. A jumble of wires dangled from the device, ending in two, ethernet jacks.

"Shouldn't you let him know you'll be sending soon? If I knew how, I'd do it myself!"

"Okay, Klaus, okay!" Turbo walked up to the keyboard and tapped in: five minutes.

The screen blanked out for a moment, then:

Remote open

Sending

Transfer complete

"Oh, shit," Turbo said. "I've got the FAX program."

248

He tapped away at the keyboard. The monitor blinked, then: Thanks, Turbo. Ready here!

Turbo waved the helmet at Klaus. Would you like to see her again? She's better than ever! Eventually, though, we can expect diminishing returns."

"No, no, I have a job to do."

"Last time you passed out."

"Turbo, just shut up and do what you have to do to make Hiro happy."

"And me happy."

"Whatever. Hector's downstairs, waiting. He hates to wait."

"Oh, Hector, he's so, erm, different." Turbo left the desk and walked up to Jody. "Are you a real boy? Man?"

"Yeah."

Turbo bent over to lay the helmet on the floor and before Jody knew what was happening, the man had jerked Jody's pants down to his knees, Fruit-of-the-Loom briefs and all.

"Oh, yesss. So big for a little cripple. Hmmmm. Just right!"

Norma looked and jerked her head away. "What are you doing to him?!"

"Oh, don't worry, Miss. I'm not going to turn him loose on you now. There is a lady in a box I'm going to turn loose on **him!** After that, he'll be mine. He'll do anything I want him to do. And that's when I'll turn him loose on you. That's what I want. After I get the videocam, of course."

"Sick mother fucker!"

"Don't worry, Norma," Jody said. "I couldn't do anything bad to you."

Turbo picked up the helmet and straightened up. "Oh, little do you know, little Thalidomide man."

CHAPTER 29
The Model Female

Hiro and Jack did not speak as they descended the stairs, Hiro holding a finger to his lips at the second-floor landing. The huge, old house was drafty and Jack could feel the cool, night air sinking down the stairwell over his shoulders. He pictured the current object of his insatiable desires, Monday, huddled up close to Mannlicher's lanky hairiness under a feather quilt in their bedroom somewhere, the draperies open to cold moonlight. Jack shivered.

But down in the basement labs, the first thing Hiro did was head for the thermostat to turn on the heat. The American-born Jap could barely contain himself, and he chattered incessantly. "The man's a red-haired, arctic bison!" He kept on swinging the helmet with the goggles as he gestured, the cord flinging around. Jack finally grabbed at it to keep the connectors at the end of the cables from knocking something off of the lab tables.

"Oh!" Hiro said. "I get carried away, don't I?" He laughed.

It was an infectious laugh and Jack laughed with him. It had been a long time since Jack had found a male he could be so comfortable with.

"I hope Monday gave you an extra pair of PJ's!" Hiro had Jack in a small swivel-chair now and was adjusting the helmet on him. "I've got Turbo online but he seems to be busy. Usually, he can't wait to share the current results of the program when you access him. Okay, right eye first. Is the pattern in focus?" Hiro was slowly turning something in the goggles, moving it out.

"Yeah, no, too far!" Jack was focusing on a multicolored grid of dotted lines, his left eye scrunched shut.

"Here, you do it." Hiro led Hack's hand up to the turret.

"Okay! Yeah, perfect."

They did the left eye.

"Can you see any light coming in from the sides now?"

"No, but the grid looks neat! 3-D! I could almost climb around in there!"

"Jack, you'll be wanting to climb **out** in a minute. I'll leave the grid on until Turbo starts sending, no, wait, I'll put on this screen saver Turbo and Manny made. You'll love it. Hang on! Ready?"

Jack nodded and leaned back in the chair. The grid disappeared and his vision went dark for a moment, then, gradually, a scene appeared, brightening slowly until it resembled daylight. Some racetrack somewhere. A dirt track with bleachers, and over the pits, a huge, Marlboro billboard. At the pits, a bright, gleaming-red, classic Chrysler roared to life. Jack jumped at the sound. He had not realized that the helmet contained speakers; it had been silent when they were focusing the lenses on the test grid.

"It's a fifty-five!"

"Fifty-six," Hiro corrected, yelling so that Jack could hear him. Hiro was at his main keyboard, a row of four boards actually, stacked one above the other like a pipe-organ console.

"Holy shit!"

"Hang in there, Jack!"

Jack's chair suddenly broke loose and skidded back a foot as he pressed backward involuntarily. The Chrysler was growing in size, the shiny grille facing him and grinning, and speaking like Jessica the toon, her voice dripping seduction. "Do you love me?" she purred.

"Answer her!" Hiro yelled, but Jack didn't hear him.

The front tires began to drip vampire-red nails, clawing at the ground in front of them. The grille was growing long, chromium eye-teeth. A wonderfully feminine laugh, low and promising. Then: "Jack, I'm a transvestite. Remember, Jack? You said to that reporter you thought we look better than real girls? Do you remember? Do you want me, Jack?"

Apparently Jack didn't answer fast enough. The Chrysler's throttle blipped and the engine roared, drowning out Jessica's voice. With another blast, the front end of the gleaming vehicle reared up into the air in a wheelie, displaying, between the twin-pipes arching over the rear axle, a hairy set of balls so heavy they were dragging on the ground. The Chrysler dropped back down and bounced, then turned and peeled forward, barely missing Jack and leaving twin tracks of spewed gravel and dirt, and an irregular, wide furrow down the middle from the dragging scrotum. Jack's chair skidded out from underneath him and he fell.

Hiro helped him pull off the helmet as Jack sat there. "Pretty realistic, huh? **Huh?!**"

They both laughed and Jack got to his feet and retrieved the chair, which had also fallen. Hiro inspected the helmet. "It's okay. You shouldn't have to readjust the focus again. The voice part, well, we have the voice pretty much finalized, but what she says turns out to be all wrong. We've found out, just recently, the human male..."

Jack shook his head. He was in a semi state of shock. Yeah, pretty realistic! He tried to listen as best he could to Hiro's enthusiastic explanation of their work.

"...just recently, that when you have the correct image of what we're programmed to go after, sex-wise, if you provide the most stimulating message to go along with the visual, the human male will drop everything, even survival! He'll kill for it without regard to his own safety, well, he'll give himself the best odds he can — in that moment — but he'll risk everything, even his life. Like when men give in to a good-looking hooker even though they know she's probably infected with AIDS. Anyway, we found the correct message by accident, well, there may be an even better one we don't know about. Listen!"

Hiro was handing Jack a simple headset. "Put these earphones on and close your eyes. Remember now, keep them closed!"

Jack did as he was told while Hiro rushed back to the keyboard.

"Jack." It was Jessica's voice again. Whispering. "Shhhhh! Jack! Jack! Do you have a knife? Oh, great, Jack." She sounded so real, so close, so...wonderful! Jack forgot all about the transvestite stuff. This was a real girl!

"Get down, quick Jack, before he sees you!" she was whispering, like from a distance. "Yeah, like that. I'm behind the wall. Crawl on over so he won't see you. Yeah. Oh, Jack, you're wonderful! Just a little farther. I'm tied to a big block of concrete back here, Jack, with an iron ring in it. I'm cold, Jack. Bring something for me to cover up in, too, okay? Please hurry. Get me away from him, Jack. Please?"

The headset went silent and Jack removed it and opened his eyes. He was sweating, and he had a hard on.

Hiro was grinning right in his face, and laughing. "Is that great or what?! Want to rescue her? Fuck her first, though, right? Spread her over that block of cold concrete? Huh? **Huh?!**"

CHAPTER 30
Sandy & The Fisherman

Sandy and Bill the bill-fisherman did lose sight of Miss Chernobyl's stern light, but only for a few minutes. Then, as more lights appeared ahead of them in the distance, Bill picked out the correct one.

"It's the flickery one because they're running broadside to the sea."

Sandy peered at the tachometers, one of which was darkened from a burned-out bulb. "Twenty-three hundred? That's it?"

"Diesels, lady."

"Name's Sandy!"

"Diesels run slower, Sandy, but they turn larger props."

"Oh! Okay!" Sandy momentarily forgot what they were doing and why they were here. They were running broadside to the sea, also. Rolling, even, four footers — the crests of the waves luminescent in the full moonlight. Sandy loved the sound of the diesels running in synch, the sound of them playing harmonics under the cockpit sole, harmonics you could feel through your bare feet. It did seem like they were keeping up, although just barely. Every few seconds or so, Miss Chernobyl's stern light would wink completely out of view, then return. Well, Sandy thought, if we do lose sight, we could call the police with the VHF.

"How many miles away are they?" Sandy was yelling and trying to sound sweet and innocent at the same time.

"Less than a mile? Their boat doesn't have enough freeboard to keep it visible behind these rollers!"

Sandy, standing on his side at the helm, allowed his arm to brush against hers as he corrected the wheel. "Wish you had a flying bridge!" she said.

"Yeah, buddy! Some day! The VHF is out, too."

Sandy felt his free arm slide around her waist, and tighten when Wet Dream broached a deep trough. "What happened?" she said, shifting her feet for balance. She allowed his arm to remain.

"We're crossing the wake of a larger boat out there somewhere."

Sandy intended to have him where he'd do anything she wanted him to do, soon, and what better way to get started? "Oh! You sound like you know what your doing!"

"Yeah."

"You ever date my sister?"

"Well. I don't know if you could call it dating. We went out in Wet Dream here a couple times."

"You ever sleep with her?"

"Noooo. Now I'm glad! Now that I've met you!"

"Awwww."

Sandy smiled to herself. Not at the easy conquest but at her choice of words.

"You're even prettier than she is!"

"Oh, no, you're just saying that."

"No, I mean it. Really!"

"Ohhhh, Bill, get real!"

"No, really!"

And so on.

"They're turning! Toward shore!" Sandy was excited. For the whole trip she wasn't sure if they were going to lose them or be able to keep up. Now, just for a second, she thought she had seen a flicker of green light beside the glimmering of Miss Chernobyl's stern lamp.

"You sure?" Bill was leaning forward, looking under the windshield he had cranked open so they could see better.

"I saw green! There it is again! They're heading in!"

"Your eyes are better than mine!"

A lot of my stuff is better than yours. "I'm younger than you are. Night vision!"

"Yeah, but..."

"But nothing!" Sandy laughed and gave the man's ribs a pat. Her own arm had been around his waist for the past fifteen minutes. So far he hadn't become any bolder and Sandy wondered if he was thinking she was being sweet to him so she could get out of paying. "Don't worry about how long this takes now, Bill. I can pay!"

"Okay, baby! Yeah! I see the bow light now!" Bill changed course to an angle which would bring them closer to shore, then reverted back to their original heading. "There's shoals out here and I haven't looked at the chart. Most of my regulars want to head straight out. If we're lucky we'll be able to follow their wake in with this moon. The sea will glow brighter where they cross the shallows."

"Okay but don't let them see us."

"No problem!"

Sandy suddenly drew herself away from the man.

"What's the matter?"

"My purse! I forgot it! Where'd I put it! It's gone!"

"Hey, Sandy! I wouldn't steal your money. It's right here under the binnacle where you put it."

Sandy bent over to look. "Oh! Yes! How stupid of

257

me."

"I wouldn't steal your money, baby."

"It's not the money. My pistol is in there."

The smile disappeared from Bill's stubbly face. He had forgotten why they were here.

CHAPTER 31
Nub-man & Turbo

Klaus was becoming impatient, angry. "Turbo, just send Hiro what he wants! You can play with these two later. When I go for your fucking supplies. **After** you print the market file!"

Turbo was standing in front of Jody, adjusting something on the helmet he had pulled over the boy's head. Jody was in considerable pain now, hanging from the wall from his nub hand, his body twisted and only his right foot able to reach the floor. The pain was worse since his pants had been jerked down with such force, the material bunched and holding his knees together. He wanted to wait for a better moment before telling this Turbo jerk that Klaus had told Hector he was going to kill him. Jody tried to hold his tongue.

Norma was more depressed than physically uncomfortable. And every time she would glance over at Jody she had to look away again. "Turbo, do you know how to shoot?"

"Well, yes, I do. Manny used to make me practice in the old days. 'No sense just letting the **jerks** have guns,' he would say."

Klaus came back from Turbo's desk and slapped her. "Bitch, shut up!"

"Mister Turbo. Do you have a gun here?"

"Well, yes, it's right over there in my..."

...desk, Norma thought. Her head slammed back into the wall, Klaus's hand over her mouth.

"Kill you now! That all right with you, Turbo?"

259

"No, it's not. Well, just so long as she's still warm when I have time for her."

"One more word," Klaus said. He mashed the palm of his hand harder against her mouth, skewing her lips away from her teeth. Then he pulled away.

"There, little Thalidomide man," Turbo said. "Do you see any light around the edges of the goggles?"

"No."

"Okay, now close your left eye. I'm going to rotate the lens on the right and you tell me when it's the sharpest."

"When what's the sharpest?"

"Oh, I forgot to plug them in. Wait here."

Klaus was back at Turbo's desk checking the monitor. "Turbo, you dumb-ass! Hiro wants to know if anything's wrong! Get over here!"

"Klaus. Hiro knows I'm always busy. You want him to know you're here? There. Do you see a pattern now? Do you see the grid? What's your name?"

"Jody."

"What color, Jody?"

"All different colors."

"3-D?"

"No. It looks flat. I still have my other eye closed."

"Good. You follow instructions well, Jody. Now. Is it getting sharper?"

"Please, Turbo. I could go through the file while you're doing this."

"Well, since you said please."

Norma thought: *And you're dead after he gets the file.* She was trying to think whether she was better off with Turbo dead or alive.

Klaus narrowed his eyes. "Please with sugar!" ("Pleese mit tzooker!")

But Turbo did not leave Jody until both sides of the goggles had been adjusted. Standing over the keyboard now, he explained to Klaus again that he was going to transmit the same video to Hiro that he was sending to "our little Thalidomide man."

"How long?"

"Oh, for as long as they can stand it." Turbo laughed for the first time. "A few minutes. Tell him there's not supposed to be any sound with this. He might think something isn't working. Tell him, Klaus, please."

Klaus shook his head. "There's no sound, little dude."

"Louder, Klaus! He has a helmet on!"

"There's no sound!"

Jody nodded his head. Norma turned and looked at him. He looked even more pathetic hanging there with the helmet strapped to his head, and his lips were tight. Suddenly, she saw his mouth relax as he began to smile. A big smile. His body was becoming tense and Norma looked past his growing erection and down to his feet. Both feet were off the ground now, the toes curling. Shit, his body was trying to turn. Hanging from the single cuff, Jody was trying to twist toward her. Norma knew that he couldn't see where she was but he remembered, of course, and was somehow trying to reach her, impossible with what little leverage he had from the short arm shackled against the wall. Drool began to run down the corners of his mouth and Norma finally had to look away again.

Just as she turned her head, with Turbo and Klaus right beside her now and watching him, she felt the hot gobs of Jody's jism splatter her legs.

CHAPTER 32
The Shopping List

Hiro kept on chattering as he tried to prod Turbo to send the latest results from the Fort Walton Beach computer. He typed:

The primordial female. The envelope please!

"Turbo's got a sense of humor. Maybe that will wake him up. I used to work with him but he got too screwy for me and I couldn't ever concentrate. Sometimes it gets hectic here."

Jack was tapping his feet, the helmet in his lap. He picked up the earphones and wanted to interrupt Hiro, get him to play back Jessica's audio.

"Once I get the embryos to crank, for instance, all hell breaks loose. That's one of our two most critical periods. The mothers have to be implanted — all of them — within three days or the embryos die."

"Mothers?"

"The sheep. The second critical period is when the clones are foaled. The ewes will drop them all over the fields. Don't need for the drug spotter-planes to see that! I keep on telling Manny: We can put them in a barn when they come to term, at least for the birthing, but I guess he'd rather chase around after Monday and me out there in the pasture with his videocam. Photographing those ratty-looking sheep licking the gorp off their hairless little human foals. Ooops!" Hiro laughed. "Did I say **human?**"

"I'm horny," Jack said. "I can't wait."

"Well, Manny said you could check out the 3's,

didn't he?"

"Yeah, but later. Business before pleasure."

"Well, we have a guest room down at the end here. But then we'd have to sneak them through the kitchen upstairs."

"That's okay."

"I can do it!"

Jack's hopes perked up. "How do you pick which ones, I mean, when you go to their barracks."

"Easy. The hungriest ones. They get fed after they do a trick."

"Oh, come on!"

"No, no, they have their regular meals, but it's never enough. But when they get out to do a trick, they get as much food as they want. After. It's a special treat for them. They let you know who's turn is next!"

"Yeah? And they don't bitch about it?"

"Oh, Jack, they're so dumb! They don't know anything else! They're dumb **and** pacific. They won't fight."

"Oh? Yeah." Jack could see himself with them now. Three of them. Piled on top of him. He sucked in a deep breath. "You say there's a guest room down here? Manny wouldn't know?"

"Yeah! No! Well, there's always the chance that he might pop up down here in the middle of the night. But not usually. He wouldn't say much, anyway. There's somebody coming now."

"Huh? Somebody coming?"

"Yup. See the box on the upper right of the screen? The number 3 in it? Blinking? Okay, it's been number 2, steady, since you and I came down here. Sensors on the stairway down and in the hall. All the computers in the house can monitor the occupancy of any of the areas. I forgot. If we brought the clones down here, they would read out. But I could override the system with a couple of keystrokes."

The squirming pile of young, blond clones on top of Jack's imagination faded from his movie screen.

Jackson's voice: "What's up, whiteys?"

"Plural?" Hiro said. "You're including me in that?"

Jack blinked. Desirey Jackson was standing in the doorway in white shorts and a bright-red, half-unbuttoned blouse. Her tight, black hair drawn to one side blooming out in a puff over an ear with a matching, red ribbon. High-top Nikes with fat, matching-red socks. Her face all made up. She looked ready to kill.

A whooof of Red Door perfume closed in around Jack's head.

"Woe!"

"Eat your heart out, Jack. Hiro, anybody find out where Klaus and Hector and them are hiding out? Abu?"

"They're probably in Brazil by now. I'm trying to get Turbowski on line."

"Turbo."

"He's probably pissed that Klaus isn't around to bring him his stuff."

Jackson pulled up a castored swivel-chair and plunked into it, hooking her Nikes on the foot rest, and hugging her knees. Arms dangling gold bracelets. Her scent worming into Jack's brain. The chair as close to him as possible, Jack thought. Bitch! God. *Fuck her in a heart beat!*

"Turbo doesn't know Klaus is on the shit list," Jackson said. She looked at Jack and drew eye contact. She shrugged her shoulders. "I don't think he does, anyway."

"Yeah, well, something's wrong over there. I wanted him to send the latest results on Miss Primeval."

"Oh, that's such bullshit. When are you guys going

to grow up."

"It's bullshit to you because women aren't wired the same way."

"That's bullshit, too. Besides, if genes can be traced back through women but not men..."

"That's irrelevant. A different subject, anyway, Desirey." Hiro pronounced her name: Dee sire EEEE, and made no attempt to hide his displeasure with her. "It's over your head. You should stick to keeping Eastland happy."

"Yeah? You know where he is?"

"No."

"Jack?"

Jack shrugged his shoulders. *Fuck you in a heart BEAT!*

"So what's going on over in Fort Walton?"

"Well, he must be okay. He sent in his shopping list a couple hours ago."

"Yeah? Great! I'll do it."

"In the middle of the night?"

"There's a big store open in San Destin. Twenty-four hours."

Jack saw the number in the box in the upper-right corner of the monitor begin to blink the number 4.

"You haven't seen the list."

"So print it out for me."

"Somebody's coming," Jack said.

Hiro punched in a few keystrokes and Turbo's message shrank on the screen and moved to the left. On the right, in a large dialog box, was Turbo's shopping list.

TURBO'S SHOPPING LIST

eggs
15a fuses, time delay
bacon
Windex
Mazola
TV Satellite Guide
cashews
Bengal roach spray
Grainola bread ("Arnold" brand)
Tide (liquid)
weenies (beef)
Playtex Living Gloves
(10 cans) Sweet Sue chck & dmplngs
(5 packs) Sams Choice p-butt cups

Hiro said: "No Twinkies. It must be the peanut butter cups fried his brain."

"I don't know about those fuses," Jackson said, leaning forward to see the monitor while Jack looked into her blouse. And you got to go to Wal-Mart to get Sam's Choice."

In a heart beat! "They have that kind at a grocery store," Jack said. "I mean, the fuses."

"Well, you can come along then!"

"Yeah," Hiro said. "Go with her, Jack. You haven't met Turbo yet."

"Yeah, well." *What about the clones, Hiro, Christ!*

Hiro laughed. "Tell him you want a shot at the goggles!"

For the first time, Jack did not laugh with him.

"The Goggles from **Hell!**" Manny said. He was standing in the doorway in pajama pants identical to Jack's, only his didn't need to be rolled up. "Yeah, Jack! Go **with** her! In your **PJ's! Here!** Take this **money!** Put it in your **pocket!** Huh? **Huh?!**" Mannlicher opened a fist and shoved a roll of bills toward Jack. "Keep the **change!**" he yelled, grinning. When Jack did not jump up for it, Mannlicher leaned forward over Jackson, his arm stretched out with the bills.

Jack snatched at the roll and looked. Hundreds. Maybe ten of them. He looked back at Mannlicher, whose face was suddenly buried in Desirey Jackson's shirt. "Woof woof woof woof" his muffled mouth was saying. "Woof **woof!**" He pulled his red head out of there and grinned at Jack. "Remember what I told you **before?** What I want you to **do?**"

"Yeah."

"Jack. You get any of **this** yet?" Mannlicher stuck his face back into Jackson's shirt. Her fingers — her long, red, pointed nails — dug into the man's wooly-red mop but with no effort to shove his head away.

"Woof woof **woof!**"

"You need to **get** you some of this, Jack! **Soon!**" He pulled his head out. His eyes were ablaze, and the grin was gone. "You **hear** me? Huh? **Huh?!** You get my **drift?**"

In his slippers and pajamas, Jack followed Desirey's long legs out to the big '79 Lincoln. Walking around the back to the passenger side, the roll of bills in his hand, he spotted Jody's homing device stuck to the rear bumper. So obvious in the bright moonlight.

She hasn't noticed this?

Probably too dumb.

Wish I had my P-38.

"How do you carry a gun dressed like that?"

"Whitebread, don' never think I ain't carryin'. No matter how I be dress'."

"Yas'm."

Jack opened the door on his side and watched her adjust her long, dark legs in the glow from the courtesy lights. And it was his job to snuff her. Could he do it? Would he do it? Jack's stomach churned with pain. Pain because he knew he was close to doing it. This wasn't just going to be Vietnam, or self-defense. This would be pure murder, for the first time in his life. It would mean going over the line. For money.

For pussy.

After radioing her way through the main gate, Jackson stomped the throttle and the acceleration shoved Jack back into his seat. He wondered how Jody's homing device could stay on, but the magnet was strong. He had provided that part of it for Jody himself. Jody. He'd be able to find the car if anything went wrong. How far was this Fort Walton lab? Well, Jody would be able to get started with an approximate fix from the top of their antenna mast on the hill at home. Would he think to do that? Yes. Jody was smart, and Jack was glad, once again, that he and Jasmine had adopted him.

But he did have to wonder about himself. The pajamas. Too timid to argue and to take the time to change clothes, but not too timid to snuff out a few citizens? His father's girlfriend? And here he was, horny for her!

I'm crazy.

I should be locked up.

It's no wonder that Dad didn't hire me sooner.

At least the heater in this old car works.

"Andrew to Whitebread!"

Jack spotted, down at his feet, the black, cloth, L.L. Bean cassette case he had bought his father several years before, for Christmas. As usual, he had bought him something that Jack at the time thought was great but that the old man would probably never use. Jack bent over, down and sideways, to reach for it.

"You think you can get in this female by startin' at the toes?"

"Ha! Wasn't even thinking about you!" Jack waved the long, slender case under her nose.

"Oh! Your daddy's tapes. Sheeeit."

"How do I turn on the interior light?"

Jackson flipped a switch. "Not for long. I hate drivin' with the light on. Nothin' in there but that dwem stuff. I don' never play 'em."

"Dwem?"

"Dead, white, European, an' male!"

"Oh, yeah, right. Like the inventors of cassettes. Ste-

269

reo. Electricity." *Gotchya!* Jack unzipped the case and peered at the selection. Beethoven's Fifth. Mozart's Requiem. Bach, Bach, Bach. The popular stuff, but still.

Daddy never once mentioned music. Not once.

It's where I got it!

From him!

Jack remembered Norma's reaction to his shoving in the Wagner opera tape on the fateful trip in Miss Chernobyl.

"Let's play the Mozart, okay?" He pried open the plastic case and saw the tape had not been rewound all the way.

"Get real, Whitebread. Any **real** sounds in there? No? Forget it."

"Yeah. Right."

Jack carefully put the cassette back and zipped the case.

I have a surprise for you, Dad!

Yeah, sure, after you snuff his girlfriend?

The interior light snapped out and Jackson's window whirred down so she could smoke a cigarette.

"Kind of you."

"Yeah. Hey, they even have clothes at this store if you want to change. Beach stuff, but better than pajamas."

"So I go in there with my PJ's? Change there?"

"Sure! Fuck 'em! I'll go in with you."

She's really not so bad, Jack.

"Okay! Thanks!"

"No pockets, huh? To put your money in?"

"No. I thought the top would have one but it doesn't."

"We can put your money in my purse."

"Okay. Well...."

"I'll give it right back to you when you get an outfit with pockets. So you can pay, you know, at the register."

"Oh, yeah, well, that wouldn't bother me. The woman paying. I mean, my ego. But thanks."

I'll have eight, nine-hundred left.

"You used to the lady paying, huh?

"The **chick** paying."

Jackson laughed. "Right!"

You can't do it, Jack.

Not this one.

It would be wrong.

And such a waste.

Jack's body shook involuntarily with a brief convulsion. He had just pictured himself standing over her body after shooting her. He saw himself drop to his knees, his hands sliding into her...

His body shook again and Jack struck his forehead with the palm of his hand, trying to knock in some sense.

"You okay, Whitebread?"

"Yeah. Yeah. Just had a bad memory."

"Vietnam?"

"Yeah."

"You don't look old enough to be a Vietnam vet."

"I lied about my age. I came in at the end when we were killing 'em wholesale."

You're a sick motherfucker, Jack.

And 'Nam had nothing to do with it.

Jackson slowed down the car. "Hey, we all gotta do what we gotta to do, right?"

"Right. You're right!"

"You okay now?"

"Okay!"

They were crossing the bridge over Cinco Bayou,

Jackson's window still down. There was the humid, funky smell of the bay, and the lights on the other side. Glittery, late-night traffic. Jackson turned left onto Yacht Club Drive.

Waste or not, there's the clones. Three of them.
Should've brought my gun.

CHAPTER 33
Sandy's Landing

It took Sandy and Bill, captain of Wet Dream out of Panama City Beach, Florida, over an hour to locate Miss Chernobyl in a man-made cove on Cinco Bayou. By now Bill was totally fascinated by his beautiful, self-confident charter and was taking orders like a good mate. When they had begun searching the private piers and marina slips, Sandy insisted they run with their lights to avoid suspicion. Now, she was telling him to turn them off.

"No, no, don't head in! Back in, silly!"

"Aye aye!"

"No, no, don't get those ropes ready. We won't be needing them."

"Lines."

"Ropes, lines, whatever. Just get close enough to the end here to drop me off. Then hand me my shoes and ease on out. Anchor off within sight, though, okay? Like maybe near this sailboat we're going around?"

Bill was running in on the starboard engine, slow, and as soon as he passed the anchored schooner near the pier where they had spotted Jack's boat, he kicked the port engine into reverse. Wet Dream shuddered for a moment and began to pivot neatly on her stern. As soon as she turned 180 degrees he shifted the starboard engine into neutral and they began to churn slowly backwards. The backwash from the huge prop swirled alongside, the froth glowing from the moon almost directly overhead. Bill was moving Wet Dream slowly toward the side of the pier Miss Chernobyl was docked on, noting that the depth must have been sufficient for the Bertram, her bow visible inside the silent boathouse. When he figured they had sufficient momentum, he put the port engine into neutral and they coasted the last twenty-five feet.

Sandy was poised at the stern now and Bill was hesitant to leave the controls to hand her the shoes. Wet Dream was heavy enough to give the fragile-looking pier a good jolt if he wasn't careful. But he had judged everything correctly and Wet Dream was nearly dead in the water when Sandy jumped the last two feet.

"Shoes!"

"Shhhhh!" Bill touched a finger to his lips. He noted she already had her purse slung over a polka-dot shoulder. He stepped to the stern and bent over for the fancy platform clogs.

"Thanks. Wait for me. Out there!" Sandy pointed at the schooner they had passed at anchor on the way in.

Bill nodded and blew her a kiss. He wondered how she would let him know when she was ready, like, would he have to stay on watch all night? He was about to open his mouth when Sandy laughed.

"You look so nervous! I'll fire a shot or something!"

"Oh, god! Well. You sure you'll be okay?"

"Why? Because I'm a chick?"

"Yeah!"

"Your problem, Bill. So, go! Go!"

Sandy already had one shoe on and was slipping into the other. She felt the pier shake as he shifted one of the engines into forward and the prop-wash shoved against the pilings.

He turned and waved and she waved back.

Men are such wimps.

She left her clogs on when she dropped down into

Miss Chernobyl for a look. Nobody there to tell her to take her shoes off, and that Arnold Schwarzenegger dude and his little, dark-looking buddy had theirs on!

On her hands and knees in the small, cuddy cabin, Sandy hoped the boat was clean because she was dragging the skirt of her dress around. When she got to the big sack and loosened the draw-string, it took all of her strength to pull it open. But the effort was worth it and a big smile spread across her face. She had been hoping it wasn't her sister Norma in there and it sure wasn't. Just some dead, smelly, ugly, foreign-looking character. Yeeech!

CHAPTER 34
Objects of Desire

Jody's body was twisted sideways toward Norma, pretzeled in a rigid contortion. His knees were drawn up as he hung from his nub hand, and his helmeted head was straining to reach her. But that's only what it looked like to the others. Inside the helmet, a three-dimensional image of either of two, alternating, ideal female sexual partners was turning, showing all sides of herself to him, and every six seconds she morphed into the alternative, ethnic selection. In turns kneeling, beckoning to him on all fours, jumping up and running, strolling back to him and smiling. Each time the alternative reappeared she was slightly different and recombinated, the computer-generated adjustments too slight for Jody to notice. It was this image in the helmet Jody was trying to reach, not Norma, whom he had forgotten all about. And when Turbo went back to the keyboard and switched off the image, Jody's body continued to work against the single hand-cuff pinning him to the wall. In the darkness of the helmet he knew that the *ne plus ultra* female was still there, still to be caught and won although he could no longer see her.

Only when Turbo jerked off the helmet and Jody was temporarily blinded by the bright lights of the lab, did he realize that he had nearly killed himself trying to reach her, and his neck was a mass of cramped muscle.

Tears ran down Norma's eyes as she forced herself to look at him once more, his crippled body twitching and his chest heaving for air.

"You even forgot to breathe there for a minute or two, little Thalidomide man."

"Nub... Nub-man. Sir."

"Sir? Mmm-hmmm. Tell me, did anything about her look familiar? Anything?"

"Yes!" Jody had to speak between lungfuls of air. "Yes sir."

"Did she look familiar, like, somebody in real life?"

"No!"

"But you said she looked familiar."

"Yes, but. I can't... I can't explain."

"If I let you down from there, will you behave?"

"Yes. Yes sir. Can I — may I — see her — again? I'll be good."

Norma looked at Klaus, whose anger was so apparent now his face was a livid red and the veins in his neck were bulging. His right hand clenched into a fist, relaxed, then clenched into a fist again. Norma felt that Klaus could probably kill somebody with one blow if he wanted to.

"Turbo, Hiro's still waiting. You forgot to send the fucking movie through the modem. You're fucking up bad, Turbo. Hector's going to be pissed. He's still downstairs waiting. Your code-name should be Terminal, not Turbo. Maybe you can give me one good reason why I don't snuff your red-headed ass."

"No, don't!" Jody yelled.

"See? He wants more! And you need your file, Klaus. We all need each other for something, don't we?"

"Yeah, and you need me to go to the store for you."

"Okay, okay, I'll get you your file and you go to the store. You go to the store first."

"Other way around, Turbo."

"Okay, then get my little man here down from the

wall for me. Let him pull his pants back up."

Klaus hesitated before he realized that he had nothing to loose. He fished in a pocket for the hand-cuff key.

"Me, too?" Norma said. "I'll be good!"

"No, no," Turbo said. "I need you for when I take my turn at the goggles. Little man — Nub-man — I'll need you to unplug the helmet when I holler, no, when you see me cum. And then you can have a turn, in this nice lady here, with or without the helmet — your choice. But then we have to let the computer go back to work. You understand? So it can go back to refining. Refining, refining, refining."

Turbo repeated himself while Jody looked at him with glistening eyes, grinning and nodding. The cuff popped open and Jody slid down to his feet between Klaus and the wall.

"Now to undress the lady here," Turbo said.

"The file!" Klaus hollered.

"Okay. Right now! Little man, would you undress her for me, please? I have to get this man his precious addresses and phone numbers."

"No, not again!" Norma looked past Jody's shoulders and watched Klaus follow Turbo down the aisle to the keyboard. "Jody, no, please."

"He said I could cum in you." Jody lowered his voice to a whisper. "I can pick the locks in your handcuffs." Louder: "He said I could cum in you with the helmet on."

"No, please!" And in a whisper: "I think there's a gun in the desk drawer."

"Yeah."

Jody looked around quickly to see what he could use for a pick. "I could come in you without the helmet, you're so beautiful!" Then, with enthusiasm he did not need to fake, Jody unbuttoned her shorts and pulled them down around her feet. Then his longer arm went for the tube top, pulling it slowly downward and watching her breasts pop out of it under her up-stretched arms. He hadn't even taken a second to examine her shaved pussy because in his adolescent dreams he had always dwelled on real, live tits in his hands and that's what he needed most now.

Norma closed her eyes and turned her head. It was easy to tell which hand had which one. The nub-hand was so much smaller.

And so greedy.

CHAPTER 35
Ready or Not

After discovering Abu's body, Sandy poked her head back out of the cuddy cabin, took a good look around, and slipped her clogs off once again. No sense making noise with them now! As for the body, she didn't know who it was and she didn't really care. It wasn't her sister.

The Arnold guy and the Latino were obviously criminals and Norma was going to need her. Need her bad. For the first time, Sandy wished it were not a full-moon night. She looked up. Clouds, but no where near the moon, which was shining clear in a big, wide open patch of sky. Out in the bayou, Wet Dream bobbed gently, her anchor-light making a semi-circled arc. The half circles of light seemed to linger through each swing and Sandy remembered she hadn't eaten for a long time, and hadn't had much sleep lately, either. When she first arrived at Norma's condo she figured she'd eat whatever Norma had available, have a little chat, and crash on the couch. Now there was all this!

A creep of fear crawled into Sandy's chest. One more look at Wet Dream out there — no sight of Bill — was he napping on a bunk or something? — and Sandy was tip-toeing down the pier to the boat house. She hadn't seen the gravel path around it yet and figured maybe there was a door in the back of the building behind the big boat tied up inside. Just as she got to the catwalk, however, she spotted the path, but not without a glance at the Bertram's dark windshield.

"Ohhhh!" Sandy clapped a hand to her mouth, her

heart pounding, and she lost her balance and almost fell into the water as she veered to the side of the little building. One of the clogs slipped out of her left hand and she stooped and caught it just in time, still, she had to whip her right hand out of her purse to catch her balance.

Whew! That was close!

Those faces in the windshield! Boy!

I need to stop skipping meals!

It'll be pink elephants next!

Sandy caught her breath, remembering the Pink Elephant bar on US-1 between Fort Lauderdale and Miami. One night a friend had brought her in the back door from the parking lot, and later, when she was drunk and he got fresh, she had exited out the front alone and saw, for the first time, the pink, concrete elephant standing there by the highway, it's glass eye glowing at her...

Snap out of it — this is real!

Those guys killed somebody and they probably have Norma!

Wake up!

The gravel hurt her bare feet and she edged her way just off the path onto the dewy-wet grass, heading toward the screened-in back porch. At the door she stopped and listened for a minute. No sounds, no TV. Everybody asleep? Some lights on inside.

She tried the screen-door and eased it open, cringing as the rusty spring twanged. Her heart still pounding, she waited another minute before closing it behind her and placing her shoes out of sight behind the mop leaning against the wall. She tried to fit her purse down into the basket of the bicycle next to the washing machine, okay, so part of the purse stuck out but nobody will notice it in the dark, right? The tiny Beretta was in her hand and that's what was going to count.

Opening onto the porch, next to the door to the house, was a wide-open, curtained window. Sandy peered in. A kitchen with a dim light glowing under the range canopy. And on the other side of the kitchen an open doorway. A man, sitting in an armchair, was writing into what looked like, from the distance, a notebook. His profile was peculiar but he had a hooked, Mediterranean nose and dark hair. It was the Latino-looking dude who had been at the wheel of Miss Chernobyl!

Sandy took a practice aim at him with the tiny Beretta, crouching, resting her forearms on the window sill. Twenty-five feet? Sandy was sure she could nail him with a single head-shot at that distance if she kept her arms steady. All the practice with the gun, hundreds of rounds over time, gave her that confidence. But what if there's an explanation? What if he's not a crook? What if Norma's not here, this is the man's legitimate house, and she kills him? Even if he has a gun and pulls it on her, he would be in the right! Self-defense!

Sandy held her position for several minutes until her legs became uncomfortable, then slowly stood up straight and tried the back door. She'd start a little dialogue first.

Locked! Sandy suddenly realized she had to pee. Her mother used to say: "Don't always be waiting till the last minute before telling me!"

I heard you, Mom.

But she hesitated to take the time to go back outside and make more noise with that twangy screen-door spring. Especially with the window open. She spotted a large, clay pot in the corner near the mop. Half full of dirt. Sandy did not take long to think about it before carefully sliding the pot away from the wall. In a second she had her panties down and was squatting over it, hoping the little hole in the bottom of the pot, if it had one, was thoroughly packed shut. And hoping the loose, dry dirt would not splatter her ass with the first burst. Fighting the stream back, Sandy tried to ease the initial flow out, and nearly screamed as she struggled to keep her balance when the back door of the house opened.

The man was lit dimly by the light from the stove as he hesitated in the open doorway. Hovering over the clay pot and with her arms still resting on her thighs for balance, Sandy bent her wrist upward, slowly bringing up the muzzle of the Beretta to where she thought the point of aim should be for a shot like this: the middle of him.

With a quick glance to the side, the man laid his notebook down on top of the washing machine. A huge, black revolver dangled from his right hand, pointing down, as he headed out the screen-door to the boat-house.

twang - BAM!

Sandy let her stream rip and felt the dirt splatter.

Norma's gun!

That's it!

Sandy jerked up the panties over her gritty, wet ass, and snicked the safety off on the Beretta. There was no doubt in her mind the weapon the guy was carrying was her sister's. Their father had given them identical pistols one Easter morning. Long barrels and black-rubber Pachmayr grips. He said to them: "Better than an Easter hat. I always wanted a lady that looked good in a big hat. Your mother would never wear one. If I were a rapist, I'd do it on Easter Sunday. Pick me out the sweetest, most innocent hypocrite bitch I could find, you know, cruise the church parking lots for one. Anyway, if you guys ever get in that position, one shot with one of these Rugers will kill him. And you won't have to testify against him in court. (Norma and Sandy had both looked at each other at that moment, both wondering for the first time if their own father was ever guilty of rape. He had said the whole thing with such unbridled enthusiasm).

Sure, there were other Ruger Blackhawk .41 magnums out there, but not many with the long, 6 1/2 inch barrel **and** Pachmayr grips. Sandy wished she had brought hers now, instead of the Beretta, whose primary virtue was that it fit easily in a purse.

Without thinking Sandy glanced at the notebook, stopped, and turned it toward the best light to see what the man had been scribbling. Two squiggly lines of Arabic on the top, or so it looked. Then two lines of something in Spanish with the word *Norma* clearly written in the middle of the sentence. The last lines were in English:

I love you, Norma, so pretty,
Beautiful, strawberry tart.

It was the Spanish, Arabic, English Rosetta Stone of contemporary lust.

Doubly convinced now, Sandy braced herself to shoot on sight — either one of those two assholes. Since she had only a .22 she would take just that extra split-second to aim carefully, then punch their brains with head-shots, through an eye or the nose if possible. She moved quickly on silent, bare feet through the kitchen and from room to room, the only sound the swishing of her taffeta, white-with-big-green-polka-dots dress. It wasn't until she was halfway up the stairs that Sandy realized she had forgotten to slide the flower pot full of pee back up against the wall on the porch.

Fuck it!

At the top of the stairs she stopped to think once more. This floor looked so different, almost like a school hallway or something. So brightly lit and so many doors!

Shoot to kill! Both of them.

CHAPTER 36
Redheads

Jody made no attempt to keep from rubbing all over Norma's naked body as he strained to reach her cuffs with the pick he had made out of a jumbo paperclip. The clip was a cheap one and kept on bending, and Jody also had to keep looking down the aisle to where Klaus and Turbo were punching up the file Klaus wanted for the printer. Within a minute, and not even close to getting the first cuff open, Jody heard the *whhht-whhht-whhht* of the printer down there churning out names and addresses.

"Give up, Jody. They'll see you!"

"Shhhh!"

Norma lowered her whisper. "Give up. Wait to look for the gun."

They saw Klaus turn his head in their direction and in a flash Jody was back to kneading Norma's tits. "Sorry," he whispered, "but..."

"It's okay, but..."

Jody mashed his face in between them. He knew that the thing to do now was head down the aisle, act interested in the computer to get near the desk. Ask Turbo for the helmet again. Anything. But he could not tear himself away from the first feel of a real woman he'd ever had.

"Jody!" Norma raised her voice. "Enough is enough!" She raised a leg and kneed Jody in the groin.

It was precisely at this moment that Sandy entered the lab. Jody was doubled over and squealing in pain, and all heads had turned toward him. Sandy, quick on her feet as always, was able to walk up right behind Klaus and with both of her hands stretched out, pull the hammer back with an audible click.

"Freeze!" She touched the barrel to the back of his head, just above the neck. Suddenly, all heads turned toward her.

Except Klaus.

"Nobody move!" With the hammer cocked, Sandy knew that just a touch on the trigger and Klaus was on his way to knowing it all.

"Sandy!" Norma yelled. "Jody, quick! Run and lock the door behind her! Get the other gun!"

Jody broke away and limped over to the next aisle so he wouldn't have to get too close to Klaus or Turbo.

"Sandy! How did you find me?! Turbo! Where's your gun?"

"What gun?"

"You said you have one. Where? Shoot him, Sandy!"

But Sandy was hesitant to move the muzzle of the Beretta away from the huge, muscular Klaus.

"In the desk," Turbo said. Top right drawer."

Jody, still in agony, worked his way behind Sandy and had almost reached the door when Hector arrived with Norma's big Ruger. Jody let out a yelp and ducked just in time. Sandy, arms straight out with the little Beretta, was already swinging around and before Hector could cock the .41 she sent two, tiny, forty-grain chunks of lead punching pop-pop through his face. Sandy did not have time to watch him crumple and she deliberately fell down backwards as she swung back to Klaus, his swinging arm missing her head as she sent three .22 slugs into his chest and abdomen.

"Ow, bitch! No!" Klaus pitched forward, clawing at

her. Sandy's next shot went into the ceiling but the last two put one in the neck just below the ear Norma had creased, and the other into his mouth at the left corner where it lodged near the base of his skull.

The Beretta's slide locked back on an empty magazine.

Klaus slammed down on top of her, his body shuddering and totally ineffective except for his sheer weight. Jody, who had just retrieved the .41 from Hector and cocked it, sighted the long barrel down between Klaus's shoulder blades.

"No!" Sandy yelled. "It'll go through him!"

Jody pulled his finger out of the trigger guard but did not de-cock the weapon. Turbo had begun to move, toward the desk, and Jody swung the Ruger that way. He watched the man slide a nickel-plated revolver out of the top-right desk drawer. Turbo, still bent over, looked up at Jody and raised his eyebrows. He had the revolver in his hand but Jody's was aimed right at him.

"Well?" Turbo slowly straightened up but without swinging his own weapon any closer toward the cripple. "You and I aren't enemies, are we?"

"Uhhhhh."

Norma screamed: "Kill him!"

"Shoot!" Sandy hollered.

Jody hesitated and Turbo suddenly raised the revolver. It was a single action, and Turbo's body doubled up as he slammed backwards into the desk before he could cock it — a 215 grain hunk of mushroomed lead lodged in his spine between his kidneys. Jody cocked the Ruger again and Turbo's head exploded. In the ringing silence after that second shot, Sandy and Jody could not hear the patter of Turbo's skull and brain fragments raining down on them from the ceiling. Jody stood with his mouth open and watched the spurts of arterial blood diminish as they pumped out of the missing top of Turbo's head.

For a moment, the survivors did not say a word.

On the blank monitor screen, a sentence began to appear, raveling out from left to right.

Give me a break, Turbo. Let the cartoon begin! – Hiro

"Hey!" Norma said. "Somebody get me down?"

Jody lowered the .41 and stepped over Sandy's blood-spattered face as she pulled herself out from underneath Klaus's body. Jody was proud. This was his day! He laid the Ruger on the desk and fished around in the front watch-pocket of Klaus's once immaculately-white jeans where Jody had seen him drop the handcuff key.

But when Jody had to reach up to Norma's wrists, he could not help brushing against her, and he could not help remembering his excesses just a few minutes earlier.

Fuck it. He released one cuff, then the other, and waited for Norma's rebuke.

"Oh, Jody, reach me those shorts, will you?"

"Gosh, I'm all full of blood!" Sandy said, on her feet now. "Hope nobody has AIDS! You're a star, Nub-man!"

Jody's heart swelled. He looked from one sister to the other, grinning. After all, just hours ago he had been in love with one of them, then the other — now both of them! Real love! He thought he could never love any female as much as he loved Sandy or Norma.

That is, until he discovered the lady in Turbo's computer.

The computer! Jody handed Norma her top and rushed back to the desk. The keyboard. Shit, he had no idea what type of program Turbo had set up here.

Quickly he glanced up and down the equipment for any stray bullet hole-damage. Then he shoved Turbo's swivel-chair back, accidentally smacking it into Sandy's legs. Without a word, he got down to punching at the blood-spattered keys.

Sandy and Norma embraced each other. "God, that was so close!"

"Shit, Sandy, how did you find me?"

"Bill, the bill fisherman, and a few other long stories! And if it weren't for Nub-man here we'd all be fresh-liver-in-a-Ziploc-bag by now!"

Jody smiled but did not look up from the keyboard. If he could just check back through the machine's automatically timed backups he could figure out how to get to the female in there.

"Could you guys hand me the helmet please?"

CHAPTER 37
Candy

Jody placed the helmet beside the keyboard so he could glance into it from time to time and see if he was getting the viewer to activate. As he tried to retrieve the program he had viewed while cuffed to the wall, Sandy and Norma were standing over the bloody bodies on the floor behind him. They were chatting away as if they hadn't seen each other for years, as if the bodies of Hector and Klaus and Turbo meant nothing. Well, they meant a lot to him. The Nub-man was a **real** man now; he had killed one of those assholes himself!

But I'm still a virgin.

"Your clothes!" Sandy said. "Yuk!" She was embracing her sister for the umpteenth time. "Norma Gene!"

"Klaus made me put them on. The big guy. Cast offs from some other bullshit of theirs. You followed us in a boat?! I thought I was good-as-dead when they brought Jody and me here. Nub-man."

"Oh, Norma, it's still anchored out there! The guy's probably asleep. Named his boat the Wet Dream! This whole Florida panhandle is an ocean of perverts!"

"**We** live here! **Jody** lives in the panhandle!"

"Perverts!" Sandy laughed. "Yeech, I can taste blood on my lips. Do any of these sinks work? This one's full of electronic shit." Sandy headed down another aisle. "Found it! Water! Soap! Paper towels!"

Jody, who was barely listening to their conversation, could taste blood on his own mouth but was too busy looking for the lady in the computer.

"Oh, great!" Norma followed her sister to the big, stainless steel lab-sink. Black, soapstone counters. "Reminds me of high-school. What I really need is a shower!"

"Big bathroom downstairs. I was looking for you there first. What **is** this place?"

"You wouldn't believe, Sandy. I think they make human clones! They sell them to rich Arabs! They were going to sell me! Or my eggs!"

Sandy had splashed water all over her face and was dabbing away with paper towels. "Don't see a mirror anywhere, do you? And that choker! Where on Earth..."

Norma had forgotten it for the first time, as heavy as it was. She reached up to touch it with both hands. Still there! Solid gold! Hers!

"I saw you on the news, sister! Kissing that head! Ha ha!"

"Well, I had an older sister to catch up to!"

"Not that much older! Oh, Norma!"

Something distracted Jody for a moment and he turned away from the keyboard to see the two women embrace again. He glanced at the door which had been closed, but was it locked? He looked down at the bodies. Turbo's revolver was lying near his feet, cocked.

I shot him just in time.

He looked at Klaus. Sandy had rolled him over when she got out from under. If anybody were to come in on them now, they wouldn't know Klaus had an automatic in his back pocket. Jody's gaze drifted back to the table he was working on and the .41 mag lying there. Four shots left.

He thought of covering the pistol with something so only he would know where it was but just then he saw something flicker on the monitor above the keyboard. He stared at it for a moment. Nothing seemed to have changed. The list of backup files he had brought up was still there, unmoving. The number in the upper right corner! It had been a **6** now it was an **8!** Jody tried to think.

Eight occupants?

"Sandy! Norma!"

Jody reached for the .41 just as a brown, slender arm pushed the door open. He cocked and raised the weapon, pointing it straight at the heart of Desirey Jackson. Straight at the vee of her half-unbuttoned, flaming-red blouse. Jody swallowed.

"Jack!" Norma was coming around the aisle, her face and arms dripping wet. Sandy was right behind her.

Desirey froze in mid-stride but her eyes were on Klaus — not on the muzzle of the .41 — Klaus, his face pale and both corners of his mouth drooling foamy, bright-red blood. Jody looked over her shoulder at his adopted father who was standing directly behind. Jack looked serious, and as Jody pulled the aim of the Ruger away from Desirey, Jack shook his head vehemently. Jody did not understand and lowered the muzzle to the floor, and with two hands (such as they were) de-cocked it.

"He's still alive!" the black woman said. "What did you do to him?!" She dropped to the floor and began to wail, cradling Klaus's gory head in her hands. Then she felt of the carotid arteries in his neck. "You killed him!"

Jody watched her run her long fingers down Klaus's silent muscles. Jack was stepping around her, waving a hand at Jody, like *come here! Give it here!*

Jody reluctantly handed Jack the .41 — butt first. "Four shots left." He looked back at Jackson. She seemed

293

to be eyeing up Turbo's revolver, on the floor but just out of reach. At the same time her hands were groping underneath Klaus's butt, the white Levi's gobbed with dark-red splotches. Jody looked back at Jack and shrugged his shoulders.

"What's going on?"

Jack turned to glance at Sandy and Norma, who had stopped at his left side. Sandy was the first to realize what was happening and her mouth suddenly formed a big, lip-sticked O. "Look out!"

Jackson was turning around and cocking the automatic Klaus had stashed in his back pocket. She looked up at Jack and got off a round into his stomach. Jack's face twisted with surprise and pain as she pumped another round into him as he tried to regain his balance and get the Ruger up. Jody hurled himself toward Turbo's revolver and nailed it. His first shot caught Jackson from behind, just below her neck and above her right shoulder blade. She pitched forward, bent over at the waist, and tried to turn and pop Jody with a small caliber round. Jack's .41 twisted up, blasting out a slug which split the back of her blouse and plowed up along her spine just under the skin. The bullet exited near her neck and exposed an ugly, pink and white-gristled furrow. This time her body flung sideways into Jody, her ass pinning down his left leg. Jody, who had shot her first from a sitting position on the floor where he'd grabbed Turbo's revolver, cocked and fired, and cocked and fired, again and again five times into Jackson's side all the while Norma was yelling for Jack not to shoot. "It'll go through her, hit Jody!"

Desirey Jackson stopped screaming.

For a moment Jody remained still, sitting there on the floor, one leg under Jackson, her lifeblood hot and running down all over him. Jody was watching his father, on his knees. Jack had dropped the .41 and was clutching his gut and looking right into Jody's eyes.

Jack thought it was the Medivac chopper. The familiar sound of the rotors, the spotlight over the grass near the screened-in porch where they had pulled him down the stairs and outside. Conscious, on his back with his head propped up in Norma's lap, he saw the chopper's spotlight swing out over the water for a second, briefly lighting up the stern of a fleeing sport-fisherman. The spotlight lighting up the brightly-painted name on the transom:

Wet Dream
Panama City

Everything seemed so sharp and clear. Eastland jumping down from the chopper. Norma bending over Jack, crying, her hair in his face. Jody and Sandy kneeling at his feet.

Why was everything suddenly so quiet? Jack turned his head and tried to brush a stray, red hair from his eyes. The rotor blades of the chopper were still. The pilot — Jack had seen him before but not with tears in his eyes — who was this guy? He was laying out the stretcher beside him, telling Norma to move please.

"No!" Jack tried to yell it out but inhaled a clot of blood instead. He had to cough but his stomach burned with each contraction. "I'm — not — going — to — make it — Baby. No — hospital! No hospital!"

Jack threw up more blood, turning his head and seeing close-up the grass beside his head slick-black with it. "Jody — tell them — what I always — say. Jody — no operating — no code. Don't let them!"

Jody tried to sound tough. "Don't take him to the

hospital."

Eastland pulled up the shirt Jack had bought not an hour before with Desirey Jackson. Airbrushed picture of a dolphin wearing sunglasses. "Lot of arteries there, son," he said, tracing the small, dark bullet holes in Jack's abdomen with a fingertip. One of them was directly under the heart. "You're bleeding internally, Jack."

"Daddy. I'm dead."

Eastland hesitated. He knew it but felt compelled to act. To go through the motions of getting him into the chopper. An act which would probably kill off Jack right then.

"Let's move him."

"No!" And after disgorging more blood at the side of his head: "Don't move me!"

Eastland felt of Jack's hands which were cold and clammy.

"Daddy, take care of Jody. Watch out for him. Just watch out for him."

Jack saw Jasmine, her goofy life, the pumping iron and the S&M clothes, the trailer full of video equipment and satellite receivers. "I understand, Baby."

Norma said: "What, Jack?"

Jody was on his knees in the bloody, slick-black grass on the other side of Jack's head now. "Don't talk, Dad."

"Let me say..." A cough interrupted him. "Last..."

"Last what, Dad?"

"Words!"

"Last words!" Norma said.

But Jack did not tell them what those words were. His eyes were dilating and his hand tightened around Norma's. He was going to say: "Goodbye, Nub-man."

He was going to say: "I love you, Nub-man."

He could see Jasmine, standing at the edge of her driveway, her tall, black Captain Hook boots, her leather shorts and bra. She was looking down at his camper in the valley near the pond, with tears in her eyes. Jack could see his camper from where Jasmine was standing. Three, identical, blond girls were chasing each other down there around the camper and his shower deck, playing tag and laughing. The girls' chores were all done and they were killing time, waiting for him to come home.

Did they feed Candy?

"That dumb, yip-yip, lap-dog," Jasmine said.

Did they make sure her dish has water in it?

Candy would never understand that he was not going to be coming home.

Jack had wanted to say more. He had wanted to say: "It's okay if Candy wants to sleep on my bed now, Nub-man."

CHAPTER 38
Retirements in Peace

"For now," Eastland said, "don't nobody go through the house and use the front door." The moon had swung farther to the west but was still high enough to shine full onto the back yard past the two-story building's red-tiled roof. They were all squatting around Jack's lifeless body. Norma, Jody, Sandy, the chopper pilot, and Eastland, who's head looked so small compared to his mustache, Jody thought, without the cowboy hat on.

"Your step-brother," Eastland said to the pilot after a long silence.

"I know, Pop. I figured it a long time ago."

Sandy, Norma, and Jody all turned to look at him. He did seem like a younger, more serious-looking Jack. Much too serious, Norma thought. She felt of her choker.

Still there. Jack never saw it.

"Nobody knows yet, do they, Sheriff?" Sandy said. "You never did call the law?"

"I am the law."

"In Walton County here?"

"No, but..."

"So nobody knows, right Sheriff?" Sandy persisted.

"Sandy!" Norma was still fingering her solid-gold choker.

"Goodness, Norma! I need to know what's going on! My ass is **not** going to jail! So who knows, Sheriff?! Nobody really?"

Eastland, still hunkered down in the circle around

Jack's body, pressed the heels of his hands hard up against his temples. Jack's eyes were staring up at the sky, the moon full in his blank face.

"Doesn't seem like any of the neighbors around here reported any gunshots, either," Norma said.

Jody looked at her. His hands, caked with soil and blood, could still feel her wonderful, hot, meaty breasts. Didn't seem like she loved Jack very much. Jody looked back to his adopted father and suddenly realized they would never do anything together again, and he burst into tears. Sandy, who was kneeling beside him, pulled Jody's head to her chest and he sobbed against her warm, motherly softness.

Sheriff Eastland was saying: "I can either lose everything now — at age eighty-five — or." He stood up, and turned, and listened. A horn honked off in the distance. A normal sound, that, and the familiar, distant rumble of cars rolling over the bayou bridge, and the soothing lapping of the sea against the boathouse pier. He walked stiff-legged in his pointy-toed boots to the wooden fence on the near side of the yard. He was trying his best to think. So many bodies all at once. It had all come down so fast. Who, if anybody, knew what?

There had been more than a few times in his long career where he and fellow officers had run up on a scene which, despite all its gory magnificence, offered no easy clues. But those scenes had been created by assholes and bums, not people with much intelligence.

Sandy and Norma he wasn't worried about right this minute. They were obviously opportunists and seemed to be as amoral as any ladies he had ever met. Desirey's family would miss her. Her car was out in front — he would have to move that first. He did not feel guilty about her, though. She had been going down the tubes fast when he offered her a chance for a better life. He would miss her, but... Nobody, not even Norma, would be missing Jack for very long, probably. Jody would. Jasmine might.

I'm sorry, Jack.

I should've cut you in a lot sooner.

Got rid of those foreign fools myself.

The Emir at The Victor was probably already on a plane. The body of Abu's wife, a secretary had in-formed him, was the servant's problem now but would bear checking. So what was he worried about?!

I'm sorry, Jack.

"Desirey's car — we have to move it," Eastland said, to no one in particular. "Like now. We have to move Jack's boat, too."

Norma said: "Abu's in there. His body. In the boat."

Eastland's stomach was churning with worry. "That makes five bodies."

"Six!" Sandy said.

"Jack's not a body, Norma. Sandy." Eastland sighed. He had been coasting along on such big plans. Big dreams. He was well off now, for a sheriff, anyway — and there was even more money to be made if Manny could be forced back to his senses. It was either going to be money and more women than an old man could ever hope for — or die in jail. No, suicide was the alternative. Well, Jack was already there, and so many of his old buddies. All of his old friends, actually. At his age, you get to bury them all.

A smile spread across Eastland's face. "Mo'Bubba, come over here, help me get a boot up so I can look over this fence!"

"Mo'Bubba?" Sandy said. She laughed, pushed Jody's face away and got up. She headed for the fence and stopped next to Eastland. "Jody! Climb up on my hands here!" Sandy locked her fingers together and waited for Jody to climb up and look over.

"Weeds. Empty lot. Abandoned house."

"Not abandoned," Eastland said." Leased by SiblTek. Kept vacant for privacy. Any signs of teenagers using the property, like for parties?"

"Noooo. Dirty swimming pool!"

"I don't think anybody knows anything went on here," Norma said. "Oh, Jack."

"The car. We have to move Desirey's car. Some-body going by in front will remember it. Big Lincoln like that with a light bar."

"What's in all this for me?" Sandy said, in her usual, cheerful voice.

Norma said: "I can keep the choker?"

Eastland moved away from the fence. "I'm so glad you pretty little gals asked."

Mo'bubba flew Norma, Jody, and Jack's body back to Jody's mother's place ("Can't miss it at night. The flashing light on top of the 'tenna mast is purple!"). Jody's job was to clue Jasmine in on what happened, comfort her, and assure her that Norma was an OK person and needed to stay down at Jack's camper a couple of days. The burial would be private. Uncle Cletus would bury his son himself. On the property. Period.

On the way, Norma found a roll of bills in Jack's pocket. More than eight hundred dollars. It made her a little airsick trying to count it down beside her leg in the vibrating helicopter so Jody wouldn't notice but hell, somebody had to pay the overdue light bill at the Cremo! She told herself that the money, sticky with blood, she would have divided up with the boy if she hadn't seen Eastland push a sizable chunk of bills in Jody's face before they lifted off.

There was no way Norma was going to go back there to her condo. Not tonight, anyway, and not until Eastland could assure her that the coast was clear and money would be provided to fix her carpet. And not until she could buy some Remington .41 magnum jacketed hollow-points so she could reload the Ruger.

Eastland didn't have the rest of it all figured out right away but he had survived other outrageous capers. A solution, if it came at all, would arrive in due course and only if he kept calm. But he did know that the bodies would have to be brought down and taken care of before dawn. So he had Sandy help him with that job first while he thought about the rest.

After he and the healthy girl had dragged the first one, Desirey Jackson, down the steps and out onto the screened-in porch at the rear, Eastland said: "Welcome to the family." A favorite expression of Monday and Manny.

"Thank you!"

Sandy looked good even in the dark. Even standing there in clothes splattered with blood and brain niblets. "You'll need to change clothes before it gets light out. Even so, you are the most beautiful helper I've ever had."

"Okay, but warning, though: I'm expensive!"

"I figured. More than your sister?"

"I keep on telling her: Charge more!"

Eastland grimaced. As they headed back up the stairs, he wondered how bad Abu must be smelling in the cuddy of Miss Chernobyl. Apt name. Good thing the box of jumbo, plastic bags in Desirey's trunk was new and unopened. Five to a box.

Sandy disappeared over the top of the steps, taking them two-at-a-time, but Eastland did his best to keep up. Most guys at eighty-five were either pushing daisies or waiting to at the nursing home, where they were too weak to tear off a square of toilet paper much less reach their ass. So he was doing OK, he figured. Could see good, too, without glasses. Could score at the firing range and in the bedroom. But this young woman sure made him realize his age.

He had wanted to take Klaus down first, the heaviest one — get that over with before he pissed out — but Sandy convinced him it was better to do the easy ones first. "Then all you have left is the one, hard job and that makes it easier!"

"Okay, kid."

When he caught up to her in Turbo's lab, Sandy had just finished frisking Hector's pockets for his money and was starting the black, plastic bag over his head. The bills she could count later. Turbo, she had already discovered, was wearing nothing under the lab coat and the coat pockets contained only a dirty hankie and a folded order blank for "HEAVY METAL" – "The Illustrated Fantasy Magazine". She had pocketed that, too, alongside the computer printout of all those foreign-looking names and addresses, which she had folded to fit among the green polka-dots in the single pocket of her dress.

HEAVY METAL! Gosh!

By the time they had Hector, Jackson, Turbo, and Klaus lined up in bags on the back porch, Eastland was about washed out. If it weren't for the scant amount of time remaining before dawn he could call Manny for help. But by the time Monday or Manny could get here it would be too late. He should've had Mo'Bubba return with the chopper but that would've only attracted more notice to all the noise and activity he was trying to hold to a minimum.

"Walk out to the pier for a minute?"

Sandy balked. Was he finished with her now? Unlike Norma, Sandy liked to check things out first. Eastland had already dropped his pistol belt when they started moving the bodies down the stairs, but...

Sandy said: "You lay your backup gun down with your pistol first."

"Woe! You don't trust me, do you? Ha! I'm the one who's neck is sticking out a mile here!"

"The gun?"

Eastland, still smiling, plunked down on the stoop and pulled a pantleg up over his boot holster. "Okay?" He handed her the compact Sig Sauer .380. "But when we're done here."

"Well, sure!"

Eastland thought he could easily fall in love with this one. He was tired and getting punchy, but this feeling was real. And how many times would that be in his long life then — falling in love for real — a hundred? They sat on a wooden locker on the pier, the moonlight partly obscured by clouds now and throwing longer shadows. The sea was more calm, also, and above the sound of the lapping of water against the pilings and Miss Chernobyl's random bumpings, they could hear a fish hit the surface here and there.

"If it weren't for all this work, this would be a beautiful night," Eastland said. "I'm building a house over down at the mouth of the Apalachicola River. Franklin County. I'm tired of being landlocked when there's so much more living on the Gulf. I'll have my boat right at my back door. And when I'm too old to cut mustard, I'll just take her out. Head toward the Yucatan with a half a tank of fuel."

"Oh, goodness, that's a long way off for you!"

"Yeah, sure. Sandy, I've lived more lives than most men and I'm thankful for that. What more could I do? How old is your husband?"

"He's twice as old as me and half as old as you."

"Heh!"

"And he bought a landlocked place which I have to live in!"

"You could come and visit me. I'm going to retire after this term and live in that house. One of my last dreams to come true."

"And that one last piece of strange, huh?"

"Yeah, you're pretty smart."

"But, Sheriff, I don't see how, at your age, there could be any strange left. I mean, like, what kind of girl haven't you had yet? Plenty of red-heads, I'm sure!"

"Heh! Well, I ain't fucked an elephant yet."

"Oh! An elephant!" Sandy laughed. She lowered her voice. "I just heard something. Shhhh!"

They listened.

Finally, Sandy said: "What about that lady we carried out. The black lady? Was she yours?"

"You could tell?"

"Oh, yes. I saw the way you looked and the way you kissed her before we pulled the bag over. I'm sorry."

"Well."

"You had tears in your eyes, too. Now I have tears in **my** eyes!" Sandy dabbed at her eyes with a corner of her dress and Eastland saw the Beretta. They sat there for a minute or two longer, leaning forward, elbows on their knees, tears in their eyes.

Only Eastland knew what his were for.

CHAPTER 39
"Bad Girls - Bad Girls"

Jasmine had not been able to get much out of Jody, and all she knew was what Eastland told her, that Jack "got in some shit over his head". At the moment, Jack's body was covered with his favorite blanket and lying in the middle of her bed in the double-wide, and Jasmine was feeling more and more abandoned and frustrated. So when she saw, on one of the surveillance monitors, the big Lincoln coming up their twisty driveway, she assumed it was Desirey Jackson.

Jasmine was in no mood for any more bullshit. She poked her head out the door and hollered for Jody, hoping he was wearing more than his usual underwear briefs. Herself, she was dressed normally, as befitted a death in the family. Black work-out leotards, plain Dollar-Store flip-flops, and chipped-red toenails.

"What!?"

The boy's voice sounded far off, like half-way down the hill toward Jack's camper. Peep-tomming that redheaded whore, Norma, Jasmine assumed. She could kill Eastland for dropping the bitch off at Jack's place earlier along with his body, just like that — with no warning — the noisy, beat-up old county chopper landing right in her collard and Chinese-cabbage garden in the middle of the night. Christ!

Didn't he think maybe she still cared about Jack? And didn't he have sense enough to know that Jody would be crying over his dad even though Jack wasn't his real father? Poor Jody, torn between that and pining after that slut down there!

And Eastland sending his Zulu girlfriend out here now instead of coming himself? I'll show her!

Ready to raise Cain with Desirey, Jasmine stomped off her little porch but held her tongue when she saw it was Eastland himself driving, no hat. With that Norma bitch sitting right beside him.

Jasmine walked up. "You're getting bald, Uncle Clit. Getting some strange?"

"Sandy here likes it. My bald head. Where's Jody?"

"Sandy?"

Eastland rubbed his eyes. "Norma's sister."

Sandy jumped out and waltzed around the Lincoln's long hood, extending her hand. She looked great, all clean and made-up in one of Desirey Jackson's Patrick Kelly originals — another delightful array of green polka-dots — only this time on a black-denim jumper. Bare feet. "Oh!" Sandy said. "We have matching toe-nails!"

Jasmine looked down at their feet and then locked eyes with Sandy. She had to smile. *Not as dumb as her sister.*

"I'm sorry about Jack," Sandy said, lowering her voice.

"Fuck 'im. He was an unfaithful idiot."

"Oh! Gosh!"

"But I still loved him, you know."

"Oh, I know! Gosh! Is Jody here? Nub-man?"

"I hollered for him but he's probably down there at Jack's, mooning over your sister. Wait, listen though. Jody's probably hurt pretty bad by Jack's — you know."

"Awwww, I know. Poor Nub-man."

"Jack adopted him against all his friends' advice, when Jody was just a tad."

"Awwww."

307

Eastland eased himself out of the Lincoln and looked up at the sky. No rain clouds. He had two men he could trust who were supposed to be coming out soon with a backhoe. To dig Jack's grave. Usually he knew what the weather forecast was going to be but...

He listened to the two women carry on for a little longer:

"Gosh, that little man of yours is so smart!"

"Yeah, I'm proud of that but look out, he's terminally horny."

"Well, he's a teenage boy!"

"**Terminally** horny. And he knows he can't get laid by anybody real. Ever."

"Get laid? Ha ha! I like you, Jasmine. Jasmine, right?"

Eastland said: "Jasmine, meet Sandy. Sandy, meet..."

"Christ, Clit," Jasmine snapped. "Hey! What about the funeral? The burial."

"Today. I have a crew coming over. We need to pick a spot. Or you need to tell them where. They're going to cover it back over right away so they'll be careful not to disturb anything."

"Who."

"Two of Jack's brothers."

"Only two? How many does he have, anyway? Oh, and you need to tell me before you leave whether they know themselves whether they're brothers. To Jack and/or to each other."

"Touché."

Sandy laughed again. "Oh! I like it here!"

Eastland said: "She needs to stay down at Jack's with Norma until everything is all settled out."

"Hey! Do I get consulted? Huh?"

"Jack's place. It is his place, isn't it?"

"Yes, yes, on paper! I'm always thinking it's still part of the same property, divorce or no divorce, you know, because of Jody. Jody thinking it's his place one day, oh, shit, what a mess!" Jasmine swiped her hands at the tears forming under her eyes.

"Oh, gosh!" Sandy said. "What you must be going through! I can stay at a motel, sure, I can take Norma with me, some motel nearby."

"No, no, it's okay. I'm just upset is all."

"I'll take her down there," Eastland said. "I have to get Jack's pickup truck and the boat trailer so I can take it over to Rasputin's. Jack's boat is tied up there. I'll tow it back here for you or Jody. Sandy can follow me in the Lincoln. She needs to go back to the Cremo where she has her beetle parked."

"Beetle?"

"I have a little VW bug," Sandy said. She raised herself up on her toes and tried to see through the woods down the hill. "Is there room to park it down there at Jack's? It's real tiny. It has flowers painted all over it like in the 60's!"

"There's room down there," Eastland said. "Come on, let's see if Norma wants to go back to her condo with us, maybe get some things, some clothes to hold her over until they clean it up and put in a new carpet..." Eastland stopped. Jasmine didn't know the whole story and that was for the best. "Well, tell Jody I missed him and that I'll be back in a little bit. Jazz, don't forget to pick out a spot for Jack. Your decision."

Jasmine let Sandy embrace her for a second, then turned her back on them.

Yeah, sure, my decision.
Like what if I don't want him buried here.
On my place!

In secret and against the law!
Did anybody bother to ask?
Why no!

She waited for Eastland to back the Lincoln out of the yard and turn down Jack's steep drive to the bottom. Then, alone with the memory of Jack's body lying cold and stiff on her bed, Jasmine walked around the double-wide toward the path to the antenna farm. It seemed like a long time ago now but Jack had given her a concrete bench and placed it beside that path, on her first birthday anniversary after their divorce. "So you can sit here and look at them," he had told her. Meaning the satellite dishes and the antenna tower she loved so much.

She stopped, and said out loud, as if Jack could hear: "Would you like to be buried here, Jack, near the bench?"

He seemed to like the spot and Jasmine turned and looked around to see if a digger machine could get in without running down any bushes and stuff.

"Right here then, Jack. Next to the bench you gave me. Okay?"

Norma didn't really want to go along but she did. As Sandy drove Jackson's Lincoln back toward Panama City Beach, following Jack's pickup and empty boat trailer, Eastland watched them in the pickup's mirrors. The women were jabbering constantly. So pretty those two were, but goddam they sure liked to talk! And it sure didn't look like they were very sad or upset about anything.

What about yourself?
You don't seem very upset about Jack!

The drive to the Gulf was a good hour through mostly open country and scattered woodlots, and Eastland thought about himself. He felt good right now about the way he had managed to sort through the few options he had and manage to come out smelling like a rose. So far. But could he say he was heartbroken over Jack's death? Jack's mother, one of Eastland's previous wives, was in a home with other Alzheimer's patients, too far gone to realize what had happened even if somebody would tell her. Tell her that her son was dead. That Jack would no longer be coming to visit. Not that he ever visited very much.

He would tell her anyway, when no one was around, next time he visited. You never know what she might be thinking inside, a brain so far gone. She would show no sign of having heard, of course — probably just keep on nodding and drooling — but she should be told and he would do it.

Sandy was applying fresh lipstick from a tube Norma found in the glove compartment. "God, this car has power! My foot's hardly touching the pedal! Here!" She handed back the lipstick.

"Wonder what he's thinking?" Norma said. "He's always looking up in his mirror."

"Yeah, I noticed. He's probably wondering what we're talking about so much!"

"Yeah! Or wondering if he should snuff us!"

"Yeah, get rid of the last witnesses."

"Yeah, no, he's wondering what we think about him."

"Oh, yeah, like if he's got a chance."

"No, well, yeah, that too, but, oh, Norma, he could hardly make it out to the boat when it was time to load that Klaus. Shit, I thought he was going to infarcate or whatever they call it."

"Heart attack? Yeah?"

"Yeah, but he made it!"

"I'll bet he can still get it up, though. I'll bet that black chick Jody shot was getting it up for him!"

"Yeah. That was terrible, shooting her."

"Well, I bet I could get it up for him, too!"

"Well, I could, too, Jeez. Big deal. Would you?"

"I don't know. Depends."

"Yeah. Then we had to get that body out of Chernobyl — Miss Chernobyl — whatta name! Daddy would love that boat I bet! Anyway, Eastland was all played out by then and I had to do most of the pulling and shoving out that little hatch-door thing whatever-you-call-it. And stink? God, the body was already rotting or something. Icky stuff oozing out all over him, too, Christ, I made the sheriff wait after we got all the shit on board the big boat and I jumped in the water and soaked all the blood and guts and that stinky, rotting stuff off me!"

"God," Norma said. She raised a hand to her neck. "I still have my choker!"

"Yeah. Bet you haven't even taken it off yet!"

"Nope! Kept it on right through my shower. Oh, Sandy, you'll love Jack's shower. That deck outside you saw. Hot water. Everything. Lighted at night! Nobody to see — so deep in the woods!"

"Yeah. Think we can both fit in that bed?"

"Just like when we were kids!"

"Yes!"

They both laughed. "Look, he's seeing us having such a good time in the mirror. Probably thinks we're both crazy!"

"No, he thinks we're bad!"

Sandy sang: "Bad girls! Bad girls!"

"Your hair still smells funny, like burny or singed

or something," Norma said.

"Shit, he's slowing down!" Sandy hit the brakes and followed the boat trailer turning left onto Highway 20. "Oh, hell Norma, we poured two big cans of gas over everything and Eastland rigged the radio to spark it off but when we got into Jack's boat away from the other one we couldn't find a radio in it so we had to go back and he set it off by tossing in this burning stick and the fire started slow at first because the gas we poured was evaporated mostly by then, I guess, and when we pulled away I was at the stern, looking and hanging on and **whooomph!** Shit, I'm lucky I still got my eyebrows!"

"You didn't wait to see if it would sink? The boat?"

"Oh, for sure! As soon as we got away a little bit he stopped and we watched. That old dude does **not** take any chances! Here we are in the middle of nowhere, no land in sight, and it's starting to get light already, right? And our little boat is going up-and-down and up-and-down — he had to keep one of the engines in gear to point Jack's boat into the wind so we wouldn't sink, he said. Sink! When we towed it out there with the big one I was looking at it all the time towed behind us and it looked like it was going to sink **then!** Waves splashing over it all the time. Then the smoke got real black for a couple minutes and then it exploded a couple times, just like in the movies! But it sank nose down. So it's starting to get light, right? And it's time to head back to land, which we could not see by the way, and these dolphins come over to us. Unbelievable! And I'm leaning over and one of them comes half-way out of the water and it let me pet it on the nose! So neat! It's like they have human brains only like they can read your thoughts! They were so neat I forgot why we were there. And then Eastland says he wished he had some cigar minnows to

313

feed them — fish-bait — and I remember where we are and he's willing to take the time to feed dolphins! So he can't be all that bad."

"Yeah, but he's a man, and he knew you didn't have anything to feed them and he wouldn't **have** to take the time, so he just said that to get you to like him."

"Yeah? Aw, well, maybe. Anyway we hauled ass after that. God, Norma, your boyfriend's boat is fast! There's bullet holes in it, you know that? Eastland pointed them out."

Norma felt a rush of pride, then remembered Jack was forever gone. She brushed away a tear.

"He's looking, Norma, he saw that! You crying. Don't cry, baby sister. We're okay now."

"Ohhh."

"One day at a time, Normie. Remember? Like now, we're both okay **now**."

"Yeah." Norma got out a Kleenex and after dabbing her face, she felt of her choker again. *Solid gold.*

"It's supposed to rain this afternoon — I heard it on the radio — but it looks like it won't right now." Sandy was going to add: *for the funeral* but changed her mind.

"Yesterday I never thought I'd ever see rain again, or the sun."

"Yeah."

"Especially when they had me locked in that mop closet in the basement. I was in there for hours and hours. I had to piss and shit in a corner, it was terrible. And no light."

"Yeah. Gosh. But here we are, baby sister! In the sunshine! Nobody can fuck with us now!"

"Yeah."

Eastland was slowing down again and Sandy almost slammed the rear of the boat trailer. They followed his right-turn around the Ebro dog track onto Highway 79. For a moment, the two sisters stopped talking, each wondering privately what dog racing was like and when they would get a chance to try it someday.

"What was Jack like? You never told me much, just that he had a boat and that he was a bounty hunter. When I thought: bounty hunter, I thought, god, Norma's got herself another asshole! Oh, I'm sorry, I didn't mean..."

"It's okay. I know what you mean. Oh, Sandy, he was, well, real nice! To me he was. And he got me doing different stuff, not just hanging around in bars, you know. And it wasn't the boat — it was where we went with the boat. Beach-combing and stuff."

"Yeah?"

"Not too many guys like that. Not that I ever met anyway."

"Yeah."

"Taking me to Shell Island just to be away from everybody, from civilization."

"Snuff Island is what they should call it now."

"Yeah. Snuff Island."

"Kissing that dead head!"

"Yeah."

"There's more."

"More?"

"Yeah! I forgot! Eastland made me promise not to tell and I said: 'Not tell my own sister?' And he said: 'Don't tell anybody anything more than what they already know. Period!' He said it real stern like. And let me tell you, he means business. So I said: 'Okay!' Okay?'"

"Then why did you just hint about it?"

"Because I'm going to tell you. You're my sister! You **need** to know, too. That sheriff is bad. Eastland. Real bad!"

"Well, yeah, but..."

"He shot a little girl right before my eyes. Well, not a little girl — a teenager."

"Huh?"

"When we first started loading up the big boat — he called it a Bertram Moppie or something like that — no, after I had to help get that rotting body out of Miss Chernobyl, all of a sudden these girls come out of the cabin of the Moppie. Triplets! Just like the one... Oh, no, not triplets but, shit, you know. More of the same ones."

"Clones."

"Clone girls. So Eastland was real surprised about it that they were there and then he gets shitty and tells them to get in your boyfriend's boat and stuff themselves down in the cuddy cabin as far up in the corner as they can. So they do, right? I mean, two of them hop right in and disappear down inside like they were told but this other one, she says she wants to go home and she doesn't want to get in the boat. Real bratty like. So she's still in the big boat and now she's bitching about how the body we just dumped there smells bad and Eastland walks up to her like nothing and pulls out his gun and holds it right to her head and pulls the trigger. **BAM!** Down she went. I couldn't believe it! The first thing I'm thinking is: Shit, I'm next, you know? And I'm turning around and the other two girls are poking their heads out of your boyfriend's boat — they saw it — and they're saying: 'I'll be good! I'll be good!' Like that. Just like that."

"Jeez. Did you try to run for it?"

Sandy hesitated for a moment. "I... I didn't do anything. I said he might as well have his other two guns."

"He had three guns?"

"Yeah."

"Well, what could you have done, I mean, really. Him being the county sheriff and all."

"I could've shot him."

"Yeah, sure."

"Yeah. But I didn't. I went along."

"Yeah."

"You at least get a gold choker out of it."

"We're getting a lot more than that!"

"We better!"

silence....

"I'd like to see that island, Norma. Sometime."

"Snuff Island?"

"Yeah. Feed the dolphins."

"Hey, we can go back there anytime we want now. In Jack's boat."

"You know the way?"

"Yeah, but his ex-wife will probably take over the boat."

"No! Jody can take it over! His son!"

"Oh, yeah. It's his boat now."

"Yeah, and he's sweet on you. He's sweet on both of us."

"Yeah, he loves us, you know that?"

"Yeah!"

Eastland looked in the mirror and saw the ladies laughing again. So pretty.

CHAPTER 40
Homunculi

"Don't worry, he'll have you back in time for Jack's funeral," Monday said. She released Jody's nub-hand and looked Dr. Mannlicher in the eye. "Right?"

"Back in **plenty** of time!"

Jody followed Mannlicher's red-hairy legs down the stairs to the basement. The man was wearing dark-green cargo shorts, the kind Jody had seen in a Cabela's sporting goods catalog his mother had at home. Jody always wanted to send for some but there was never enough money left on his mother's credit cards, so she said. Now, with this new job he was promised, there would be. Jody would be able to order anything he wanted.

Lights clicked on automatically as they walked around the water heater and the central heating unit. They passed the laundry room and stopped. Jody squinted his eyes at the ancient row of shelves, stuffed with musty newspapers and old magazines.

"Check it **out!**" Dr. Mannlicher yelled, his ruddy face glowing in the incandescent light. He mashed a button on the keyboard of his portable radio, a unit which looked identical to the one Jody had seen Uncle Eastland use sometimes, and the wooden shelves shuddered and began to slide down the wall. The movement revealed a steel door the color of gray cement.

"Like in the **movies?** Huh? **Huh?!**"

"Neat," Jody said.

"Come **on!** It's **marvelous!** Any **questions?**"

"Well."

"Well **what?!**"

"Using sheep. I mean..."

"**Sheep** don't know how to dial **911!**"

The door led down a brightly lit, florescent hallway. Long. Nearly white, clinical-looking floor tiles. Clean. The steel door clicked shut behind them and the damp, basement smell gave way to the scent of filtered, mechanically driven air.

"Come **on!**"

Mannlicher's river-rat sandals slapped against the waxed tiles. They passed several closed, steel doors painted the same, antiseptic, bright-cream color as the walls.

"**Wait!** You're a **kid!** Kids **talk** too much, with each **other!** How do I know you won't **tell** anybody about all this! Huh? **Huh?!**"

"I don't know any other kids. I need the job. I need the money."

"And I **owe** you! Your **daddy** did his **job** and I **owe** you! But once you join the **family** here, you need to **know!** One word leaks **out** and you're **what?**"

"Dead. History."

"Louder!"

Jody raised his voice. "Dead!"

"Dead as a **duck!** Okay? Keep a tight asshole now!" Mannlicher led them through the fourth door on the left.

It was a laboratory, not unlike Turbo's although this one was much neater. And there was no extra, electronic equipment in the unused sinks. Jody looked around trying to spot a helmet with a set of goggles.

"Huh? **Huh?!**"

"Neat."

"Neat? **Neat?!** It's **wonderful!** You want this **lab?**

Huh? You recognize all this **equip**ment? You know how to **work** this shit?"

"Soon as I figure out the programs!"

"The **programs? Show** me a program!"

Jody hesitated, then walked up to the nearest keyboard. He recognized the UPS unit above it immediately and hoped whoever used the computer last had it switched through the battery backup. He pressed the button and immediately the machine began to boot and the monitor lit up. Jody ran through the file manager. It was going to be a piece of cake. Whoever set up the system had apparently saved most of the laboratory files in the root directory. Somebody who knew biology better than computers. Piece of cake! Jody highlighted a single sub-directory named:

PROTPSSM

Here, he hoped, there would be an index or guide to all the rest. If the directory wasn't password protected.

Mannlicher, hunching over Jody's head from behind, clamped a steel hand over Jody's good shoulder. "Protopossum!" he yelled. "**Boy** do you have a nose for **pussy** or **what!?**"

Jody was about to bring up the directory on screen but Mannlicher stopped him. "Wait, wait, plenty of time for **that.** I just wanted to **see.** First thing **tomorrow** I want you to back **up** everything here. I don't **know** anymore what the fuck **Hiro's** been **doing** but I want **everything** backed **up** in case **you** fuck up, we have it all on **discs!** Burn some **CD's!** O-**kay?**"

"It looks like this has an old tape-drive backup, too."

"**Tape**-drive? What the fuck is a **tape** drive? Huh?"

Jody tried to explain but Mannlicher interrupted. "Okay! O-**kay!** After you back**up** I want you to figure out the **hookup** to the Fort Walton **Beach** lab. **Tur**bo's lab. **Okay?** Then I want everything over **there** copied in **here** and put on **our** drives. Would that be **better?** Should we do **both?** How can I keep **up** with all this **shit!?**"

"Wait, okay, here's the optical drive."

"**Optical** drive? **What?** Do we have some of **those?** What the **fuck** is an **optical** drive!? No, no, not **possible** on **discs!** That unit over in **Walton** has been running twenty-four hours a **day!** For **weeks!**"

"Yeah, but..."

"Weeks! Figuring out who the female **proto**possum is! What she **looks** like!"

"I saw her."

"You **saw** her!?"

"With the helmet."

"With the **helmet?!**"

"Turbo made me."

"Turbo **made** you!?"

"Yeah. She was so beautiful!"

"**Beautiful!?** Is that all you can say? **Huh!?** What color was she **this** time?"

"Like she had a tan. And her hair was silvery but then it changed, well, like..."

"Just her **hair?!** Hiro and Turbo thought they're so **smart! Listen!** The **reason** the **color** can't be re-**solved** on that **whore** in the **computer** is because the **original** Eve had different color schemes **built in!** That's the way it's **supposed** to be! It's what God **wants!** You believe in **God? Huh?**"

"Well, no."

"**Yeah?** okay, well **fuck** him then! Oh, SheHeIt's **out** there all right but you'll never see the fucker in **church!**"

"Well, I don't think there is one."

"What? No **Creator?** Who was there before the big **bang!** Who was dishing out the **hydrogen** atoms, huh? **Huh?!**"

"Ummmm."

"She was **beautiful?** That's **all? Huh?!**"

"Oh, yeah!"

"See, every man wants **different** from what he's got at **home!** Assuming **most** men have monochrome **house**-holds!"

"Monochrome? Oh!"

"All one **color!** Remember two-toned **cars?** Huh? There was a buying **frenzy** when **they** first came out! All this present-day one-**color** stuff is just snobby, elitist **shit!** Are the **snobs** going to paint their **shutters** the same color as the **house** now? The **roof?** Huh? **Huh?!** The ladies don't want to **hear** this but males **evolved** to tramp around in the **greener** grass! We can't **help** it!"

"Yeah."

"I **love** it! Hey! Should we all **castrate** ourselves? Be stuck with **wives?** Who **cheat?**"

"Well, um."

"Poor **Turbo!** Oh, Nub-Kid or whatever I'm supposed to **say,** hey, that's all **my** fault. And **Hiro's** fault. Right now **he's** up on the top **floor** where he **lives!** Pouting! His **mother's** probably jumping all round the **room** on all **fours** and **hooting** like a **monkey!** You know she **does** that? She's **crazy!** He should've **told** Turbo. **He** says **I** should've told Turbo. That fucking **Klaus** and **Hector** were on the **hit** list. Turbo didn't **know!** He didn't **know!** I'm so **sorry!**"

"Turbo was mean. He hung me on the wall. He hung Norma on the wall."

"**Norma?** He hung **Norma** on the **wall?**"

"And he..."

"He was just **experimenting** or something, **right?**"

"No, I don't think so. He said he was going to rape Norma."

"Rape? He said **rape?!**"

"Well, not in so many words, but..."

"Fuck her in a heartbeat my-**self!** Would **you?** Huh? **Huh?!**"

"Well."

"See? **See?**"

"Um, yeah but..."

"But **what?** Huh? What kind of **chicks** you get, Nub-Boy? Huh?"

Jody stammered. "I — don't."

"That's all **over** with **now.** You **know** that? **Okay?** And I **owe** you, because of Jack. And I **need** you because you're a **cyber**-head, **okay? Huh?** I'm going to take **care** of you. And your **mother!** What's your mother **like?** She take good **care** of you? **Huh?** What's she **like?**"

Jody could not think of a way to describe Jasmine. He thought: *A lot like you!* but didn't say it.

"Huh? No, wait, **tomorrow** we need to go over to Fort **Walton** and clean **up!** No, we can do that **tonight.** You and me and **Monday!** Can you help with **that?** This one **time?** A little **dirty** work? I'll be right **there** with the mops and sponges with you, **right? Huh?**"

"Yeah, sure."

"I'll pay you in **cash.** I **owe** you, Nub-Person!"

Jody suddenly remembered his conversation with Jack, when this all started, and Jack's dreams about the clones.

"What about the clones?"

"The **clones? Girls? Huh?** You want to be paid off in **pussy?** Give up all that **cash?** I don't be-**lieve** this shit! Fourteen years **old?** Do I look like I'm **crazy?**"

"Yes."

Mannlicher suddenly turned toward the door. "Come **here! Wait!** If you turn that thing off like **that** you might loose a **file!**"

"I know how to turn it off. We didn't add anything, anyway. It'll all still be there."

"Oh? Yeah? **Pussy?** I swear!"

Jody followed Dr. Mannlicher out to the hallway.

"Nub-man! This is **Hiro's** lab, right next door here to **yours!** He keeps it locked but as soon as he's through **pouting...**" Mannlicher lowered his voice. "One of these days, when you get all settled with your equipment — that was Turbo's old lab we were just in — I want you to figure out how to access Hiro's password-protected files. What's the matter?"

"Your voice just changed. Like you sounded like another person. That's all."

Mannlicher kept it up, leaning closer. "There's this little man inside of me, with this real, serious voice. Whenever I get into shit over my head, I let him do the talking. He's talking now. Shhhhh." Mannlicher was bending over, his large, clean and jagged teeth inches from Jody's face. "That little man is my savior. He knows every step I make. Knows every hair on my head. He makes sure the authorities never get a clue."

Jody had to back up a little bit and he could feel his heart pounding. He felt like he was in the presence of evil. For the first time since Turbo hung him on the wall, he could feel real evil.

Mannlicher suddenly smiled and straightened up. "The cops can't touch us, Jody. You know why? They don't have a **clue!** And you're not going to be the one to **give** them a clue, **either!** Dig? You **dig?!**"

"Yes sir. I wouldn't want to."

"Oh, you **know** it!"

Jody followed the man down the hall the way they had come, back up the stairs to the kitchen. Monday was sitting at the table with a cup of coffee and a platter full of freshly baked chocolate-chip cookies. She reached over and tapped on the chair next to hers and Jody eagerly sat down.

"Welcome to the family, Nub-man," she said. "Manny made these cookies himself just an hour ago. They're still warm."

"I read the **directions** on the chocolate **chip** bag!" Mannlicher said. "Then my pussinal **manager** here starts **eating** them before they can even cool **off!** Are they **good?** Huh? **Huh?!**"

CHAPTER 41
The Garden of Eden

Jody saw that it was getting close to noon, and he was worrying about getting back home in time to help bury Jack. He and Mannlicher and Monday had finished off the entire batch of chocolate-chip cookies in the kitchen, the husband and wife team laughing at Jody's stories of his home-life with Jasmine and some of the escapades Jack had barely survived. The Mannlichers were genuinely taking to Jody, and seemed to be loving every minute.

"But Jack didn't survive this last one," Mannlicher said. His voice sounded sincerely subdued. "I'm so sick about that."

"We'll take good care of you, Nub-man," Monday said. "You'll see."

"And we have a surprise for you!"

"What about your mother, now? Can we trust her? Should we be taking that kind of chance?"

"Ask Uncle Cletus. Anyway, she has a lot of pornography tapes and stuff at home and she doesn't dare fuck up. She likes those little-boy clones you have, too."

"Little **boy** clones! **Huh?**"

Monday looked just as surprised as her husband. "My babies?"

"She has a tape of them running out of a building coming right at her — at the camera. She plays it over and over all the time."

"Little **boys?** Running at the **camera?**"

"Yeah. We have this Saint Bernard, his name is Bernie, and we have this tiny Russian videocam, a critter-cam. We strap it to his neck and it transmits to a repeater we can bungee to a tree so we can record the movies at home, and..."

"I heard **enough!**" Mannlicher said. "Should you be **telling** us this?"

"Now? Sure!"

"How many **tapes?**"

"Just one."

"I want it de-**stroyed!**"

"Yes sir."

Monday said: "A Saint Bernard? I saw him!"

"She **likes** those hairless-balled little-boy **monsters?** Well, of **course** she would! **They're** horny as **billy** goats!"

Jody said: "She'd be your slave."

"What's her name, Jody? Nub-man?"

"Jasmine."

"**Jasmine!** You mean, the stuff they anointed **Jesus** with?"

"No, Manny, that was frankincense and myrrh."

"Frankincense and **myrrh?!** Well, Jasmine? **Welcome** to the **family!**"

Jody smiled. Then he remembered once more that Jack was dead. Gone forever. The tears came to Jody's eyes even as he kept on smiling.

"We're going, too," Monday told Jody. "So don't worry about the time. I just called and your mother asked about you, but she said the crew just arrived but they haven't started the hole yet. We'll drive over there pretty soon. I'm sure your mother wouldn't appreciate a lot of strangers standing around her place waiting. She sounded nice on the phone!"

"**I** sound nice on the **phone!**" Mannlicher said. "Come on, Nub, there's **more!**"

Jody didn't hear. He was thinking: *the hole.* "Is Sheriff Eastland coming here first? He said he would take me back home."

"Who **knows?!**"

"Manny. The boy just lost his father."

"And he has no **god** to bitch to, **either!** Jesus H **Christ!** Well, that's not a problem **I'll** ever have! I tell **off** the one **I** believe in! Nub! Tell you **what!** You're a neat **kid!** Huh, wife?"

Monday nodded. She had moved behind Jody's chair at the table and was massaging his neck and shoulders.

"Hiro has us wired **big** time! T-line **and** satellite! Tell you what. You find out how to complete **high**-school on **line** and we'll **pay** for it! See how many **college** credits you can get, **too!** When you have **time!** O-kay? Huh?!"

"Yeah! Thanks!"

Jody had trouble meeting the intensity of Mannlicher's eyes and he glanced away to a Bavarian barometer nailed to the wall between a faded PLAYBOY centerfold, blond twins, and a November cover featuring a set of triplets from Brazil. Hansel & Gretel in one door of the little, brown, plastic hut, with the witch emerging. "Witch is coming out," Jody said.

"So scien-**tific!**" Mannlicher said. "See those **triplets?** PLAYBOY knows! When I was still in **college** we used to buy **girlie** magazines at the **news**paper stand on the **corner** and they had **twins** featured one time, in DUDE or ESCAPADE or some such, and **then** a couple months **later** I read that a rich, German **industrialist** had offered those twin chicks **ten** million **Deutsch**-marks if he could marry **both** of them!"

"Live with both of them," Monday corrected.

"What-**ever**! That's like four million **dollars** then! That planted the **seed** in my **mind**! It gave me the idea for all of this wonderful **stuff** we're working on here! But sometimes I **forget**! I lose the **objective**! Like when some of the T-**threes** went bad, the Pod-**Threes**. I thought, hell, we can salvage what's **left** and **sell** them! Indi**vid**ually! How **dumb**! I **forgot**! In the **real** world **single** chicks are **free**! We couldn't **give** them away!"

Mannlicher looked up at Monday and she made a face.

"Is Hiro coming?"

"No, I don't **think** so. I didn't offer to take his **mother** along. He's up in his room **pouting**!"

Monday shrugged. "He's upset about Turbo, I think."

"**Turbo**! So am **I**! Doesn't Hiro think I have feelings, **too?!**"

"Jody," Monday said. "Hiro's okay. He has the whole, top floor. He'll show you one day. It's really nice up there."

"Watch out for the **mother**!" Mannlicher yelled. "She'll sneak **up** on you! Don't bend over to pick up the **soap**! Okay? **Huh?!** Come on **outside** with me for a minute, Nub. I want to **show** you something only Monday and Hiro and I know about. Well, **Turbo** knows!" Mannlicher let out a mean, rolling, howling laugh.

"Only the Shadow knows!" Jody said.

"Aw-**right**! Hey! You're **okay**! How did you **know**! You're too **young**!"

"Uncle Clit has all these old radio tapes."

"Uncle **Clit?**"

"Sheriff Eastland."

"Sheriff **Eastland!**"

"Manny." Monday said. "I think it's time for some help from one of your friends."

Jody guessed that she meant a tranquilizer or something like that, and he started humming the Beetle's tune: "A Little Help from my Friends".

"Oh!" Mannlicher jumped up from the table and pulled out a prescription bottle of pills from the butter compartment of the refrigerator. He popped one and placed the bottle back. "Can't eat **margarine** any more! Too much **cholesterol!** I could **die!** And that would be **bad!** Just **think** about it. Jody? Can I call you Jody now that we **love** you to **death? Huh?** Just **think** about it. I suddenly die of a **heart** attack, and Monday commits **suicide** because she can't live with**out** me, and there you **are.** You walk out the back door. Barracks after **barracks** full of horny little bitches and you're the **only man!** Huh? **Huh?!** Well there's Hiro but he's too busy feeling **sorry** for himself! Hari Kari for **him!** Seppuku! Come on **outside** with me! Not **all** the hangars are full of **clones!**"

"Are you sure, Manny? Today?"

"Hey! For my boy here, **every** day's going to be a new surprise. **Every** day!"

They stopped just outside the second-closest building to the old house. Jody was ready to go back home. It was wrong to just rush back at the last minute in the nick of time to lower his father into the ground. He had pictured spending some time with Jack alone. To thank him for everything and tell him how he'll miss him.

"This is not like the other buildings on the inside," Mannlicher said. His voice was low and subdued now, almost a whisper. "You'll notice the lights will be out except for the globe over the big terrarium in the middle, okay? No talking in there, either. Okay? I might, but you keep quiet, so nobody knows you're with me. Got that?"

"Got it."

"Now when we first go in, you'll see that we have to look at the terrarium from behind this shield. The shield runs along the whole inside of the building and it's one-way glass, okay? From behind it we can see in, but anything in there can't see us."

"Mmmm - hmmmm."

"Oh, and you should know. When we move after the clones are all sold, this is the only project we're taking with us. Plus all the lab equipment and our clothes, of course." Mannlicher waited for a smile before continuing. "You can help us work out the details on that later, okay?"

"Mmmm - hmmmm. You're not making any more clones?"

"Well, maybe after we move we might come up with a new model. Okay. Take off your shoes here, outside. They're used to hearing only my footsteps." Mannlicher bent over and looked Jody in the eye. He had a kindly smile this time, and he gave the boy a happy and confident thumbs-up. Then he eased open the little side-door they were standing beside and waited for Jody to remove his sneakers. He gave the boy a gentle shove.

The huge building was dark and humid inside. Just as Mannlicher had described, there was a single, bright globe of light hanging near the roof over a huge, green platform nearly the length of the building. Covering the platform was a clear dome. Jody inched forward in his stocking feet along the narrow passage between the long side of the building and the smoky, glass shield.

He could see that on the near side of the dome over the terrarium a mist had formed. Mannlicher, impatient with Jody's progress, moved past him and pulled Jody along by the hand until they had circled the platform to where the mist had cleared. Inside was a tropical diorama of what looked like real plants and ferns growing up and down the sides of artificial mountains. There was even a little stream of running water coursing along a narrow valley and disappearing underneath a rock. Jody could hear the nearly-silent hum of an electric water-pump. He pressed against the one-way glass shield to get a better look.

Mannlicher pulled him away and whispered into Jody's ear. "Go down to the observation point next to you and I'll take the farther one. Shhhhh."

Jody looked. Just ahead was a depression in the shield with just enough room for one person. A bubble, really, with the far side of it nearly touching the terrarium dome. Jody eased on in there and got as close to the display as he could. To his left he could see another observation bubble but he could only make out the shadow of Mannlicher as the man occupied that one.

Jody expected something spectacular but could not figure what that could be. Jack and he had made a small terrarium once, out of a 30 gallon aquarium, with a little lake with sandbanks around it that Jody had constructed. A couple of little rocks and a flat one for the lizard they put in there to sun himself. A flat piece of glass on top enclosed it all. But one day Jody had left the contraption out in the sun and forgotten to give the lizard water — he was young then and he called the lizard "Lizzie" — and the reptile died. Jody was heartbroken. Besides, he had been feeding it regularly and was waiting for it to have eggs or babies.

This terrarium was huge, and there was so much to see! Little paths leading into the woods. A hole in one of the mountains, about halfway up, that looked like a real cave, even with some soil erosion at the mouth of it where whatever lived there came and went. Jody stared. What was the big deal? Probably a big rat farm or something like that. Well, Dr. Mannlicher was being nice about it. Showing him this because he was a kid. Kids liked stuff like this.

Does he have his own kids? Did he build this for them to watch? Probably has lizards in here, too, and the kids can watch the rats kill them. That would be something somebody like Mannlicher would think of.

Jody strained his eyes. No sign of life other than the green plants, and the mosses and lichens....

Something moved! Something white! Jody had been scanning the far right of the table, just past where the mist was forming on the dome, when in his peripheral vision he saw it on the far left. But what? He was staring now at the other side. Suddenly Jody's mouth dropped open. On a flat rock, almost out of sight for the tall grasses growing around it, were reclining a naked, white couple, a man and a woman, perfectly formed, the man bearded and with hair almost as long as the woman's. He was propped up on his elbows and looking around, and the woman, eyes closed peacefully to the bright globe above them, was lying back. The female was so beautiful!

Jody stopped breathing. It was hard to tell but they appeared to be not much more than a foot tall.

Jody heard Mannlicher cough and watched in awe as the couple jumped up and sprang from the rock, disappearing into the woods. Mannlicher came over to Jody's bubble and stood behind him.

333

"They must have done something wrong," he whispered. "You see how guilty they looked when they heard me?"

Jody nodded his head. His chest was tight and he remembered to breathe. A finger jabbed between his shoulder blades and Jody allowed Mannlicher to take his head in his hands and turn his gaze to another direction. The cave in the mountainside. A shadow moving just inside the opening. A wiggling, bewhiskered nose. The sniffing nose of a small ferret! Jody jumped with fear.

"Hey!" Mannlicher whispered. "He can't get out of there!"

"I was scared for **them!**"

"Oh! Yeah! Shhhh..."

Jody cut his voice to the barest whisper. "Can that thing kill them?"

"If they're not careful, sure! Don't worry, we can make more. Hiro has hundreds of them in the freezer! Embryos, you know. Of the people, not the ferrets!"

"Aren't we supposed to be quiet?"

Hundreds of them.

"They can hear **me.** They hear me talking all the time. I don't want them to know about **you.** Explain later."

Jody nodded, his eyes glued to the cave. The ferret, apparently satisfied that prey was nowhere nearby, receded back into its lair. Jody scanned the rest of the jungle for the couple.

"I named them Adam and Eve."

Jody nodded.

"Sometimes they fuck on top of that rock they were sunning themselves on. Table-top fusion! I love to catch them at it! I have **dominion!**"

"Mmmm - hmmmm."

"It's their favorite place when they're not busy hunting for food. They can see all around their little world from that rock. Anyway, they've already shit up everyplace else in there. The other day I finally commanded them to make little, wooden shovels to carry around, bury their doo-doo from now on. That's in the Bible."

"They understand English?"

"Shhhh." Hell, yes, I'm not about to teach them **Hebrew!**

"Sorry," Jody whispered.

"They don't know what to think of me yet. They hear me talk, to them and to others, but they can never see the others. Like you today. That's in there, too."

"In there?"

"In the Bible."

"Oh."

"Are you ever going to show them the real world?"

"After we move we can raise more. Would you like that? Hiro has another batch that'll grow to just about two feet tall. But I want these two here to stay inside the terrarium. I'm waiting for them to develop religion. I want to see what they come up with — see what kind of dumb-shit stuff they teach their kids!"

"Mmmmmm."

"Their kids are going to Mars! Tiny astronauts! The girls are going to be the Sirens of Titan!"

"Like in Kurt Vonnegut's book?"

"You're so smart! Yes, but think about it! We can watch Eve running around in there with her brats hanging from her tits by their teeth!"

Teeny little kids. Jody pictured it.

Eve breast-feeding them.

A glimmer of light came from the side-door —

335

Monday coming in after them — motioning for the two males to come out. Jody liked her and hoped she would never find out how horny he always was — how he was always thinking about sex. But he remembered Jack had told him one time: "Girls know how we think. That's why they wear bras. That's why they keep covered up. They know what we're thinking about all the time."

Mannlicher put an arm around Jody's good shoulder. "Come on, son. We can watch them again later. Let's go take care of your daddy.

CHAPTER 42
The Cute Hand

Jody was dressed properly for a change, (sneakers, jeans, a red-flannel shirt) for the cooler weather which had sprung up after Jack's funeral. He was sitting on the concrete bench near the grave, which was out of sight of the driveway. It had been only a few days but already fresh, green shoots were springing from the sod which had been replaced over the burial mound. But the first freeze of the winter, due any day now, would take care of that, well, maybe not. The winter before they had not experienced a freeze almost the whole season, until the beginning of March.

Uncle Clit still hasn't brought the boat back, Dad.

Jody could picture Jack, leaning back in the chair down in his camper, nodding his head, like: "That figures!"

Jody suddenly pictured Jack on his back, wrapped in his favorite blanket down there under the dirt. In his best jeans and his favorite "EAT MORE POSSUM" T-shirt. Wearing all his old biker rings studded with turquoise, and his waterproof Timex. Jody wondered how long the watch would keep on ticking down there.

"They forgot to pick me up this morning again, Dad. This is the second time!"

"That's life, Nub-man." Jody could almost hear Jack's voice.

"Sandy left right away, Dad. Right away."

"Well, you know how it is."

"And Norma left this morning." Jody wiped away a

337

tear with the back of his hand. But the tears kept on coming and he had to whip out a handkerchief. "Norma is so pretty, Dad."

"Yeah."

"It doesn't seem like she misses you very much though."

"Girls look at things a little different than we do, Nub-man."

"Maybe. Norma didn't want me hanging around. I forgot that she might be missing you."

silence....

"They didn't give me a clone to sleep with yet, Dad. First he told me he owed you, but now he just smiles when I mention it. And Monday said I don't have enough room. But that was before Norma left. Remember that first morning when we talked about them? How it would be?"

"Yeah. That was nice."

"Yeah. Oh, Hiro and Manny figured out how to grow people small. Real small. And they don't have to drop the temp at certain times to make them turn out dumb, like the clones. They turn out dumb by themselves, but not real dumb. Manny says the intelligence level is not totally relative to brain size, just partly. Neat, huh? He calls them Adam and Eve. Monday says they're moving everything to the mountains soon, but she didn't say where. I'm guessing Utah or Wyoming. I don't really want to leave here but I've never been anywhere else, so...."

"You need to go, Nub-man."

"Yeah. But they won't have Uncle Cletus there to be the sheriff, so they're not going to put up a lot of buildings and stuff. No more clones. Just the miniature people. Manny says he's going to get the government to buy them one day. For astronauts."

"Too small to have sex with, huh?"

"Well, I thought of ways. Anyway, it would be fun to have Eve running around all over me while I lie on my back, I thought of that. And she has hands."

"Neat."

"Yeah. Wish Norma liked me better, or Sandy, you know, because Norma was your girlfriend. Mama said for me to bring her sheets up to wash but I'm going to leave them on one more day. I'm going to sleep in them tonight down at your place." Jody suddenly regretted telling his father that. It didn't seem right. "Manny said I can take any of my own stuff I want along when they move."

"Your satellite dish, too?"

"Oh, no, he's going to buy me a new setup. He says all our stuff is way outdated, anyway. And he said Mom can visit when she wants to. He said exactly: 'If she doesn't stay too long.'"

"Ha! Don't blame him!"

"Yeah." Jody straightened up on the bench and looked around. Did he hear a car coming? "I got to go now, Dad. I think somebody's coming."

"Remember what I used to tell you about when you're alone. If you're outside, don't go running up right away. They'll be looking at the trailer, and you'll be watching them from where they won't know. Then, after you're sure they're cool, show yourself."

"I remember."

"I still have enemies looking for me. People I put in jail. People who don't know I'm dead."

"Right."

Jody shut up and cocked his ears. He had tried to talk his mother into driving him to the feedlot but no, she was busy cleaning up the double-wide — she was planning to maybe start dating again — and there was no reason to be carrying him to work when The Mannlichers had promised Jody transportation. "And Uncle Cletus is coming."

"Uncle Cletus is coming?"

"Yes, sometime today if we should be so lucky!"

Jasmine was not usually so crabby. And ever since they buried Jack her attitude had been getting more and more critical of Dr. Mannlicher, and Monday, "...his screwball Indian".

"But, Mama, they treat me like I'm normal!"

Jody figured she was getting pissed because she felt ripped off. "My silence and cooperation ought to be worth something!"

Jody thought he heard Jack's voice again. "They promised me three of them, Nub-man. Three!"

"What? Oh, Dad, Mama says she might start dating again. She wants me to start sleeping down at your place. Either that or at the farm, the feedlot they call it. As soon as Norma was gone Mom drove down to the camper and loaded up your fridge for me. I mean, loaded! A whole gallon of peanut-butter-chocolate ice-cream for the freezer. A whole box of those frozen Mississippi Mud Pies. Bananas. Cans of mixed nuts. A whole bunch of those ham & scalloped potatoes things you can microwave. Two boxes of my favorite cookies, those Fudge Oreos."

The sound of a vehicle was distinct now, turning into their long, twisty drive from the highway. At first Jody could not place it — the familiar sound of it — then it clicked. Jack coming home in his pickup pulling Miss Chernobyl on the trailer!

Just in case it wasn't Eastland Jody stayed put for a

minute, and waited for the crunching of the tires on the gravel near the last turn. A thought punched up Jody's heartbeat. If it wasn't Eastland and Miss Chernobyl, he needed to move. Jody eased himself to his feet and turned around. Shit, from where he was he couldn't see anything. Plus he'd left his gun in the briefcase he had packed for the trip to the feedlot.

"Be back later, Dad."

Jody snuck around the thick scrub to the path leading to Jasmine's back door. From there he spotted Miss Chernobyl's twin stern-drives poking out past the near corner of the trailer, the stainless steel propellers dazzling in the sunlight. He heard his mother's heavy, brisk footsteps inside heading for the front door, and the screen-door whack shut behind her. A squeal of delight.

Then his mother's.

Jody instinctively crabbed his body into a crouch, then took off around the far corner to the front yard. He stopped cold behind Miss Chernobyl's long, sleek, fiberglass hull. Just off the front porch, his mother was trying to handle two, squirming, dark little boys wearing white shorts and no shirts. The wiry-headed rascals were hanging from her, one of them already up on her shoulders and straddling her neck. Eastland was leaning back against Jack's pickup, a big smile on his face. Still no cowboy hat — when had he decided to give that up?!

Eastland spotted Jody and made a serious face, then leaned forward in a mocking way and beckoned Jody to come over.

"Well, come on, Nub-man! I brought you something!"

Jody's heart slammed in his chest. He strode up to the pickup in a near run, straining his eyes to see where they were. For a painful, crushing moment, Jody suddenly thought he was about to be disappointed again. The clones were nowhere in sight.

The pickup was spattered with mud and the hood flecked with white spots of dried sea water (Jack always kept it super-clean). Bernie had gotten out of the double-wide and was barking at the tailgate.

Eastland did not move, but his head followed Jody as the boy walked past him and looked down into the truck bed.

"Can we get up now?"

"Can we get up?"

"Can we take off the blindfolds now?"

"Can we?"

Lying on their sides on some blankets, knees sort of drawn up, were two, red-headed girls with black-corduroy blindfolds tied around over their eyes. Their hair was long and their faces were pretty and they both had cute, identical bodies. Tight jeans and little, green muscle shirts. Jody stood at the side of the pickup with his mouth hanging open.

Their arms looked all goose-bumpy.

"They're cold!"

"We're cold!"

"Can we get out now?"

"Can we get out?"

Eastland, grinning, grabbed Jody by the sleeve and jerked him around. "Let down the tailgate."

"Oh, yeah, sure!"

The tailgate on Jack's truck had always been a problem. The latch was bent and Jack himself usually took two hands to jerk it open. Jody usually couldn't do it at all but this time he had it snatched open with his one, normal hand. It came down with a bang. The girls apparently did not recognize the sound and both of them quickly doubled up and covered their faces with their hands, still lying on their sides. Their hands had pretty, long, red fingernails.

"Are they."

"Yours."

"Oh, god. To keep?"

"God? You Jody?" Eastland laughed. "Yes but only if you follow all the rules."

"You mean, like hide them when planes fly over and stuff? I can do that. I promise!" Jody was too excited to do anything more but stand there and jabber. "But if somebody drives up, I mean, do they have to hide, you know, if..."

"Same as always, Jody. You don't even have a mail-box out there on the road. Anybody drives in here is trespassing anyway, and since Monday dyed their hair red and gave them kinky perms. No freckles, though. No green eyes."

"She dyed their hair?"

"She said you'd like it."

"Oh, I **love** it! Thanks!" Jody was still frozen there, at the tailgate. The girls slowly withdrew their hands from their faces.

"These are the same ones as the decapitated..." Jody stopped himself. "The blond ones?"

"Yup. Now listen. They may look a little different now, but their fingerprints are all the same. Get it? They either stay confined or they have to be whacked. Snuffed. Got that?!" Eastland gave Jody's nub-arm a se-vere pinch. "I already told them the woods here are planted with mines, land mines, so they don't get ideas."

"Oh, yeah, good. I don't want anything bad to hap-pen to them."

"So don't take their blindfolds off till you get them

down the hill. They don't need to know where it's safe to walk." Eastland was speaking in a loud, clear voice and Jody loved it, nodding his head to everything the old man was saying. "Now they have that little pier down there they can fish in, and I already told them that the pond itself isn't mined, just the shore on the other side. You might want to teach them how to catch a mess of crappies, huh? And what chores they need to do every-day."

"See?" Jasmine said. "You should've listened to your mother!"

Jody whipped around. Jasmine had walked up behind him, minus her little-boy playtoys. Jody had no idea what she had done with them and he didn't care. "What?"

"I told you to wash those sheets this morning!"

"Oh! Shit!"

"We can use a machine!"

"We know how much soap to put in!"

"There's a machine down there?" Eastland said.

"No. Jack always used mine."

"They don't need to be coming up here. Rule number one. Keep these two girls separated from the boys at all times! If Manny ever thinks for a minute there's any risky kind of bullshit going on here he'll snuff them all in a heartbeat."

"Yessir," Jody said.

"What about you, Jasmine?"

"Are you kidding? I wouldn't trade those two little guys for two golden Sylvesters!"

"Sylvesters?"

"I'll explain later, Uncle Clit." Jody suddenly jumped at the old man and reached around his .45 Colt and gave him a good hug around the waist with both arms, such as they were.

"Okay!" Eastland said. "Out you come!" The girls groped their way to the tailgate on hands and knees.

"Jody, you lead them down there, one on each side or one at a time, whatever. I've got to go. If anything at all goes wrong, shoot them. Jasmine, I need to borrow the El Camino."

"Shoot them!?"

"They're not human."

"Shoot them? Uh-unh."

"Either that or shoot yourself. I'm serious."

"I'll make sure I won't have to."

"You better."

Jody barely heard him. He was enthralled as he watched the girls slide off the tailgate to their feet. Such nice little asses. Little waists. Pretty belly-buttons. God!

They stood there right next to him, their arms crossed over their chests. They were shivering.

"Did they bring clothes? They're cold."

"Some. Look behind the seat. Remember! Take them down there first, before you take their blindfolds off. I'll set their clothes and stuff in your father's boat so Bernie doesn't chew them all up. Let them warm up with a hot shower while you get the clothes. We can bring them more tomorrow. The gas working down there? The tank full? It's going to get cold tonight."

Cold.

The twins buried under the covers with me.

"Just had the propane filled," Jasmine said. Jody had forgotten she was still standing behind him.

"Come on, guys!" Jody worked himself between them and reached for their hands, one on each side. He reached for the one on his left, first, because that arm was so short.

345

Of course they still could not see him.

"What's this?"

"What?"

"Cute little hand!"

"Seems the same to me."

"No! Here! Feel!"

Jody swallowed hard as the two girls mashed to the front of him and traded hands, both of them feeling of his short arm.

"Oh, on the right side!"

"No, the left side, dummy!"

"I'm not dumb!"

"Are too!"

"Are not!"

Shut up!" Eastland hollered. Jasmine laughed and quickly covered her mouth. The girls shut up, but just for a second.

"I get the cute hand, ha ha!"

Jody beamed. It was the one on the left said it.

"We're hungry," both of them said after they had tired of running all over Jack's place at the bottom of the hill. For fifteen minutes they had raced here and there, as soon as Jody had the blindfolds off. Testing the perimeter by stopping whenever he yelled for them to stop.

"Far enough!"

"We can't walk in the woods?"

"Only the first ten feet."

"Oh."

"Ten feet."

"A little longer than you are. Lie down on your back and stretch your hands over your heads with your feet on the edge of the lawn. If your arms were just a little longer, the mine would blow your hands off."

"Okay!"

"Thanks! Okay!"

"We saw a mine go off once."

They ran up and down the pier, got in and out of Jack's little johnboat (Jody told them he'd get the oars later — take them out on the pond before dark).

"Oars?"

"Oars?"

They were so cute! So beautiful! All his life Jody had dreamed of having a normal body. Now he wouldn't trade places with any normal man. The first minute, after the blindfolds were off, they had checked him out, inspecting his nub arm, taking tentative little grabs at his crotch, feeling his hair. Jody's happiness was almost more than he could bear.

"Your hair is nice!"

"We just got ours colored!"

"It's red now!"

"And kinky!"

"Do you like it?"

They compared his little arm in length to the wooden dildoes they practiced with, so they said. "Your arm is bigger!"

"Yes! Bigger! Make a fist!"

"Oh, neat-o!"

"I get him first!"

"Who says?!"

"We can both have him first!"

"Oh, yeah."

"My name is Jody."

"Jody?"

"Jody?"

"Jody, can we use your arm, too?"

347

"We're hungry."

"Mmmm - hmmmm."

"Hungry." One of them pushed Jody down on Norma's crumpled bedding and laughed while the other one worked on the laces of his sneakers.

"We get special treats if we do a good job!"

"Treats? Like what?"

"Food!"

"Food!"

"Yummy stuff!"

It took her a long time but the first sneaker finally fell to the floor. The girl on top of him had his shirt unbuttoned and was trying to get it and the T-shirt underneath off at the same time. Her wonderful hair brushed against his face and her scent mingled with Norma's from the bed.

"Like ice-cream and chocolate sundaes and stuff!"

The other sneaker clunked to the floor. Jody tried to hang on as both of them got to tugging at his socks. He had wanted to get them out on the shower deck first — with him out in the hot water together — but that idea seemed to have lost its appeal.

Jody was waiting for the dryer cycle to end, not on Norma's bedding, which he had already done and brought back down there, but on the clothes the girls had worn over in the back of the pickup. Candy, Jack's little lap dog, lay on the ground beside him, asleep. As the rivets on the girls' jeans clicked around the dryer drum, Jody was still trying to think what to name the girls. But the memory of their happy, female voices kept on intruding on his thoughts.

"Is the big boat yours?"

"We know this island. We saw it there once."

"Oh, yeah, you can camp there, too!"

"There's dolphins you can feed! They come right up to the boat!"

Shit, he wished the dryer would hurry up. He'd have to get his own, that's for sure. And some toys and stuff the girls could play with. Well, if he was going to be moving with the Mannlichers soon....

Suddenly, Jody wasn't sure he wanted to go along with them out west.

Sick of the stomping around he could hear from inside the double-wide, the giggling and his mother's screeching, Jody walked out to the edge of the drive where he could look down the hill. The trees were casting long shadows now and the late-afternoon air had the clean smell of winter with it. Candy trotted up beside him and looked at Jody with an inquisitive whine. Down below, two, identical, red-headed girls were chasing each other around the camper and his father's outdoor shower deck, playing tag and laughing. The girls' chores were all done except for folding the laundry, and they were waiting for Jody to come back home.

Epilogue

Leviticus 27:3-5

And thy appraisal shall be of the male...fifty shekels of silver... And if it be a female, then thy appraisal shall be thirty shekels.

Numbers 31:15

And Moses said unto them [after the battle], have ye saved all the women alive?

Numbers 31:17,18

Now therefore kill every male among the little ones, and kill every woman that hath known man by lying with him. But all the women children, that have not known a man by lying with him, keep alive for yourselves.

Deuteronomy 21:18-21

If a man have a stubborn and rebellious son, which will not obey the voice of his father, or the voice of his mother...then shall his father and his mother say unto the elders of his city: "This our son is stubborn and rebellious, he will not obey our voice"...and all the men of his city shall stone him with stones, that he die...so shalt thou put evil away from among you.

THE SHEEP CHILD

Farm boys wild to couple
With anything   with soft-wooded trees
With mounds of earth   mounds
Of pinestraw   will keep themselves off
Animals by legends of their own;
In the hay-tunnel dark
And dung of barns, they will
Say   I have heard tell

That in a museum in Atlanta
Way back in a corner somewhere
There's this thing that's only half
Sheep   like a wooly baby
Pickled in alcohol   because
Those things can't live   his eyes
Are open   but you can't stand to look
I heard from somebody who...

...

But this is now almost all
Gone.   The boys have taken
Their own true wives in the city
The sheep are safe in the west hill
Pasture   but we who were born there
Still are not sure.   Are we,
Because we remember, remembered
In the terrible dust of museums?

Merely with his eyes, the sheep-child may
   Be saying   saying

      I am here, in my father's house.
      I who am half of your world, came deeply
      To my mother in the long grass

      ...

———

The last few lines here make me wanna cry. The excerpt is from an early poem by James Dickey, and first published in *The Evergreen Review*
   ...with permission from the author ca 1972 FIU, and the inspiration for this novel, which was a long time in coming. – *John Aalborg 2.February.2013*

Books by John Aalborg & Bleep-Free Press
eBook versions Published by Smashwords

Harry & Ivory

Lowboy #22

Gulf Coast Stories

Children of The Lambs

All are available at Amazon.com

————————

Critical acclaim for "Gulf Coast Stories":
If Raymond Chandler and Ernest Hemingway had a baby, it would be John Aalborg, or at least this great collection of short stories. Witty, gritty, hard hitting and great fun, Aalborg has a way of telling a story that just keeps you reading. His own lifetime on the road and living large come through with every plot, character and twist. You can see it all in your mind as you read. His descriptions are vivid and so very real. I love short stories, I teach a course at college on how to write them, then publish an anthology of each course's work and I wish Aalborg had been one of my students!
— Perry Gamsby, author and publisher
"StreetWise Publications" - Sydney, Australia

In addition to his novels and internationally published "Over The Road" articles — including Newsweek
and Cosmopolitan — Aalborg wrote the Axel McKay
radio-play series aired coast-to-coast, numerous magazine publications of trucking experiences in foreign
countries, and he continues to write a monthly road
column by "Mo'hammer and Cheater".

Author's notes:

A sequel featuring "The Garden of Eden" and the miniature humans — including the serial characters Norma, Sandy, Nub-man, and the Mannlichers — is presently in outline.

It is common practice for paperback books to contain several pages of boring tributes of questionable provenance. Of all the unsolicited praise I have received for this story — much of it in comparison to the pulp fiction greats — I feel compelled to quote below *the most sincere review* I have ever received, a comment typed by a reader from his KindleDX and currently found in the Amazon catalog. This book is also *fun* to read? Why not?!

This review is for: Children of The Lambs - An old myth brought to life by rogue science! (Kindle Edition):
"typing on a kinle dx is akin to torture but read the book itt will be fun and games; and isnt that why youre reading this blurb right now?"
– Murray L Winship

Back Cover Blurb

Forget the ageless rumor that oil-rich sheikhs have harems filled with blond slave-girls snatched from the streets of England and America, never to be heard from again. Something new: the Kingdoms of Crude and wealthy, German satyrs are paying cash for the best that rogue American technology can offer. Clones shipped from the Port of Panama City, Florida. Replicas of female humans. Bred to be beautiful, whiter than the local beach sand, factory fresh, and dumb as dirt.

And now, in batches of twenty: half-breed, shiny-dark, boys. Clones which are monkey-like only in their behavior. Greed and paranoia, however, rule the clandestine clone lab. With all this money to be made, who can afford to wait for the underage siblings to look more grown-up? Are they legal if they don't pass the Turing Test? And how many people who know too much will have to die?

Jack Rebman thinks this exciting enterprise is perfect for his dependable, offshore power-boat, "Miss Chernobyl". Little does he know that SiblTek© has its corporate eye on his new girlfriend, Norma G. So fine! Flaming-red hair, blue veins showing through her peaches-and-cream, and freckles you can taste with your eyes closed. Beauty and brains for one, low price. Tough, mouth-wateringly appealing, straight-shooting Norma Gene.